HOLDEN'S RESURRECTION

GEMINI GROUP

RILEY EDWARDS

Holden's Resurrection

Gemini Group 6

Riley Edwards

Cover design: Lori Jackson Designs

Written by: Riley Edwards

Published by: Riley Edwards/Rebels Romance

Edited by: Rebecca Hodgkins

Proofreader: Julie Deaton, Rebecca Kendall

Holden's Resurrection

ebook ISBN:978-19515670-9-5

print ISBN: 978-1-951567-12-5

First edition: October 27, 2020

To my family - my team – my tribe.
This is for you.

1

"Seriously?" McKenna Swagger glanced over her shoulder and narrowed her eyes. "But, you just moved here."

I'd thought a lot about why I'd moved to Maryland. When I was packing up my house in Virginia Beach, I'd had a hundred reasons why I wanted to leave. But only two of them were true. The rest of them I'd made up to make myself feel better for uprooting my daughter to chase some fantasy that Holden Stanford and I could finally get back what we always should've had.

That wasn't going to happen.

Holden made it painfully clear the last time I saw him. That'd been a month ago.

My gaze moved to the kitchen table where my daughter, Faith, sat, and my heart constricted.

Another move.

Another change.

Not that she remembered all the upheaval after her father had died. As a matter of fact, she didn't know Paul. He died while I was pregnant with her. I'd buried my husband and a week later found myself alone in the hospital giving birth.

Not that my parents hadn't offered to be in the room. My mom was pissed when I told her I didn't want anyone with me and complained that all her friends had been in the delivery room with their daughters and even daughters-in-law, so I was making her look bad. Paul's mom wasn't pissed—she didn't bother to come to the hospital and neither did his sister. It was no surprise they hadn't shown. They'd hated me from the start.

"It won't be until summer, I can't move now in the middle of the school year," I explained.

"Charleigh—"

The doorbell cut McKenna off.

"I'll get it." Faith jumped up from the table.

"No, sweets. Let me get it."

Without argument, she sat back down and picked up the marker she'd abandoned and resumed coloring. That was my kid, always polite, never back-talked, rarely complained. And as strange as it made me, I hated it. It was almost as if she knew that since her birth, I'd been on the edge of a nervous breakdown and she didn't want to push me off the cliff. Even as an infant she'd been perfect.

"It's my landlord. I'll be right back," I told Micky and swiped the invoice the furnace guy had left earlier that day before I headed toward the stairs.

When I moved to Kent County, Maryland, I rented an apartment above a real estate office in what the locals called the "downtown" area. It didn't resemble any downtown area I'd ever seen in the city. It was quaint. Historic. Quiet. In another life, it would've been the perfect place to live. Hell, six months ago when I moved here, I thought this was where I'd stay and raise Faith.

Now, I knew I needed to leave.

I was weak. I couldn't face Holden. Actually, I wasn't facing Holden at all because he was avoiding me.

I opened the door expecting Mr. Travers. However, the man standing in front of me was most certainly not my sixty-five-year-old landlord.

"May I help you?" I asked, and not for the first

time wished I had a peephole or a window in my front door.

"Charlotte Towler?"

It had been so long since someone had used my given name it took me a moment to answer.

"Yes. May I—"

"You've been served." The man shoved a large envelope at me, leaving me with no option but to take it or watch it fall to the ground.

"Served?"

"Have a good day."

The man strode off without another word.

Served?

What the hell?

I stepped back into the small entryway and closed the door.

The outside of the manila envelope was blank. I opened the clasp and shook out the documents. My blood iced in my veins.

Son of a bitch.

Son of a stupid, mean, hateful bitch.

NOTICE OF REQUEST FOR VIRGINIA REGISTRATION OF A CHILD CUSTODY AND/OR VISITATION DETERMINATION FROM ANOTHER STATE.

That *bitch.*

I quickly scanned the first page. Paul's mother, Beatrice, was named as the requesting party, and Paul's sister, Patricia, was named as the other interested person. I flipped to the next page and the thick layer of ice that had formed around my heart cracked until more anger than I'd ever known invaded it.

Freaking bitch.

I dashed upstairs, found my phone, and looked at Micky.

"I have to make a quick call. Will you keep an eye on Faith?"

"Of course I will. Is everything okay?"

"No. Please make sure she doesn't go upstairs."

Micky's face softened and concern washed over her pretty face. I'd always liked Nixon Swagger. At one time, he'd been a good friend, then everything went to shit with Holden. After that, I made a series of bad choices—though Faith had come from one of those choices, so I couldn't regret all the decisions I'd made. But, those decisions had put Nixon, along with Jameson, Weston, and Chasin right in the middle of a mess. While supportive, they'd come down mostly on Holden's side, and I couldn't blame them.

I hadn't lost them per se, but I had lost the closeness and I'd definitely lost their respect. Then after

Paul's death, I'd lost them all in a new way. They avoided me the best they could, only coming around to fulfill what they considered their duty to Paul's child and widow. Those interactions hurt so badly; I'd put a stop to them all together, insisting I didn't need their help. Which was a big, fat lie. I needed the support. I missed their friendship. I just plain *missed* them.

I was happy they'd all found women who complemented them. Especially Nix. He'd been the one to harbor the most guilt about Paul's death. It wasn't his fault, but he'd never seen it that way. McKenna was perfect for Nixon.

I'd barely gotten them back and I was going to give them all up again.

"I'll explain in a minute," I told her and turned to Faith.

And like always, my daughter was on high alert.

"Mommy—"

"Everything's fine," I lied. "I need to make a phone call, then we'll make another batch of cookies."

"And finish decorating the Christmas tree?" Faith asked.

"Yes, we'll finish the tree," I promised.

A tree that Faith and I had picked out alone. I'd

strapped it to the roof of my car, then dragged it up the stairs all by myself and set it on the stand. Same thing we did every year. Just me and Faith.

I jogged up the stairs to the third floor wondering what it would've been like if Paul hadn't died. Would we still be together for Faith's well-being? Or, would Paul have finally called off the farce of a marriage and divorced me? Would I have been able to continue to live a total lie? By the time I made it to my room, I had no answers to the questions that had plagued my mind for years. But there was one thing I knew for certain—had Paul been alive, his horrendous mother and sister wouldn't be an issue.

Paul despised them. He would never have allowed them around Faith.

But Paul wasn't around to shield his daughter from their malice. And each year, the Towler family became more vindictive. More hateful.

Now they wanted to take Faith from me.

Over. My. Dead. Body.

I swiped the screen of my cell and knew I should take a minute to calm down. My mom called me a reactor, meaning I reacted before I thought. My best course of action was to have my attorney answer this latest court filing and not allow myself to get sucked back into their sick game.

But that wasn't the type of person I was. I thought the Towlers had learned their lesson the first two times they dragged me into court. Both cases they'd lost.

Total waste of time and money.

I pushed on the Devil Bitch's contact and waited.

"What?" Patricia answered.

"Unfit? That's your new play, really?"

"Totally. First, you keep my *niece* from her family, then you move her to Maryland so you can chase after the man you cheated on my brother with—"

"I never cheated on your brother," I cut her off.

"We have witnesses, Charlotte," she sneered.

"Well, they're lying."

"We're gonna get Faith, and when we do, you're never gonna see her again. We'll make sure she knows you never loved Paul. He was a meal ticket. After that other one dumped you, you needed another free ride. That money was supposed to be ours. Not yours."

Right. The money. Paul's death benefits. It always came down to the money.

"Paul's life insurance isn't yours and it's not mine. It's Faith's."

Guilt ate at my heart. *Was it really Faith's?*

"It should've gone to my mother. She earned it."

"You're disgusting."

Who thought like that? Who actually wanted their child's death benefits? What kind of mother behaved like a vulture waiting to collect money that meant her son was dead?

Beatrice Towler, that was who.

She was horrendous and she'd taught her daughter to be a greedy, money-grabbing cow, too. It was a miracle Paul had turned out the way he did. Just because it wasn't a love match between the two of us, didn't mean he hadn't been a good person. He was. When I'd found out I was pregnant, he insisted on marrying me. He'd loved Faith from the very first moment I'd told him.

He would've been an excellent father.

"And you're a whore who got knocked-up on purpose to trap my brother. And once you had his ring on your finger, you lied and cheated on him. I wouldn't be surprised if Faith wasn't even his."

That was so far from the truth it was laughable. Though I wasn't laughing, I was feeling homicidal.

Hindsight being what it was, the very first time they'd called me a whore and denied Faith was Paul's daughter, I should've told them they were right. Maybe that would've been the time to come clean. But there'd been a reason Paul was so eager to marry me and claim Faith even though he knew the truth. I should've signed over Paul's life insurance and walked away, keeping my daughter protected from Paul's family.

But I couldn't do it.

Paul hated his family with a passion. He never wanted them to have a penny of his money. Before he'd married me, all of his money was to be donated to the Navy SEAL foundation. Maybe that's what I needed to do. That would be the right thing to do. I hadn't touched any of it. I couldn't, not when I still had secrets that could ruin everything.

"This is a waste of time. You're not getting near Faith."

"We'll see," Patricia said in a know-it-all tone. "She's as good as ours. We have pictures of you cheating on Paul."

Pictures?

That was impossible. I never cheated on my husband and I never lied to him. Paul was very aware I was in love with Holden even though I was married to him. As I said, we were not a love match; Paul and I were friends who'd slept together once, in a drunken one-night stand. Then we did what he felt was best for my unborn child.

Or did we?

Paul had spent the last eight months of his life in a loveless marriage.

And I've spent the last eight years mourning the loss of a friend I'd done wrong, while harboring so much guilt there were days I wasn't sure I could breathe. Then there was Holden. I'd never stop grieving the man I loved.

"You're full of shit, Patty."

And with that, I hung up.

I wouldn't put it past them to make up more lies about me and I was sure they knew plenty of shady people who they could get to lie for them, too. But pictures? Bullshit. They didn't have any because none existed.

For the five millionth time, I wished Paul was here.

And for the five millionth time, I was reminded I was all alone.

Me and Faith.

The dynamic duo.

No matter what, the two of us would be okay.

2

Something was going on.

Holden heard it in Nixon Swagger's curt tone when he'd called and told him to come into the office early. He saw it on Jameson's face when he'd mutely passed him in the hallway. The vibe in the Gemini Group office was tense—the atmosphere so thick, Holden Stanford could guess what the problem was, or more to the point—who.

Charleigh Towler.

The woman drove Holden mad. He avoided her at all costs. Truthfully, he avoided her daughter, Faith. The very sight of the little girl cut so deep, hurt so badly, he couldn't bear to be within a hundred feet of her. Her cute face and pretty brown eyes sent Holden reeling back to a time and place he couldn't afford to revisit. For years, he'd wished Faith was his. Cursed the universe for taking away his chance while dangling the one thing he'd wanted so desperately in front of him. Family. Something Holden would never have.

But Faith was not his, she was Paul Towler's. She was Charleigh's. She was theirs.

Fuck life.

"She's moving." Holden heard McKenna tell her husband as he approached Nix's office. He stopped just before the door and listened. "She said she was going to wait until the school year was over, but she'd made up her mind."

"That might not be a bad idea."

"Nix," Micky huffed. "That's a horrible idea. I don't want her to leave. Plus, with those people trying to take Faith from her, she needs to be close so we can help her."

Holden's anger skyrocketed.

"Those people" could only be Paul's mom and sister. It wasn't the first time they'd fucked with Charleigh. Almost two years ago, Holden went down to Virginia to help Charleigh when Beatrice Towler tried to sue Charleigh. It was a bogus lawsuit and had been thrown out, but what came after had been bad. Bea and Patty harassed Charleigh and scared Faith so bad the little girl had refused to go to school.

It seemed they were at it again.

"You know we're not going to let that happen. I've already called a friend to look into the pictures they supposedly have of Charleigh. Though I can tell you right now, she never cheated on Paul, and if there are pictures, they're fakes."

What the actual fuck?

A sick feeling Holden hadn't had in a long time roiled in his stomach.

Flashes of memories he didn't want.

If only his team knew the truth.

The whole situation was twisted and fucked-up. It had been one gigantic disaster and Holden couldn't deny his part in it. He was the catalyst that ruined four lives. His mistake had sparked a chain of events that would forever mark him.

Fucking hell.

There were a great many number of things that needed to change around Gemini Group before this situation got worse. The women seemed to be taking sides and it was causing friction. Especially between Genevieve and McKenna.

Holden was close to Evie. He'd almost died

protecting her, and from that grew a tight bond. Not that he wasn't close to all his friends' wives, but he was closest to Evie. So naturally, she'd side with him. Bobby, being Evie's best friend, would take Evie's back in her crusade to keep Charleigh away from Holden. Evie knew the pain it caused him every time he was forced to see Faith.

McKenna loved everyone. She was also deliriously happy with her husband and daughter, Holly, and wanted the people she loved to have what she had—bliss.

That was not in the cards for Holden. He lost his chance when he lost Charleigh.

Though, 'lost' wasn't the right word. He'd left her. Then she betrayed him in the worst way and sealed their fate.

Holden stopped eavesdropping and passed by Nixon's office door, relieved that his friend didn't stop him. He was in no mood to discuss Charleigh's problems. Though he owed it to her to put a stop to them once and for all.

He'd just sat down behind his desk when there was a knock.

"Yeah?"

"You gotta minute?" Chasin asked as he walked in and closed the door behind him.

"By all means, come in and make yourself comfortable."

Chasin took a seat, completely unaffected by Holden's snarky remark.

"I know this isn't something you wanna hear about," Chasin started and Holden braced. "Charleigh got served with custody papers. Beatrice Towler is claiming Charleigh's an unfit parent and wants sole custody."

"Say again?"

Holden hadn't thought the bitch would go that far. He'd assumed she was once again trying for visitation.

"Charleigh didn't want to share, but Micky pointed out this case wasn't about her but Faith, and that little girl needs all the help she can get. Charleigh finally agreed and let us read the documents. It's all bullshit. Beatrice claims Charleigh was having an affair. They have pictures. But they're taken out of context."

Apparently, Holden hadn't braced enough because he felt like he was going to come out of his skin.

"What's that mean?"

"Nix put in a call to Rhode Daley. After he left the teams, he started to do some PI work, mostly for an outfit called Takeback. Anyway, I just talked to him. He found the pictures. They're of me and Charleigh. Like I said, they're taken out of context."

Holden was at a loss for words and the oxygen in his lungs seized.

"How in the fuck are there pictures of you and Leigh-Leigh?"

"This is the part you're not gonna want to talk about."

"And what part is that, Chasin? The part where you were fucking—"

"Don't go there, brother. You know that never happened so don't say shit just because you're mad at yourself for the epic fuck-up you instigated."

Good Christ.

He hated it, but Chasin was right. Everything that had happened all started because he'd fucked up.

"Then what don't I want to talk about?"

It was a stupid question, considering Holden didn't want to talk about *any* of it.

Chasin leaned forward, placed his elbows on his knees, and speared Holden with fiery regard.

"I suppose you don't want to talk about any of it, but particularly the reason why I was visiting Charleigh."

"Christ, Chasin, cut to it."

"Those pictures were taken a few hours before Paul and Charleigh's wedding. She called me and asked to meet her at Red Wing Park. She was having second thoughts. Or maybe she was having third and fourth thoughts." Chasin paused and Holden didn't like the way his chest tightened. "Charleigh admitted that even though you'd broken it off with her that the two of you had slept together on more than one occasion in the five months you'd been apart. And she was worried that the baby she was carrying might be yours."

There it was. That constant ache of wanting made itself known, and Holden felt his feet itching to run. The child who had plagued his thoughts for years, the child he wished was his.

"Yet she married him," Holden spat.

The remark was wholly unfair. Holden knew Faith was Paul's, and the snide comment against Charleigh was uncalled for. But to this day, hearing about Charleigh marrying Paul burned.

"Don't go there. The whole situation was as fucked as it could've been. You left her without an explanation. You were with her for years, brother, and one morning, you wake up, pack your shit, and tell her it's over. You were miserable, wouldn't talk to us about why you'd left her. You crashed at my place, Nixon's, and Weston's. Then for five months, you strung her along. You fucked her when *you* wanted but refused to talk to her otherwise."

"And during all of that, with my head as fucked-up as it was, I didn't fuck anyone else. She did," Holden lamely defended.

He knew he didn't have a leg to stand on; he'd screwed Charleigh over. He'd done everything Chasin accused him of doing and then some. There was more he'd done, hurtful, mean things he'd said in his quest to make Charleigh hate him. He had needed her gone, and he was too weak to let her go. So he'd set about making her hate him. And Paul was right there, ready to pick up the pieces.

It didn't work.

Nothing ever worked.

Not even when she married someone else did Holden stop loving her.

"Why was she at the bar that night with Alison?" Chasin asked.

Hell to the no. Holden wasn't going there. That might have been the single biggest screw-up of his life. He'd said horrible things to Charleigh that had driven her to seek out Nixon's then-girlfriend, Alison, who was a conniving bitch. Charleigh got trashed, and by the time Holden had found her to apologize for what he'd said, he saw her and Paul stumbling out of a cab and into her place.

Five hours later Holden watched Paul exit the apartment that at one time he'd shared with Charleigh. His friend—his teammate—had fucked his woman in his own goddamned bed. Though it wasn't his bed and Charleigh wasn't his woman by then—he'd thrown it all away.

"Tell me about the pictures." Holden changed the subject.

With a long-suffering sigh, Chasin answered. "We were sitting on a park bench and Charleigh was crying. One picture is of her head leaning on my shoulder. There's another of me hugging her, and right before we parted ways, I kissed her on the forehead. All innocent and taken out of context. I was consoling a friend who in a few hours was marrying a man she didn't love while leaving the man who she did behind."

Holden knew Chasin was telling the truth. Unlike Paul, Chasin would never touch Charleigh. They'd been close friends. Hell, Charleigh had been close to his whole team. She was friendly and likable. Never nagged or bitched, was always up for a good time. She could hang with the guys and drink beer or sit with the women and gab with them. Everything about Charlotte Axelson was perfect. His Leigh-Leigh, the only woman he'd ever love.

But she wasn't his—she was Charleigh *Towler*—Paul's widow.

"And now, the Towlers are using those to what, prove Charleigh's an unfit parent?"

Paul's mom and sister, the White Trash Twins, as Paul not-so-lovingly had called them.

"They're using the pictures to try to claim the money he left her and Faith. They're using her move to Maryland to prove she's unfit," Chasin explained.

"That's absurd."

From everything Holden had seen, Charleigh was a good mother. She loved her daughter and had worked hard to provide a nice home for the two of them. Before they'd moved to Maryland, Charleigh had a nice two-bedroom condo in a decent part of Virginia Beach. She'd had a good job that paid well. All of which she'd given up to move to Maryland after Holden had been shot.

Now she and Faith lived in an okay apartment above a real estate office three blocks from the Gemini Group office. Gone was her view of the beach, her friends, her job, Faith's school. Charleigh had given up everything and uprooted her family to be closer to him.

All because he'd been shot. A reminder that life was short. Though Holden didn't think she needed to be reminded. She lived with the knowledge every day. Her husband had been killed in combat before he had a chance to meet his child.

Holden shook that thought away quickly.

"How are we gonna play this?" Holden found himself asking even though he knew he shouldn't be involved.

"Daley's digging into Beatrice and Patricia now."

"Tell him to crawl so far up their asses Charleigh has enough to bury them. This is the third time they've pulled this shit. It ends now. Have Daley send me the invoices, I'll take care of them personally. I want those two bitches leashed and neutralized."

"Right." Chasin smiled. "Anything else?"

"Yeah, I don't want her knowing I'm involved."

"Holden—"

"Don't you think I've fucked up her life enough? She doesn't need to know I'm sticking my nose in her business. The last time we had words, it wasn't pleasant, but I think she understands that there's no going back, there's no fixing what I broke."

"Yeah, I heard about that," Chasin admitted. "Though I also know the last time the Towlers pulled their shit, you waded in and fixed that for Charleigh."

"Obviously, I didn't do a good enough job because here we are and they're at it again."

Holden needed this conversation to be over. He didn't want to think about his trips down to Virginia Beach, and the latest screwed-up game he and Charleigh had played.

A game that had broken him.

"What else do we have going on this week?" Holden asked as he shuffled through the papers Micky had put on his desk.

Chasin gave Holden an unhappy glare but gave him his play.

"Jonny's got a case he needs help on. He'll be in tomorrow. Jameson just left to head to Philly to pick up a bond skip and Weston's finishing up his latest assignment."

Holden had been pleased when Weston had literally drawn the short straw and was assigned the job of following a cheating husband. Those were boring as fuck, and by the end of the case, you were put off sex for a good long while. Spying and taking pictures of two people doing the dirty made you wish eye bleach was a real thing.

Being as Holden wasn't having sex, maybe he should've saved Weston and taken the assignment. But then the team would've been deprived of hearing Weston's incessant whining about the old man pumping away at his twenty-years-his-junior side piece.

Nothing like watching old man balls swing with a Viagra erection.

"When's Weston due back?"

Chasin's mouth tipped up into a devilish grin. "Around two. I'll bring the popcorn to the debrief. Old Mr. Thompson's meeting with his latest piece at eleven. It should be a nice long session. Weston's gonna be in a fit."

Chasin wasn't wrong, Weston would bitch and complain about his afternoon live-action porno shoot. Just what Holden needed—entertainment to get his mind off Charleigh.

And if he was lucky, hearing about Mr. Thompson's escapades would put him off sex and quell the ever-growing ache Charleigh's proximity created.

3

"I don't know, Char. Does that say Barnyard Chic or Farmer Jane?" my client, Lizza Powell, asked.

That was Lizza with two z's.

Normally, I loved my job. In Virginia Beach, I'd worked for a large event planning company. When I moved to Cliff City, I decided it was time to start my own business. Which had worked out wonderfully. I loved being my own boss, I loved executing my vision and seeing my clients' faces light up with happiness the day of the big party.

But every once in a while, a Lizza with two z's came along and made me want to drown myself in a bathtub full of vodka.

I wasn't sure what Farmer Jane was, and if she

called me Char one more time my head was going to explode.

Char.

Like I was a *char*broiled meat patty.

I took a deep breath, plastered a fake smile on my face, and tried again.

"Lizza, we could move the party from your barn to the main house, but Sydney's guest list is nearing a hundred. It'd be a squeeze, but we could make it work."

"No, no. Syd wants the barn," Lizza sighed then finally came out with the truth. "I just don't want people to think we're *poor*."

And there it was, the difference between new money and old money. Lizza and her husband were nouveau riche—they'd recently acquired their wealth and it showed in everything they did. Not only was it nauseating, but it was also exhausting to deal with.

"I can assure you no one will think you're poor."

It was becoming increasingly harder to swallow the bitter taste of disdain.

"Maybe we should hang crystal chandeliers." Lizza pointed to the ceiling.

"You could, and it would certainly be a lovely addition to the voile that will be draped along the rafters. You'll need to hire an electrician to wire outlets."

"Yes, yes, yes." Lizza spun in a circle. "I'll have Stone call someone. That's what we need. A touch of elegance. Very Martha Stewart."

"Yes, very," I agreed and fought the need to roll my eyes.

And for the record, Stone was not Lizza's husband's real name. It was Steve, but she called him Stone because it sounded "classier".

"Perfect. Then I'll wait to hear from the electrician and adjust the sheets of fabric as needed. Was there anything else you wanted to go over?"

Please God say no.

"You're sure about the caterer?" she pressed.

"He comes highly recommended and both you and Sydney enjoyed the tasting," I reminded her.

"Yes, well, I just want to make sure he's in line with who our friends hire."

Sweet mother of God, I'm going to strangle this woman.

"Mrs. Goldman from your yacht club recommended him, so I'd say you're fine on that front."

"Right. I forgot. I just want everything to be perfect for my girl's party. You only turn fifteen once."

Right. This fifty-thousand-dollar party was for a fifteenth birthday, and not even a *quinceañera.* Totally new money. And the way Lizza went through it they'd be in the poor house sooner rather than later.

"Everything will be perfect," I promised, then added, "So perfect, no one will be able to stop talking about it."

"Yes, that's what I want. The party of the decade."

Yeah, I knew that's what she wanted. People like Lizza had zero self-esteem and needed others to stroke their egos. Sadly, she was passing this trait down to her pretty teenage daughter.

Speaking of daughters, I needed to end this meeting and go pick up mine from Jameson and Kennedy Grant's house.

"I have to get going, Lizza."

For a moment she looked like she was going to argue, then at the last second thought better of it. It was a Saturday—not only that, the Saturday before Christmas—and she was lucky I'd come out at all to deal with her latest hissy fit.

"Yes, of course."

No "thank you for coming out" or "I appreciate you dropping everything, finding a sitter for your child" not even a "sorry to bother you on a Saturday".

Nothing. Pure entitlement.

Annoying.

It had taken nearly the entire drive to Jameson and Kennedy's for me to put my irritation aside. The only good part about my impromptu meeting was Faith got to spend time with Kennedy. My daughter loved helping Jameson's wife make jam and honey. Now that it was winter and there was no garden to tend to or wild berries to pick, Kennedy was teaching Faith the art of bread making. Today was sunflower seed bread. Faith would totally love that. My heart constricted at the thought of moving her away from the people she'd bonded with.

I wish she could've had this her whole life. Good men to help protect her. Good women to help me guide and teach her. Even Chasin's fiancée Genevieve was kind to Faith, though it was very obvious she disliked me. But that hadn't stopped the former country megastar from giving Faith guitar lessons. And Bobby, Genevieve's best friend, was a riot of laughs and was welcoming and friendly to my girl. Though she was firmly in the I-hate-Charleigh Camp.

As long as they were nice to my daughter, they

could hate me all they wanted. I deserved most of their ire. Most—not all. Though I did understand why they'd shifted all the blame from Holden onto me. Holden was theirs; it was natural they'd protect him from an outsider. But part of me did wonder if they knew the whole truth.

You know the saying, 'there are two sides to every story, and then there's the truth?' They only knew Holden's side and I found it doubtful he'd been forthright.

By the time I pulled into the Grants' driveway, my heart ached. When would I stop loving Holden? Would there ever be a time when I could move on and not pine for a man who didn't want me? After all of these years, I still loved him the way I did the first time I saw him. So at this point, it was a good bet I'd die loving him. That thought made me sick to my stomach. Faith would grow up an only child of a single mother, who never taught her how to love a man or be loved by one. She'd grow up without a family. It would always be just her and me.

I hadn't even exited my car when the front door opened and Tank the giant German Shepherd that Jameson should've named Giganto—the dog was that big—came barreling across the yard, Faith's little legs trying but failing to keep up.

"Mom!" Faith shouted. "Auntie Kennedy's baby kicked. And I felt it."

The "auntie" designation was new and I wished with all my heart that I could find joy in my daughter's closeness with these women. But all it did was grind me to dust. I was going to selfishly yank her away from the first healthy family she'd ever had.

Good God, I'm a horrible mother.

"You did?" Faith came to a skidding halt in front of me, Tank danced around, his tail thumping my thigh with such force I'd be surprised if I didn't have a bruise. "I see you, Tank." I reached down and gave his soft fur a rub.

"Can we get a Tank?"

"No, sweets, we live in an apartment."

"Then can you have a baby in your belly so I can feel it kick all the time?"

Dagger to the heart.

"Nope. I already have my best girl. No more babies for mommy."

"But you can have a baby in an apartment."

Good Lord, twist the knife.

"You sure can. But lucky for you, Kennedy already has one in her belly so you can feel hers kick."

"I guess you're right." Faith's lips twisted but she dropped the subject.

"Hey. How'd it go with L-I-double-Z-A?" Kennedy asked as she made her way to my car.

"About like I assumed it would go. She wanted to triple-check that her fifteen-year-old would have the premiere party of the decade. I shouldn't complain; between my fee and my commission, I'm making a fortune on this party. But it feels so wasteful to spend all that money on one day. It works out to being a little over ten thousand dollars an hour."

Money I certainly needed since I was moving again.

"My whole wedding didn't cost ten thousand dollars."

Neither did mine, but I wasn't going to comment. "That's 'cause you're smart. I hope little miss was well-behaved."

"Pal-leeze. You know she's always a doll. The bread she made is in the oven and she entertained Tank while Jameson put together baby furniture."

As if Kennedy's words summoned her husband, Jameson came out onto the porch, and when his gaze settled on Faith chasing Tank, his whole face softened.

This was a new look for Jameson. In all the years

I was with Holden, the one adjective I never would've thought to use when describing Jameson was gentle. He'd always been surly, broody, grumpy, and that was how he behaved around friends. If the man didn't like you, watch out, he could be downright menacing. I was happy to see that whatever had weighed him down had been lifted. Kennedy was a sweetheart. I loved that Jameson had found himself a good woman.

All of them had.

And one day Holden would, too.

On that thought, I shivered, and it had nothing to do with the bite of the December chill. No, it was pure bitterness. Holden would move on and I'd stay in the vicious, unending triangle I'd created.

"Is there a reason you're standing out in the cold?" Jameson boomed.

Kennedy rolled her eyes and shook her head before she called back to her husband. "It's not *that* cold." It was indeed *that* cold and the puff of vapor proved it. "I know everyone thought I was weird waiting so long to announce I was pregnant, but I knew this would happen. He just can't help himself; it's like his protective instincts have kicked into overdrive."

I wish I knew how that felt. Someone loving you

and their unborn child so much they'd worry about something as small as you being cold. Sure, Paul had loved Faith, or maybe loved the idea of having a daughter. Everyone who knew him called him a good dad, but that was purely because he told anyone who would listen how excited he was about having a child. There was no doubt he would've spoiled and loved Faith. He understood what dysfunction looked like—his family was horrible and he was eager to start his own and give his child everything he never had.

But that never happened.

Now I was left alone to deal with the vipers whose sole mission was to make my life miserable and steal my daughter for her money and to punish me.

"Jameson's right, it's cold. You should get in the house."

"You're coming in, right? Faith's bread should be done any minute."

Shit. I didn't want to go in. Over the months it had become increasingly harder not to fall in love with Kennedy. I adored Micky and it would be hard enough to leave her. But there was something about Kennedy's personality that made me want to unload my burdens. She was tough and smart and I figured she'd be the type of friend who would tell you to pull your head out of your ass if you were doing something stupid. Like, say, still being madly in love with a man who hated you.

I needed friends.

I needed a tribe of women I could trust and lean on, and in return, I'd repay the favor and be a loyal friend.

But it wouldn't be the wives of my dead husband's teammates.

Sometimes, life sucked.

Sometimes, everything crashed in and you couldn't see a way out.

Tank barked and my head turned toward the dog dancing around Faith, pushing her onto the grass as an SUV pulled into the driveway.

I didn't have time to think about what a great dog Tank was. Not when my heart was thundering in my chest. It was time to leave.

"Faith, sweets, time to go."

My daughter's head swiveled between the Suburban slowly making its way up the lane to me, then to Kennedy, then back to the SUV.

"Okay."

Faith ran across the yard and stopped in front of Kennedy. "Thank you for teaching me how to make bread and for letting me feel your tummy and for letting me play with Tank."

"Don't you want to..." Kennedy paused as she glanced at Holden's SUV. Understanding dawned. "I'll bring your bread by tomorrow and we'll do a taste test."

Jameson had come off the porch, his large frame strung tight as he stalked down the brick walkway. At the same time, I heard a door slam behind me but I refused to look. I knew he'd gotten out of his vehicle. Faith moved closer to me and I prayed Holden hadn't blocked me in because I needed to leave, and it would suck to have to go all Dukes of Hazzard and drive over Kennedy's flower beds, but I totally would.

"What's wrong?" Jameson called out.

"I tried calling but you didn't answer. Jonny needs us." Holden's voice slammed into me and my eyes drifted closed.

Would hearing his voice ever stop hurting?

Once upon a time, his voice had soothed me, lulled me to sleep at night, made me feel safe and loved. It could also turn me on and make me want to rip his clothes off. But none of those applied anymore. All I felt was pain. Deep, biting, razor's edge pain that sliced my soul.

"Sorry, I was working on the baby's room."

In an effort not to look over my shoulder, I stared at Kennedy with laser focus, therefore, I didn't miss her flinch.

God, why is everything so uncomfortable?

"What's Jonny got going on?" Jameson inquired.

I didn't want to know what Jonny Spencer had going on that would require Holden to drive out to Jameson's house. Jonny was a local cop, a super-nice guy with beautiful sorrow-filled blue eyes.

"Two missing teens."

My arm tightened around Faith's shoulders and I pulled her closer.

"You're gonna find them, right, Uncle Jameson?" Faith asked, and I watched Kennedy snap to attention.

I really, really wanted to look back at Holden to see what had made Kennedy go stiff but I didn't dare. I had a pretty good idea he had the same pained expression he always had on his face when he was around Faith. But when he heard her speak or when she called one of his teammates "uncle" that pain turned indignant.

Something worth noting—Faith never called Holden "uncle". As a matter of fact, since we'd moved to Maryland, she'd only spoken to him directly a handful of times. During those exchanges, he'd been soft and cautious with her. On more than one occasion, when he thought no one was looking, I'd caught him staring at her. Not with loathing or hurt, but studiously watching her every move.

The fuck of it was, I'd never stopped wondering about Faith's paternity. I'd always wondered, even after I had to seek Holden out to tell him I was pregnant and he'd exploded. In my moment of deepest shame, he'd denied the baby I was carrying could be his and told me to go find Paul. I never lied, I never cheated, I never tried to cover up my drunken mistake, but even if I had, Holden had seen me and Paul together.

Yet, I still loved him.

How in the hell was that possible?

"Gonna do my best, beanpole."

Faith beamed at the nickname Jameson had given her.

Then Jameson said to Holden, "Give me a minute and I'll be on the road."

I heard Holden slam his door. Seconds later, he was reversing down the lane.

Kennedy gave me a pitied look and my stomach revolted.

Screw pity.

Yeah, it was time for me to make a change. Another big, huge, life-changing decision. I couldn't take these people away from my daughter. This was what she needed. Good, strong men around her. Sweet, loving women who would teach her to make bread and jam. We were staying.

Fuck Holden Stanford.

Fuck him and his cruel words. Fuck him for leaving me. Fuck him for never loving me the way I should be loved. And mostly fuck him for turning his back on me.

Fuck that. Fuck him.

No more. I was better than this sad sack of a woman. I was a good person. I was a good mom.

Holden dumped me.

He ran away without an explanation.

If he didn't like me around, screw him, he could run again—he was good at it.

4

Holden was on his bed in his Airstream. Alone. Which was how he preferred it. These days it seemed he couldn't go a day without someone mentioning Charleigh or Faith. He'd managed to keep physical distance between the three of them but that didn't mean the universe wasn't punishing him. There was something new every damn day. Faith said this, Charleigh did that, her business was going well, the Towlers weren't backing down. He couldn't get away from hearing about them.

There was a knock on the door and Holden wondered why he hadn't gone to Bora Bora for Christmas. All of his friends were married and either had kids, had one on the way, or were thinking about reproducing. He was the odd man out. Nothing and no one was keeping him in Kent County for the holidays.

"Yo, Scrooge McDuck, what are you doing?" Bobby's voice filled the small space.

Well, not all of his friends were married. Roberta "Bobby" Layne wasn't officially attached to anyone, though she was giving Jonny Spencer a run for his money.

Holden opened his eyes and found Bobby already in his Airstream looking around.

"One day you might walk in here uninvited and get an eyeful," he warned.

"You lock the door when you do that." Bobby smirked. "Everyone's already at Alec's. Are you coming?"

After last year's Christmas extravaganza, Macy, Alec's wife, had declared that brunch at the Hall house would be a tradition. At the time, Holden was all for the new ritual. He had great friends who'd all found great women.

But this year, the last place Holden wanted to go was to Alec's house. There'd be too many smiling, happy people there.

And *she'd* be there.

"You can't avoid her forever," Bobby continued.

"Sure I can," Holden snapped. Then he sat up

and sighed. "Sorry. It's Christmas. I shouldn't be an ass to you."

"How very altruistic of you. Listen, I know Evie pretty much hates her, which means I'm supposed to, too."

Holden couldn't hide his wince. He hated how everyone had taken sides. The men had remained neutral—they were stuck between duty to a teammate's widow and daughter and their friend. Logically Holden understood their predicament—hell, he was as confused as they were. The bastard Paul told Holden of all people to take care of his wife and child while he drew his last breath.

It was the most fucked-up thing anyone had ever done to him.

Fucked-up in ways none of the others could ever understand. Holden knew things the others didn't.

A funny thing happens when someone dies, especially when that person dies a hero—suddenly all of their transgressions vanished. All the shitty things they'd done while they walked this earth were wiped clean and they were held in high regard. No one wanted to speak ill of the dead, but Paul had been a dick while he was alive.

Not just for what he'd done to Holden, but what he'd done to Charleigh. Paul Towler was a wolf in sheep's clothing. And for years, Holden had bit his tongue every time he heard what a great man Paul had been. Bile churned in his gut when people talked about what a great father he would've been. He wasn't great at anything but being an obsessive prick who'd fixated on Charleigh and waited until she was at her most vulnerable to strike. And the worst part was that Holden had played right into Paul's hands. It had been Holden who'd brought Leigh-Leigh low, giving Paul the perfect opportunity to take advantage of her. Then he'd fucked up again when Leigh-Leigh came to him and told him she was pregnant.

Holden swayed as the guilt and self-disgust rocked him.

He'd let his pride, ego, and doubt override his love for her. He should've calmly told her the truth. Instead, he'd turned her away and sent her straight to Paul.

Such a dumb fuck.

Now he'd never know if he and Charleigh could've made it through. He'd never know if his love for Charleigh was so deep he could've raised another man's child. Instead of taking the time he should've, he'd burned his world to ashes.

"Did you know that Chasin's named in the

lawsuit? The Towlers are claiming Charleigh and Chasin were having an affair behind Paul's back," Bobby went on.

"Evie has nothing to worry about. That never happened. Chasin and Charleigh were friends. Those pictures are not what they seem."

"She knows that. And that's not why she doesn't like her. She's worried about you."

Not wanting to have this conversation while sitting in bed, Holden stood.

"Evie has better things to do than worry about me. All of you do. I'm fine. And she shouldn't hate Charleigh." It was time to end all this division. "What happened was a long time ago. It was my fault and it's way past time everyone moves on."

"I don't think Charleigh can move on," Bobby quietly told him. "I understand why Evie's taken your side; the two of you are close. She's insanely protective over those she loves. To her, Charleigh's an outsider who causes you pain. But she's torn because she likes Faith."

Punch to the throat.

Knife to the heart.

Everyone enjoyed being around Faith because she was a sweet, polite kid who always seemed to have a smile.

"Holden, I hate to tell you this, but I don't think you can move on, either."

"Trust me, I've moved on."

Bobby's hands went to her hips and her eyes narrowed. For a short little thing, she could be seriously scary. When the woman was pissed, it was best to get out of her way and let her burn it out.

"Why are men so dumb?"

"I feel like that's a trick question."

Her eyes narrowed further. "It's not. It's a rhetorical question. I wasn't looking for an answer because there is none. Your definition of moving on is sexing up every woman you can find. That's not moving on. That's fucking away your cares. And by the by, Holden, most women don't like to be bedded and have the man bedding them thinking about another woman while they're doing the deed."

Well, Bobby was right about one thing, he had spent years trying to fuck his cares away. However, it didn't work. Nothing did. Not time, not war, not moving to a different state, not his work, nothing. Charleigh was never far from his thoughts. Charleigh and Faith.

Years and years of guilt had piled so high he was ready to collapse. The weight had compounded and multiplied until he was under maximum load and the ground beneath his feet had crumbled away, leaving him in constant freefall.

"I wasn't trying—"

"Save it. That's exactly what you were doing. Why'd you leave her?"

Holden snapped straight and shook his head.

"Bobby, it's cool of you to care. You know I love you, but you need to back off."

She seemed to consider his words, then in true Bobby fashion, decided to plow ahead.

"Right. Like Nix, Jameson, Weston, and Chasin have done? Back off and let you live in your Airstream all alone stewing and suffering by yourself? Is that what you mean?"

"I'm not stewing," he denied. "And I'm not suffering."

"That's a bullshit lie and you know it."

It certainly was. It was a big, fat, fucking lie. However, he did more than stew and suffer. He grieved and ached for all he'd lost. He sat alone agonizing over the stupid choices he'd made. But at the time, he'd felt like it was the right thing to do. He thought he was giving Charleigh what she needed to be happy.

"Bobby," he warned in a low growl. "Drop it."

"No. Your time's up. One of those men should've

pulled your head out of your ass when you left her. I get that men don't do touchy-feely, and things like emotions cause allergic reactions in tough macho men. But seriously, Holden, it's been a long time and you still love her. She loves you. You love each other." Bobby gave him a scathing look that told him she thought he was a dumbass. "So unless she did something so heinous, which I doubt because you said it was your fault, I don't understand why you won't try to fix things with her. So, tell me, why'd you'd leave her?"

"It's none of your business."

"Bull-shit. Bullshit. You're like the obnoxious big brother I wish I never had. Which means it's my duty as the pseudo little sister to make it my business. But more as your friend, I owe it to you to stop you from purposefully hurting yourself."

Holden found it increasingly difficult to hold his temper in check. The last seven months had taken a toll. It was one thing to live with the shame when Charleigh and Faith lived in another state. It was easier to pretend he hadn't screwed over a good woman. No, *easier* wasn't the word, nothing had been easy. Nothing could ever erase the indignity of his actions.

And that was part of why there was no fixing

what he'd done. He didn't deserve Charleigh's forgiveness.

"Holden—"

"She wanted kids. Lots of them," he sneered.

"And? You didn't?"

Hell yeah, he did. He wanted to give Charleigh everything she wanted. A big family, lots of love and laughter. He wanted to be a dad. Wanted it so badly, that when she came up pregnant his whole world shattered.

"I can't have kids."

A sour taste coated his tongue and his heart hurt so fucking bad his hand moved to his chest to massage the ache.

"What?" Bobby's face crumbled and all the attitude left her features.

"I couldn't give her what she wanted. What I wanted. One night we were lying in bed and she was whispering about our future. The house we'd live in, the family we'd make, the adventures we'd take our kids on and it hit me, I couldn't give her that. There would be no family, no adventures, no kids."

"Jesus, Holden, did it ever cross your mind the two of you could've adopted? You could've used a donor and had children that way?"

"No," he admitted. "Nothing crossed my mind

except I couldn't give my woman what she wanted. I lay in that bed, next to the woman I loved more than anything, wanting nothing more than to be able to give her a family. And after she fell asleep in my arms my mind wouldn't shut off. All I could think about were my shortcomings. All the pain she'd go through because of me. Adoption doesn't always lead to a happy ending. Birth parents can change their minds and take the baby back. I didn't want that for her. I wanted her to be happy. I wanted her to find a man who could give her everything I couldn't. I didn't want fertility doctors and disappointment. So I let her go. Only, I didn't know how goddamned painful it would be."

Never having admitted the truth, Holden felt like he'd run a marathon with a hundred-pound ruck on his back. His chest heaved and his muscles ached just from uttering the words. No one knew why he'd left Charleigh. No one knew he'd been exposed to radiation and he'd had to go to appointment after appointment to be tested and prodded.

"Whoa, whoa, whoa. Hold up." Bobby took a step in his direction, her face red with fury. "You didn't get to make that decision for her."

Suddenly facing the happy, smiling people at Alec's Christmas brunch didn't seem so bad. Actually, facing a firing squad would be preferable to discussing his sperm count with Bobby.

"We're not—"

"You know what?" Bobby exploded. "You're right, we're not...I'm so unbelievably pissed at you right now. I cannot believe you made an important life-changing decision *by yourself*. I cannot believe you're *that* guy. I love you, Holden, and once I'm over the shock of you being a total asshole, I'll be back. And when I am, we're finishing this conversation, so you'd better find a pair of big boy underwear, Holden, because I'm gonna make you fix this. If for no other reason so you both can move on."

With that ass-reaming, Bobby turned and stomped to the door. Her hand arrested in mid-air as she reached to push open the door. Her neck craned, and her face was bleached when she asked, "Do you still love her?"

Fucking hell.

"I'll love her until the day I die."

"Holden," she grumbled, but it sounded strangled and full of pity. "You need—"

"That's a hard no. And I mean that, Bobby. You do not go there. Not with me, not with Evie, not with anyone. I've fucked Charleigh's life enough, I will not do that to Faith, too."

"You owe it to Charleigh to tell her the truth. After all these years you're still hurting her. Think about that, while you're sitting in here stewing and suffering."

That was all he'd thought about for years. Wondering. Questioning. Doubting. Yearning. Aching.

He heard the metal door slam. His shoulders slumped forward and he hung his head in shame.

Holden was damn near rock bottom. There was no farther he could go in his humiliation. He'd disgraced himself, he degraded Charleigh, and he'd thrown his future away. All because he was an asshole.

He'd left Charleigh unprotected.

Paul Towler had known exactly what he was doing that night.

Fucking bastard.

It was time to pay the piper.

The truth needed to come out.

5

I was taking the last ornament off the tree when there was a knock at the door. I glanced at the clock and only twenty minutes had passed since Kennedy had come to pick up Faith. I pulled my cell out of my back pocket as I made my way down the stairs. No missed calls. Maybe Faith had forgotten something.

I opened the door and was met with the most dazzling pair of soulful eyes.

Then I remembered I'd turned over a new leaf and was actively, painstakingly, falling out of love with Holden. I'd even deleted his number from my phone. I hadn't seen him since the Saturday before Christmas, and even then I hadn't laid eyes on him. It was now a new year and I was determined to move on.

He also wasn't going to run me off. Faith liked her school, liked her new friends, loved McKenna and Kennedy like crazy, enjoyed the music lessons from Genevieve, and when Silver wasn't working, Faith liked to hear about all the "big boats" she got to pilot. And my daughter had bonded with Macy's daughter, Rory.

If Holden wanted me gone, that was too damn bad. He could eat a bag of dicks and choke on them.

"I'm busy," I said and started to shut the door.

Holden's hand shot out, preventing me from closing it.

"No, you're not. Kennedy picked up Faith and you're home by yourself."

I rocked back, wondering how he knew where my daughter was. Something I would contemplate further when I wasn't face-to-face with the man who'd inflicted the most pain I'd ever felt in my life.

"Just because Faith's not here doesn't mean I'm not busy."

"I need to talk to you."

Hell. To. The. No.

"You've got some brass balls coming to my door telling me you *need* to talk to me when the last time we exchanged words I told you I still loved you and you told me you didn't care. I heard you, Holden.

You don't care. I get it. I've kept my distance and I'll continue to do so."

"We can't go on like this, Leigh-Leigh."

Good gracious, that hurt.

"Don't call me that. And we can go on like this. You ignore me, I ignore you, and everything will be fine."

"And what about Faith?"

The day was sunny, albeit as cold as a witch's tit, but at that moment when he uttered my child's name, I could've sworn bolts of lightning sizzled across the sky and thunder crashed.

"Don't you dare bring my daughter into this conversation. You pretend she doesn't exist and—"

"But she does exist." Holden pushed the door open wider, forcing me to take a step back. My heels hit the bottom step and I started slowly walking up them backward. "And the Towlers are pulling their bullshit. She needs to be protected."

No freaking way.

Not now.

"I can't believe you." My statement was barely above a whisper. "After all this time. With everything going on, you're gonna do this now?"

"You're misunderstanding me."

The hell I was.

He was gonna try to take her from me.

He was gonna...I couldn't even think about what Holden was gonna do. My stomach bottomed out and I pitched forward. Before I could lose my balance, Holden was in front of me. His hand gripped my biceps and it felt like I'd been zapped. For years, I would've done anything to have him close. Now I didn't want the reminder of how his hands used to feel. Holden had always been into PDA—both public and private displays of affection. If I'd been close, he was touching me in some way. I used to live for those touches. Now his hands on me felt tainted. Everything we once had was poisoned and diseased. Ruined.

But my daughter wasn't. She was clean and bright and I wouldn't let him infect her.

"Get your hands off me." I jerked free and tromped up the stairs, resigning myself to the fact that if Holden wanted to have this particular talk, I wasn't going to be able to stop him.

However, I could control the conversation.

When we both made it into the living room I stopped, gathered my thoughts, and turned to face him. Then I let 'er rip. I should've taken more than a moment to think about what I wanted to say. I shouldn't have allowed my emotions to get the better of me. I shouldn't have done what I always did.

Unfortunately, no matter how badly I tried to forget what Holden did—tried to stop loving him, and move on—I couldn't.

"You know, you rolled out of our bed one morning and left me without an explanation. Yet, I was still stupid enough to let you come home, have sex with me, and spend the night holding me just to have you roll out and leave again. Over and over I let this happen, hoping—no, praying—you'd tell me what was wrong. That you'd let me help you. But you never did. Then when I begged you to stay, to stop leaving, to fix us, you told me I'd never see you again. You told me to forget you. And for days, I called you and fucking begged you to talk to me. You never, not one time, picked up or called me back. You did all of that and I still loved you. God, I'm stupid. Stupid and clueless."

"Leigh-Leigh—"

"No, Holden. Hell no. Fuck no. I've spent ten years loving you. You don't get anything else from me. Nothing. I don't care why you're here, what you need to talk to me about. You've ceased to exist for me *and* for Faith. You don't get her. You don't get to talk about her. You don't deserve to know about her."

Holden flinched and nodded. "You're right. I don't deserve her. Maybe if I hadn't been a dick when you told me, we could've worked things out. But I'd lost everything—"

"*You* lost everything?" I cut him off. "You? Are you fucking kidding, Holden? I was pregnant, scared, and you turned...me...away."

"I saw you with him!" Holden shouted. "I fucking saw you take him back to *our* house. You fucked him in *our* bed. *Ours*, Leigh-Leigh." His deep voice had taken on a hard edge—fury had taken hold, making it rumble as he finished. "I sat outside and watched that motherfucker leave my house after fucking my woman."

Fire hit my chest and my lungs singed as I inhaled.

"Oh, no, you're not putting that on me. I'm done feeling guilty. I'm done wearing the big, huge scarlet letter, everyone thinking I did you wrong. The day you left me, that apartment stopped being *our* home. When you refused to tell me what was wrong, that bed stopped being *yours*. I was at that stupid bar because I was heartbroken. I was lost. I was sad. And I thought you were gone forever. I had way too much to drink and did something I'm not proud of. But I got Faith out of it so you'll never hear me apologize."

"You got everything you wanted that night and I lost the woman I loved forever."

My vision blurred as every cell in my body turned to ice.

"Fuck you. You threw me away long before that night."

"She's not mine," Holden whispered and I froze. "I wanted her to be. I wish she was. Every fucking night I go to bed and wonder what our lives would be like if she was. I wonder if she'd have brothers and sisters. I wonder what kind of dad I would've been. I wonder what it would feel like to hold my child, rock her to sleep, watch you love our child. But none of that matters because she's not mine."

"There you go, Holden, denying she could be yours. But you're right. The only thing that matters right now is when I tracked you down and told you I was pregnant, you rejected us and told me to go find Paul and never bother you again. Which was what I did. And you know the shittiest part about that? Paul, a man who was merely a friend, not the man I loved and spent two years living with was excited I was pregnant. Over the moon happy. He knew the truth. I never lied to him. Yet, he still, claimed my child even though there was a possibility it wasn't his. He insisted we get married." A foreboding wave of violence was pulsing from Holden. I felt the cold seep into my bones but I ignored it and went on. "But, the man I loved, the man I wanted to marry, have a family with, spend my life with, turned me away."

"She can't be mine because I can't have fucking kids, Charleigh."

My world tilted and my legs turned to jelly. Holden couldn't have kids?

But before I could recover from his soul-crushing blow, he angrily continued, "I bet the asshole couldn't wait to marry you."

"What's that mean?"

"It means from the moment he met you, he was gagging to get in there. Everyone but you saw it."

Why were we talking about Paul when he'd just dropped a life-shattering bomb?

"Let's talk about—"

"No, Leigh-Leigh, he wasn't a *friend*. Not to me, not to you. On more than one occasion, I had to have words with him, to tell him to keep his distance."

"What?"

Paul had been friendly. He was always hugging, wrapping his arm around someone's shoulder. He'd been a little touchier than I normally would've liked and had zero sense of personal space. *But that didn't mean...*

"And not just me. Jameson straight out told him if he didn't stop touching you, he'd break his hands."

"What?"

I didn't want to discuss Paul, I wanted to know why he thought he couldn't have children. But he seemed hellbent on slandering my dead husband.

"Jesus Christ, really? Honest to God, Leigh-Leigh, he was always putting his arm around you."

"So? He was friendly."

"You ever see him do that to any other females that came around with one of the guys?"

Off of the top of my head I couldn't, but I'd see him plenty of times in bars put his arm around women...before he took them home for the night.

Wait.

I didn't like the insinuation that Paul had done anything wrong. He'd never tried anything inappropriate until that one night I was at the bar with Alison. By the time he showed up I was already three sheets to the wind.

I only vaguely remembered what happened that night.

"Paul's gone and you're trying to paint him as some sort of villain. He didn't do anything wrong, either. We weren't together. As a matter of fact, before we left the bar I remember him asking me if I was sure you were done with me."

Wrong thing to say. Way wrong. The hostility rolling off Holden was so thick I was surprised I hadn't choked. But when his face screwed up in disgust and his hate-filled words filled my ears, my world rocked.

"Don't you *ever* defend that asshole to me. He's gone so he can't answer for what he did to you. But make no mistake, he did wrong. He's not the villain in this story—that's me. I fucked up. But he's the fucking devil. He fucked you over so badly, you can't even begin to dream of all the ways your perfect husband screwed you over. And I hope for your sake when he came home to you and took you to your marital bed he gloved up."

"Are you saying—"

"I came here to make you an offer," he cut me off. "Our investigator in Virginia Beach called and informed me Beatrice has taken a second mortgage out on her house. She's prepared to fight to get Faith away from you. They've hired a PI in Virginia to try to dig up dirt on you, which they won't find because I already dug and there's nothing *to* find. Which means they'll make shit up. Word is, he's on his way to Maryland. Again, they won't find jackshit. You're a great mom, you have a good job, you give Faith a nice place to live."

"What's your offer?" I croaked, still stuck on the fact that Bitchface Bea had taken out a second mortgage on her house.

I couldn't afford to fight them unless I used Paul's money. I hadn't used a dime of it since he died and I never wanted to, but I would to keep Faith safe.

"They don't want Faith, they want Paul's death benefits."

"No shit, Sherlock. But they're not getting the money. And before you say something shitty and insult me, I haven't touched it. I never wanted it, but Paul would roll over in his grave if those bitches got it. He hated them. He never wanted them to have it."

"You're willing to risk Faith to protect a dead man's money?"

"How dare you?" My temper flared. "How fucking dare you, Holden."

"Give it to them and I'll replace the money. I'll make sure you and Faith are taken care of."

"No way. I don't want your money, either."

"Leigh-Leigh, think about Faith."

"Don't you dare tell me to think about Faith. She's all I think about. Every decision I've made since I found out I was pregnant has been about her. What was best for her."

"You're making a mistake. Trust me when I tell you Paul's not worth this. He's not worth your loyalty. Faith is the only one who's important. I can set the two of you up, you'd never have to worry about money. Just give them what they want and all of this can be over."

"Sure. It will all be over. You'll what, pay me off? Give me all your money so you can feel better about yourself? How you left me broken. Will trading money in a bank account erase the guilt? Because it sure as hell won't help me. I don't need Paul's money and I don't want yours. It won't fix my broken heart. It won't make me any less lonely. It won't do jack squat for me except tie me to you. Why'd you leave me, Holden? Why'd you destroy us?"

"Because I loved you. I tried to let you go. I tried to do the right thing. But I loved you so much I'd only make it days before the ache was so bad I gave in and went to you. I wish like hell I could've given you everything you wanted. Goddamn, do I wish that when you came to me and told me you were pregnant that I could've pulled you into my arms and kissed you and been excited with you that we were getting everything we wanted. But instead, in that moment all I could see were *my* failures. Paul could give you something I never could. I know I fucked up. I know I can never make up for what I did to you. But think about Faith. I can free you from those assholes and there will be no strings attached."

With that, Holden turned and jogged down the stairs, leaving me standing in my living room reeling.

It was too much.

Too much information. Too much hurt. Too many memories.

My heart sank and I dropped to the floor.

What the hell just happened?

6

Holden was walking back to the office when his cell rang. He didn't bother to pull the vibrating device from his pocket. After the blow-out with Charleigh, he was in no mood to speak to anyone.

With every step he took, anger and frustration thrummed through him. He'd said more than he'd intended, and in doing so he'd told Charleigh something he never should've. Not that he'd said it outright, but the implication was there and she was a smart woman. She'd put it together and either think Holden was behaving like a jilted lover—therefore lying—or she'd know the truth.

For years, he'd remained silent about a lot of things. Too many things. The reason why he'd left her was at the top of the list. Paul cheating on

Charleigh was a half-click down. Something Holden never understood was why, after Paul finally got what he wanted, did he defile it in the worst way? The fuck of it was, Paul hadn't been careful. It seemed that anytime the asshole had shown up where Holden was, he'd made a whole production out of picking up a woman. For the life of him, he could never figure out his play.

Why would a man deliberately try to sabotage his marriage? Unless he wanted Holden to tell Charleigh so Paul could deny it, accuse Holden of lying, and drive the wedge in deeper. It had been unnecessary, Holden had done that all by himself. There wasn't a wedge between him and Charleigh, there was an abyss of pain between them.

A chasm that Holden had dug with one incredibly bad decision.

How had his life spiraled so far out of control?

The vibrating stopped only to start again, and with a petulant sigh, he yanked his phone out and saw Nixon's name on the display.

"Yeah?" Holden rudely snapped.

"I'm not even gonna bother asking what's crawled up your bunghole because I'm fairly certain you're finally coming to terms with the multitude of ways you fucked up, which would mean that stick that's been up your ass is being twisted."

"Is there a reason you called?" he asked as he crossed the intersection.

"Jonny's here."

"Know that. I'm looking at his truck."

Holden continued to scan the street and saw Chasin's Charger and Weston's Jeep parked in front of the office.

"We'll wait for you to brief." Nixon hung up and Holden slowed his pace, needing all the extra time he could get before he faced his friends.

By the time Holden entered the office, his thoughts were no less heavy.

He'd screwed up again. Damned if he did, damned if he didn't. There was no winning this battle and his best course of action was to stay away from Charleigh. He'd caused enough turmoil and pain.

"Conference room," Nixon unnecessarily called out.

Holden shoved all thoughts of Charleigh to the back of his mind and locked them up where they belonged—in a box marked, do not open. Unfortunately, the padlocks were weak, the catches too flimsy to keep him from accessing the memories anytime he wanted. Which was daily. He had an unhealthy fixation on his past. It had been the only time in his life he'd truly been happy. It was hard not to lie in his bed and remember all the reasons why he'd fallen for Charleigh. And when the pain of losing her inevitably came, he used it to punish himself for being such a bastard.

"What's going on?" Holden asked when he entered the room.

Everyone was there: Weston, Jameson, Chasin, Nix, Alec, Jonny, even Micky was sitting at the large table with her laptop open in front of her.

"Jonny's got a case he needs to work through," Nix answered.

This wasn't unusual. Gemini Group had worked with the Kent County Sheriff's Department many times.

"This is technically Vaughn's case but something's not sitting right," Jonny started.

Vaughn Holbrook had been on Alec Hall's team when they'd served in the Navy. They'd been stationed in San Diego so Holden had never crossed paths with the man. But Nixon had when he'd gone to California for training. Vaughn had separated from the Navy before any of them had and spent years wandering around until Alec had reached out and pulled him into the fold. Nixon offered the former SEAL a job at Gemini Group but he'd declined and joined the sheriff's department.

One could say Vaughn wasn't open to connections. The man made Jameson look friendly and in comparison made Holden seem well-adjusted. However, by all accounts, Vaughn was a good deputy who simply enjoyed solitude and isolation. Holden could understand the need for both. That was one reason he lived alone in his Airstream.

"Does this have to do with the two girls from a few weeks ago?" Holden inquired.

They'd found the girls, unharmed but freaked the fuck out. They'd been no help identifying the man who'd taken them.

Jonny scrubbed his hands over his face, and when he looked up, regret was clearly visible. "We're missing something. The pieces are all here."

"What's your gut telling you?" Jameson inquired.

"Not sure. But something is not right."

Jonny slid a file folder to the middle of the table. "This is from a year ago. A report was filed by the parents of a seventeen-year-old girl. They waited until she was two hours late for curfew, then they started calling her friends. An hour later, they called the KCSD to file a missing person report. She was found a few hours later sleeping in her car."

"Out drinking and didn't want to go home and get busted by her parents?" Weston tossed out.

"If her shirt hadn't been torn, two fingernails hadn't been broken, and pure terror wasn't in her eyes, I'd say yes. But that was the story she gave to us and her parents."

"Her parents didn't question how her shirt was torn?" Nixon asked as he picked up the file and opened it.

"They did. She told them she was at a party with some girlfriends and they were jacking around and she accidentally ripped her shirt. The parents were overcome with relief that their daughter was safe, they didn't question whether or not she was actually unharmed."

Holden glanced at the report Nix had pulled from the file and waited for Jonny to continue.

"Next one, missing person report filed by parents when their sixteen-year-old was three hours late coming home. She showed up when the deputies were there taking the report. Unfortunately, both officers were in the house so they didn't see the car that dropped her off. Her story was, she had a boyfriend who lived in Delaware, they'd lost track of time. However, the deputy noted her makeup was smeared and it looked like she'd been crying. Her skirt had blood on it, and she wasn't wearing shoes. In that case, the dad was so pissed he asked the officers to leave. The last thing they noted was faint bruising on her wrists and ankles."

Jonny paused and pulled out another file.

"This one." He stopped again and cleared his throat. "Was my case. Six months ago, I was on shift and got called out to a noise complaint out on Perkins Hill Road. The caller said it sounded like cars were racing. Something that happens on that stretch of road a lot. We went out there, and indeed there was a group racing, but there was also a large gathering of cars in front of the Morgan residence. Two squads took care of the boys racing and I went to the house. The Morgans were out of town, leaving their eighteen-year-old son, Tyler, home alone. Kids scattered like cockroaches, a few were given alcohol citations, and the two twenty one year olds were given a summons for distributing alcohol to minors."

Jonny looked around the table, shook his head, then glanced back at the report. "Molly Buchannan. I found her outside about thirty feet from the main house, behind a barn. When I walked up she was adjusting her clothes. I gave her a moment to get herself presentable and walked her back to the house. Mascara was running down her cheeks, she had scratch marks on her arms, and she was visibly terrified. She was also sober. She swore she was just embarrassed she'd been caught with her boyfriend and nothing had happened. Since she was sober, not breaking any laws, I had no reason to detain her. I did follow up with her parents and they said she was upset with herself because her friends had talked her into going to the party and there was drinking going on. I had no evidence a crime had been committed so there was nothing further I could do. But there are some things you just know in your gut but can't prove. Whatever had happened to her was not consensual."

"Playing Devil's advocate here," Weston said. "But getting caught by the cops having sex with your boyfriend would probably freak any teenage girl out."

Undeterred by Weston's comment, Jonny continued.

"Three months ago, a fourteen-year-old girl was reported missing at midnight when her mom heard a car stop in front of her house. The way the mom tells it, she had a bad feeling and went to check on her daughter. She found her daughter missing, the bedroom window unlocked and left open a couple of inches. The mom wasted no time calling the KCSD. The girl called her mom at five the next morning asking her to come pick her up from McDonald's. Her story was, she'd snuck out and gone to a party in Queen Anne county. She refused to give any names because she was a freshman and they were seniors and she didn't want to snitch. She'd rather take the heat from her mom than be shunned at school. Kimberly Lot committed suicide last month."

Jesus fuck.

"Any prior issues with mental health?" Holden asked, then followed up with, "How did she look when you picked her up from the McDonald's?"

"No prior issues on record. It was a shock to her teachers, coaches, and family." Jonny held Holden's gaze and he braced for Jonny's next answer. "We took Kimberly's mom to pick her up and all it took was one look at the girl's dead eyes to tell she'd been violated. We brought in a female deputy and social services but Kimberly insisted nothing had happened, she was just scared her mom was going to be mad since she snuck out. And she said she was upset because the girls she thought were her friends left her at the McDonald's instead of driving her home."

Before Holden could process the horror of a young girl taking her life and the possibility of what could've been done to her that night, Micky spoke.

"You have a pattern. Every three months to the day." Micky looked up from her laptop. "You also have a type. All blondes, all in high school. There's a reason these girls aren't reporting what happened to them. My guess would be he's much older and someone in a position of power, or perceived power. The girls are scared of him—he likely threatened to harm them if they talked, maybe told them no one would believe them, or he could've threatened their families."

"That's my opinion as well," Jonny agreed. "And the two girls we found, they were taken three months after Kimberly. Both blondes."

"If you're working a profile, Elliana and Ayla don't fit. They said they were together the whole time."

"Upping the thrill factor," Jameson tossed out, and Holden's stomach revolted at the suggestion.

Holden hadn't been with Jonny, Nixon, and Weston when they'd found the girls but he'd heard the story they'd given Jonny and it didn't add up. From start to finish, it sounded like bullshit. The girls said they'd been at a bonfire with a group of friends when they'd wandered off and gotten lost. Holden and Jameson had searched the stretch of beach they'd claimed to have been at and there was no evidence of a bonfire or a party. And there was the small detail that the road they'd been found on was over ten miles away from where the party had supposedly happened. Not to mention there were a lot of hours unaccounted for between the mid-afternoon when neither set of parents could get ahold of their children and when the party started. And another long stretch of time from when they'd wandered away from their friends and when they were found.

"Have they changed their story?"

Jonny frowned and nodded. "So many times, I've lost count."

"What about the nine-one-one caller?" Nixon inquired.

After hours of searching, they'd caught a break when the 911 call came in from a motorist that two young girls were walking down a dark country road in the wee hours before dawn. The caller was a man, had told the dispatcher he didn't want to approach and scare the girls but he'd keep them in his sights until units could arrive.

"His name's Cory Saddler. He said he didn't see

anything. No other cars on the road, he didn't pass anyone else walking. Just Elliana and Ayla."

"Do you know this guy?" Weston asked.

"I know of him," Jonny answered. "His daughter, Miranda, graduated a few years ago. Went to Ole Miss on a full ride."

"Academic?" McKenna rejoined.

"Soccer. Cory coached rec soccer until Miranda went to the high school, then he started coaching there. He still does."

A tingle of concern hit Holden and he glanced at Nixon. The apprehension he saw there confirmed he wasn't the only one who didn't like the sound of the 911 caller having ties to the high school.

"What was Cory doing out on Caulks Field Road at four in the morning?"

"Leaving for work. He lives in Rock Hall and works in Annapolis. He leaves early to avoid the Bay Bridge traffic."

"That's mighty early," Weston noted. "As in two hours earlier than he needs to. Is he married?"

"Divorced."

"Did you ask his ex-wife if this was normal?"

Jonny's face bleached and he shook his head. "No. I didn't question anyone in regard to Cory.

Why would he call in the sighting if he had something to hide?"

"Cover. Establishing doubt," Micky started. "He'd call it in to do exactly what you're doing right now—dismissing him."

"I'll contact his ex-wife."

"What do you need from us?" Nixon shuffled the papers in front of him.

"I need a fresh set of eyes. If this is what I think it is, we have just about two months before he'll find his next victim. Something happened to one or both of those girls and they're lying through their teeth. Something also happened to the other four girls but they're shit scared and won't talk. Vaughn and I are working it on our end but Kent County's experiencing a crime wave and we're low on resources. I can't give this case the manpower it deserves. I need your help."

"Anything you need," Alec joined the conversation. "How open is Kimberly Lot's mom to talking to the police? She might be the key."

Jonny's guilt-ridden gaze went to Alec and Holden felt bad for the man. This last year had not been good for him personally, and by the sound of it, he was taking hits professionally as well.

"She is, or she was, a single mom. Kimberly's

father lives in Florida. As expected, she's completely undone. We offered victims assistance and she turned it down. Her house is on the market and last I heard she wants away from Cliff City as fast as that can happen. She might be open to talking, but I recommend sending in McKenna."

"I can do that. I'd be interested in looking around Kimberly's computer and phone."

"Appreciate your help on this. I'll leave the files. Let me know if you need anything else. Vaughn knows I was coming here today to ask for help. He's good but he's new, so he appreciates the help as well."

Jonny stood and the rest of the men followed. Holden and Chasin stayed in the conference room with Micky while the rest of the team walked Jonny out.

"How'd the talk go?" Holden looked at his friend and shook his head. His conversation with Charleigh still churned in his gut, the bitter taste of his words still on his tongue.

"We're not going there."

They were stuck in a never ending circle of grief, and no matter what Holden did, he couldn't find the off-ramp. He had no clue how to end their misery.

She needed to move on and find a good man, not only for her but for Faith as well.

Saliva pooled in his mouth at the thought.

And with all due haste, he hightailed his ass out of the office.

7

"So," Kennedy started, and I turned from watching Tank chasing Faith around the backyard to my friend. "Time to spill."

"What?"

"I've given you ample time to get to know me. You trust me with Faith. So, now it's time you spill the beans."

She was asking about Holden.

Shit.

The last thing I wanted to do was dig through painful memories—not only because the shame that came with that time in my life was something I'd tried hard not to think about. I glanced back at my daughter and my heart started to throb. My daughter was the best thing that had ever happened to me. But the heartbreak that surrounded her conception still stung.

"You're hurting and stressed out," Kennedy went on. "I can see it, we all can. But today it's worse. Did the Towlers do something new?"

I needed a friend. I had to talk to someone about what was going on or I was going to explode.

With one more glance at Faith to make sure she was happily occupied with Tank, I launched in.

"Holden came over."

"Today?"

"Twenty minutes after you left. He showed up, said he wanted to talk, and pushed his way inside my house."

Kennedy gave me big eyes and said, "I kinda thought he was avoiding you. I know, you know, that *we* all know, you and Holden used to be together, then you...well...you...um..."

"Got pregnant and married Paul. Who happened to be one of Holden's teammates and friends," I offered in an effort to put her out of her stammering misery.

"Well...I'm sure it's way more complicated than that. I'll be honest with you, I was curious, I mean we all are about what happened. I asked Jameson but he wouldn't tell me anything. McKenna knows some, but obviously not directly from Holden."

I was surprised to hear that. I'd actually thought that Holden would've happily painted me as the bad guy.

"You're surprised to hear that," Kennedy noted.

"Yeah. I figured the way things ended, he'd be all too happy to make me sound like a cheating bitch. Which I'm not. I never cheated on him."

I fidgeted on the wrought iron chair, pulled my scarf tighter, and wondered if I was doing the right thing. Kennedy was married to Jameson. Holden and Jameson were close, they worked together. It probably wasn't right unloading my burdens on her.

"I'm sorry. I didn't mean to make you uncomfortable. It's just that I know what it's like to have the weight of the world on your shoulders and no one to talk to. If you don't want to talk to me, I get it—"

"No," I rushed out. "You're Jameson's wife. I don't want to put you in a weird place and I don't want you to think I'm talking trash about Holden because I'm not. He's your friend."

"Who's *your* friend?"

Kennedy's question made my eyes sting. I'd lost most of my friends when Holden and I broke up, and the few who had hung around turned their backs on me when I found out I was pregnant. My whole life had revolved around Holden.

I eventually found new friends but they were more work acquaintances. All they'd known was, I was a widowed single mother. And when I moved, they'd dropped off, too.

"Damn, Charleigh, I didn't mean to upset you."

"You didn't," I sighed. "I don't know how my life got here. I'm stuck. Some days it feels like the morning I woke up and found Holden packing. Other days it feels like being with him was a lifetime ago. We've been apart longer than we were together and I can't stop loving him. What's wrong with me?"

Ten minutes with Holden and I was right back to the sad-sack in love with a man who'd kicked me to the curb. No self-respecting woman would allow herself to throw her life away.

"Nothing's wrong with you," she whispered. "Why'd he break up with you?"

"No clue."

"What?"

I slowly exhaled before I told her the truth. "I don't know why because he refused to tell me. One day everything was good. The next morning, I woke up and he was packing. He just said he couldn't be with me. For months I begged him to tell me what was wrong and he never would."

"What an ass," she mumbled and my stomach knotted.

"He's not," I defended, hating that Kennedy thought that. "We shouldn't talk about this. It's really not cool of me to tell you this. I don't want you to think badly about him. And Jameson probably wouldn't be happy if you...I don't know, took my side, or got mad at Holden. And seriously, I don't want anyone taking sides and I really don't want Jameson mad at me. You all have been really good with Faith. I can't take that away from her."

"What about you, Charleigh?"

"What about me?"

"Who do you have?"

God, there was that question again. The one I didn't want to answer because I had no one, and admitting it made me feel like more of a loser than I already did.

"I have Faith."

"Your daughter doesn't count."

"She totally does. She's all that counts. I can't risk upsetting you and Jameson. She needs good people in her life. I'll figure it out, I always do."

"I don't like knowing you're hurting and you don't have anyone to turn to."

"Maybe there's a reason I lost all my friends when I lost Holden. Maybe I'm as horrible as they all thought I was—being with one man and getting knocked up by another. Maybe I've spent all these years blaming Holden for leaving me and breaking my heart so I wouldn't have to face what I did. Maybe they're all right, it didn't matter that Holden dumped me and shattered the perfect future I thought we were going to have. I'm still the bed-hopper, the slut that got drunk and had a one-night stand that resulted in my daughter being conceived. It's all my—" I clamped my mouth shut and closed my eyes when I heard Kennedy gasp.

Oh, shit.

Fuck me running, I said way too much.

Way. Too. Much.

"Could Holden—"

"He says no. But I didn't hide anything from him," I rushed out. "Paul knew, too."

Kennedy's brows hit her hairline. Then they pulled together and her face slowly turned red.

"You wouldn't have told him if there wasn't a chance," she scoffed.

"Kennedy, please—"

"What a dick."

"Please don't say that. Please—"

"I swear to you, I won't breathe a word to anyone, but I'm seriously pissed at Holden."

"You don't understand. It was complicated. Everything was messed up. Then my parents got involved and it got more twisted until I did the only thing I could to get everyone off my back. Maybe if I hadn't been rushed into marrying Paul, Holden and I could've worked it out."

It had been the perfect storm. Holden had told me he never wanted to see me again. I'd slept with Paul, then I'd spent weeks feeling like a disgusting bitch for letting it happen. I found out I was pregnant. Holden had flipped out. My parents had freaked out and demanded I be married before I was showing so they wouldn't be embarrassed around their friends. Paul asked me to marry him, then we'd rushed everything because he and his team were leaving for training and he wanted us married before he left. It was the craziest ten days of my life. I couldn't think straight, so I agreed.

That was when I knew there was no fixing me and Holden.

We were over—forever.

"I'm not even talking about Faith right now. I'm

pissed he broke up with you and didn't bother to tell you why. Who does that?"

"He told me the baby couldn't be his."

"Right," she snapped. "Were you having sex with him?"

God, would I ever stop feeling the shame of bed-hopping?

"The week before," I admitted and braced for her repugnance.

"Damn, Charleigh, you look like I'm gonna judge you. He broke up with you. You didn't do anything wrong."

"I was drunk and—"

"Stop. I don't care if you were stone sober. You did nothing wrong. You weren't together with Holden and slept with someone else. That doesn't make you a bad person."

"But Paul was—"

"Jeez, why do women always have to shoulder the guilt? Have you ever stopped to think that if Paul was such a good friend to Holden he never would've touched you? Obviously, Paul wasn't thinking about his friend when he crawled into bed with you."

No, I hadn't thought about it like that, mainly because I'd been too busy beating myself up. To be honest, I hadn't thought about much except how badly I'd felt that Paul had been stuck with me the months before he died.

"I can't do this," I announced. "I'm sorry, Kennedy. I appreciate you offering to be my friend, but trust me, if you knew all the screwed-up things I did, you wouldn't be offering." I stood up and swiped at my tears before they started to roll down my cheeks. "Please, don't be mad at Holden. We both messed up. It was both of our faults."

"I don't see how you can think that."

"Because he was mine and I missed something. Something big. I thought everything was great but it wasn't. There was something wrong and I missed the signs. Or maybe he'd been telling me in his own way he was unhappy and I ignored it."

"Or maybe he's a dumbass and should've talked to you."

"I just want to stop loving him," I whispered. "I want to forget. I never should've moved up here, but after Holden almost died I couldn't stop myself. I had to know. I had to try to get him to listen to me one more time. It was selfish. I uprooted my daughter. I infiltrated his life. And now that I'm here, I can't bear to take you all away from Faith. So, please, don't be mad at him. Just pretend I never told you."

"Charleigh." Kennedy reached out and I stepped back.

"Please."

"Okay. I won't be mad."

My mother was wrong, I wasn't a reactor. I was a ruiner. Everywhere I went I ruined people's lives.

8

"Yo!" Chasin called out as he opened the door to Holden's Airstream.

He really needed to start locking the door. Actually, he needed to hook his rig up and move it off of Genevieve and Chasin's land.

"Dude. Knock much?" Holden pulled his head out of the fridge. Not technically—however, he straightened after a solid five minutes of staring even though it was mostly empty.

"Evie's in her studio," Chasin informed Holden, as if that was an excuse not to knock. "I've given you a week and you haven't said anything."

"About?"

"Charleigh—"

"Don't go there." He slammed the door and

pinned Chasin with a stare. "No more talking about Charleigh."

"Brother, it's eating you up. It's time we talk about what happened."

"What happened is I fucked over a good woman and I'm gonna pay for that for the rest of my life. There's nothing more to it. And shut the damn door if you're coming in, I'm not trying to heat the outside."

Chasin closed the door but made no move to come farther in.

Good. That meant he wasn't planning on staying, which if Evie was just across the yard in her music studio, Holden wasn't surprised.

Genevieve Ellison-soon-to-be-Murray, or better known by her stage name Vivi Rush, had a set of golden pipes. There was a reason she'd climbed to the top of the charts when she'd released an album. However, she'd given up the fame to do what she loved to do—write music and help new artists. She and Chasin had converted an old barn into a kickass recording studio and office for Evie. The bottom floor also had a badass bar and lounge area.

Sometimes when she had bands she was producing over, they'd sit around the firepit in the space between Holden's Airstream and the studio and throw back a couple of beers and jam. Sometimes the whole gang would come over and sometimes it would only be Holden and Chasin joining, sitting back to enjoy a live show.

"I've waited a long time to ask you this," Chasin started. "Why'd you never tell Charleigh about Paul cheating on her?"

Holden tried but failed to keep his frame from going solid. He contemplated playing dumb, however, there was zero chance Chasin would fall for that line of bullshit.

"How'd you know?"

"Saw him the night we were at The Dog right before we took that trip to Tennessee. That was what, a month into their marriage? Asshole didn't even try to hide it."

The normal anger that accompanied thinking about all the fucked-up shit Paul had done flared to life. That night at the bar, Paul had been particularly open about taking a blonde out the front door only to come back in a half-hour later with a smile.

"Everyone else know?"

"My guess is Nix suspected it, but you know him. The way Paul died, he likely erased every bad thought he ever had about the man. Jameson was never Paul's biggest fan. He wasn't thrilled when

Paul got shuffled into our squad when CJ left so he didn't pay much attention to Paul. But Jameson was there that night, so I'd say he didn't miss Paul flaunting that shit in front of you. But—"

All the hair on the back of Holden's neck stood on end.

"Wait. What? You think he was flaunting picking up a woman in front of me?"

"Actually, I think he was taunting you with it. Paul never did hide the fact he was jealous as fuck of you. You beat him at pretty much everything."

Jesus fuck.

"Seriously? I knew he had his eye on Charleigh, but she's gorgeous so I didn't think much about it."

Chasin was quiet for a good long stretch before he seemed to win some internal battle and said, "I screwed you over."

Holden's brows knitted together and his muscles bunched at his friend's admission.

"Come again?"

"That day in the park when I met with Charleigh. She told me straight out she loved you. I should've advised her not to marry Paul. But she was a wreck. Her parents were down her throat about the kid being born without a father. You'd pushed her away. Paul was pressing her hard to get married and do it before we left on that workup. She was so scared I didn't know how to tell her."

Acid bubbled as vile thoughts ran through Holden's head.

"Did he...get her pregnant on purpose?" The question left a sour taste behind and more anger grew.

"I think he knew she was at the bar with Alison and hightailed his ass over there looking for his shot. There was only one thing he could do to hurt you and that was to take Charleigh. I think her winding up pregnant was icing on that particular cake. With her trapped, he'd win."

"Jesus Christ. Fucking hell!" Holden exploded.

With his body taut and his temper rising, Holden thought back to that night. The team had all been at Weston's place playing poker. Holden was coming back to the table from grabbing a beer when he heard Nixon mumbling this was his last hand, Alison and Charleigh were at The Dog and drunk, and he needed to pick them up. Nix had made his statement quietly, not meaning for Holden to overhear. By that time, no one was mentioning Charleigh's name in front of him. Before the hand was dealt, Paul had stood and announced he was done for the night.

Paul had heard Charleigh was drunk and left.

Son of a bitch.

"I saw them that night," Holden admitted. "When I left Weston's, I went to her place to apologize. I couldn't live with what I'd done to her and I needed to tell her the truth. Then I saw them get out of a taxi. I sat outside like a stalker and waited until Paul left."

"Christ, Holden, you never said you saw them."

"I've never said a lot of shit I should've. I never told Charleigh about Paul fucking other women. I never told her why I left her."

"Why haven't you?"

"Because it no longer matters."

Holden barely recognized his own voice. Defeat laced every word. He'd fucked up and lost her and now it felt like he was losing her all over again. A feeling that was so crippling he wasn't sure he'd survive. Hell, he didn't deserve to survive it. He'd earned every twinge of pain, every stab of regret, every twist of the knife when he looked at Faith.

"I think it matters a lot, Holden. It's been years and neither of you have moved on. If nothing else, don't you think you owe it to her to come clean so she can find some semblance of happiness? I've watched her since she's moved here. She's not living. She works, she gives everything to Faith, she smiles on cue when she's with us, but she is miserable. And I'm not even gonna start on how you live your life—but, brother, it's painful to watch. Don't you want to find a woman and have a family?"

A trail of agony slithered down his spine.

Family.

Holden wasn't capable of having a family—that option had been taken away from him courtesy of the Navy.

"No, Chasin, I don't want either of those," he lied.

The truth was, all Holden had wanted was to build a family with Charleigh.

"Holden—"

"Trust me, a family is something I will never have."

That wasn't a lie. Holden would never have what he'd desired most. He was utterly incapable of making one.

The two men stood in the tiny space and locked eyes. Holden allowed his friend to see every ounce of remorse and pain he felt. When Chasin clenched his jaw, Holden knew he saw it.

Before Chasin could question him further, he changed the subject. "Who's going in with Micky tomorrow?"

The team had decided to delay reaching out to Kimberly's mom until they had more information. There was no need to cause the woman anymore pain than she'd already experienced if Jonny was wrong and the incidences weren't linked. No one wanted to cause the grieving mother undue stress.

However, after a week of investigating, the team felt Jonny was right and it was time for Micky to make contact with Kimberly's mom.

"No one. She wants to go in alone. It's her opinion Donna Lot wouldn't be comfortable with any of us there."

Holden nodded his agreement. They'd discussed some of the questions Micky was going to ask and he didn't think any mother would be comfortable discussing her daughter's possible abuse in front of a man, especially one she didn't know.

"I hate for Micky to take it on herself, but it's the best play."

Once again, the men fell silent, a host of emotions flickering in Chasin's gaze. His right eye twitched—Chasin's tell that he was annoyed—and Holden braced.

"I think you need to tell Charleigh who Paul really was."

That was not what he thought his friend was

going to say. He was also not going to get into another Charleigh conversation.

"That's not gonna happen. I already let a few things slip. He's dead and gone. I'm not going to dishonor the memory of her husband." The flavor of his words made him wince.

Her husband.

Charleigh had married the bastard.

His beauty Leigh-Leigh had a lying, cheating asshole for a husband and that was Holden's fault, too.

"Hold—"

"You should go see what Evie's up to," Holden cut him off.

"Stubborn fuck," Chasin muttered and exited.

He wasn't stubborn, he was finally being smart.

Hours later, Holden was in bed on his back staring at his favorite picture. Leigh-Leigh sitting in his lap, her thick brown hair loose around her, a beautiful smile on her face, her eyes brimming with happiness. She looked so happy. He looked like a man who knew he had it all.

Then he threw it away.

9

"Do you think when me and Rory are done, can you take us to get milkshakes?" Faith happily chirped.

It had been a long, exhausting week and I was looking forward to Aurora Hall coming over to play with Faith all morning. With Rory over, Faith would be occupied and I could finally have time to look over the paperwork my attorney had mailed me.

For the last two weeks, I'd slept like shit. All I could think about was what Holden had said. Which was counterproductive to me, trying to live my life *not* thinking about him. I couldn't be bothered to give much thought to Holden knowing Paul had been cheating on me, when the Towlers were now having me followed.

It was on that thought, I answered my daughter,

"Not today, sweets." Faith frowned and I quickly went on, "But I will order you pizza with extra garlic knots and we have root beer."

"Can we make floats?"

"You sure can."

"Yippy!" Faith squealed and started for the stairs. "I'm gonna get the dollhouse so it's ready when Rory gets here."

I watched as my excited daughter bounced up the stairs to get the wooden dollhouse she and her friend would spend hours gluing together, and reminded myself that was why I was fighting the Towlers. I was protecting that exuberance and free spirit. They didn't want her, they wanted to punish me. They didn't love and care about her well-being, she was a pawn in their disgusting game.

The PI the Towlers had sent to Kent County to dig up dirt on me was not a very good one if Nixon had found him hours after his arrival. Nix had called to tell me the investigator was in town and he'd send me a picture so I knew who to look for. He'd also ensured me he'd had a chat with the man and made it clear he was not to approach me or Faith. If he did, I was to call Nix or one of the other guys right away. So far, I'd seen the PI but he hadn't gotten close. Even if I hadn't received the picture, I would've been able to spot the man. He wasn't exactly inconspicuous. Though, if I hadn't known who he was, I would've marched my happy ass straight to him the first time I saw him lift his camera in my direction and kicked him in the balls.

I couldn't say I was pleased some creep was taking pictures of Faith and me, but I could say I was mighty happy that even though Beatrice had taken out a second mortgage she still couldn't afford the best. This lawsuit was going to eat through my savings quickly enough as it was.

My gaze went out the window and I smiled when I saw the piles of snow. Later today, after Rory and Faith were done putting together the dollhouse, I'd take them outside to build a snowman. There was a small courtyard between my front door and the restaurant next door—it would be the perfect place to let the girls have some fun without worrying about Alec losing his mind because his daughter's picture had been taken.

There was a knock at the door and a tingle went up my spine. I knew that feeling, the same dread I had whenever Holden was near.

"Is that them?" Faith yelled down the stairs.

I turned and found her looking down at me from the landing.

"No, baby. Rory's not getting dropped off for another few hours."

"I thought maybe she was early."

"Nope. Macy would've called."

Without further complaint, Faith rushed back up to her room.

My plan to ignore the door was dashed at the very loud pounding.

I wanted another altercation with Holden—never. But more than that, I didn't want to have one with my daughter around. I wasn't a very reasonable person on a good day; being confronted by Holden's presence sent me over the edge, straight to insanity. I was still in deep denial, telling myself I no longer loved him.

Now I couldn't stop myself from thinking about how destroyed he looked when he told me he couldn't have kids. *No way he'd lie about that, would he? No.* I quickly shoved that thought aside. Holden could be an ass but he'd never lie about that.

I wanted her to be.

I wish she was.

God, why did he have to say those things? It had taken all of my strength not to rush to his side and pull him into my arms. Despite everything he'd done to us, it killed to see him in so much pain.

But I couldn't. He didn't want me to console him. He didn't want me to touch him. He didn't want me, period.

How the hell could he blurt out something so huge, then not elaborate, not talk about it, not tell me if that was why he'd left me? And if that was the reason, I didn't know how I felt about that. *Furious* came to mind, but so did *sadness*.

Time. I just needed more time and one day I'd forget about him. But when the third knock came, I knew today would not be the day he started to fade into the back of my mind.

No, today was going to be the day I made it clear, he was never to show up at my house uninvited, and since I'd never invite him, he'd never be welcome.

I was on the bottom step when the fourth bang started.

"Keep your pants on."

I threw the door open and froze.

That single moment of extreme fear was a moment too long. I started to slam the door but a very large man shoved it open.

Then my world went black.

Faith.

"Charleigh."

Someone called my name. Though it sounded like I was in a tunnel. A long, dark tunnel. I was running, trying to get to the end—I had to get to Faith but I couldn't do it. Every time the end drew near, the road in front of me would lengthen and I'd have farther to go.

Why was Faith running from me?

"Why isn't she waking up?"

There it was again, a whisper of a voice. I wanted to wake up and get out of this nightmare.

"I'll be back."

Holden.

He was there. Was he taking Faith? Why couldn't I catch her? Where'd she go?

10

Holden had known terror. He'd known dread. He'd felt the gut-clenching fear of a firefight, moments when you weren't sure if you or the men by your side would make it out alive. But he'd never felt those things when they were coated in love. Seeing Charleigh's blood spilled in the foyer of her apartment had almost been his undoing. In the single most difficult moment of his life, he had to hold himself together. Push away every emotion so he could find Faith. He couldn't think about what had happened to Leigh-Leigh or he'd lose control.

"Are you sure you want to go before she regains consciousness?" Chasin asked when they stepped out of Charleigh's hospital room.

Fuck no, he didn't want to leave her side. But he

knew Charleigh would put Faith before herself. That was the only reason he was leaving her in a hospital bed with a fractured skull and a concussion.

"Faith's been gone for three hours, it doesn't matter what I want. I need to find her," Holden replied, nearly choking on the words.

"Where are you gonna go? We have no leads," Chasin reminded him.

They had jackshit because when Macy had found Charleigh, she was sprawled out on the floor, a pool of blood waterfalling down the stairs where Charleigh had cracked open her head. After a call to 911, she called Alec, who called the rest of the team and everyone descended on the scene at the same time.

Faith was gone.

They'd looked in every closet, under every bed, in the cabinets, in the attic space, anywhere and everywhere Faith could've hidden, they looked.

Just gone.

And no one saw a thing. There were no security or traffic cameras in the area. They had nothing to go on. Except Holden did. His gut screamed the Towlers had taken her. The question was, how had they overpowered Charleigh. Beatrice was old, Charleigh would beat the hell out of the woman if she'd threatened to enter. Patricia might be able to take Charleigh, but with Faith on the line, he doubted it. Besides, Charleigh had no defensive wounds.

No, she had a fucking possible fractured skull and a missing child.

"I'm going with you," Chasin said.

"I need you to stay here with Charleigh."

"The rest of the team and the women will be here."

Holden grappled with how to explain to his friend why he needed him to stay with Charleigh. He didn't understand it fully himself but he needed Chasin to keep her safe.

"She's closest to you." Holden pointed out.

"She's close to all of us."

"No, she was always closest to you. Before she married Paul, she sought you out. And then there's Genevieve..."

"Are you saying what I think you're saying?"

It was no secret—Genevieve pretty much hated Charleigh. Bobby was a tossup. That left Micky and Kennedy to keep Charleigh calm, though Macy and Silver would pitch in. But Holden needed Chasin to monitor the situation.

"You know Evie, you know Charleigh's not her

favorite person, but I am. She'll worry about me and likely that's gonna make her on-edge. I need you to keep Charleigh safe until I can bring Faith home."

"Evie would never hurt Charleigh," Chasin snapped. "But you're right, Evie's gonna be worried for you."

"Let's hit the road." Chasin and Holden turned to find Jameson stalking toward them. "I've got my truck loaded up."

"I'm—"

"Heard what you said to Chasin and I agree, she's closest to him so he should stay. But that doesn't mean you're going alone."

Holden didn't have the time or patience to argue about who was going or staying. Moreover, Faith didn't have the time. He needed to get on the road—he should've done it the moment he'd realized Faith had been taken—but he'd needed to lay eyes on Charleigh before he left.

"You're gonna find her."

Chasin's proclamation hit him square in the chest and threatened to crack the reinforced walls he'd built. He couldn't allow a single twinge of emotion to color his anger. He had to stay completely detached or he'd find himself crumbling under the debilitating fear. His friend meant well, but none of them had any idea how close he was to breaking down.

Holden had seen the blood, had watched Charleigh get loaded into an ambulance, he'd searched her house, he'd heard the doctor's assessment. The woman he loved more than anyone else on earth was lying in a hospital bed and her daughter had been kidnapped. With each breath he took he'd disconnected, he'd separated from the overwhelming agony. He had to, he owed it to Charleigh.

To Faith.

Sweet Christ, Faith. He couldn't go there. Couldn't think about how scared she had to be. Absolutely could not think about what she'd seen. Did someone carry her down the steps? Had she closed her eyes so as not to see her mother bleeding out from a head wound? Had she been forced to walk down the stairs and step over her mother's prone body? Had she stopped to try to wake up Charleigh? Had she kicked and fought?

Stop.

Holden shoved his thoughts away and stared at Jameson. Before Kennedy, the rage on his friend's face was typical. The perpetual scowl was so normal, no one paid it any mind. But after Kennedy, that deep frown had vanished. Jameson had found happiness. He'd found love, acceptance, a good woman he was smart enough to make his wife, and they were making a family. It had been so long since Holden had seen Jameson's anger surface, it startled him. A stark reminder of how fucked the situation was.

"We're headed to Virginia Beach. I'll call Rhode on the way. Keep me up to date with Charleigh."

That was all he could ask. He couldn't bring himself to tell his friend to tell Charleigh he loved her, that he was sorry he couldn't sit by her bedside. Though he desperately wanted to stay.

Faith. Everything had to be about Faith.

"Brother, you're gonna give yourself a heart attack if you don't calm down," Jameson griped.

Not taking his eyes off the long stretch of roadway in front of him, Holden gritted his teeth. They were thirty minutes outside of Virginia and Holden was losing patience. He wanted to yell at Jameson to drive faster. He wanted to rail at Rhode for not finding anything useful at Beatrice Towler's house. But having a bitch-ass temper tantrum wouldn't help. What if they'd wasted three hours driving south? What if Holden's hunch was wrong and he'd put Faith in more danger? She'd been gone six hours.

"Do you ever remember Paul mentioning a vacation home? Or a place his family vacationed?" Jameson asked.

The mere mention of Paul had every muscle tightening.

"Wasn't close enough to the man for him to share his vacation plans. Nix or Weston might know, those two seemed to be the only ones who could stomach listening to his bullshit."

That was because Nixon had been their leader, he'd felt it was his job to pull the team together, to keep them a cohesive unit. Nix had managed to do that while they were on the battlefield—there was no room for personal dislike if you wanted to stay alive. However, stateside had been a different story. Paul had been an outsider, his constant ego-driven need for competition had gotten old fast. He was exhausting to be around. Weston had seemed to be the only one in the group who could put up with him on a personal level. Chasin had tried at times but it never lasted long. Jameson had straight out disliked Paul from the beginning—he'd actually had words with Nix to try to get Paul placed on another team.

"What if—"

"Don't go there," Jameson cut off his morose thought. "Rhode didn't find anything at Beatrice's house. He hasn't been to Patricia's yet. If he doesn't find anything by the time we get there, we will. They have her, Holden, we both know it. We just have to find where they took her. And there's a possibility they'll call in a ransom demand. They want Paul's death gratuity and life insurance."

Christ. Holden hadn't thought about a ransom. He picked his phone up off his lap and dialed Nixon.

"Yeah?" Nix answered.

"Do you have Charleigh's cell?"

There was a beat of silence and Holden knew Nix was putting together the pieces.

"Fuck. I don't know. I didn't think to look for it. I'll ask around and if we don't have it, I'll send Alec to her apartment."

It was on the tip of his tongue to ask about Charleigh. The warring inside him had grown to an all-new high. Holden wished he could clone himself. He'd never felt such a crushing need to be in two places at once.

"There's been no change here. How far out are you?" Nix tore through his inner turmoil.

"No change? Are the doctors concerned? She should've woken up by now."

Or maybe it was better she was unconscious and not caught in a living nightmare. Leigh-Leigh would freak out when she woke up and found Faith had been kidnapped. She would lose her ever-loving mind and probably need to be sedated. Yeah, maybe it was best she was asleep.

"They've assured us that she's stable and her body's doing what it needs to heal. I called her parents. They're on their way up. I held off as long as I could but there will be things that doctors will need consent for and her mother had medical power of attorney."

All sorts of horrible visions invaded Holden's mind.

"Consent to do what? I thought she was—"

"Slow down, brother," Nix admonished. "Charleigh's gonna be fine. But her parents had the right to know. There's some scans the doctor wants to do, that's all."

Holden didn't believe his friend. There was more going on. However, he was grateful for the temporary lie. He had to push back the fear and find Faith.

"We're almost there. I'll be in touch soon."

He disconnected without thanking Nixon for

watching over Charleigh. *Separate. I have to keep everything separate*, he reminded himself.

"This isn't the best time to bring this up, but we need to talk about it."

Holden braced for the onslaught of guilt and anger to explode—part of what he'd been trying to avoid. He couldn't let his guilt prevent him from accomplishing his mission.

"I'm barely holding on," he admitted. "And every minute that passes, my fingertips slip closer to the edge. I can't go there. If I think about Faith, about what I've done, the years I've wasted, I will not be able to control myself."

"I think you're already out of control. That's why we need to talk about this now. Before we find her and you lose all sense of reality. You're going to need to keep a tight rein on your anger. Faith cannot see you unleash the beast."

Jameson was right about that. Faith couldn't see the type of man he really was.

"You take Faith and get her safe. I'll handle the rest."

"No, Holden. You're taking Faith and I'm handling the rest."

"James—"

"I know why you left Charleigh."

It took Holden three long, slow blinks for Jameson's words to penetrate his brain. He knew? That was impossible.

"You might think you know, but you don't."

"I do. You likely don't remember telling me because you were so trashed it's a miracle you didn't die of alcohol poisoning. You came back to my place after Charleigh told you she was pregnant and you started drinking. By the time I got home, you were fucked-up and ready to talk. I'd never seen a man so destroyed. You told me everything, including being a royal dick and sending Charleigh to Paul." Jameson paused and he let out a long sigh. "Damn, Holden, I tried to talk you around, begged you to let me call Charleigh and stop her so you could explain. I was reaching for my phone, not caring what you wanted, but something you said stopped me."

"What'd I say?"

"Actually, it was more the way you looked. I'm not trying to unman you right now, but when the toughest brother you know breaks down in tears and pleads with you, it's hard not to cave. You told me that you wanted it to be yours so badly that you couldn't witness her carrying Paul's child. At the time I didn't get it, I thought there was a chance the baby was yours and I couldn't understand why you wouldn't want to know. But I did understand you were in extreme pain. I thought I was doing the right thing. I see now, I did wrong. I shouldn't have let your alcohol-clogged mind make decisions about your future. I should've sobered you up and made you talk to her."

"She can't be mine," Holden croaked. "I knew it then, just like I know it now. I can't have a family."

"I know that," Jameson conceded. "You told me what the doctor said, but doctors can be wrong. No matter how slim the chance, you should've found out. If she is yours, you've lost eight years that you'll never get back, and you gotta know my part in that weighs heavy."

It didn't surprise Holden to hear that he'd told Jameson the truth. He could still remember the day Charleigh had followed him from outside the compound's gate. He'd spotted her the moment she'd pulled away from the curb. He hadn't seen her since the night he watched Paul take her home. That hurt, but what hurt the worst was when he told her the week before that he was putting an end to their fucked-up non-relationship and he never wanted to talk to her again. He'd devastated her with his words. Her tears had been like a thousand razor blades slicing his flesh.

When Holden had pulled into a shopping center and parked, Charleigh had followed. But, there was no missing the tentative steps she took to stand before him. She'd never looked more beautiful. And when the words "I'm pregnant" fell from her lips, Holden's life ended. Totally and completely imploded. Despair wound around his heart and his soul died.

His life was over and he'd lost the woman he adored. She was having another man's baby. Irrational hate had consumed him. He hated Paul Towler. Hated the world. Hated himself. Pure unadulterated hate enveloped him as he came to the understanding his future had vanished.

And in all the years since, all of the days he'd live without Charleigh, he'd never stopped loving her. All the minutes that had passed had never stopped him from wishing that Faith was his. But he'd been right that drunken night—the truth couldn't set him free. It killed him. The doctor hadn't made a mistake. And a DNA test would've been the nail he couldn't withstand.

11

An hour later, Holden, Jameson, and Rhode stood in Patricia Towler's kitchen shuffling through a stack of legal documents. Their play to kidnap Faith becoming more apparent with every page they turned. No amount of money was going to help them win a case against Charleigh. Holden had read a letter from a lawyer outlining the reasons his firm wouldn't take a case they'd deemed unwinnable, therefore Hodgkin and Associates believed it would be ethically wrong to file the suit.

Holden had to admit, he was surprised a lawyer had turned down a case. However, the Towlers had found a new law firm, one that didn't care if they couldn't win. And after racking up the billable hours, they'd recently sent the Towlers a letter explaining that after further examination, there was very little possibility the court would find in their favor and urged them to drop the case.

So why'd they send the PI to Kent County to follow Charleigh after they'd received the letter from the attorney?

"What do we know about the PI? Chad Bullock, right?" Holden asked.

"He's mainly a fuckwit," Rhode said. "Ambulance-chaser type."

"How did Patricia and Beatrice hook up with him? Does he work with the lawyer?"

Jameson's gaze lifted from the loan documents he was looking at. "What are you thinking?"

"I'm trying to piece this together. The lawyer advised them to drop the case, then they hired a PI. I want to know where they found him. I want to understand who this guy is and if he's an accomplice, or if Patty and Bea used him to keep tabs on Charleigh until they could strike."

"You think he nabbed Faith for them?"

"Yes."

The admission made Holden's stomach knot up. It was one thing to run every possible scenario; it was another to conclude that an unknown man had taken Faith. Somehow, thinking the Towlers had the little girl was an easier pill to swallow. They were total money-grabbing assholes, but Holden didn't believe they'd hurt Faith, they'd keep her safe until they could ransom her. Faith being held by a strange man made him sick.

"How much of a mess can I make?" Rhode asked.

"What do you mean?"

"In here. Do you care how we leave the place?"

Rhode's intentions became clear. Holden gave zero fucks how big of a mess they left. He knew the Towlers were behind Faith's kidnapping, and the sooner they found her, the better. If that meant Rhode tore the place apart while he searched, so be it.

"Do your worst, brother."

A satanic smile formed on Rhode's face before he stalked down the hall toward Patty's bedroom. The house was decent enough, not great, not horrible. However, it was better than he'd expected since Patty didn't believe in working all that hard. One thing Holden did remember about Paul was he despised his lazy family. He'd complained about them ad nauseum. Apparently, one or both of the women would hit him up monthly for money. He'd also bitched about his sister's poor choices in men. More than once, Holden had heard about the deadbeats Patty brought into her life, and Paul hated how he always had to clean up the mess after they took what little money she had—which was probably Paul's money—and dumped her.

During those times, Holden had been happy he was an only child, and while his parents had divorced when he was a teenager, their split had been perfectly amicable. Compared to some of his teammates, Holden's family life had been utterly boring.

Holden's mind whirled with possibilities. But he knew down to his bones Patty had a connection to the PI and it had to be personal. Rhode said the guy was a fuckwit, ambulance-chaser type, not a criminal mastermind. No, the architect would be Patty. She was a conniving bitch, but she'd need muscle behind her.

Jameson's voice filtered through the living room but Holden ignored his friend's phone conversation and glanced around the room looking for any signs a man lived there. Anything that would tie Chad to Patty.

"Nixon's going to the hotel now. We'll know in twenty minutes if Chad's still in Kent County,"

Jameson said as Rhode came back into the living room.

"A man's living here. There are clothes in the closet."

Holden's heart rate ticked up and he strode to the kitchen. Jackpot, the garbage can was full. Without delay, he dumped the contents on the kitchen floor and used the toe of his boot to shift through the mess. He knelt and picked up a balled-up receipt and smoothed it out. Seconds later, Holden tossed the grocery receipt and continued to comb through the trash.

Once the trash in the house had proved to be useless, Holden and Jameson went to the garbage can outside and tore through those bags.

It took twenty minutes for Holden to finally find something. But when he did, he hit paydirt.

"They're in Charlottesville," Holden announced, holding a wrinkled, sullied booking confirmation. "Reservation under Chad Bullock."

"Before we head out, let's have Micky work her magic," Jameson suggested.

Holden didn't want to wait another second. He wanted to get on the road and go get Faith but he knew Jameson was right. McKenna Swagger could hack into the hotel's security feed and computer systems to find out if Chad had checked in. They'd also have a clearer picture of what they were walking into.

His every instinct screamed for him to run to the little girl as fast as he could. She had to be scared out of her mind, even if her grandmother and aunt had her. Holden closed his eyes and remembered the last time Faith had been forced to see them. The Towlers had filed for visitation, and a guardian ad litem had been assigned to Faith. The overworked GAL had meant well when she'd set up a series of supervised visitations. According to Charleigh, the first two visits had been awkward but not traumatizing. No, the Towlers had saved that for the third visit, when they'd explained to Faith in front of the court-appointed social worker that from then on, Faith would be spending more time with them. Beatrice made her faulty play when Faith had expressed she didn't want to spend weekends with her grand-mother, and certainly not the whole summer, which was what the Towlers had wanted. Bea didn't back down—she argued with Faith, then turned to Charleigh and bitched her out, accusing her of a whole host of nasty shit.

That was the last time Faith had been in the same room with Bea and Patty. But, it had left a lasting effect. One that Holden had gone down to Virginia to deal with when Patty and or Bea kept showing up at Charleigh's condo, demanding to see Faith.

Holden had thought he'd made himself clear the last time he saw Beatrice. A pang of regret hit his chest. Beatrice Towler was a Gold Star Mother, her son had given his life in protection of his country. That meant something to Holden; even if he didn't personally like the man, there was no disputing he'd died a hero's death. Paul had been a teammate, and Holden had held his hand while he died.

And during Paul's last moments of lucidity, he'd given Charleigh back to Holden. He'd also asked Holden to take care of his daughter. The memory was so vivid, Holden could smell the stench of sweat and blood, he could hear the artillery blasts, taste the fine-powdered sand and debris in his mouth as he tried to swallow the inhuman request.

Paul could've asked Nixon.

But he didn't—he'd burdened Holden with more regret, more pain, more torture.

So in the end, Paul Towler had won. He'd instigated the biggest *fuck you* he could, then died.

Since that day in the desert, Holden had broken every promise he'd made to the dying man.

But today, he'd finally start fulfilling it. Holden would get Faith back, and once she was safe with her mother, he'd protect her any way he could. Charleigh could try to stop him, but Holden was done licking his wounds. He'd been a coward for far too long. Now Faith's life was in danger and he had to wonder if that was his fault. Had he done everything he'd promised Paul, would Faith be missing?

Fuck, no, she wouldn't be.

If he hadn't been such a dumbass, he would've checked his ego and made things right with Charleigh, even if *right* only meant taking care of Faith.

Holden's eyes came open when his phone shrilled.

Kennedy's name flashed on the screen.

"Charleigh okay?" Holden asked by way of greeting.

"Holden," Charleigh breathed.

"Leigh-Leigh, are you—"

"Please find her."

"I will," he promised. "We have a lead."

"I know McKenna's looking at security tapes from a hotel. I saw her."

"Saw who?"

"Faith." The word came out as a whispered sob. "That PI was carrying her."

Christ Jesus. Why had Micky allowed Charleigh to see that?

"Charleigh, you don't need to see that. Let Nixon and the guys handle everything. You need to relax. You have a—"

"No. I need to help. Nixon's not here and McKenna wanted me to ID the guy. He was carrying Faith, but she wasn't moving. Do you think... oh, god...what if..."

"Stop, baby, don't do that. I'm gonna go get Faith and bring her home to you, and when I do, she's gonna be just fine."

That was a lie. Faith wasn't going to be okay—she was going to be emotionally traumatized. The poor girl had probably been drugged as well.

"My parents are here," she moaned and Holden almost cracked a smile.

Charleigh had never had a good, loving relationship with her parents; they were both too domineering for that, her mother especially. The woman always had something to say about appearances and keeping the family in good standing with their country club friends. Holden had found it exhausting but he'd kept his mouth shut because Charleigh loved them.

No longer the dutiful boyfriend who felt the need to make a good impression on the people whom he thought would one day be his in-laws, he felt no such responsibility. He also had nothing to lose.

"I'll talk to Chasin, he can run interference. Kennedy's level-headed and she can help."

"I think Kennedy's not so level-headed when it comes to my mother," Charleigh whispered.

That meant Zoe Axelson was behaving badly. Holden gritted his teeth in an effort not to say something that would make the situation worse. Once his jaw started to ache, he unclenched and said, "You do not take on their bullshit, Leigh-Leigh. Use Chasin as a buffer—you know he'll do anything you ask. Right now, all you need to do is relax so you can recover. I'll bring Faith to you as soon as I can. But fair warning, when I get there I will not stand for anyone—and that includes your mother—bossing you around and making things worse. I get I'm not her favorite person, but for now, all of that shit will be set aside for Faith."

"Please, just bring her home."

"I will, Leigh-Leigh, that's a promise."

He heard her suck in a breath and a fresh sob tore through her.

"I'm so scared."

"Know you are, honey. But you're surrounded by good, strong people. Use them. Let them keep you solid until I get there."

"Okay, Holden."

"Gonna let you go so I can get on the road." There was a long pause, and as much as Holden didn't want to rush her, he needed to talk to Jameson and Rhode and make a plan. "Leigh-Leigh?"

"Be safe, Holden. I'll be waiting."

His eyelids drifted closed and his heart burned. But before he could respond to her plea, Charleigh was gone.

God, how many times had she whispered those exact words to him before he'd left on an exercise?

Too many to count. But it never got old. It meant she cared, she loved him, and wanted her man to come home to her. And every time he did, she was always waiting.

12

Holden's hands shook with pent-up aggression.

"Almost," Jameson muttered from his seat behind the wheel.

They were parked behind the Glen Hotel on the western side of Charlottesville. After a two-and-a-half-hour drive, *almost* wasn't good enough. Faith had been away from Charleigh for going on ten hours.

Holden was fresh out of patience, and each minute he had to sit in the car and wait for Nixon's call felt like he was enduring the worst torture. Faith was so close, yet they couldn't rush the building. They planned on grabbing the girl without disrupting the hotel guests nor did they want to put Faith in anymore danger than she already was.

Jonny had made some calls to the Albemarle County Sheriff's Office. The sheriff herself would be meeting them with three deputies to haul Beatrice, Patricia, and Chad in. That was not Holden's first choice. He wanted to beat the ever-loving fuck out of Chad. He wouldn't have laid a hand on the women but he would've happily landed a verbal smackdown before Rhode called the police to turn them over.

"The sheriff is on her way," Jameson unnecessarily reminded him. "They're going in soft. If Faith's awake, they don't want to scare her. Rhode and I will cover the back, the deputies will cover the front. You're going in with Sheriff Knox. Faith's coming home with us. Just stay calm."

Holden wanted to remind Jameson he had not been calm when Kennedy had been kidnapped. But that would've been an asshole thing to do, so instead, he nodded and stared straight ahead.

A black SUV pulled into the parking lot and Jameson's phone pinged with a text.

"They're here. It's go-time."

Before Holden could move, Jameson grabbed his bicep. "I mean it, keep your shit. Faith's gonna be scared, so she needs you calm and collected."

Unsure if he'd be able to remain calm, Holden turned to look at Jameson.

"Maybe you should be the one to go in."

"No. It needs to be you."

Arguing meant wasting time. Time that Faith didn't have.

Jameson's phone dinged again and his face went hard. "Chad's on the move. McKenna's still monitoring the cameras. Go. We gotta get into position."

Holden jumped out of the truck and headed toward the sheriff. Jameson went the opposite direction.

"Holden Stanford," Sheriff Knox greeted.

"Yes, ma'am."

"We've been briefed," she continued. "I've been told you have a permit to carry but I'm going to ask you to keep your weapon holstered and let me take the lead."

Nothing about the rescue was going as he wanted. Keeping his weapon holstered meant he was vulnerable, Faith would be unprotected, and he'd have to trust someone he didn't know. His mind rebelled at the thought, but he still found himself agreeing. He'd do anything that would get him in that hotel room and to Faith faster.

"Ma'am, I will keep my weapon holstered with the caveat that if I feel my life, your life, or Faith's life is in danger, it comes out."

"That'll do," she sighed. "I have more units on standby. As these things go, I felt a show of presence would endanger the child and other guests."

"I understand. But you should know, Chad Bullock has left the room."

The woman's face went tight and she quickly called in the update to her deputies.

"Let's head up."

The walk into the hotel was silent and he was happy for the reprieve. Jameson was right, he needed to find it in himself to remain calm for Faith's sake. She didn't need to witness him going gonzo on Beatrice and Patricia. No, Faith needed him steady, in control. He needed to be her safe place until he could get her back to her mother.

The manager met the sheriff in the lobby. They exchanged a few hushed words while Holden scanned the area. No Chad. *Where did that fucker go?* Finally, the manager handed Sheriff Knox a keycard and the man went back behind the desk. Holden followed behind the sheriff and waited for the elevator. Once they were inside, Sheriff Knox quickly gave Holden a rundown.

"The rooms beside the Towlers have been vacated. Mr. Null called them and upgraded the guests to suites. The rooms across from them are vacant. That doesn't mean this is a free-for-all, but the rooms are empty."

Holden bit back his smartass retort, remembering his only objective was rescuing Faith.

"I'll knock and you stand out of sight. If they don't answer, the front desk will call and explain there's a problem with their room and they need to be moved. I don't want to enter blind. But I will if it comes to that."

Again, the night was not going how Holden wanted. It would've been so much easier to just kick in the door, knock some heads—well, knock one head, zip tie two bitches up—and take Faith. But to end this once and for all, Charleigh needed the Towlers arrested.

"Understood," Holden acknowledged.

"Mr. Stanford, I'll get your daughter back."

Every cell in Holden's body froze. His daughter? What the hell had Jonny told the sheriff? Old wounds threatened to take him to a place he couldn't go. If he needed to pretend to be Faith's dad to get her safely home, he'd do it. The pain that the thought created was secondary to getting into that room.

The elevator door slid open and he shoved all

hurt aside as he walked down the hall. Four doors down, Sheriff Knox cleared her features, everything about the woman softened. She no longer looked like the county sheriff but instead an average citizen, completely unassuming in her presentation. Even her clothes were average.

The sheriff knocked on the Towlers' door. Anticipation thrummed through Holden as he waited for a response. *So close.* Faith was right there behind that door.

Almost there, Leigh-Leigh, he thought, praying there was some way for Charleigh to know her daughter would be coming home soon.

"Who is it?" Patty called through the door.

"Hi, my name is Janie, I'm in the room next to yours. I found this in front of your door." The sheriff held up the keycard. "I think you must have dropped it."

What felt like a lifetime later, the door slowly came open and Sheriff Knox moved quickly, shouldering her way in. Patty was face-first against the wall with both hands being cuffed behind her back when Holden rushed into the room. Beatrice was moving toward the bed where Faith was on her side, her eyes closed.

"Don't think about it," Holden growled and

blocked Bea's path. "Turn around and put your hands behind your back."

"I have rights!" Bea screeched. "She can't have her."

"Hands behind your back," Holden repeated.

"I know who you are," the old woman seethed. "You were with Paul. Did you let my son die so she could steal his money? I bet you didn't even try to save him. It's all your fault. All of this. I never understood why my son wanted that slut. But you had her and he never could think straight—" Beatrice didn't finish spewing her venom; a deputy approached, cuffs out, ready to make an arrest. "I have rights," she repeated.

"You do," the deputy said. "The right to remain silent."

"That woman—"

"You kidnapped a little girl after you knocked her mother unconscious, you crazy bitch," Holden snarled. He stood away, allowing the deputy to deal with the woman, and knelt by the bed.

Holden brushed Faith's golden brown hair off her face and gently felt for a pulse. He hadn't realized he'd been holding his breath until he found a steady, strong heartbeat.

Thank God.

"Faith, honey, wake up." Nothing. The little girl didn't move. "Faith. Time to wake up, honey."

"There's an ambulance downstairs," Sheriff Knox shared.

"I'm taking her down."

Holden scooped the little girl off the bed as the sheriff protested, "Wait for the paramedics to come up."

Not a fucking chance.

"Find out what they gave her." With that, he carried Faith out of the room.

He glanced down at the girl's precious face and his chest tightened. How could so much pain be caused by something so beautiful, so sweet, so innocent?

Christ. He had to stop thinking about the past. Faith was blameless, and if Holden was being honest, so was Charleigh. She hadn't done anything wrong, it was all him. His actions had set the chain of events into motion.

Holden slowed his pace, adjusted Faith's weight, and pulled his phone from his back pocket. Clumsily, he unlocked the screen and hit the green icon on the last incoming call.

"Holden," Kennedy answered.

"Let me talk to Charleigh."

"Did you get her?"

"Kennedy, babe, respect, but give the phone to Charleigh."

A moment later, Charleigh's breathy voice came over the line.

"I have her."

"Thank God," she wailed. "Is she hurt?"

Holden's stomach roiled and for a second, he considered lying.

"I don't think so. She doesn't have any visible wounds, her heartbeat is strong, but, Leigh-Leigh, honey, they gave her something to make her sleep. I don't know what that is yet. I'm taking her down to the ambulance now. But I wanted you to know I have her."

"Don't leave her, Holden. Please. Do not leave her side. If she—"

"Honey, I gotta hang up, the elevator's here. I'll call you as soon as I know something."

"Please don't leave her."

"I promise you I won't leave her side."

"Thank you. Thank you so much for finding her."

"Gotta run, Leigh-Leigh. Call you soon as I can."

"Kay."

Holden quickly shoved his phone in his pocket, not even checking to see if the call disconnected.

"Come on, baby girl, let's get you checked out."

Faith didn't stir.

13

"I can't believe you're trusting *that* man with my granddaughter," my mother griped.

My eyes drifted from my mother to Kennedy. One look at my friend told me she was done with my mom's complaining. McKenna, on the other hand, looked like she felt sorry for me. Thankfully, Nixon and Alec had both left with my father before my mom started in again. Neither man seemed real happy with Zoe.

As for me, I was at the end of my rope. There were so many emotions flowing through me I couldn't hold onto one of them long enough to process it and move to the next. They all mumbled together into a ball of extreme unease, and my mom was making it so much worse.

"Enough, Mother."

"Charlotte," she snapped.

The warning was clear. Even at my age, Zoe Axelson thought she was the boss of me. Actually, she thought she was the boss of everyone. That hadn't gone well for her when I was with Holden. He'd never been outright rude to her, but he made it clear he wouldn't put up with her shit, and part of that shit was the way she spoke to me. Needless to say, if she didn't like Holden before he broke up with me, she despised him after. She said it was because he broke my heart, but that wasn't the truth. She hated him because she'd thought there was a possibility he could be Faith's father. Neither of the potential baby daddies—and yes, that was what she'd called Paul and Holden—were good enough to mingle with the Axelson family. But at least Paul had died a hero.

My gaze went back to my mother, and the rope I was barely holding onto slipped from my fingers and I was in a freefall. Not a single iota of compassion for *me*. Not an ounce of sympathy that I was lying in a hospital bed with a concussion while my baby was three hours away from me. No empathy that my child had been stolen from my home. Not a goddamn thing for me or my daughter. It was all about her and her hatred for Holden. And her contempt for me, how I, as a grown woman, got pregnant before I was married and how that made *her* look.

Fuck that.

"I think you should go home," I told her.

"Really, Charlotte. And how would that look? Your father and I in Virginia while you're in the hospital?"

"I don't much care how it will look, Mother. And if you didn't activate the country club phone tree and tell everyone I was in the hospital, no one would've known."

"You're our daughter, those are our friends. They'd be upset if they couldn't support us in our time of need."

Seriously?

I had no words. Absolutely none. My mother's selfish need for attention knew no bounds.

"I want you to leave."

"Charlotte—"

"Either you leave or I'm calling hospital security and I'll ask them to escort you out. Think about how that'll look."

"You'll do no such thing," she sneered.

"What's going on?" My father's voice boomed in

the small room and a wolfish smile tugged at my mother's lips.

She wrongly thought since my father was back she'd have an ally, that together they could bully me into whatever Zoe wanted. And why wouldn't she? My whole life I'd backed down, I'd chosen the path of least resistance, which meant I gave in because I didn't want the hassle.

I'd trained my parents, particularly my mother, to treat me like shit. I'd taught her that if she pushed hard enough, I'd roll over like a dog.

Yep. I was a doormat that read: *Please walk all over me, Zoe Axelson.*

Not today.

"Edward, please talk some sense into your daughter. She's being ridiculous." My mother actually tilted her head back and sniffed.

Stuck her nose in the air like those of us beneath her stank.

God, really?

"What's this, Charlotte, why are you being difficult?"

"Well, Father, since you asked, I'll tell you. I'm being difficult because I made it clear I was done listening to Mother's disparaging remarks about Holden."

"That boy again. I thought we were long past mentioning his name. Your mother has a right to say what she will about the louse who left her daughter with child and ran off."

When I hit my head I must've been transported back to the nineteen-forties when men used words like "louse" and "with child". That was the only explanation for my father's highbrow display. And make no mistake—that was what it was. All a show for the other people in the room. Edward Axelson had to believe he was the most cultured person in any given company and he didn't care how he went about flexing his perceived superiority. While my dad needed to feel like wealth and class at all times, my mother had to feel like she was in charge of a room. It was her way or her way.

"My child was kidnapped," I screamed and I immediately regretted it. Stabbing pain radiated from the back of my head around to the front, like ice picks were gouging out my eyes.

"Char—"

"Don't talk to me. Get out."

"That's preposterous," my father returned. "We will do no such thing."

My eyes drifted closed, not because I couldn't stand to look at my selfish parents any longer but because my head felt like it was going to explode. Pressure had built and the pain was becoming unbearable.

"Mr. and Mrs. Axelson, I'm going to have to ask you to leave, please."

I didn't need to open my eyes to know my doctor had come into my room. *Thank God.*

"That's not going to happen," Edward argued. "My daughter has sustained a head injury. She's obviously experiencing an episode. I have medical power of attorney, you can't ask me to leave her room."

There was a moment of silence and I wondered if my doctor was contemplating all the ways to strangle my pompous father or if he was going to cave. I hoped she'd call security and have them thrown out. Maybe Kennedy could record it for me, so one day when my head didn't feel like it was splitting in two I could watch it and laugh myself silly.

"Sir, I have every right to ask you to leave when you are upsetting my patient. Furthermore, the medical power of attorney no longer applies. Charlotte Towler is awake and cognizant. Now, if you'd please exit the room, I need to examine her."

"I'm not leaving." My father stubbornly dug in.

"Then you leave me no choice but to call security and have you escorted out. However, I must warn you, if that happens, you will not be allowed in for the duration of your daughter's stay."

"I want to speak to the hospital administrator."

"Certainly. If you'd like to wait in the waiting room, I will page Dr. Blackburn and ask her to come down."

"I will—"

"Leave, Father," I croaked. "I don't have the energy to deal with you and Mother."

"Char—"

"Leave. This isn't about her and what her friends will think. This isn't about you and paving her way to get her what she wants. This is about my child. I'm scared to death, my head hurts, I want to see my daughter, and I'm stuck in this bed. For once, please listen to me and take her and leave."

"We'll be at the hotel," my father clipped.

"Edward," Zoe snapped.

"Come, dear, Charlotte needs her rest." I opened my eyes, shocked at my father's acquiescence. "When Faith arrives, we'll come to pick her up. She will be staying with us."

There it was. He wasn't accepting my wishes, he was maneuvering to get control.

Um. No. That wasn't happening, either.

"That won't be happening. Faith is staying with me. I appreciate you making the drive up, but as you can see, I'm fine. Holden is bringing Faith home and when she gets here, she will not be leaving my sight. You should head home."

My father's face turned a scary shade of red but he didn't get a chance to chastise me. My mom stepped forward full of hatred and indignation and proceeded to tear me down.

Typical.

"Here we go again. Didn't you learn the first time? That man is nothing but trash. What kind of man asks a woman to live with him before he marries her? What kind of man lives off of a woman? Then you come up *pregnant*." My mother's lips curled in disgust. "And he leaves you. Now you're stupid enough to trust him with Faith? He doesn't love you, he never did." My mother stepped closer to the bed and jabbed her finger at me. "I'm warning you right now, young lady, if you invite this man back into your life, you're cut off."

Cut off?

How can you cut off someone who takes nothing from you?

"What exactly will I be cut off from, Mother? I've never accepted financial help from you. And since we're talking about Holden, let's get one thing straight—the years we lived together I lived off of him. He paid all the bills, not me. He took care of everything. Every last bill he paid. You can hate him for breaking my heart, but don't rewrite history and make him into something he's not. And as far as Faith goes, he didn't abandon her. He's not her father. But he is the man who saved her today. He is the man who tracked the Towlers down and rescued her. And he's the man who is right now taking care of her and trying his damnedest to bring her home to me."

"So naïve. It's like I didn't even raise you."

Kennedy's phone rang and my attention sliced over to her. Embarrassment seized my lungs. I'd been so wrapped up in my parents, I'd forgotten she was quietly sitting next to my bed.

"Yeah, she's right here, but you're gonna have to hold on a moment while the doctor calls security." There was a pause and Kennedy's normally pretty face turned hard and her gaze lifted to my mother. "Because the Axelsons are in her room, and after several attempts to ask them to leave they're still standing here upsetting her. She had to yell at them which caused her a great deal of pain, yet Mrs. Axelson has decided that saying bad things about you is more important than her daughter's health. They've also eluded to taking Faith. Charleigh has made it clear she doesn't want Faith to go with them." Another pause. "Right. I'll tell them."

Kennedy hung up and a broad smile replaced her earlier frown.

"I wanted to talk to him," I complained.

"He's calling Nixon, Alec, Weston, and Jonny. He said he'd call you right back."

"Why is he calling them? How's Faith?"

Kennedy's smile vanished and compassion filled her eyes.

"Faith is fine. They'll be on their way home soon. As to why he's calling in the guys...he said over his dead body would someone take your daughter away from you. Faith's awake and asking for you and Holden said that he will make sure Faith gets exactly what she wants. He also said if your parents weren't on their way back to Virginia by the time he got here, he'd personally escort them home."

"Really?"

"Well, I was paraphrasing and I left out all of the curse words, but that was the gist of what he said."

"Oh my God," my mother snickered. "I see it already. You're falling for his crap. It's all over your face. Can you believe it, Edward? Your daughter would choose a foul-mouthed piece of—"

"That's enough, Mrs. Axelson," Nixon said as he entered the room. "I believe Charleigh's made her wishes clear. The doctor has asked you to leave, now you're going to leave."

Great. Perfect. Now my night of fear and humiliation was complete. Nixon, Alec, Weston, and Jonny had all filed into my room with matching expressions of dislike.

"I will not be told what to do by a roughneck. And if you think to put your hands on me, I'll sue you."

"Just go, Mother. I want to call Holden back and talk to Faith."

"Ma'am." Jonny stepped forward and flashed his badge. "This will be the last time you're asked to leave before I arrest you for trespassing and harassment."

"I'm not harassing anybody."

Sweet mother of God, please make her stop.

"Charleigh? Is Mrs. Axelson harassing you?"

"Yes."

"Well," my mother huffed, up went her nose back in the air, and I wished I'd been born into a normal, decent family. "We'll see. We will see.

When that man leaves you broken and these people all abandon you, do *not* come home to your father and me. You will not be welcomed. And when that child of yours grows up and turns out to be just as ungrateful as you are, I will not feel sorry for you. Remember, Charlotte, you reap what you sow, and you just bought yourself a plantation of trash."

With that, my mother turned on her ridiculously expensive high heels and strode out of my room with her head held high. And like the good lap dog my father was, he followed.

"Can I use your phone to call Holden back?" I asked Kennedy.

She tilted her head to the side and her eyes softened. "Do you want to talk about what happened first? That was pretty harsh."

"That was nothing," I told her. "Harsh was when they called me a slut and told me I was an embarrassment to the Axelson name and I needed to find a suitable man to marry before I was showing or everyone would know I'd been whoring myself out."

"Seriously?"

I shrugged and lifted my hand, silently asking for Kennedy's phone. "It's just the way they are."

Kennedy placed the phone in my hand and her gaze went across the room. I was consciously trying to forget the others in the room. I didn't want to look, didn't want to see the anger in their eyes. One thing my mother was right about was, Holden's friends would get sick of all the drama and chaos I brought to the group. They wouldn't all abandon me at once, but they would start to distance themselves from me.

I pressed the call button and put the phone up to my ear.

"Did they kick those assholes out? Swear to God, if they've upset her, I will—"

"It's me," I cut him off.

Tears pricked my eyes but inside warmth bloomed. That was *my* Holden, the old Holden, the one who had shielded me from everything. Hearing his fury on my behalf made me remember all that I lost.

Will the pain ever go away?

"Are they gone?" he asked. His tone was much softer than it'd been.

"Yeah, Jonny threatened to arrest my mother. In true Zoe fashion, she said her parting shot and walked out like she owned the place and it was her decision. How's Faith? What did the doctor say?"

That was what had started the whole argument with my mother earlier. Faith had to be checked out by a physician, and since I wasn't there in person to consent, I had to assign Holden medical power of attorney. I hadn't thought twice about it when I was brought the papers to sign. He was with her and I trusted him to do right by her. My mother had gone ballistic.

"She's fine." I could hear the smile in his voice and tried my best to ignore it. "They found doxylamine in her system. It's an antihistamine and the main side effect is drowsiness, which explains her ten-hour nap. She's awake but groggy. Sheriff Knox understands that Faith's not to be questioned until you're present. The Towlers are being held in Albemarle County until Jonny can arrange to have them brought back to Kent County. Jameson and Rhode caught Chad sneaking out the back. He's in county lock-up as well. All three of them have clammed up and asked for lawyers. McKenna should've already been in contact with your attorney to explain the situation and Jonny has filed for a restraining order. As soon as the judge signs it, he'll bring you the paperwork. That will be for both you and Faith. Even though we don't believe you or Faith are in danger with the Towlers in custody, Jonny has posted a deputy outside your door and he made arrangements with the hospital to allow Faith to remain in your room with you for the duration of your stay. As soon as Faith's doctor signs her discharge papers, we'll be on our way back to you."

She's fine.

Faith was fine.

That was all I could process. The rest—all the arrangements Jonny had made—barely filtered in. Not because I wasn't grateful, but because my baby was okay and that took up everything I had left.

"How much did she see?"

"Leigh-Leigh, honey, I haven't asked and I won't. She'll need her mama when she talks about that. Right now, all we're doing is test what flavor Jell-O she likes best and slowly getting something in her belly. So far, she likes strawberry the best and spit out the lime. Everyone's taking good care of her. One of the nurses went to the pediatric unit and brought her down a stuffed sloth and a book. Between Jell-O tastings, we've been learning about the rainforest."

I felt it happening. My throat clogged with emotion and the sob tore from my soul. Holden was reading to my baby, feeding her Jell-O, and taking care of her discharge paperwork. No one had ever cared for Faith like that but me. God, why did it have to be Holden who was taking care of her? Why was I still being punished? I was supposed to be untying myself, falling out of love, and now I'd never forget the kindness he was showing Faith. I'd never, ever forget he'd rescued her.

"Charleigh?" he called.

"Thank you."

"There's nothing to thank me for."

He was wrong. There was so much gratitude welling up inside of me it was overwhelming. Faith was safe. She was being well cared for in my absence. And she was coming home.

14

"Holden?"

"Yeah, doll?"

Holden looked over at Faith when she didn't continue, her pretty face illuminated by the screen of his phone. He was sitting in the back seat of Jameson's truck next to the little girl, something she'd demanded with a savage scream. Without another thought, Holden had gathered Faith in his arms and held her until her little body stopped shaking with fear, then he'd climbed into the back seat next to her and held her hand. Once she'd calmed down, he'd downloaded some games onto his phone so Faith had something to occupy herself with. That was two hours ago. They still had a little over an hour to go.

Some of the tension had ebbed once they were on the highway headed back to Maryland but he knew he wouldn't be able to fully relax until he reunited mother and daughter.

That was the newest lie he told himself. The truth was, the knot in his stomach wouldn't unwind until he saw Charleigh. Yes, he wanted to see mother and daughter safely together, but the last time he'd had eyes on Charleigh she'd been unconscious. He'd spoken to her over the phone almost hourly to update her on Faith, so logically he knew she was okay, but he still needed to see her.

"I'm hungry."

Well, damn, Holden wasn't sure what to do with that. The doctor had given Faith a clean bill of health and no restrictions, but he didn't have the first clue what to feed an eight-year-old. Not to mention, it was nearing on midnight.

"Hey, Jameson, can you stop at the next fast food place you see?"

"Mommy says I'm not allowed to eat fast food."

"Well, kiddo, at this time of night that's all we got."

Faith lifted her eyes and the tiny, rebellious smile hit Holden like a semi. Honest to God, how was it even possible for this girl to smile about anything hours after she'd been rescued from a kidnapping? But that wasn't the only thing that had hit Holden square in the chest with such force, he was happy he was sitting down or he would've been knocked on his ass. That small smile, the one that said Faith was down to break all the rules—consequences be damned, was one he would swear he'd seen before. The same grin that had pissed his mother off and told his teammates he was getting ready to do something crazy.

Or was it wishful thinking? Was it his mind playing tricks on him because for years he'd wished Faith was his?

Coveting your neighbor's wife was a sin—surely coveting your dead teammate's daughter was as well —but it still didn't stop Holden from staring at the little girl in fascination.

"Mommy gets me milkshakes on special occasions," Faith announced.

"Okay..."

"I think you saving me from having to live with Grandma and Aunt Patty is bigger than me getting straight As. So I don't think Mommy will say anything about me eating McDonald's."

Holden smiled down at the girl.

"I like the way you think, doll."

"I'm a good thinker."

Jameson chuckled, Faith smiled hugely, and Holden's heart swelled.

It was a horrible idea to get close to Charleigh's daughter. The pain would be atrocious. But right then, sitting next to Faith, he wanted to know everything about her. He wanted to spend the next hour hearing her talk. And he really wanted to see her smile.

So that's what he did. Jameson pulled through a McDonald's, Faith ate her Chicken McNuggets, sipped her milkshake, and Holden listened to her prattle on about anything and everything. By the time they pulled into the hospital parking lot, he knew her favorite food was Charleigh's homemade tacos, her favorite movie was Barbie Island Princess, her favorite animal was a dog, and she wanted a Tank of her own. He'd learned that Faith wished her mommy would grow a baby in her belly so she could feel it kick like she'd felt touching her Aunt Kennedy's belly. Faith had been clear she never wanted to see the mean Towlers again and she didn't like her other grandparents because they weren't any fun. Her favorite color was red, her favorite person was her mom, and she loved math, hated spelling, and she wanted to be an astronaut when she grew up.

And somewhere deep inside of himself, in a dark place he'd never admit to out loud, he felt sorry that Paul would never know those things about his daughter. But Holden was immensely grateful he did. Even if Charleigh never allowed Faith around him again, he'd never forget all of Faith's favorite things.

FROM HIS SEAT in the corner of Charleigh's hospital room, Holden looked away from mother and daughter cuddling on the small, twin-sized bed down to his watch and stood.

It was after three in the morning; the last seventeen hours had been harrowing but it was the last two that had taken it out of him. Witnessing Charleigh and Faith's tear-filled reunion drained nearly everything he had left.

Kennedy had stayed by Charleigh throughout the whole ordeal. McKenna had stayed until Chad and the Towlers were taken into custody. However, when Jameson, Holden, and Faith arrived at the hospital they were greeted by the whole team, sleepy kids included. The gesture had hit him hard—they'd all come to welcome Faith home. No one except Nixon had gone up to Charleigh's room, but in a show of support, they'd all gotten out of bed, awakened their children, and had been waiting for them in the parking lot.

Faith seemed to bloom under the attention. The girl was simply amazing. She passed out hugs, smiled, then very sweetly asked if she could see her mom.

Two things had struck a chord, and if Holden was being honest, both washed over him with staggering force—neither he'd ever forget. Even though Faith had gamely hugged the crowd, she remained close to Holden. And when she was ready to go up to her mom's room, Faith had reached out and held his hand. It wasn't until they entered Charleigh's room did Faith let go of his hand and rush to the bed. But Charleigh hadn't missed the handholding. Her eyes had done a scan of her daughter, pausing on their clasped hands. Tears formed that she'd swiped away before smiling brightly.

Nixon, Jameson, and Kennedy left shortly after Faith climbed up next to Charleigh and yawned. Surprisingly, the girl hadn't fallen asleep—instead, Holden had settled into a chair and soaked up every word Faith said. The rambling commentary covered everything except what had happened. Though she did rat Holden out about her midnight snack. When Charleigh's gaze went to Holden and her pretty lips twitched, his heart swelled.

Getting too close wasn't smart, but it was too late. Faith Towler had wormed her way into his heart, and that hurt worse than all the years he'd studiously avoided her. Maybe he could play the doting uncle. Maybe he could spend time with Faith like Nixon did. Maybe he could come up with a cute nickname for her like Jameson had.

Maybe, just maybe, he didn't have to give up Faith.

Or, maybe he needed to walk away now before they were all drowning in more pain.

The thought made Holden's chest physically ache.

Yeah, it was way too late to pull away now.

"I'm gonna head home and let you two get some sleep."

"No."

Never in all his life had he seen anyone move as fast as Faith. She practically jumped from the hospital bed into Holden's arms. Her limbs wound around Holden like a rabid spider monkey. Her little arms wrapped around his neck, and with surprising strength, she choked the hell out of him.

"Whoa, doll," he wheezed.

"Don't leave me."

That was not a timid request—it was an unholy demand. Her voice was hoarse and full of panic, her grip didn't loosen, and her body shook.

"Faith," Charleigh started.

"You can't leave. You can't, you can't, you can't."

She was working herself up into a tizzy and Holden would do or say anything to calm her down.

"Okay, I won't leave."

Holden's eyes went to Charleigh and his lungs seized. Silent tears streamed down her cheeks. But when Leigh-Leigh's gaze lifted and their eyes locked, Holden learned a whole new meaning of hell.

He knew his Leigh-Leigh. Back in the day, he'd made it a point to know her every look. He could read her body language and know exactly what she was feeling. She'd hidden nothing from him. His woman was an open book. And right then, he was transported back to a time he'd never thought he'd be in again. Only now, despair coupled with the longing he saw.

Yearning. Fear. Anguish. Hope.

Holden knew he had to make a decision, and

quick. But with Faith wrapped around him and Leigh-Leigh giving him that look, he had no choice.

He'd tried to walk away. He'd tried to give her a life. He'd tried to do the right thing.

But he wouldn't be able to do it a second time.

15

They made a pretty picture.

That was my shameful thought as the vision of Holden holding my daughter turned watery.

I had to remind myself Faith was home, she was safe, and she was unharmed. Patricia and Beatrice were in jail. So was that Chad asshole who'd hit me and knocked me out. As soon as I'd opened the door and saw Patty standing behind him, I knew I was in trouble. Actually, I'd sensed the trouble before I'd opened the door. All of my instincts were screaming that there was danger behind my front door. Yet, I'd stupidly opened it anyway, thinking it was Holden I was sensing.

Even as disoriented as I was, when I'd woken up,

I'd been frantic to talk to Holden, to tell him who had Faith and beg him to find her. Once Kennedy calmed me down, she explained Holden had been in to see me but didn't stay. At first, my heart sank to a new level of despair. Then she told me Holden wasn't at the hospital because he and Jameson were already searching for Faith. Holden had blindly gone on the hunt for my kidnapped child. With me unconscious, they had no leads. But Holden had known who'd taken Faith, and he went to Virginia prepared to do whatever he had to do to get her back for me.

And he did. He'd found her and brought her home.

Now my child was clinging to Holden like he was her lifeline. Not me—Holden. She'd leapt out of my arms into his and wrapped her tiny body around his much larger one, and from my position on the bed, I could see her trembling.

I'd hated the Towlers for years, but never had I wished horrible things upon them like I did now. I hoped they were sitting in a jail cell, scared out of their minds. I hoped they were uncomfortable. I hoped that a great many awful things happened to them while they rotted away behind bars. This time, they'd gone too far. This time, they'd awakened the vicious mama bear, and I would stop at nothing until they were ruined. They'd never see Paul's money. They'd never, ever see Faith again. I would fight until my dying breath to ensure my child wouldn't have to endure another second with them.

"Faith, honey, it's late. Holden's been busy all day. Maybe we should let him go home and get some sleep."

"No."

No. Just no. That was all my daughter squeaked out as she clung to Holden.

My gaze lifted and met Holden's steely eyes. The ever-present pang of loss and grief hit me, but unlike all the other times, I couldn't hide it. I was emotionally spent. My child had been kidnapped. *Kidnapped.* Stolen from my home, and I'd been powerless to protect her. The stress, fear, and pain of the day bore down on me and I couldn't stop the tears. Relief and frustration mingled together. Anger and the deepest terror I'd ever felt boiled until I wanted to lash out and hit something, or scream, or flip the universe off for being so cruel.

"Leigh-Leigh?"

God, he needed to stop calling me that. Every time he said it another crack in my heart formed.

That stupid nickname was like salt in a very open wound. One that would never heal. The gashes would always be there, bleeding, exposed, gaping.

"Babe?"

I blinked and Holden came back into focus. His features had softened, the look reminiscent of days gone by. Days and nights when he only looked at me with love and care.

"Everything's gonna be okay," he continued. "Faith's home and no one's gonna hurt her. Promise, Leigh-Leigh, both of you are safe."

I wanted to tell him not to make me stupid promises he couldn't keep. I wanted to tell him to fuck off and leave me alone. But I couldn't with Faith there. I couldn't say anything I wanted to say, which included irrationally blaming him. I wasn't sure what I was blaming him for—nothing was his fault. But in that moment, seeing the man I'd loved for what felt like forever holding my daughter after he'd rescued her, but not before he'd left me and broken my soul, all I could see was red.

Fury and anger welled up. Just as I opened my mouth to say something that would likely scare my daughter, Holden spoke again, "Take a breath, Charleigh."

I clamped my mouth closed and glared at him. I

hated that he was intimately familiar with my temper. I hated that he knew I was going to lose it and say something I'd regret later. Not because my words would be untrue, but because Faith didn't need to hear.

Once Holden ascertained I had a hold on my tongue, he turned to Faith.

"Let's get you back into bed with your mama." Faith shook her head, the movement barely there since her face was buried in his neck. "I'm not going anywhere, but you need to get some sleep. So does your mom."

"You'll stay?" Faith mumbled against Holden's throat.

"I'll stay."

"I don't want you to go."

"Faith, I promise you I'll be here when you wake up. I'm not going anywhere."

"You'll protect Mommy?"

Holden's eyes snapped back to mine and a look I'd never seen flickered. Then it was gone before I could process it.

"With my life."

My breath hitched and my throat clogged.

I didn't need time to process his statement, I

needed to unhear the fierce determination in his voice. I needed to forget the defiant resolve in his tone. Those words were spoken to Faith but they were not for her, they were for me. Holden was telling me, without actually telling me, he was planning something. The man standing before me was the old Holden—my Holden. Not the cold, distant, Holden who had been far from my reach for years.

I wanted the faraway Holden back, the one I was determined to get over. The one who wanted nothing to do with me or Faith. I had to move on for me, for my daughter. I needed to build a life for us and find happiness.

This Holden, the old Holden, the thoughtful, protective, caring man, was dangerous. I'd taken one look at him and fallen in love. A single glance in his direction and I knew he would be the man I'd marry. Obviously, I'd been wrong. So very wrong. But there was still one undeniable truth, I'd always love him. It was like a sickness I couldn't get rid of. Holden Stanford was my other half. From the second I saw him, something clicked into place. I'd never believed in soulmates until him.

Before I had Faith, I'd been willing to fight for him. I'd given it my all and I'd failed. Now, I had to protect my daughter from my dysfunctional heart. I wouldn't allow her to get close to Holden only to feel the sting of his deflection.

No way. No how. I'd keep Faith safe at all costs.

Tomorrow, I'd thank Holden for all of his help. Then I'd make a plan to extradite him from our lives. It should be easy—he hated me—but the look on his face no longer said revulsion. It said something new and that scared the hell out of me.

Holden walked to the side of my bed, and with his gaze still connected to mine, he kissed the top of Faith's head before he laid her next to me.

Bastard.

"Get some sleep."

I pulled Faith closer and she settled on her side with her little arm over my chest, her head resting on my shoulder, and I held on tight.

My girl was home. She was safe. She was physically unharmed.

Nothing else mattered. Not the revenge I'd vowed on the Towlers, not Holden, not my heart, not the battle I had on my hands. Not a damn thing other than my girl.

Then why couldn't I get the sight of Holden and Faith walking into my room hand-in-hand out of my mind? Why couldn't I stop the replay of Faith holding onto Holden? Why couldn't I stop the mental images of how perfectly she'd fit in his arms, from assaulting me?

Why in the actual hell couldn't I stop loving the man who'd destroyed me?

16

Holden stayed silent and watched as Faith came awake. Mother and daughter had slept cuddled together on the small twin-sized hospital bed. Twice, a nurse came in to wake up Charleigh and check her vitals. Neither time did Faith even twitch at the intrusion. Both times, Charleigh turned her gaze to the corner where Holden was sitting and didn't hide her irritation that he was still there.

However, Holden ignored her. He'd spent years living under a mountain of regret, years wishing he'd done everything differently, without knowing how or if he should explain to Charleigh why'd he'd done what he'd done. Sometimes, things are better left in the past, but in the hours he spent looking for Faith and the hours he spent after he'd found her, he'd come to a decision—he needed to make things right.

Though, sometime in the wee hours of the morning as he stared at Charleigh and Faith sleeping, his objective changed. He wasn't only going to make things right; he was going to make them his. Which meant he was going to turn the water under this particular bridge into raging rapids of emotional turmoil. He'd have to confess everything. Six months ago, that thought would've made him sick to his stomach. Hell, six days ago, he would've rather run away than fess up and tell the truth. Admitting he couldn't have children was only the tip of the iceberg. There was so much more, things that Paul had said and done that he'd kept to himself. Only after Chasin and Jameson had spoken with him did Holden understand how deep Paul's hatred and jealousy ran. He knew the guy didn't like him, even knew he had a thing for Charleigh. But he never thought Paul was so manipulative he'd take advantage of Charleigh.

It seemed Holden had been wrong about a lot of things.

The little girl's eyes shot open and Holden's gaze collided with hers. It wasn't the first time he'd taken in Faith's appearance, not even the first time he'd felt relief she didn't look anything like her father. She was a carbon copy of Charleigh. Only, not as outgoing. Faith was more stoic, like he'd been as a child. But there was something different about this moment. Holden fought back a shiver as Faith stared at him. Assessing, evaluating, judging. He held perfectly still and waited to see if he measured up. The girl was no dummy; she sensed more than Holden wanted her to. In the rare times he'd been around her, she'd always kept her distance. During those times, he'd been grateful Faith hadn't been friendly with him. Hadn't wanted to get close or talk to him like she did the others. Now, the thought made him sick. He hated he'd given her reason to be leery around him.

Holden knew he'd never deserve the child's friendship or Charleigh's forgiveness, but that didn't mean he wasn't going to try. He'd worm his way into their lives, fall to his knees and beg, lay himself bare and tell Charleigh everything. He couldn't live another day without Charleigh knowing the whole truth.

Faith gave Holden a lopsided smile that made his heart constrict and she nodded her head as if she approved of his silent musings. He immediately returned her grin and watched as she nuzzled her mother's chest. The sight took his breath. Leigh-Leigh and Faith. Mother and daughter. Their love was beautiful—perfect. And he wondered if there was room for him in their circle. Could he fix everything he'd broken? Could he earn a place in their hearts? Did he have that right, or should he settle on friendship? The thought of being nothing more than a friendly "uncle" now felt abhorrent. He wanted to be more.

"Morning, pretty girl." Charleigh's sleepy voice filled the room and hit Holden square in the chest.

He hadn't heard that raspy voice in so long he'd almost forgotten how sexy she sounded first thing in the morning. Only, she'd greeted him with a "Morning, handsome" and the words were normally accompanied by her hand stroking his chest. Charleigh was a maximum contact sleeper; when they were in bed she was always touching him. Hell, even when they were out of bed she liked to be close. Something that Holden loved. Wherever they were, there was no mistaking she was his. And he proudly claimed her. Charlotte Axelson was downright beautiful, but it wasn't her beauty that had drawn him to her, it wasn't even her beaming smile. It was simply *her*. She was beyond explanation—call it her aura, her spirit, her energy, or whatever New Age description, but there was something about Charleigh that drew you into her atmosphere, and once you were there you hoped to God you never fell from it.

He'd been perfectly enthralled until he realized he couldn't give her the life she wanted. He couldn't give her a family without heartache and disappointment. If he'd stayed with her, she wouldn't have a perfect daughter who looked just like her. One she nurtured and grew in her womb. She would've never experienced childbirth. Instead, any children they had would've come with lawyers, paperwork, social workers, and heartbreak.

What if she wanted more children?

Jesus, the very thought made him break out into a cold sweat. Nothing had changed. Not that he'd been back to a doctor since he'd received the crushing news he'd never be a father, but he still couldn't give her what Paul had.

Faith mumbled something unintelligible just as the door slowly opened and a nurse appeared.

"Good, you're awake. My name is Anne and I'll be taking care of you this morning." Anne's gaze went to Faith's and her smile brightened. "I heard we had a special little angel on the floor this mornin' takin' care of her momma. But no one told me how pretty she was." Faith snuggled closer to Charleigh and sheepishly looked at the nurse. "Would you mind sitting with your daddy for a few minutes so I can check your momma over?"

"Oh, he's not her father," Charleigh corrected.

Anne's face turned a light shade of red and her eyes went wide. "My apologies. They look so much alike, I just assumed."

"Um...he's a..." Charleigh stammered but said nothing more.

"It's fine," Holden cut in. "Faith, doll, you okay sitting with me while Nurse Anne checks your mom over?"

Wordlessly, Faith nodded and got off the bed. Holden held his breath, waiting to see what Faith would do. When she walked right to him and climbed onto his lap, his lungs started to burn. *Christ, why does that feel so good*? There was no hesitation from Faith but Charleigh's eyes immediately narrowed as she took them in.

Holden lost Charleigh's attention when the nurse started asking her questions about pain level and dizziness. He stopped paying attention to the nurse when Faith tapped his cheek.

"I'm hungry."

His eyes lowered and he took in the little girl. Did she look like him? He'd never thought so, but then he never wanted to look too closely, instead choosing to believe she was a mini-Charleigh. But now that she was close and he could see the light flecks of brown in her eyes, flecks that he saw every time he looked in the mirror, he wondered. As impossible as it was, he couldn't stop himself from scanning Faith's face for any hint of himself. It was futile, and in the end, it would only cause Holden extreme pain, but he couldn't help himself. He'd wished—hell, he'd prayed for years—that by some miracle she'd been his.

Praying, wishing, and hoping was pointless and it led to nowhere.

"As soon as your mom's done with her checkup, I'll get you something."

"Pancakes?"

Holden smiled.

"Is that what you want?"

Faith nodded and continued with her breakfast order. "With syrup. And bacon, too." There was a pause, then she snapped her eyes back to his and quickly added. "Please."

"Sure thing, doll. Pancakes and bacon it is."

There was another moment of silence and once again Holden felt like he was under heavy scrutiny. The little girl had an uncanny way of making him want to fidget. No one made Holden uncomfortable, but then not many people had the balls to stare him down. Faith did. Which was a weird thing to say about a child, but it was true nonetheless. Like Charleigh, Faith seemed to have an iron constitution.

"You need something, darlin'?"

"You forgot the syrup."

Holden couldn't hold back his roar of laughter. "Right. The syrup."

"You have the same dimple I have when you smile." Faith's head tilted as she stared at Holden's cheek.

He didn't have a dimple per se, but he did have a small indent, so slight people often overlooked it. Not *this* little girl, though.

"See?" Faith continued, and tipped her lips up into a toothy smile.

It was there, ever so slight, the same as his.

A dangerous emotion clogged his throat, making his nose sting. He didn't want to admit it felt a hell of a lot like a possibility, when there was none. But he couldn't deny it when wishful thinking filled his chest. Then came the excruciating letdown, the knowledge that no matter how many similarities he made up, Faith wasn't his. It wasn't genetics that she had flecks of gold in her eyes or an indentation in her cheek, it was simply a coincidence. A lot of people had specks in their irises and dimples in their cheeks.

"You sure do," he croaked out.

He was saved from further study when the nurse announced she was done and the doctor would be in soon to talk to Charleigh about discharging her.

Unfortunately, that meant while Holden was no longer under Faith's examination, Charleigh had turned her critical consideration his way.

Mother and daughter had the fault-finding glare down to a science.

"I'm not sure they have pancakes in the hospital cafeteria, sweets," Charleigh said and arched an eyebrow Holden's way.

"They don't have a cafeteria in this hospital, period," Holden returned. "What do you want for breakfast, Leigh-Leigh?"

Tiny creases appeared on Charleigh's forehead, warning him she was irritated. But before she could tell him in a kid-friendly version to go fuck himself, Faith spoke.

"Leigh-Leigh? Grandmother and Grandfather

call her Charlotte. But she hates it when people call her that. Everyone else calls her Charleigh."

"I know."

"You do?" Faith's nose scrunched, and for a millisecond, Holden thought about holding his tongue. Then he decided he didn't want to. He wanted Faith to know how well he knew her mother.

"I do. I've known your mom a long time."

"I know *that*. You've been to our house in Virginia."

"Yup. But I knew your mom before you were born."

"You knew my dad."

It was a statement. Of course, Faith knew Holden knew Paul, but it was still a dagger to his heart. A stabbing, piercing pain that had him rethinking his plan to get close to the duo.

Fucking Christ. He couldn't do it. He thought he could, but he hadn't taken into consideration that Faith might have questions about her dad. None of the guys had ever mentioned if Faith had talked about Paul—not that they would. Faith and Charleigh had been a no-go topic.

Holden swallowed down the sour taste and answered. "I did."

"I never met him."

He heard a choking sound coming from Charleigh but didn't dare look away from Faith.

"I know you didn't, doll. And I'm sorry you never had the chance."

"Grandfather says you can't miss something you never had."

Sweet Jesus, Charleigh's dad is a dick.

"That's not true. I'm sure you miss your dad."

Faith squirmed uncomfortably. He wasn't sure what that meant but he did know he didn't want to discuss Paul. At least, not until he figured out a way to lock his hatred for the man down so Faith would never know what a douche the guy had been.

Shit. He shouldn't have even been thinking that while Faith was on his lap.

What was wrong with him?

The man was dead and gone.

Years had passed but Holden still couldn't forgive Paul for what he'd done. Especially what he'd done to Charleigh.

Not knowing what else to say, Holden's gaze slid to Charleigh. She stared back at him with a look that said *help me*—or maybe it said *go to hell.* Whatever the message, the tears brimming in her eyes were Holden's undoing.

In an effort to move the conversation along, he rewound to breakfast.

"Are you ready for pancakes, syrup, and sausage?"

"Bacon," Faith corrected.

"Oh, right, bacon."

Holden winked and Faith was back to smiling.

"Leigh-Leigh?"

"I'm not hungry."

Faith leaned in close to Holden. In a horrible attempt at a whisper, she announced, "Mom's grouchy before coffee."

"She is," he readily agreed.

So many memories assaulted him; bringing Charleigh coffee in bed; watching her shuffle into the kitchen, her hair disheveled but never looking so beautiful, wearing a deep frown until she saw coffee was made; Leigh-Leigh kissing him sweetly when he made her a mug just the way she liked it.

Holden could recall everything about Charleigh. Every single little detail. From her favorites, to the freckles on her stomach, to the places she loved to be touched.

"How about we get her some?"

Faith nodded and smiled. Without delay, Holden grabbed his phone off the roll-table that was covered in Faith's medical records from the night before and dialed Nixon.

"Everything good?" Nix's tired voice came over the line and Holden internally frowned.

Damn. It was still early and his friend hadn't left the hospital until late.

"Yeah, sorry, brother, I should've checked the time. Go back to sleep—"

"I'm up. What do you need?"

Not for the first time, or even the hundredth, Holden thought about how lucky he was to have such good friends.

"Faith's up and hungry. I don't want to leave. Would you mind picking up pancakes and bacon and don't forget the syrup?"

"Yup. What else?"

"Two extra-large coffees. One black, one with about two inches of creamer and five sugars. A toasted everything bagel with extra cream cheese. Oh, and an orange juice."

"Got it. I'll swing by Sam's then be in. We need to talk about where Charleigh and Faith will be staying."

Shit. Goddamn. Holden had forgotten about that. Charleigh would be released today and there was no way in hell they were going back to that apartment.

But Holden's Airstream was barely big enough for him.

"I'll make some calls."

"No need," Nix told him. "Genevieve already made arrangements. Her uncle's house is available. The security there isn't great but they won't be walking into the scene of the crime, so to speak. And with the Towlers and that dickweed behind bars, I don't think they're in any danger. It's yours for as long as you need it."

He owed Genevieve huge.

"That's perfect. Thanks."

"Don't thank me. Evie's been running around with Bobby getting the kitchen stocked and making sure the place is set up. She even went to Charleigh's and packed clothes for both of them. McKenna says Evie's pulling out all the stops to make sure they're comfortable."

That wasn't surprising—even though Charleigh wasn't Genevieve's favorite person, she was kind and thoughtful. Holden scratched a call to his friend onto his mental to-do list. A call that would include explaining some things to Evie, key points he'd left out of the story that he didn't want her to know—but it was time to come clean.

"I'm sure I'll see her at some point today."

"Bet on it. She's...feeling guilty for giving Charleigh the cold shoulder. Especially after Bobby talked to her at Christmas. I guess the last vestiges of her grudge wore off yesterday. She feels like shit."

So it seemed Bobby had shared.

Fuck.

"She shouldn't, but I'll talk to her."

"Right. See you in thirty."

Holden disconnected and Faith looked up at him. "How'd you know that an everything bagel is Mom's favorite?"

Because I've toasted them for her hundreds of times.

"Told you. I've known your mom a long time. I know she loves extra cheese on her pizza but she doesn't like cheese on her hamburgers. She loves baked potatoes but hates potato salad and only likes fries from McDonald's. She's not a fan of eating in the morning but she loves bagels and her favorite meal of the day is lunch."

The little girl's eyes widened and she asked, "What's her favorite soda?"

"That's a trick question, doll. Your mom doesn't drink soda, she drinks iced tea with Sweet'N Low. But, she despises sweet tea. She says it's too sweet."

"Wow. That's cool. You know, like, everything about her."

"Pretty much."

Holden heard Charleigh make a disgruntled sound but he kept his eyes on Faith. She was smiling up at him as if he'd brightened her world.

But his eyes stayed glued on that damn depression on her cheek.

17

How did I get here?

Not here in this hospital bed, but here—*here.* The here and now. The here where Faith was sitting on Holden's lap listening to him tell her stories about when we were younger. The here where my daughter was hanging on his every word completely enthralled. The here where every muscle was tight and my skin prickled.

I'd thought I'd been pushed to my limits before. Just yesterday, I'd been hit over the head. When I'd woken up and learned my child was kidnapped, I thought I'd finally been shoved over the edge into a dark abyss of anger and fear and I'd be lost there forever. But then I found out Holden had gone after Faith, and there was a part of me that knew he'd find her, and I found the will to keep myself together.

But this?

The two of them together—smiling and joking and having a grand old time at my expense. This I couldn't handle. This was too much for my peace of mind. This was everything I'd ever dreamed of and my worst nightmare all rolled into one.

He's going to hurt her.

Faith would fall in love with him just like I had... and she would be crushed when he walked away.

I had to get out of here. I needed to get the two of them apart and explain to my kid that she shouldn't get attached to the man who would charm her, make her feel like she was the most important thing in the world, make her believe she was beautiful and loved, only to tear it all away and leave her in shambles. Leave her wondering what she'd done wrong, where she'd failed, how she could've been so wrong to love him so much and believe they'd live happily ever after.

There was a tap on the door. It slowly opened and Micky poked her head in.

"Morning. We come bearing gifts."

Micky walked in followed by her husband. Both had their hands full of white paper bags, but I only had eyes for Nixon. *Coffee. Thank God.* Maybe after I sucked down some caffeine my head would clear and I'd be able to formulate a plan of escape. The only problem with leaving the hospital was going home.

"Yay. Pancakes," Faith squealed and my eyes left the drink holder in Nixon's hand and landed on my daughter's pretty face.

Happy. That was the only way to describe her. How was that possible? It hadn't even been twenty-four hours since she was taken from me and she was smiling and calm.

Holden.

It was all Holden. His presence. His gentle teasing. His strength.

Damn.

"Pancakes, butter, and bacon," Nixon announced and Faith's smile faded.

"He's kidding, doll," Holden said and hugged her tight. "Nix would never forget your syrup."

With a heavy heart, I watched Faith tip her head back and grin at Holden. The smile so sweet and innocent, it made my insides seize. What the hell was going on? Why was he pulling her into his web? Holden knew exactly what he was doing. He might be a promise-breaking, heart-crushing jerk but he wasn't stupid. He *knew* Faith would eat up every word he said.

Nixon's chuckle cleared my thoughts.

"Stop teasing her," Micky chastised. "We brought you coffee, Charleigh. How are you feeling?"

"Better, thank you. Just waiting on the doctor so we can go home." Nixon and Holden exchanged a look I couldn't decipher but instinctually I knew it was about me. "What's the look for?"

"What look?" Holden asked.

"Don't play dumb. You just gave Nixon a look. What's going on?"

"Nothing, babe. Drink your coffee and we'll talk after the doctor comes in."

"No way."

"Leigh-Leigh, drink your coffee and get some food in your stomach. You didn't eat anything yesterday so I know you're starving." *How does he know I hadn't eaten yesterday*? "I know you didn't eat because I asked." Holden answered my unasked question. "We'll talk after *breakfast*," he amended.

My daughter nodded like she approved of this plan and I wasn't sure I liked her and Holden on the same team. And as much as I wanted to argue and tell Holden he could shove his heavy-handed directives straight up his ass, I refrained. There was a time and a place for me to explain to Holden that nothing had changed. I was grateful for his help, but we were going back to avoiding each other until I could figure out my next move.

And I still had to deal with my parents. My mother would rather die a thousand deaths than ruin her mother-of-the-year persona. I would be shocked if they actually went back to Virginia Beach empty-handed. She cared more about her country club friends' opinion of her than her daughter's or granddaughter's well-being. It was vitally important to her that she see Faith before she left so she could report back to her crew the state of her "precious grandchild." Pure bullshit. Neither of my parents actually cared about us. They cared about their reputations.

Nixon was unearthing Faith's pancakes when I felt Micky tap my hand with the cardboard cup. "Here."

"Thank you. I appreciate you bringing Faith something to eat," I returned.

"It was no problem. We were coming in anyway."

"Where's Holly?"

"We dropped her off at Weston and Silver's."

It must be nice to have close friends as neighbors.

Weston and Silver lived on a piece of property that bordered Nixon and McKenna's. It was the same with Alec and Macy and Jameson and Kennedy. Actually, Chasin and Genevieve bought Nixon's old farm, making them neighbors with Nix, Micky, Weston, and Silver, too. Bobby lived in a repurposed old shed on Chasin and Genevieve's property. They'd remodeled the old building into a kickass guest house. And of course, Holden lived there, too, in his Airstream.

He hadn't owned it when we were together and I'd never been inside, but I'd heard from the others that he'd redone and modernized the interior. As much as I didn't want to be, I was curious what it looked like and why he chose to live in a pull-behind trailer and not in a house or apartment. However, I never asked and I never would. The less I knew about the new Holden Stanford, the better.

I didn't want to know what he'd been doing in our years apart. I didn't want to know if he'd fallen in love, had his heart broken, or been the one to break more hearts. I didn't want to know if he spoke to his parents or if either of them had remarried. I didn't want to know if he and his dad had worked out their differences about Holden being in the military. Nope. I didn't want to know anything. Not a damn thing that would strengthen the connection I felt. It was better for me not to know anything.

That wasn't to say I didn't break my own rule sometimes. In a moment of weakness when he and I were alone after he'd come to Virginia to help me out with the Towlers, I asked a few questions. None of which he answered. That also wasn't to say that after a few drinks I hadn't tried to kiss him. The ill-fated kiss was so embarrassing, I shoved it down into the darkest recesses of my mind in an effort to forget that as soon as my lips had brushed his, I felt the bond we shared snap back into place. Holden hadn't. He quickly jumped back like I was the most hideous, vile creature to ever walk the earth.

Yet, I couldn't stop loving the man. I needed shock therapy, or a brain transplant.

I sipped my coffee, hoping the warm liquid would provide much needed armor for the day ahead. Nix, Micky, Holden, and Faith talked amongst themselves while I sat quietly and listened. Actually, I wasn't listening. I was watching. The words they were saying didn't penetrate. But the way Holden absentmindedly handed Faith a napkin did. The way my daughter happily sat on Holden's lap while she ate her breakfast certainly did. The way the two of them looked content hit me with a force so painful I wondered what I'd done that was so horrible I'd be punished in such a way.

One night of drunken sex had given me my beautiful child. I'd never regret it, never wish it hadn't happened. But that didn't stop me from being heartbroken that the years Holden and I had made love, the years we'd had wild, fantastic sex, hadn't resulted in me being pregnant.

She can't be mine because I can't have fucking kids, Charleigh.

My sinuses started to sting just thinking about Holden's admission. Why hadn't he told me when we were together? Why hadn't he been honest? For years, I wondered if Holden was really Faith's biological dad. I tried my best not to but that didn't mean I hadn't looked for similarities. She looked nothing like Paul. Not her hair color, her eye color, her skin tone. Not her mannerisms, nothing. No part of her resembled the Towlers. But there'd been plenty of little things that had reminded me of Holden. Now I knew it was all in my head, wishful thinking, stupidity.

Knowing the truth once and for all didn't make me feel any better. It felt like I was standing in that damn parking lot confronting Holden all over again. His anguish and anger plain as day, his hatred surrounding me when he told me to go find Paul. And now I knew why.

"Momma?"

I blinked and looked at Faith through watery eyes.

"Yeah, sweets?"

"Why are you crying?"

Shit, goddamn, shit.

I could lie and say I had a headache but I feared that would land me another day in the hospital. The truth wasn't an option.

"Sometimes, doll, after something really scary happens and after you know everything's okay, all the emotions you were hiding come out," Holden explained.

"Why would you hide them?"

"Because sometimes hiding is the only thing that gives you strength."

My eyes drifted closed and I wondered who Holden was speaking to—me or Faith?

He certainly hid a lot from me.

"Yesterday, your mom had to be strong for you even though she was scared and hurt. All she was thinking about was you. Now, she sees you're safe and all those feelings she was hiding are coming out."

"But she didn't need to be strong. She sent you."

"She was still scared for you, darlin'. That's what moms do. They worry. Now you're home safe and sound and she's so happy and relieved all those emotions are coming out."

I wished with all my might that was why I was crying. Not that I wasn't happy and relieved my daughter was home, but I hadn't begun to process everything that had happened. I would do that when I was home in my bed with Faith tucked next to me. I'd finally give in to my fear and anxiety when no one could witness my breakdown.

The bed jostled and I opened my eyes to find Faith climbing up.

"It's okay, Mom."

I slowly exhaled and gathered my daughter in my arms, feeling guilty she was the one consoling me.

"You're right, everything is just fine. We're gonna be okay."

And one way or another I would make that so. We'd be okay. Together, we'd get through the aftereffects of what the Towlers had done. Together, we'd move on. We always did.

Holden stood and jerked his chin toward the door. Nixon moved in that direction, but before Holden could take two steps, Faith sat up.

"Where are you going?" The panic in her voice couldn't be missed nor could the way Holden's body went rigid.

"I'm gonna step out into the hallway with Nixon," he told her.

"No. You can't leave."

I sat frozen and watched as Holden loosened his muscles and softened his features. Everything about him transformed before my eyes.

"Last night I promised you I wasn't leaving. I keep my promises. I'm not going far. I need to talk to Nixon in the hall but I'll be right outside the door. No one will come in here and I'll be right back in."

Liar, liar, pants on fucking fire. Holden did not keep his promises. He broke them without explanation.

Faith nodded and laid back down, tucking herself in the crook of my arm with her face turned toward the door.

Damn him.

He had no right to make promises to my daughter.

"Be back, Leigh-Leigh."

I bit back the request I felt like I'd made a million times for him to stop calling me that dumb nickname and remained silent. The jerk smiled and shook his head as if he found me amusing.

As soon as I was out of this hospital bed, I was letting him have it. Then we'd see how amusing he found me when I told him to go fuck himself.

The door closed behind the men and Micky made a strangled sound. Her eyes went wide as saucers when she said, "Uh-oh. I know that look."

There was nothing I could say in reply with Faith in the room. And even if my daughter wasn't present I still wouldn't have said anything to McKenna. She was Nixon's wife. Holden's friend. She probably wouldn't like hearing what I had to say about the big jerk.

"Can I ask you a favor?" Micky murmured.

My heart sank. After all that she and the others had done for me and Faith, I would do anything she requested.

"Anything."

"Go easy on him."

Anything except that.

"You don't know what you're asking."

"I do and I don't. I know him. I know he's a good man. A good friend. I also know he's in pain. He has been since I met him. He covers it up with a smile, but it's there just under the surface. I see it when he looks at me and Nix, or Jameson and Kennedy, or Weston and Silver, or Chasin and Evie. But I see it most when he watches Alec with Rory, Joss, and Caleb. And I see how he looks at Holly and Dylan. I don't know the whole story and I'm sure he's the one at fault. So, I know I'm asking a lot, but please—go easy."

"Who's in pain, Mom?"

If there was ever a time I needed a black hole to open up and swallow me, it was now. I didn't want to think about why Holden watched Alec with his children. Or what McKenna meant about *how* Holden looked at her daughter or Weston's son. I didn't want to know he was in pain or figure out why that was. I had to get over him and move on.

"Holden," I answered.

"Why is he in pain? Did he get hurt?"

That was a loaded question I wouldn't answer.

"I don't know, honey."

McKenna's gentle smile was meant to be reassuring but it did nothing but confuse me. My feelings for Holden were complicated. I knew I would love him for the rest of my life but everything about us was muddy and tarnished. Our love had been stained by betrayal. First, Holden leaving me, then my night with Paul.

There was no fixing it. Once a mirror was broken, you could search for all the pieces and try to glue it back together but there would always be that one tiny sliver that would be missing. The spiderweb of cracks would always be visible. I'd been naïve thinking we could repair what had been broken and be together. Holden was right. He'd been smart to keep his distance and push me away. He'd moved on with his life and I'd stupidly stayed in the past.

My problem was, the past was so beautiful I didn't know how to let it go.

18

Charleigh was going to blow her stack. Holden felt it coming. Of course, she'd wait until Faith wasn't around before she unleashed her wraith—but it was coming nonetheless.

"I love it here," Faith announced, and Holden pinched his lips in an effort not to burst out laughing.

Faith was looking up at the ceiling with her arms spread wide, twirling around the great room of Evie's uncle's house while Charleigh looked on in horror. She'd been discharged from the hospital an hour before —she hadn't suffered a fracture, just abrasions and a minor concussion—and from the moment the doctor had left her room, Holden saw the trepidation seep in. Charleigh being Charleigh had kept it locked down.

The woman would never admit she was scared as fuck about going back to her home. The place where she'd been bashed over the head and her daughter taken.

No, not the new Charleigh. Instead, she'd blanked her expression and prepared to take it on the chin. Holden's Charleigh would've turned to her man and been honest. She would've told him she was scared and clung to him tight knowing he'd protect her.

He'd fucked up in a good many ways, but one of the worst fuck-ups he'd perpetrated was turning his back on a good woman. And since he'd done that, she'd changed in ways he didn't like. She was still the spitfire she always was, but now there was a weariness to her that he hated.

He'd done that. He'd hurt her. He'd screwed up so badly she'd been on her own, forced to handle everything herself. Not only for her, but for Faith as well.

"This isn't necessary," Charleigh complained.

Holden got close and lowered his voice.

"It is and you know it."

When her brown eyes settled on his, he saw it. Relief. She'd never admit it. As a matter of fact, Charleigh was going to fight it and pitch a fit. But, he much preferred that over the fatigued worry he'd seen earlier.

"We're not your problem," she hissed.

"You're right, you're not. Because me looking after you and Faith isn't a problem."

"You know what I mean." Charleigh continued to hiss, but this time she narrowed her eyes and flattened her lips.

"No, Leigh-Leigh, I don't know what you mean. You're not taking Faith back to that apartment. At least not right now. First, she doesn't need to be there. Second, you're not ready to go back there. And before you deny it, remember who you're talking to. I know you. I saw it the second worry crept in. We'll stay here a few days and go from there."

"We?"

"Yes, we."

Those narrowed eyes turned to slits and she shook her head. "You are not staying with us."

"I am. I promised Faith I wasn't leaving. Besides, look around, this place is huge. There are five bedrooms. Evie stocked it with enough food for a month."

Something passed over Charleigh's features. Her shoulders snapped back, and a look of defiance took over.

"We'll go stay with Jameson and Kennedy."

What the fuck?

"You'll go stay with Jameson?"

"Kennedy," she corrected. "She won't mind and Faith will be comfortable there."

Holden's eyes sliced to the little girl who was still dancing around the room, then looked back to Charleigh.

"She looks pretty damn comfortable here."

"Well, I'm not."

The little girl danced over to them. "Can I go upstairs and pick out my room?"

"No."

"Yes."

Charleigh made a grunting sound and Holden chose to ignore it.

"After you pick your room, I'll take you up to the roof," Holden told Faith.

"The roof?"

"Yep. There's a widow's walk."

"What's that?"

"It's like a deck but on the roof. You can see all around Cliff City from up there."

"This place is awesome. I wanna live here forever."

Holden shot Charleigh a smile and she returned a scathing glare.

At least he had Faith on his side.

NINE HOURS LATER, Holden sat in the kitchen. Since Charleigh had taken Faith upstairs to go to sleep, the house had been too quiet. Normally, he reveled in silence and preferred to be alone. But the house was too big, too quiet, too lonely with Faith and Charleigh moving around. Without Faith's constant chatter.

Not much had changed in the hours they'd been there. Faith had excitedly checked out every room. Charleigh had followed behind her daughter, disgruntled. Holden had taken Faith down to the dock, but without being able to get in the water there wasn't much to do out there. Then he'd made them dinner, and throughout their meal, the only conversation had come from the eight-year-old. She'd told Holden all sorts of stuff—from her new school, the friends she'd made, the teacher she didn't like, her favorite subjects. When she'd exhausted all things school-related she'd moved on to wanting to play softball in the spring. Charleigh had remained noncommittal about Faith playing, and only spoke when Faith had asked her a question.

Charleigh's wariness was back in full force and Holden was second-guessing his decision to push his way into their lives. He wanted in—that had not changed—but he'd begun to wonder if he was causing more harm than good. He hadn't given her an option when they'd left the hospital. He hadn't asked if she was okay with him staying—mainly because he knew she wasn't but he hadn't thought she'd retreat into herself.

All of his friends were married. They had homes and wives to take care of, but he knew if he asked, one or all of them would come over and stay with Charleigh and Faith. Of course, there was Jonny; he was single and a cop so maybe she'd feel more comfortable with him staying. The thought rankled. Holden didn't want anyone but him watching over the girls. He didn't want any of his brothers getting closer to Faith. Nor did he want to give Charleigh more time to dig a deeper channel between them. It was deep enough as it was and so wide the bridge he needed to build would be difficult.

The truth will set you free.

Christ, he wished that was true. Unfortunately, the truth would just hurt her more.

Holden heard her footfalls before he saw her.

When she stepped into the dimly lit kitchen, his breath arrested.

Fucking hell.

Charleigh stopped and stared at him from across the room. Neither said a word as each assessed the other. She looked so damn beautiful. And suddenly Holden was transported back ten years. A bevy of memories assaulted him. How many times had he watched her putzing around their apartment looking exactly like she did right then? Contacts out, glasses on, hair pulled up in a messy knot on top of her head, oversized tee on, and though he couldn't see them he knew she'd be wearing cotton sleep shorts. Even when it was cold—not that Virginia ever got as cold as it did in Maryland—she always slept in a tee and shorts or nothing at all. If she got cold in the middle of the night, she'd tangle her legs with his and burrow close.

Who had kept Charleigh warm in his absence? Who had she welcomed into her bed? Homicidal rage thrummed through his veins at the very thought of another man touching her. And wasn't that fucked-up, considering he'd been with other women? Though for him those women meant nothing. They were a warm body and nothing more. That was not

Charleigh. Paul notwithstanding, she was not a one-night-stand type of woman—and she'd married the motherfucker, so she *really* wasn't the type of woman to sleep with a man and walk away. Which meant anyone she'd had in the years between meant she'd cared for them, maybe even loved them. Had they met Faith? Did the little girl talk to them about school? Did they make her pancakes in the morning? The urge to ask Charleigh for a list of the men she'd been with so he could track them down and kick their asses was strong. The need to erase both of their pasts hit him hard.

"We need to talk." Charleigh broke the silence.

He whole-heartedly agreed but was having a hard time vocalizing his agreement. He was too angry to speak. Royally pissed at himself for what he'd done, seriously fucking pissed at Paul, mad at the universe for taking away his ability to give his woman what she wanted, and now he was irate at the thought of her sharing her bed with some bastard.

"Holden?" she snapped.

He cleared his throat and nodded.

"What do you want to talk about?"

"Me and Faith are leaving in the morning and going to Kennedy's."

"No."

"What do you mean, no? You don't have a say."

"I sure as fuck do."

Charleigh's features turned to stone and she stomped farther into the room.

"No, Holden, you don't. You have no say. And this shit you pulled bringing us here...no, let's back up, the shit you pulled playing nice with Faith was unbelievably uncool. But you making my daughter promises you're not going to keep is beyond fucked. You wanna jack me around, fine, go ahead. I know you think I deserve it after what I did to you, but don't you dare bring my child into your games."

There was no missing Charleigh's righteous indignation, but it was unwarranted and it was high time they got a few things straight.

"I'm not playing games," he started and stood, "and I'm not jacking you around."

Pain washed over her pretty face. He fought the need to go to her and pull her into his arms. He figured he had one shot at getting this right, one chance to start to heal the breach he'd created, and touching her would only fuel her outrage.

"You've made it clear you hate me," Charleigh said with a hitch in her voice. "*Painfully* clear, Holden. I moved here...never mind why I came—"

"I know why you moved here, Leigh-Leigh," he

cut her off. "And I don't hate you." Holden stepped around the table. His heart was hammering in his chest. It was time to come clean. Time to put all his cards on the table and stop hiding like a pussy.

"Could've fooled me," she mumbled.

"I tried," he admitted. "I tried so fucking hard to hate you." Charleigh paled and stepped back and he knew before he was done he was going to wreck her if that one small admission made her look like he'd sucker-punched her. "You wanna know why I went to your wedding? Because I thought watching you vow your life to another man would make me stop loving you. I thought that when I heard you say the words to Paul I desperately wanted you to say to me, I would finally hate your guts. But it didn't work. I hated that prick with everything I am but I couldn't stop loving you. I went to two barbeques at your house for the same reason. I thought seeing you with him would help me get over you. Seeing you *pregnant* with his child would finally kill what I felt for you. It killed all right, it killed so fucking bad, I broke. He had everything I loved. He had you and his baby and the life I wanted with you. He had *everything* and I had not a goddamn single thing that was worth a damn." Holden stopped and tried to gather his composure, but now that the words were flowing he couldn't stop them.

Good or bad, he had to get them out—purge the poison that had been eating at his innards for so long he couldn't remember what it was like to breathe clean. Before he could process the look on Charleigh's face, more poured out of him.

"He got you. He won. He had the world in his bed and what did he do? Fucked every available piece of pussy he could find, and he did it in front of me. He rubbed my nose in it and taunted me. A silent dare for me to go to you and rat him out so he could deny it and make me look like a crazy fool. You were at home with his kid in your stomach and he was getting blowjobs in his truck. Stupid motherfucker. And if that shit isn't whacked enough, the prick had to go and die. His last words on this earth were him giving you back to me. He had the balls to ask me to take care of *his* wife and child. His, Leigh-Leigh. His wife. The woman I loved more than my own life belonged to another man. I will go to my grave hating that fucker and loving you. For years, I tried everything I could to stop thinking about you, stop loving you, stop my body from craving you, stop my hands from remembering the way your skin felt.

"Nothing worked. Not women, not alcohol, not

seclusion, nothing could make me hate you. And straight up, baby, I tried. I wanted to so badly. I tried hard. I blamed you, Faith, Paul, God, anyone and anything I could, but the truth is, all of it is my fault. I did this to us. I walked away when I should've stayed and talked to you. So, no, this isn't a fucking game, woman. I'm not jacking you around or making promises to Faith I don't intend to keep. This is me fighting for what should've always been ours."

When Holden was done, his chest heaved like he'd run fifteen miles in the sand but it was the tears streaming down Charleigh's cheeks that left him breathless. He'd been so caught up in his furious attempt to clear his conscience, he hadn't stopped to think about the blows he was delivering.

Fuck.

"Leigh-Leigh—"

"I knew," she snickered. "I knew he was stepping out on me—like you said, he didn't hide it. Though I didn't hide I was in love with a man who was *not* my husband. I couldn't stop myself from lying in my marital bed and crying. I was married to a man I barely knew, was in love with you, and I was pregnant with a child I wanted to be yours. You think I care he was getting blow jobs in his truck? You think I care he was out carousing? From the day I married him I was emotionally cheating on him with you. And not that it's any of your goddamned business, but I don't blame him."

What the hell?

"He told you he was fucking around and you didn't care?" Holden asked in utter shock.

What woman didn't care her husband was cheating on her?

"He didn't have to tell me. I didn't miss the perfume, the lipstick, the scratch marks on his back. You think he was taunting you? You're wrong. That was him punishing *me*. He had a woman in his bed who loved another man and wouldn't go there with him. So he'd go out and find it elsewhere, then the next day make sure he was up and walking around shirtless before I left for work so I could see the evidence of his cheating. I never said a word, so he did it more and more. Hickeys, bite marks, you name it. It didn't faze me because all I was thinking about was you and who you were with."

Holden's world tilted. All the fucked-up things Paul had done to Charleigh flitted from his head until his thoughts zeroed in on one thing—she wouldn't go there with him. What the hell did that mean?

"You wouldn't go there with him?"

Charleigh reared back and shook her head.

"None of that matters. Faith and I are going to—"

"It matters a helluva lot. Are you telling me that you never fucked that asshole?"

"Obviously I did, Holden, the evidence of that encounter is sleeping upstairs," she sneered.

A deep growl emanated from his soul, the sound so feral, Charleigh took a giant step back as Holden advanced.

"You know what I'm asking, baby."

"That's none of your business."

Something ugly started to blossom in his chest. An ugly, selfish happiness he should've been ashamed to feel, yet he couldn't bring himself to feel anything but warmth at the knowledge. Holden didn't need her to admit it, but he still wanted to hear the words come out of her mouth.

"Tell me, Leigh-Leigh, did you marry that prick then keep yourself from him? You said marital bed, so I assume you slept next to him. So you shared a bed but not your body?"

They were standing close, so close Holden could smell the faint scent of her lotion, so close all he had to do was lean in a few inches and he could take her mouth. Yet, he controlled his urges and stayed perfectly still. She, however, didn't. Her hands were shaking, her chest was rising and falling, and her lips were trembling.

"You're an asshole," she whispered. "I see that makes you happy. That I married him but never consummated my vows. That I slept next to him but cried over you. Yeah, I can see how that'd make a dick like you happy. Does it make you feel good to know that he held me on our wedding night while I mourned the loss of you? My face was buried in his neck, his arms were around me, and I cried all night long."

Holden ignored the vision of Paul holding Charleigh. Further, he tried and failed to stop his hands from reaching out and cradling her face. His palms were met with wetness. She tried to pull away but he held her still.

"I am a dick," he admitted. "A Grade A asshole. But not one thing you've said makes me *feel good.* I haven't felt good since the night before I rolled out of our bed and left you. I haven't felt alive, I haven't felt happy, I haven't felt anything but anger and pain."

"Why'd you leave me?"

Charleigh's question turned Holden into a ball of remorse.

"I told you why," he deflected, not wanting to talk about anymore of his failures.

"No, you didn't. You gave me some excuse."

"Excuse?"

"Yes, Holden, an excuse. So why'd you really leave me?"

His hands dropped from her face and he stepped back.

"Right," she snickered. "You're quick to talk about all things me and Paul, but when we get down to you and the real reason you left me, you close down. Wanna know what I think? I think you left me because you didn't love me, and when I started talking about our future you got cold feet so you bolted."

Anger flashed and Holden lashed out. "Right. That's why I couldn't let you go and kept coming back trying to sort my head."

"No, you came back to fuck me. Tell the truth. For once tell the goddamn truth, Holden. Stop being such a coward and come clean. I thought I was going to spend the rest of my life with you. I gave you everything, you owe me. Put me out of my misery and—"

"I was scared!" he shouted. "I was paralyzed with fear that once you found out I couldn't have kids, you'd leave me. Or worse—you'd stay, then you'd resent me for not giving you a family. So I left you before you could leave me. I left so you could find a *real* man. I didn't come home to you to fuck you, I came home because I couldn't breathe without you. I came home because I was so lost I didn't know where to turn. I love you so damn much I can't—"

"You stupid, stupid, dumb man." Charleigh's pain-filled whisper stopped Holden's rant. "You ruined us for no reason. You destroyed my life for nothing."

"Baby, please, try to understand." Holden paused and wracked his brain for what he wanted her to understand.

Why he'd been scared.

Why he'd been a spineless prick.

Why he'd run from the best thing that ever happened to him.

"You selfishly, singlehandedly demolished me. And the worst part is, if you would've told me, if you would've asked, I would've told you that you were enough. We were enough. If all I ever had was you, I would've been happy. But you didn't give me that. You didn't give me the choice. You took control and left me powerless."

"Baby, you wanted kids. You told me you did. That night, you were going on and on about all the places we'd go, all the adventures we'd have. I couldn't give you that."

Her tear-streaked face tilted up and sorrow-filled brown eyes met his.

"You mean you *can't* give me that."

The verbal sucker-punch left Holden without oxygen. There it was—he *still* wasn't good enough, he was *still* half a man, he *still* couldn't give her what she wanted.

Nothing had changed.

Charleigh would always be lost to him.

He felt it the moment it happened—all hope drained out of him and the shutters slammed shut.

He had no choice but to let the woman he loved go.

19

I couldn't believe what I was hearing even though it was the second time Holden had told me why he left me. The first time left me reeling, wondering at the possibility that the man I loved would really leave me over something...hell, I didn't know what to call it.

Insignificant? Though I could understand how it would be crushing to him, it didn't mean the end for us.

Small? Although it was a big deal not being able to have children.

Selfish. Yeah, that was what I was looking for. Selfish as fuck. He took himself away from me instead of letting me be there for him. He left me instead of staying and allowing me to prove to him I loved him no matter what.

This time, hearing him say it was downright devastating. On top of everything, he knew about what Paul was doing, which was salt in the wound. It finally hit me, how little he'd trusted me.

"No, Charlotte, I can't give you what you want."

Calling me Charlotte was a low blow. No one but my parents called me by my full name. And he knew how much I hated it.

"There you go, Holden, doing what you do best—putting distance between us. Run. You're so good at switching off your feelings you should teach a class. You're a master at masking your emotions and making the people around you feel so unimportant and immaterial that I doubt you even realize you do it."

"What do you want me to say? I left you because I wanted you to have—"

"Fuck. You. You left because you didn't trust me enough to talk to me about something big in your life. You left me because you didn't want to admit to me there was something medically wrong with you. You left me because you didn't trust that I would love you in any way I could have you. Don't push your insecurities onto me and make this about me. We could've adopted. We could've gone to a fertility doctor and had a family. Or guess what, we could've just lived our lives together and had wild adventures, just the two of us. But you didn't give me the option. You stole that from me. You took yourself away from me, and for the last eight years, I've lived in hell wondering why. And now that I know, I wish I didn't. I wish I could go back to wondering why you didn't love me enough to fight for us."

My hands came up to cover my face and my fingertips dug into my throbbing forehead.

"You still won't fight," I mumbled from behind my palms.

"What was that?"

I dropped my hands and looked Holden dead in the eyes.

"You still won't fight for us. I waited for you. Every day, I waited and prayed you'd come back and tell me so we could be together. Eight years I waited."

"I'm here, Leigh-Leigh, standing in front of you telling you I never stopped loving you."

"So?"

Holden's eyes widened before they hardened. "So?"

"Yeah, Holden, so what you never stopped loving me, what does that matter? Nothing has changed. You still can't have kids." I threw my hands up in frustration. "Just because you're admitting it doesn't mean shit. How long before you leave me again? Only this time, I have Faith to consider. You're still not willing to fight for us."

"I sure as fuck am," he growled.

Please, he could save his caveman grunting for someone who gave a shit.

"Bullshit. I just watched you shut down. You're ready to give up and walk away because I pointed out you still can't have kids. That's not fighting, Holden, that's being a—"

I didn't get to finish my sentence because Holden was in my space, walking me backward until my butt hit the counter. Then his hands went around my waist and he lifted me off my feet and plopped me down on the granite surface. Holden wasted no time spreading my legs and stepping between my thighs.

This was something I'd forgotten about him, how unbelievably annoying it was that when we were arguing about something he wanted to be in my space. Not in a threatening manner. In a way where all there was to focus on was my face.

"That's me wanting you to have your heart's desire. I'll give it to you, I was selfish. I did leave you because I was insecure. But I didn't want you to have to go through the possible heartbreak of adoption. I didn't want you to get a baby and have it taken away from you. I didn't want you to have to go through doctors' appointments and disappointments."

"Liar. *You* didn't want to go through the *possible* disappointments. *You* didn't want to take the chance of us getting a baby and having it taken back. Don't blame me."

Holden's body went statue-still before it started to vibrate. His face contorted and I jolted when the scariest, nastiest, most chilling sound rumbled from his chest and out of his throat. The noise didn't sound human, he wasn't forming words, it was animalistic and painful to hear. But that wasn't what tore my heart in half. It was the big, fat tears that leaked from the corner of his eyes. I sat frozen in horror as they rolled down his face in rivers.

"Honey," I whispered and lifted my hands, but before I could reach his face to wipe away the tears, he caught my hands, trapping them between us.

"I couldn't do it." He licked his lips and waited for my gaze to lift before he continued. "I couldn't do it, Leigh-Leigh. I wanted a family with you so badly I knew I would break if we'd adopted and the birth mother changed her mind and took our baby from us. I read so many books on adoption and that's the first thing the experts warn about. It's a possibility. I couldn't see you with our child then have it taken away from us. I wanted Faith. I didn't care she was Paul's. I wanted to lie and pretend she was mine. But I knew if Paul asked for a DNA test she'd be taken from me. But the God's honest truth is, I would give anything if she was ours. I want her to be ours so fucking badly." Holden's voice hitched and I swallowed down the lump in my throat. "I'm gonna fight for us, baby, but Faith's it. There'll be no more kids. That part hasn't changed."

I had waited so long to hear him tell me he was going to fight that my first instinct was to give in and tell him all was forgiven. Only I couldn't.

"What's changed?"

"Faith."

"What?" I tried to pull back but Holden dropped his forehead to mine.

A sure sign I wasn't going to like what he had to say because he didn't want to look me in the eyes while he said it.

"I couldn't face her. Fuck, Leigh-Leigh, I didn't blame her, but seeing her was a knife to the gut. She represents all that I want. Everything I wanted for us. I couldn't look at her without feeling sorry for myself. Then I'd feel overwhelming guilt because she's innocent in all of this. The circle was unending. I wanted to fight for us, for you, hell, for *her*, but I couldn't even be in the same room without...fuck." The words sounded tortured as Holden spoke.

He was talking about my daughter. My child. And as much as I didn't want to understand because she was mine, I did. I could put myself in his shoes. If the roles were reversed and he'd had a baby with another woman, I wouldn't be able to be around that child. I could lie to myself and say I was better than that and a good, decent person wouldn't feel that way, but that would be bullshit. I'd avoid Holden and his child. I'd do whatever I could to never see them together. The pain would be unbearable.

Some of the anger waned as the heart-wrenching pain crept back in.

Would I ever feel whole again?

"Faith hasn't changed, Holden."

"No. But I have. She's not mine but she's yours. She's a part of you. I want to get to know her better. I can't walk away from you again. I physically cannot do it. It's always been you for me—always Leigh-Leigh. And I know I'm it for you. If I wasn't, you would've moved on. You would've picked up the pieces I broke, dusted yourself off, and found someone. I know you, that's the kind of woman you are.

You're strong and resilient. You wouldn't have waited all these years for me if you didn't love me in a way that will never die. We have to try to make this right."

Music to my ears. Words that fed my soul. I'd waited so many years to hear him tell me he loved me and wanted me back. So many damn years.

"I'm sorry, Holden, but I can't."

"Baby," he rasped.

God, the pleading in his voice was going to kill me.

"I get it—all of it. I understand why you avoid us and it pains me to say, I would've done the same thing. Seeing you with someone else's child would kill me. But, I have to think about Faith. She's already attached to you. It will only get worse the longer she's around you. I can't chance her well-being, Holden. I know the pain of you leaving better than anyone. I know what it feels like to have you, then have nothing. I don't want that for her."

"I'm not going anywhere. Didn't you hear me? I said I can't walk away. I've missed you so damn much, I ache. You're all I've thought about. Leigh-Leigh, please give us a chance."

"I heard you say you wanted to *try*. That's not good enough. Trying means testing the waters.

Trying means there's a possibility you walk when you realize Faith is still Faith. She's a part of me but she's always a part of Paul, too. One day, that will crash over you and we'll be right back where we were, you not being able to look at her. And, Holden, I love you with every cell in my body. I love you so damn much. But I love my daughter more. She comes first."

I felt Holden's swift inhale and his body between my legs had once again gone solid.

"I don't need that knowledge to crash over me. There's not a day that's gone by that I haven't remembered who her prick of a father is."

"And that right there is why this is not ever going to work. You can't even say his name without venom."

"Damn right, I can't. The asshole preyed on my woman. Waited until the right moment to take advantage of her. Then he screwed her over. He had you in his bed and he stuck his dick in any barfly that would look at him. Unforgivable. He was a disgrace to the uniform he wore and the gold pin on his chest. He knew nothing about honor, commitment, or brotherhood. He was a spineless, selfish asshole."

Nothing I could say would make Holden understand that I didn't care Paul was out getting laid. I was his wife on paper and nothing else. I wasn't sleeping with him. I didn't love him. We were barely friends. My marriage was a sham from start to finish. Something I allowed my parents to talk me into because I was scared and weak. I didn't care what others thought of me, I certainly didn't care what my parents' country club friends thought. But I did care about the child growing in my belly. Back then I was a young, freaked out, scared girl. I hadn't been thinking straight. I thought marrying Paul was the best thing to do. If I was in the same situation today, I would've gone at it alone. I wouldn't think twice about raising my baby by myself.

Being the man that he was, Holden would never fathom why a man would cheat on his wife. Even if the marriage was a farce.

"Here's what you don't get—Paul might've been all of that and more, but Faith will never know those things. To her, he will always be the hero who died in combat before she was born. To her, he will always be the man who was excited to become a father and a man who loved the mere thought of her being born. That is what she'll know of him. That is all I can give her and she's damn well getting it. She asks questions, Holden, and how are you going to answer them when you can't keep the disdain out of your voice or the hatred off your face? What happens when she asks me to look at pictures of him? How will you react to that? I wish things had been different for us. My biggest regret is not barring the door so you couldn't walk out. I should've fought you and made you stay until you told me what was wrong. If I could go back I would, and, Holden, that's saying something because you leaving me gave me my daughter. But I still think about it—where would we be right now if I'd fought? This can't work."

Holden pulled back and his angry brown eyes held me hostage. God, he was so beautiful. Mad, playful, happy—he was so good-looking it hurt to look at him. Of course, when he was mine it didn't hurt; I could and did spend a lot of time staring at him.

"I don't know where we would've been. But I do know where we're going. Fair warning, baby, I'm fighting."

"Holden—"

"Strap in, baby, and armor up, because we're going into battle."

"Wait—"

"No more waiting. No more lying. No more pretending. No more living in hell. Fight with me,

Leigh-Leigh. Fight and bleed for what is meant to be ours. No more regrets."

"Please—"

Holden shook his head and stepped back.

"I'm gonna win," he said authoritatively and walked away.

I didn't call out his name. I didn't jump off the counter to chase him down and make him see reason. No, I sat frozen with a stupid smile on my face and fear in my belly.

20

"You have to go, sweets."

Charleigh's voice drifted up the stairs as Holden walked out of the bedroom he'd slept in last night. Actually, he hadn't slept. He'd tossed and turned. Plotted and planned until the sun came up, then he'd showered in the en suite bathroom, the whole time wishing Charleigh was with him in the lavish, marble shower big enough for two. Part of that wishing was fantasizing about how dirty he wanted to get her before he soaped up every inch of her lush body.

Leigh-Leigh was a fan of shower sex, hell, she was a fan of sex in general and she was good at it. Not a woman before or after compared to her. Since he'd had her last, she'd lost some weight. Weight she didn't need to shift off and he'd do his best to help her put it back on. The woman had a body made for fucking. Thick thighs that felt so damn good to be between. Full, heavy breasts that swayed when she rode him. An ass that jiggled when he pounded it from behind. Every inch of her beautiful. Every freckle, every blemish, every mark she complained about made her the most perfect woman he'd ever seen.

Last night, she'd retreated but she hadn't kicked him out. And she very well could've. There was no longer a physical threat to her or Faith. He didn't need to be there to protect them. Yet, she hadn't tossed his ass out uncaring he'd promised Faith he wouldn't leave. He had no right to Faith; Charleigh was her mom, and if she didn't want Holden around, she would've made that happen. Yet, she hadn't. But even if she had, he wouldn't go far. He'd sleep in his SUV in the driveway if he had to.

"But I don't want to." Faith's voice pitched high on the last word and Holden frowned.

He hadn't been around the little girl a lot—in truth he'd made an art of avoidance—but he'd never heard her argue or even raise her voice.

Once he hit the foyer, his gaze landed on mother and daughter standing off.

"What's going on?"

Faith rushed to him, hitting him with all her weight, then wrapped her arms around his middle and held on tight.

"I don't want to go to school."

"Why not? You told me you like school."

"I'm not going," she said defiantly.

"Sweetheart, you have to go," Charleigh tried, her face a mask of concern.

It took more effort than Holden had anticipated to pry Faith off of him so he could kneel in front of her.

"Why don't you want to go to school, doll?"

Faith shook her head.

"Are you scared?"

She nodded.

"Of what?"

That got Holden a shrug.

"I can't help you with what you're afraid of if you don't tell me."

Charleigh moved close to her daughter and Holden looked up as she placed her hand on Faith's shoulder.

Something profound slammed into him. An emotion he wasn't ready to give over to yet. A feeling that was huge and wanted. This was what it would be like if they were a family. Holden and Charleigh bracketing Faith between them, keeping her safe. Together as a team. That right there was what he'd always wanted. It didn't matter that Faith was not his blood, he'd still bleed for her. It didn't matter he didn't share DNA with the little girl, he'd still teach her and guide her. And if she allowed him to, he'd show her love and affection.

But first, before he could execute his plan to win his family, he needed to see to Faith.

"Faith, honey, no one's going to hurt you." Charleigh broke the long stretch of silence.

"I know. Holden told me they were in jail."

"Then why are you scared?" Holden inquired.

Faith's eyes lifted to meet his. Holden held his breath to stave off the discomfort that had bloomed in his chest. *Those eyes.* Big, brown, puppy dog eyes that, praise be to all things holy, were not blue like Paul's. Instead, rich and sweet and made Holden want to melt when she looked at him.

"Honey—"

"I don't want you to leave," Faith blurted out.

"I'm not going to leave," Holden assured her.

"You're gonna leave," she proclaimed.

"Doll, I'm going to go to work while you're in school, but I'll come back over when you get home."

Charleigh made what Holden was now deeming her signature disgruntled noise—a cross between a grunt and a choking sound.

"If you go to work, then Mom will be alone."

Holden finally got it, and when he did, he didn't stop the broad smile that pulled at his mouth.

"So, you're worried about your mom." Holden waited for Faith to nod, then he continued. "She won't be alone, doll, she'll be going to work with me today."

"What?" Charleigh's voice pitched much like her daughter's had earlier and that made Holden smile bigger.

Damn, she's cute.

"Jonny texted me. He needs to talk to you. I told him I'd bring you into the office with me."

"I have work to do," she protested.

Holden didn't take his eyes off Faith because now that he'd opened himself up to the little girl he couldn't stop looking at her. He wanted to soak up her features, he wanted to learn all of her tells, he wanted her to know she could depend on him.

"You can use my office," he told Charleigh.

"I have appointments."

"Then after you talk to Jonny, I'll take you to them."

"I don't need a bodyguard, Holden."

"You're right, but if it makes Faith feel better, you're getting one."

There it was again, Charleigh humphed and Faith smiled.

"She hasn't had coffee yet," Faith whispered conspiratorially.

"Well, that explains a lot."

"You both remember I'm standing right here, right?" she snapped and Faith giggled.

"Yeah, baby, there's no way to miss the pre-coffee grumpy Charleigh."

Holden winked and told Faith, "You get ready for school and I'll get your mom coffee."

"You promise you'll be here after school?"

"Promise."

Faith looked over her shoulder at Charleigh and nodded. "I'll go to school."

He wasn't sure if Charleigh was praying for patience, fighting an eye roll, or planning to murder him as soon as Faith left the room. What he did know was, she was the picture of natural beauty. Further, he knew he was going to catch shit for making more promises to Faith. Which he intended to keep doing indefinitely. Each day, he'd make a new promise to stay until it was simply a given he wasn't leaving.

He needed to sort his Airstream and find a house to rent. A nice place with a yard for Faith. And a dog. Jameson had mentioned how much Faith loved Tank. It wasn't beneath him to bribe Faith into wanting to live with him. Nothing was off-limits, he was willing to play as dirty as he needed to in order to win.

"I'll help you find some clothes."

Faith turned back to Holden, leaned forward, and kissed him on his cheek.

"Thank you."

Faith skipped off, Charleigh stared down at him in horror, and Holden felt like his legs were going to give out as he stood.

"That wasn't cool, Holden, and you know it."

"You don't win wars by being cool, Leigh-Leigh. You win them by pulling out all the stops."

"My daughter's not a tool to use in this war."

"You're right, baby, she's not a tool. She's the prize I'm gonna win. Her and her momma."

Charleigh shook her head and her eyes turned glossy.

"She's not a prize, either."

Without thinking, Holden stepped into

Charleigh's space, his hands went to cradle her cheeks, and he held her where he wanted her as he leaned in close.

"Wrong. She's the ultimate prize. You both are. The jackpot, the trophy, the medal, the windfall. The family I will go to war to earn, then once I have, I'll spend the rest of my life protecting. There's not going to be anything cool about it, or fair, or decent. I warned you last night, baby, but I see you didn't prepare. I'm gonna wear you down by any means necessary. Together, we're winning this. Together, we're gonna finally find happy. Together, we're gonna be whole so we can show Faith that when you love someone, you go the distance. I forgot that, baby, but mark this—I remembered."

Holden closed the small space between them and brushed his lips against Charleigh's, the faintest graze that left him wanting more. "Now, go get your daughter ready for school and I'll make coffee."

"Holden—"

"Shh, Leigh-Leigh. If I wasn't sure, I'd walk out that door. If I didn't know you loved me down to the deepest part of your soul, I'd leave you be. If I didn't know I was ready for Faith, I never would've made promises. I'm a dick, not a piece of shit. I'd never hurt that girl. And I'll never leave you again."

Charleigh's forehead wrinkled but she didn't say a word, not in protest or in agreement. She simply walked away unconvinced.

THE LAST TWO hours had zipped past in a blur. Being as Holden didn't have children, he had no idea the amount of effort it took to get one pint-sized human up and out the door. In the preceding hours, his respect for Charleigh had grown tremendously. Through all the wrangling, the directing, and finally corralling Faith out to the car, she hadn't broken a sweat. Holden was impressed. Which had led him to think about his friend, Alec Hall, who quite literally had an infant daughter sprung on him without warning. He'd gone from a single man to a single father in a matter of days and Holden hadn't seen him skip a beat. Sure, Alec had struggled a bit in the sleep department but he'd never heard the man complain. Nor had Alec thought twice about taking in a child he hadn't known he helped create, until her mother had died, thrusting Alec and Joss together with only a letter explaining her conception.

The point was, Holden was mentally tired from nothing more than driving Faith to school. He hated that Charleigh had performed the morning ritual on her own for the last eight years. Holden learned that morning that before Faith had started school, she'd gone to full-time daycare. He didn't want to think about those early years when Faith needed to be dressed and fed in the mornings, meaning Charleigh would have to get up extra early to get Faith and herself ready. At least now for the most part Faith was self-sufficient. She could feed and dress herself, and she needed less coaxing to keep on task, though she still needed reminders about the time, and even that wore him out mentally.

"You know this is ridiculous, right?" Charleigh complained, breaking the silence.

Holden pulled into the parking lot behind Gemini Group's office. Which, incidentally, was catty-corner from Charleigh's old apartment. She might not know she wouldn't be going back but he did, therefore, it was her *old* place. He'd find something more suitable for them all within the week.

"Nope. I don't see how spending the day with you is ridiculous."

"Seriously, Holden. Stop playing games. My apartment is right there. I have work to do."

He barely stopped himself from telling her she was never, not ever, stepping foot back into that apartment. She might think it wouldn't bother her, but he knew differently. It had taken him months to be able to go back into the house where he'd been shot. He'd almost died that day and would've if Genevieve hadn't stayed by his side quelling the blood flow.

"I have a perfectly good office you can use. No one will bother you. After you talk to Jonny, if you need to go out, we'll go."

"And *I* have a perfectly good apartment, right across the street."

Her attitude fed the loose hold he had on his temper. Holden was already on edge remembering the yellow tape the deputies had used to keep looky-loos from getting too close.

"No, Leigh-Leigh, *you* have a crime scene. One you're not going to be subjected to, and Faith sure as fuck will never step foot back in the place where she saw her momma bleeding on the floor."

"Holden," she whispered and placed her hand on his forearm.

"No, Leigh-Leigh, there's nothing you can say that's gonna make me be all right with you going over there. You might think you're fine, but I guarantee, the second you open that front door and see those stairs it's gonna hit you what happened there. You don't need that, and Faith doesn't *ever* need to feel that. We're staying at Evie's uncle's house. We can use it for as long as we like. After that, we'll figure it out."

"Right." Charleigh pulled her hand away and placed it on her lap.

The way she'd said "right" was like how most women said "fine". Something was wrong and he didn't think it was because he was acting like a protective caveman. If anything, Charleigh had softened when he'd mentioned not letting Faith back into the apartment.

"What's wrong?"

"Nothing."

Translation: Everything, you big dummy.

Holden knew her "nothings" like he knew she was best left undisturbed until she consumed enough caffeine to jack up an elephant.

"Baby, you do know that in all the years we've been apart I haven't forgotten one thing about you."

"What's that supposed to mean?" she snapped again.

"It means that back then, when you told me nothing it meant something. So something is wrong. If memory serves and I know it does because again, I remember every single thing about you, it would take me a minimum of fifteen minutes to pull it out of you. So, baby, save us some time and tell me what's pissing you off."

"Nothing's pissing me off."

Holden sighed and sat back, but didn't bother turning off the engine. It was cold outside and without the heater running they'd be freezing their asses off within five minutes.

"Why are we just sitting here?" she asked after a few moments.

"Because likely whatever has pissed you off will require privacy while I sort you out."

"Sort me out?" Her eyes narrowed dangerously on Holden. "What's *that* mean?"

"Leigh-Leigh."

"My name is not an answer."

Well, at least she wasn't bitching anymore about him using his nickname for her.

"Tell me what's wrong and I'll explain what sorting you out means."

The woman was lucky she was cute as hell when she was being stubborn. If not, it would likely annoy the ever-loving shit out of him. And he knew unequivocally she wasn't going to budge when she crossed her arms over her chest and settled back.

So...guessing it is.

"Are you pissed I don't want you going to your apartment?"

"No."

Holden wanted to laugh; by answering his question she'd essentially admitted she was pissed about something.

"You mad I don't want Faith there?"

"No."

"Then you're mad we're staying at Evie's."

Her pause told him that was closer to the mark.

"I'm not mad, I'm just...confused as to why she's letting us. She's hated me since she picked her head up off Chasin's shoulder in the hospital when your doctor came in to tell us you made it through surgery."

Shit.

He'd fanned that hatred. Now he needed to fix it. But first, he needed to be honest with Charleigh.

"I haven't been right for a long time. Even before I was shot and you came to Kent County, I was pulling into myself. Everyone saw it but no one was talking to me about it. After my trip to Virginia when you went to court and the Towlers were giving you problems, I retreated completely. My head was so fucked-up I didn't want to be around my friends. They'd all hooked up with great women, they were starting families, and I was wallowing in self-pity."

Holden fixed Charleigh in his gaze so she'd understand. "Evie and I are close. She doesn't trust many people because she's been burned so many times, but when you're in, you have her absolute love and loyalty. That's Evie. That's my friend. And, I may have abused that friendship, now that I'm looking back."

This was the hard part—the way Charleigh looked at him after that statement told Holden to run. But, if he did that, if he stopped talking right now, he'd not only lose his Leigh-Leigh, he'd be betraying one of his best, most loyal friends. "After I heard you'd come to the hospital to visit me, or more to the point, after I heard you'd brought Faith with you, I had what amounts to a hissy fit. I lost it and Evie was there to listen as I broke down. As I said, she's loyal. Without meaning to, the things I said turned her against you without her getting to know you."

He leaned toward her. "That's gonna change, baby. First, I'm gonna talk to her, but more importantly, she's gonna see me happy and she'll change her mind. But just to say, Evie going all-out making sure you and Faith were set up with a safe place to live was her attempt at reaching out. She was there when I was shot. The first few times she went back to that house, she freaked the hell out, totally inconsolable. She didn't want that for you or Faith. But I see how staying at what amounts to her family home is an issue. So this afternoon before we pick up Faith, we'll move into a hotel. There's one in town with an indoor pool. We'll tell Faith we moved there so she can swim." Holden paused and thought of something. "She *can* swim, right?"

"She can," Charleigh croaked.

"Good. Then that's what we'll tell her."

Charleigh shook her head and quietly said, "We don't have to leave."

"We do, baby. I'm not having you stay somewhere you're not comfortable."

"It's not that. I guess I'm still upset that when you were shot, I was in the waiting room worried out of my mind you were going to die, and she was sitting by your bed and I wasn't allowed. Even when you were moved out of ICU, Genevieve made it clear you were to have no visitors."

Holden cringed. He'd done that, too.

"That was *me*. I asked her not to let anyone in. I'm sorry, Leigh-Leigh. I'm being as honest as I can be. I tried everything I could to stop myself from loving you. I tried to hate you because it hurt so fucking bad to get through each day knowing I'd never be where I am right now. Baby, you're hard to get over. Every day was a struggle. Like I said, I'll talk to her. We'll go to the hotel."

"Seriously, Holden, it's fine." She let out a deep breath before she gave him a wan smile. "You know me, always reacting before I think things through. Regardless of what she thinks of me, it's really cool she's letting us stay there. I should be thanking her, not shoving her kindness in her face. And us leaving would make me petty and mean. I'm neither of those things. But thank you."

Christ.

Had they'd done it?

Had they navigated their way through that minefield and come out with all their limbs intact?

Thank Christ, they had.

And she wasn't angling to get him out of the house.

"I'd do anything for you, Leigh-Leigh. Anything. If you change your mind just say the word and we'll go."

Holden drank in the sight of her sitting next to him. He hadn't lied when he said he never thought he'd ever be close to her again—not physically and certainly not emotionally—yet there he was, staring at her and planning a future he never thought he'd have. One with her and Faith.

It had only been a few days since an unexplainable switch flipped. Perhaps it was seeing her bloody and unconscious. Maybe it was Faith being in danger. Or maybe he finally grew a pair of balls and manned up. Whatever the cause of his epiphany, he wasn't letting her go this time.

On that thought, he tagged her around the back of the neck and pulled her face to his. This time when he brushed his lips against hers, he let them linger. Not a real kiss, but a promise.

Holden slowly let her go, enjoying the low-grade burn. He'd keep fanning the spark until she caught fire. It would happen and soon, all he had to do was be patient and coax her into remembering how good they were together.

Hell, yes, I'm gonna win.

21

I was either the stupidest person alive or the smartest. There would be no in-between. Bliss or bane. Those were the only two outcomes.

In under twenty-four hours, I'd allowed Holden under my skin. Not that I'd ever fully worked him out, but sometime in the middle of the night as I lay in bed next to Faith, I questioned my motives. Why was I really pushing Holden away after pining after him for so long? My daughter was a consideration, a big one, the most important one. But the truth was I was using her as a crutch to forestall possible heartbreak. I'd survived Holden's rejection once, but I didn't think I'd survive a second go-round.

I'd been on the fence when I'd woken up. Then seeing Holden interact with Faith pushed me close to the ledge. When we were in his car talking about Genevieve and why I was uncomfortable staying at her uncle's house, he'd quickly come up with a solution. It wasn't the solution that made me stop waffling. It was his honesty. He'd been uncomfortable admitting he'd spoken badly about me to Genevieve, yet he came clean and took responsibility. Maybe I should've been mad he'd made me out to be the bad guy, but I wasn't. I was happy he had close friends who were loyal to him. They'd stuck by him, unlike all of mine who'd deserted me as fast as they could. I was grateful to Genevieve for saving his life, then sitting vigil by his bed as he recovered. I'd wanted to be the one he'd opened his eyes to, but I understood why it had been her.

I glanced over at Holden as he walked us into the breezeway from the parking lot to the front of the office. And make no mistake, he was walking us. As soon as we exited his truck, his hand wrapped around mine and he led the way. There was something comforting about him being in control. It was silly, but now that I'd decided to take a flying leap off that fence I'd been teetering on, I was going to allow myself to relish in all things Holden. The nuances that made him the man he was. Like holding my hand and taking control of something as small as walking us through a parking lot while he scanned the area for hidden dangers. Something he'd always done. I was safe and well-loved when I was with Holden.

This was it, no more wavering. No more vacillating or making excuses. If Holden was going to fight to fix what had broken between us, I wasn't going to stand in his way. But I wouldn't be telling him that. There was a lot he needed to prove to me. A lot of it had to do with Faith and some of it had to do with him telling me he didn't want kids. That was a problem. I wanted more. It wasn't a deal breaker and I needed to tread carefully considering he was the one who couldn't have them. But the truth was he would need compelling reasons for me to give up wanting siblings for Faith. And being scared wasn't a good enough excuse. Neither was wanting to protect me which is what got us into this heartbreaking situation in the first place. He had to trust we were strong enough to get through anything, even the possible devastation of being given a baby only to have him or her taken away. He had to believe down to his soul we could get through anything, as long as we had each other.

"What's wrong?" Holden asked.

"Nothing."

"Then why are you looking at me like I have a booger on my face?"

My face heated at the unladylike snort that slipped past my lips.

"Damn, I missed that sound," Holden muttered.

"What sound? Me sounding like a pig?"

"No, baby, the sound of you amused."

My mouth clapped shut and tears stung my eyes.

"Don't be sweet before I have to face Jonny," I commanded.

Holden's head tilted slightly as he dipped his chin, and a hank of his unruly in-need-of-a-haircut hair fell on his forehead. My hand itched to brush it aside. I wondered if it was as soft as it looked. When we were together he was still in the military, and even though he was a SEAL and in some assault teams it was standard practice for them to grow out their hair and beards, Holden's team wasn't one of them. He'd always worn his in military standards, meaning close-cropped. There was never enough for me to run my fingers through it, or grab a handful when his head was between my legs.

"What are you thinking about?"

"How you've grown your hair out."

A sexy smirk formed and he bowed down, lowering his lips to my ear.

"No, you weren't. You were thinking it's now long enough for you to grab a fistful and keep me where you want me."

Heat bloomed hotter on my cheeks and I struggled to keep my hands to myself.

"Same thing."

"Right." He chuckled.

Jerk.

"I could forgo the hair-tugging and yank on your ears. You know, for old times' sake."

I shrugged like it was all the same to me when in actuality, I *really* wanted to test out his new, longer 'do.

"Baby, when I get my mouth between your thighs you won't be thinking about where to put your hands. Just that you better hold on."

"Cocky."

"Am I wrong?"

No, he wasn't wrong. In my experience, albeit limited, a man had to like going down on his woman or he wasn't any good at it. Holden didn't like it, he loved it. He made an art out of oral sex. There hadn't been a single time when his mouth was between my legs I hadn't gone crazy. For him, going down on me wasn't a prelude to sex, it wasn't foreplay to work me up, it was all part of the glorious experience. And he'd had no problem waking me up in the middle of the night to get me off with his mouth and fingers, only to roll over and be done without getting anything in return.

Without warning, an unhappy, miserable thought popped into my head. How many women since me had the magnificent pleasure of his mouth?

God, I didn't want to go there. It was none of my business and the answer would likely make me want to vomit.

"We should go. Jonny's waiting."

Holden pulled his head away from my neck and his eyes narrowed.

"What's put that frown on your face, Leigh-Leigh?"

I shook my head, not wanting to answer.

He studied me a few beats before his hand came up and he stroked my cheek with the back of his knuckles.

"Wish I could tell you there hasn't been anyone since you. What I can tell you is, I've never loved another woman. I've never fallen asleep or woken up next to any of them. I've never held another woman in my arms and been so content I never wanted to leave. You are the only woman I've ever made love to. The only one who I was myself with.

Just you, Leigh-Leigh. You've always had my heart."

Damn it all to hell, I didn't want to cry. I knew there had been others, we'd been apart for a very long time—years and years and years. He wouldn't have been celibate. But sweet baby Jesus, it hurt hearing it.

"Beyond that, I'm not gonna give you an accounting of the last eight years. All you need to know is none of them were you and, baby, that's all you need to know. I've loved you and only you since the day we met. And if you're thinking you need to explain or tell me about the men who have been in your life—don't. I don't wanna know."

Well, that was good because it would've been awfully embarrassing to admit that while he was getting laid, I was not. There hadn't been anyone since the night that I'd made my daughter. That was the one and only time I'd ever slept with Paul.

The humiliation of that night hit me. Not only had I drunkenly taken Paul back to my apartment, I'd had sex with him without protection. The next morning, I'd woken up before him with my head pounding. The walk of shame to my bathroom felt like it was ten miles and not the ten feet it really was. When it hit me that Paul was in my bed in only his boxers and I was wearing his t-shirt, I'd nearly burst into tears. Once the shock had worn off, I'd obsessively searched for a condom wrapper. When I didn't find one, even going as far as rummaging through the trash and looking to see if Paul had taken his wallet out of his back pocket—which he hadn't—I started to pray. Really, *really* prayed, like I never had before, that in a moment of sober clarity he'd gotten up and flushed the wrapper *and* the spent condom.

"Baby?" Holden murmured.

"Yeah, I don't want to talk about the past."

"Charleigh, we're looking forward."

"Okay."

Something that looked like relief washed over his features before he gave me my third lip touch of the day. Holden knew what he was doing. He was a good kisser, and even the slightest brush of his mouth did wonderfully-crazy things to my dormant girly parts. And effectively wiped clean the last remnants of self-recrimination over my drunken one-night stand.

His hand fell from my face, found my hand, and once he twined our fingers together he started walking toward the sidewalk that would take us to the front door of his office.

"Why'd you leave the Navy?" Holden's step faltered and I quickly backtracked. "Forget I asked."

"I left because it was time."

"Oh."

I'd never given much thought to Holden leaving the military or what he would do after.

"That's not me dodging your question, Leigh-Leigh. I didn't get out for some traumatic reason. It was just time. My body had been beaten and worn down too many times to count. There were a few missions I almost didn't come home from...fuck."

"Don't do that," I sighed. "I know Paul's not your favorite person, but what happened to him was horrible. But—"

Suddenly, I was yanked to a stop and Holden was staring down at me with the fiercest expression I'd ever seen.

"I despised the man. But when we went out, he was my teammate. I had his back—we all did. And when he took that bullet, I worked on him the same way I would've if it was Nixon. Maybe harder knowing he had you and a baby at home waiting for him."

"I wasn't implying...Holden, I would never think that of you," I whispered.

He nodded and stepped back but I tugged him forward and waited until his fiery eyes met mine. "Seriously, honey, it never crossed my mind that you wouldn't've tried to save him. You're a good man. A good teammate. I was going to say, but I don't want what happened to him to stop you from telling me about your experiences. It might make me the world's worst person, but I got over his death a long time ago. He was my husband on paper only. We were just friends and I mourned him as such. He wasn't my lover. He didn't have my heart. He was just Paul."

Holden's face softened and he gave me a small smile that didn't reach his eyes. "I overreacted."

"You didn't. You thought I was questioning your integrity."

"I know you better than that. I was wrong. Let me apologize so we can move on."

"Okay."

And once again, we were on the move. This time, he didn't stop until we made it up a narrow staircase, only pausing on the landing to open the door and wave me through. That was when I got my first look at the Gemini Group office. I'd walked past the street-level door plenty of times. I'd sat at the park across the street while Faith tossed pennies in the fountain and stared at the building wondering which second-floor windows belonged to them, but I'd never been in the office.

Holy wow. Holden and the others must've charged a whack for their services if they could afford a place like this. The reception area, minus an actual receptionist desk, was beautiful. Tall arched windows had a perfect view of Fountain Park and the courthouse. The farthest wall was exposed brick, the floors were worn hardwood, the ceiling was stamped tin square tiles, and the furniture, though sparse, was handsome and looked expensive.

I only had a moment of contemplation before Jonny, Nixon, and Jameson joined us.

"Morning," Nixon greeted and I winced at his disheveled appearance.

"Long night?" I returned.

"Yeah. Holly was up half the night."

I could remember those sleepless nights like they happened yesterday. For the first two years of Faith's life, I felt like I was walking around in a fog. Dazed and confused was the best way to describe my state of mind back then. I was fumbling through, trying to learn how to be a mom with no example of what that looked like. I had a cold, distant mother, not a loving mom, and I refused to follow in her footsteps.

"Teething?"

"Yup. Two bottom teeth coming in at the same time. She's miserable."

"Poor thing."

Nixon jerked his chin in agreement then asked, "Faith okay this morning?"

No, she hadn't been okay until Holden had talked to her. My normally sweet, people-pleasing daughter had turned into a scared, stubborn little girl. Another reason to hate the Towlers. They did that to her—made her so afraid she didn't want me left alone. She'd seen me hurt and had been taken and drugged.

Faith had talked about what happened while I was in the hospital. I let her lead the conversation just like Beth, who Jonny had sent from victims assistance, instructed me to do. Holden and I were silent as she recounted what she remembered. Throughout this, Holden looked like he was going to go on a murder spree. Thankfully, Faith was too young to feel the anger coming from him. I, however, felt every spark of fury.

"She was worried about Charleigh being left alone," Holden responded before I could. "We're following Beth's orders and not pushing her to talk about what she saw. I get we have to give her time, but she has to start processing what *she* went through, how *she* feels, and what happened to *her*.

Right now, Faith's all about Charleigh and I don't think that's healthy."

Holden was right. I thought about that while Faith was getting dressed.

"The way Beth explained it is, what Faith's dealing with is two-fold," Jonny interjected. "What happened to her and what happened to her mom. Faith has to feel safe before she can deal with her trauma. Charleigh is what makes her feel safe. Once Faith knows her mom is okay, she'll open up. But she can't do that until she believes Charleigh is all right."

Good Lord, that hurt my heart. I was the parent. It was my job to protect my child, not the other way around. I was supposed to be Faith's safe harbor, her shelter, yet, she was so worried about me she was bottling up her emotions.

"Again, I get that. We're working on Faith seeing that Charleigh is well taken care of and that there's nothing to be afraid of so she'll open up. What I'm saying is, I don't like coming downstairs seeing Charleigh and Faith in a standoff, with Faith refusing to go to school because she doesn't want her mom to be alone. That conversation should've been about how Faith didn't want to go to school because *she's* afraid *she'll* get kidnapped again. So any other advice Beth has for us about how to move this process along would be appreciated."

There were a lot of "we's" in Holden's statements along with an "us" thrown in there. The use of the pronouns made my heart thunder in my chest. I wasn't used to "us" and "we"—it had always been "me" and "I". I took care of Faith. It was I who would get her through the latest trauma the Towlers had inflicted on my child.

"I'll ask her to call you and Charleigh."

You and Charleigh.

Before I could protest or question or remind Jonny that Beth should call me, not Holden, his gaze went to me and he launched into what was going to happen.

"Chad Bullock and the Towlers are being brought back to Kent County. The State's Attorney has set up a bail hearing for the day after tomorrow. Your attorney has been notified. He said he'll be calling you this afternoon once he gets our report. At my request, there's been a restraining order drawn up; you need to sign that before it can go in front of a judge. It will be granted. Once you have the RO, your attorney will need a copy."

The kernel of fear that was still sloshing around in my belly expanded until I felt like I was going to pass out. I didn't want those people in the same county as Faith. I didn't want them near me. I didn't want restraining orders or more court appearances. I wanted them gone. Just gone. Out of my daughter's life for good.

"Baby, they're not going to get near you or Faith," Holden said.

But I didn't believe him. They would. They'd get to us somehow. They always did.

"If they make bail..." I let my sentence hang, unable to think about what would happen if they were let out. "Can't they stay in Virginia?"

"I'm sorry, Charleigh. The crime happened in Kent County so they have to face charges here. But Holden's right, they won't—"

"You don't understand," I cut Jonny off. "They will. They play games. They'll call me. They'll send me letters. Patty will email me. I wouldn't put it past them to stay just outside of the restraining order but make sure I see them."

God, I hated them.

"None of that will happen this time," Holden promised. "You and Faith will always have someone with you. Micky will monitor your emails. I'll check the mail and we'll get you a new phone number."

"I don't want a new number. I want them to

leave me alone," I raged. "They want the money." Holden stiffened next to me and I knew what I had to say next would probably piss him off but I was so over the Towlers I didn't care. "Paul would roll over in his grave if I gave it to them. He hated them almost as much as I do. I don't want the money, I never did. I just refused to give it to them because Paul made it known he didn't want them to have it. It's in an account at Navy Federal."

I looked at Nix and his face had gone blank. He didn't like to talk about Paul's death. All these years later, he still blamed himself for Paul getting shot. "I don't want the money, Nix. Can you arrange for it to be donated to the Navy SEAL Foundation? There's a little over three-hundred thousand in the account."

"Charleigh." Nixon softened his voice and his eyes skidded to Holden before they came back to me. "He wanted you to have that money to help with Faith. Think about her future."

"I am thinking about her future. One that doesn't include the Towlers kidnapping her for ransom. One that doesn't include them dragging my ass into court once a year using her as a pawn to get their hands on money that Paul never intended for them to have. I want it all gone."

"Charleigh—"

I shook my head to stop Nixon from speaking. I didn't want to hear it. Nixon didn't understand but Holden did. I turned to look at the man at my side. His face was a blank mask, no emotion evident—by all accounts, he looked like we were discussing the weather.

"Make it go away," I demanded and he flinched. "You know, Holden."

"Baby, that money is Faith's. He wanted his daughter to have it."

The tremble in his voice told me that one sentence cost him huge.

Paul was dead, he didn't get a say. As shitty as it was for me to think, it was the truth.

"He would want his daughter safe." My fist clenched and I fought back the urge to scream.

"Charleigh's right," Jameson joined the conversation. "And, Holden, don't pretend like you hadn't already thought about her handing that money over to Patty and Bea to buy them off. I know you did. Putting aside all of our personal feelings, the best thing for Faith is if that money is gone."

Thank God for Jameson.

"They're facing jail time," Jonny rejoined.

"You don't know these people, Jonny. They're leeches. They'll be right back at her as soon as they're out. I know Paul was trying to take care of Faith but for the life of me, I don't understand why he'd strap Charleigh with the burden. He knew what his mom and sister would do. Donate the money and be done with them. They didn't want a relationship with Paul when he was alive—they used him as a bank—and they don't want Faith. It's all about the money."

"I'll make the arrangements," Nix told me.

"Thank you."

I glanced at Holden hoping I'd find him more relaxed. After all, he'd come to me and told me to get rid of the money. It had been his idea. But he didn't look calm, he looked angry.

"Holden?"

"This is one of those times when reality smacked me in the face. I need a minute, Leigh-Leigh, and I'm asking you to give it to me." My shock must've registered on my face because he leaned forward, dropped his forehead to mine, and whispered, "I need you to trust me to sort myself out."

"Okay."

As soon as the word was out of my mouth, Holden sagged against me.

"Thank you, baby."

The shock I felt had nothing to do with him

telling me what he needed and everything to do with him admitting it in front of his friends. He wasn't hiding how he felt.

He wasn't hiding *us*.

Holden was fighting.

22

Holden glanced at the door as Micky walked into the conference room.

"Sorry I'm late. Holly wouldn't go down," the tired-looking woman explained.

"Is she all right?"

The concern in Nixon's voice made Holden's lips twitch. He'd never doubted Nix would be an excellent dad, but he'd hadn't thought his friend and former team leader would turn into a puddle of goo over a tiny baby. But he had. Holly Swagger had her daddy wrapped around her chubby little baby finger.

"Yeah, Charleigh rocked her until she fell asleep."

Holden wasn't sure if he wanted to rush upstairs to Micky and Nixon's office to witness what he was positive was a beautiful sight, or run from the vision of Charleigh holding little Holly. This was another one of those times when life crashed around him. He'd seen Charleigh with Faith a few times when she was an infant. He'd seen Charleigh in the final stages of her pregnancy. Sights that had gutted him and made him feel worthless.

"Good. Before we start, I called Sam Thrift at the foundation. Apparently, with a donation that large, there have to be some provisions made. He's working on it."

"What donation?" Micky asked and Nix looked at his wife.

Christ. The hits kept coming, and if Holden didn't roll with them as they came they'd start stacking up until they piled high and crushed him.

"Charleigh's donating Paul's life insurance and death gratuity to the Navy SEAL Foundation," Holden explained.

"So the Towlers will leave her alone," Micky surmised. "There are other ways. She can keep the money."

Holden clenched his jaw in an effort to keep his trap shut. This was a no-win situation for him. He didn't want Charleigh to keep anything of Paul's, but that was him being a selfish prick. Nix was right, that money would go a long way to setting up Faith. He wanted to know but had refrained from asking why Charleigh hadn't used that money. Or, maybe she had. The standard death benefit alone was a hundred K tax-free, but Holden didn't know how much life insurance Paul had taken out. But the way Charleigh made it sound, she hadn't touched any of it and wouldn't.

Holden's phone vibrated, pulling him from his thoughts and the conversation between Nix and Micky.

He glanced at the display and stood.

Rhode.

"Sorry, I have to take this," he told the others and connected the call as he made his way out of the room. "Rhode, what's going on, man?"

"When I was searching Beatrice's house, I found a box of papers. I took it with me to look through in case we didn't find something at Patty's. It was Paul's," Rhode said and Holden's step faltered.

"And?" Holden asked, even though he had absolutely no interest in hearing about a box of Paul's shit.

"I went through it. There's some stuff you and Charleigh need to see."

Holden braced and inquired, "What kind of stuff?"

"The kind you need to see in person, brother. The bad news is, I'm tied up this week, and you have to know that if I could, I'd break away and drive up this afternoon. But this case needs my full attention and I won't risk mailing the box. It fucks me to say this because I'm sitting on some important information you all need, but I need seven days, then I'll be up."

"Tell me," Holden ground out.

"Not over the phone. Trust me, Holden. You and Charleigh need to *see* it."

"If this is some fucked-up sex tape or pictures of him with other women, Charleigh knows he was cheating on her and I don't ever need to see that shit."

"Nothing like that."

Holden took a deep breath, hoping to clear some of the disdain from his voice when he said, "Honest to God, Rhode, I don't give the first fuck about some box of Paul's that his mom kept. And I don't want anything jacking up what Charleigh and I are building. So I have to ask, what's in the box?"

"Trust me, you want to look through this box in person."

"Rhode—"

"A week, brother, and I'll be up."

"Fine," Holden snapped. "What case are you working on?"

"Bad shit, man. Really bad. A thirteen-year-old girl was rescued a month ago. She finally broke and told the police there were two other girls with her. I'm working with a group to go in and get the other girls. We have a lock on their location, but this operation is linked to a bigger cartel, so we have to go in easy."

"Takeback," Holden offered.

"Yeah, how'd you know?"

"Nixon told us about the group and asked us if we were all right with him offering up our services to the organization if they needed extra guys. They do good work, dangerous work. Be safe out there."

"Will do. We've put together a great team. See you in a week. In the meantime, get your woman back in your good graces."

"Trying."

"Don't try, Holden, just do it."

"Copy that."

The line went dead and Holden pocketed his phone and looked at his shoes.

He really didn't want that fucking box, but he

had to admit he was intrigued. Rhode knew who Leigh-Leigh was and understood what she meant to him. There was no way he'd purposefully bring trouble, but there was no guarantee how Charleigh would react to any information about Paul.

Christ.

The punches just kept coming.

"SORRY TO INTERRUPT," Charleigh said as she stood in the doorway of the conference room. "It's almost time to go pick up Faith. I don't have my car keys—would it be all right if I borrowed a vehicle?"

Holden looked down at his watch. *Damn, where had the time gone?*

"She's out at two-thirty, right?"

"Yeah."

"We're almost done."

Across from him, Weston leaned back in his chair and stretched, reminding Holden they'd been sitting around the table for hours going over the reports Jonny had left. Vaughn had interviewed Cory Saddler's ex-wife, the do-gooder who'd called in Elliana and Ayla walking down a dark, country road in the wee hours of the morning. His story had partially checked out. According to the very happily ex-Mrs. Saddler, Cory did leave for work very early. Though by her account it wasn't to beat the traffic, it was so he could fuck his side piece before work. The other catch was he didn't work on Sundays. Jonny was working on getting his schedule. The sheriff was doing his best to get the information he needed without alerting Cory he was asking for it. Jonny was also adamant about treading on the side of caution so small-town gossip didn't flare up and ruin a man's reputation if it wasn't warranted.

Holden, however, had a sick feeling in the pit of his stomach and wanted to go at Cory full-force. With just under two months until a sick pervert struck again, every instinct was screaming to go hard, push Cory until they were either satisfied he was telling the truth or they caught him in another lie.

None of the men were pleased with the reasons why the ex-Mrs. Saddler was so immensely thrilled she was free of her husband. Not only had he been a cheat but he'd also been an asshole. She'd shared voice mails she'd saved from Cory. Some of the calls had been direct to her cell, some to their daughter, Miranda's, and a few were left on the home answering machine. When Jonny had played them earlier that day, Holden watched as Jonny clenched his jaw while they'd listened to a husband and father verbally abuse his wife and daughter. Cory Saddler was a mean son-of-a-bitch.

So, yeah, every part of Holden was raring to teach this dick a lesson in manners.

"I can go by myself," Charleigh protested.

"I can take her." A new voice entered the conversation and Charleigh paled.

"Hey, baby, what are you doing here?" Chasin asked and rose from his seat. Holden followed suit.

"I was in the neighborhood and wanted to check on Holly. McKenna told me they had a rough night," Evie said.

It was then it hit Holden just how tight the women were. Evie and Bobby were the latest additions but they'd been brought into the fold and fit right in. It was almost as if Holden couldn't remember a time when all six women weren't close.

Fucking hell. Now he got it—why Charleigh had been so uncomfortable. She was the outsider and he played a large part in why that was. She'd formed a friendship with Kennedy and he'd heard that McKenna had gone to Charleigh and Faith's apartment to bake cookies. He couldn't remember the details about how that came to be, because he'd been studiously avoiding all talk of mother and daughter.

Rory and Faith were friends, they went to the same school, though Faith was in a grade above Rory, and he only knew that because Rory had told him all about it. Holden also knew Evie liked Faith and had given her a few guitar lessons. That knowledge came direct from Evie when she'd warned him so he wouldn't be on the property when the duo showed up. At the time, he'd appreciated the warning. His Airstream was only a few yards away from Evie's music studio.

Why hadn't he kept his mouth shut?

"'Preciate the offer, but I'm done for the day," Holden said.

Evie's mouth twisted in indecision before she stood tall, and Holden held his breath, not liking the look on his friend's face.

"Okay, I'm just gonna address the elephant in the room—"

"Genevieve," Chasin warned.

"Please, none of you men give Charleigh enough credit. She's not some wilting flower with no backbone."

Fuck.

Charlotte Axelson was the exact opposite of a wilting flower. That was the problem. When Charleigh got mad, the shit that flew out of her mouth was enough to cut a man down at his knees. Holden didn't want to witness two women he cared about—one he loved more than anything—go toe-to-toe, and by the expression on Charleigh's face, she was ready for battle.

"Leigh-Leigh, baby—"

"What?" she snapped. "She's right. If she's got something to say, I'm all for it."

"Fuck," Jameson muttered, knowing exactly what Charleigh's tone meant.

Genevieve sighed and looked at Charleigh.

"What I meant was, they all want to cushion this conversation for you, but they don't need to because *you* don't need them to. Besides, all the conversation is going to consist of is me apologizing for being a bitch to you and poking my nose into something that's not my business. But I hope you can understand that I was being a friend to Holden when he was in a great deal of pain. That, I won't apologize for, but I never should've turned into the Queen Bitch and froze you out. I didn't like doing that, but I didn't want to take the chance that if I was around you, that I'd like you. Then that would really suck, because I love Holden, and I wanted to be on his side. Clearly, things have changed, and now that they have, I was hoping we could start over. I really love your daughter—she's a great kid and I'd like to be allowed to come over and see her."

Jameson had visibly relaxed now that a Charleigh-Evie-Smackdown was obviously not going to happen. Chasin was smiling. Nixon, Weston, and Alec were staring at Charleigh expectantly. And Holden was ready for just about anything. It was a crapshoot what his woman would say.

But he shouldn't have worried.

"Faith would love that."

"Would tonight be all right? And can Bobby come? She's been asking, too."

Charleigh looked at Holden and his heart swelled. "We'll be home, right?"

Christ.

Square to his solar plexus, the softest blow he'd ever felt. Silky smooth but so damn painful—the most exquisite pain warmed his being.

"Yeah, baby, we'll be home."

"It's kind of strange, me telling you that you can visit your uncle's house." Charleigh sheepishly grinned. "Would you like to stay for dinner?"

"We'd like that."

"If Chasin, Evie, and Bobby are going over for dinner, you know McKenna's gonna horn in on that. And there's not a chance Kennedy's gonna stay away. If four out of the six girl posse's getting together, then Macy and Silver will not be left out," Nixon stated. "Why don't we order in? It'll be easier to feed the horde and less clean-up."

Holden stopped paying attention to the others around him as they planned dinner. He only had eyes for the woman standing a few feet away with a broad, beaming, beautiful smile on her gorgeous face.

That was his Leigh-Leigh.

Top-to-toe stunning. Easy-going, stubborn, sweet, spitfire, wild and gentle. A mash-up of traits that made her perfect.

23

"Leigh-Leigh?"

"Huh?"

My eyes focused on Holden's happy, smiling face and I couldn't hold back my sigh. He'd had that look for the last two hours and it made him insanely good-looking. I hadn't seen him look so carefree in... well...since the night before he left me. We'd been at a get-together at one of our friend's houses. All of the guys were there and more from another SEAL platoon. Holden had always been happy back then.

"You okay?"

"Yeah, why?"

"You look a little overwhelmed."

My gaze went across the room to Faith, who was standing in front of Jameson and Weston animatedly telling them a story. She, too, had had a smile on her face for the last two hours. This was what I'd always wanted for my daughter. A room full of honorary uncles who she could entertain. Men who would protect and guide her. Women who could be examples of strength.

"I suppose I am, a little."

Holden frowned and stepped closer. "Say the word and I'll tell them to leave."

"No."

"I don't want you to be uncomfortable."

"I'm not," I told him, then decided since he'd shown me honesty, I owed it to him. "We haven't had this."

"Had what?"

"This." I motioned around the room. "Since...it doesn't matter."

I stopped myself from explaining, which would surely put Holden in a bad mood.

"Don't do that, Leigh-Leigh. Tell me."

"I don't have friends like this. I forgot how loud a room full of people could be. I forgot what it's like to be surrounded *by* friends. Faith's never had this. I like it. I love seeing her happily flitting around from person to person talking to them. I love that she's comfortable with all of you."

Holden was silent for a moment but I wasn't fooled. He was smart—just because he wasn't verbally responding didn't mean he wasn't mentally putting the pieces together. It was easy for him to figure out that I lost this—friends gathering for a spur-of-the-moment good time—when he left me. He could further surmise that I lost what little I had left when Paul died. Neither of us needed to say it. Instead, he smiled and gathered me in his arms. And I appreciated him not casting a pall on the night by pressing the conversation.

"They are loud. But now that there are kids running around, they've calmed down some."

This seemed to be true. I hadn't seen anyone shotgun a beer or break out the whiskey and pound shots. All of the guys had beers in hand and the women ranged from glasses of wine, beer, and of course, Kennedy was drinking water. But no one was drunk. Back in the day, two hours into a party, one of them would've been well on their way to three sheets to the wind. Usually Jameson; he hadn't been fond of crowds, his coping device had been copious amounts of liquor.

I searched out the big man and smiled. What a difference eight years made on the surly, brooding man. Jameson was damn near the picture of sunshine and roses.

"Are you laughing?" Holden asked.

"Yes." I pinched my lips together, which only made my body shake harder. "I was thinking about Jameson. He's happy."

"Ah, you noticed."

"It's impossible not to. In my mind, I was describing him as sunshine and roses."

Holden chuckled.

"I would love to hear you tell him that."

"Um, no. I don't care how much I've seen him smile, I'm sure the big, bad, grouchy bear is still in there somewhere."

"You'd be right. Though since he found Kennedy we rarely see that side of him. Now he's more like a bear who's had his teeth pulled but we haven't figured out a way to declaw him."

I didn't think it was possible to declaw Jameson, especially with a baby on the way. His teeth might even grow back extra-long so he could bite anyone who dared harm his child.

"Holden?"

"Yeah, doll?"

It had taken me a few seconds to process my current situation. When I did, I tried to pull out of

Holden's arms, but he held tight. My daughter had never seen me in a man's arms—never, ever seen me with a man, period, in any way. Somehow, I'd been so lost in all things Holden, I'd missed her approach, and Holden wasn't letting me go.

Shit.

"Holden, me and Rory want to play with my Barbies but we can't get the tape off the box."

"I'll be right there."

"Rory!" Faith shouted. "Holden's helping."

I didn't hear the other girl's response. I was stuck in a dumbfounded stupor. Why hadn't Faith asked me? She always asked me for help.

"Gonna go help the girls."

I nodded against his chest and closed my eyes.

Faith asked Holden.

Holden said yes.

He didn't stiffen the way I had when she'd caught us hugging. He didn't jump away from me or offer Faith another solution—say, a solution that didn't include him cutting the tape off her box. He'd readily agreed.

The hand that had been resting on my hip moved between us until I felt his fingertips under my chin gently tilting my head back. I opened my eyes and found Holden's brown eyes blazing.

"So beautiful," he whispered before he lowered his mouth to mine and kissed me.

Not a brush, not a skim of his lips against mine. But an honest-to-goodness kiss that included his tongue sweeping my bottom lip. Sweet baby Jesus, I was a sucker for that tongue swipe and he knew it. In the past, that had been a promise of good things to come. It'd been his way of telling me when he couldn't otherwise verbalize what he was going to give me, but there were good things on the horizon.

Shit.

I wanted those good things. I wanted all that he had to offer. I wanted to jump for joy and throw caution to the wind and go for it. But I had to be smart and think of Faith. Slow and steady was a better option. Faith needed consistency, she needed to be eased into this situation. I needed to know Holden was all-in and serious about finding us again.

But my body had other plans.

"It's still there," he murmured.

"What is?"

"Us. That need to whisk you away and worship you. Soon, baby, I'm gonna remind you what it's like to be breathless."

With that, he walked away to help Faith, leaving me...well, breathless. I wanted to call out and tell him I didn't need to be reminded—I'd never forgotten.

"Whoa, Nelly. I know that look."

I twisted and found Bobby standing next to me with what could only be described as a shit-eating grin. She looked like an older version of Hayden Panettiere—petite in height, blonde wavy hair that brushed her shoulders, and a smile that could win awards.

God, why do I have to be surrounded by beautiful women?

"What look? I don't have a look," I protested.

"Girlll..." Bobby drawled out the word, her Tennessee accent more pronounced than normal.

"What are you *girling* about?" Evie joined.

"Charleigh here's denying she has the look," Bobby offered and Evie took me in.

"You so have the look."

"What look?"

"Like you're happier than a dead pig in the sunshine," Evie returned.

"What?"

Both women looked like they were fighting back a laugh when Evie dropped her voice and unleashed the full drawl of her Southern twang. "Girl, you look as happy as a tick on a hound dog."

"I think you've gone crazy," I noted.

"That's right," Bobby started. "Fat and sassy, makin' plans to eat that boy up."

"Yeah, both of you have lost your minds."

Evie got close and hip-checked me, making me stumble to the side before I regained my balance. "We're joking with you. What we're tryin' to say is, you look happy."

"Maybe that's what you're sayin', but I'm sayin' she looks like she wants to get that man into the nearest bed and give him a go. Not that any of us would blame you for dragging him off. That man is fine. Please tell me he's as good as he looks."

My mouth dropped open at Bobby's forwardness and Evie busted out laughing. The sound rang out in the room and my cheeks heated.

"You don't have to answer that," Kennedy said as she entered the conversation. "Bobby has no concept of basic decency."

"I take offense to that. I'm decent."

"You're nosy."

"There's a difference between nosy and indecent." Bobby pointed out.

"What are we talking about?" McKenna asked.

"About Bobby being nosy," Evie supplied.

"Ah. Has she asked how big Holden's—"

"No." Evie laughed. "She hasn't gotten that far. She just wanted to know if he was good in bed."

McKenna nodded as if that was a normal question then confirmed my thoughts when she added, "I can see why she'd ask."

"*Thank.* You," Bobby snapped and put a hand on her hip. "It's only fair, y'all are getting some, I'm the one on the longest dry spell in the history of dry spells."

"Think I got you beat by about eight years. I haven't had any since the night my daughter was conceived."

Four women sucked in lungfuls of air and I wished I could pull the words back in. Why had I shared? Damn. *Damn.* Damn.

"You're born-again. The first time Holden gets in there, it will be like poppin'—"

"Bobby," Evie chastised.

"What? Why is everyone so sensitive? I'm right. A woman goes that long and things close up."

"Close up? Oh my god." Kennedy laughed. "See? No decency."

"Holden will be careful," McKenna proclaimed and my face burned.

It burned so hot, I wanted to run away and never face these women again.

"Why does Charleigh look like she's overheating?" Macy asked.

Goddamn. Could it get any worse?

"Because Bobby told her that after like eight years of no sex, her vagina is closed." Kennedy's matter-of-fact tone only made me more embarrassed.

"Like, closed for business?" Macy inquired. "Because from what Alec told me, Holden's in it to win it. So the "Closed for Business" sign might have to come down. I'd start dustin' it off now."

Macy said that. Sweet, mother-of-three, unassuming Macy just said I needed to dust my vagina off. The nervous laugh bubbled up so fast I couldn't stop it from bursting out of me in a rush of high-pitched hilarity that rocked me so hard, I had to bend forward and hold my stomach.

This went on for so long I couldn't breathe and my stomach muscles started to ache. Sweet Jesus, these women were insane.

"Oh my god," I wheezed.

"Does that mean you're ready to answer my question?" Bobby pressed.

"What question?" Macy, late to the game, asked.

"If Holden's good in bed," Kennedy repeated. "He looks like he'd be."

"Oh, shit." Nixon's voice boomed and I snapped

straight.

"Hey, honey." McKenna smiled at her husband innocently.

"What's wrong?" Holden joined our huddle.

And there it was, it *could* absolutely be worse.

"Nothing," I squeaked, and Bobby snickered.

"Leigh-Leigh—"

"Did you get the box open?" I rushed to change the subject.

"Yeah. What's wrong?"

"I told you, nothing's wrong."

"Baby, your face is on fire and you look like someone's been force-feeding you lemons."

"Oh, for God's sake. She's fine, macho man. We're not torturing her," Bobby sighed.

Nixon chuckled and Holden's gaze went to his friend. "They're totally torturing her. They're on step one of the initiation process."

Oh, Lord, there was more?

If step one had me ready to bolt, I wasn't sure if I'd survive step two.

"What's that mean?" Holden asked and moved closer to me.

A wide smile formed on Nixon's face. He hadn't missed Holden positioning himself—and neither had I. That was a typical Holden maneuver—if he'd even caught a hint someone wasn't being nice to me, he moved in for the kill.

"Brother, you're moving in the wrong direction. If I were you, I'd get my ass out of here. When I walked in, Kennedy was asking if you were good in bed. That's step one."

"I was not," Kennedy objected. "I was repeating Bobby's question. I told her she didn't have to answer."

"Nice, throw me under the bus for asking the question everyone wants to know."

"I don't want to know," Micky lied sweetly.

She so wanted to know, too.

"You asked how big his—"

The growl that came from Nix had Bobby snapping her mouth closed, and once again I couldn't stop the bubble of laughter.

McKenna narrowed her eyes on Bobby. The death stare did nothing to stop the smirk on the other woman's face.

"I think I should leave," Holden croaked, and I glanced up at him.

Holy sweet mercy, Holden was blushing.

"Are you...are you..." I couldn't get the sputtered words out of my mouth to form a complete sentence because I was bent over in laughter.

"Charleigh," he grunted.

"I can't...believe...you...are," I said through my amusement.

"Like I said, we need to beat feet before the scorecards come out. I know one of them has a size chart hidden somewhere."

Holden's groan only fueled my mirth but I was sober enough to tell him. "Don't worry, honey, I have your back."

"Thanks," he grumbled.

"Great. Now Holden's slot will go unfilled," Bobby groused.

And I was left wondering if there really was a scorecard, and if there was, did I want to see it?

"That might work in Holden's favor depending on the order of names," Nixon teased.

"We sort by size," Bobby deadpanned.

"Well, then there's no need to shuffle—you can scratch Holden in on the bottom."

My eyes widened at Nixon's comment. Was he being factitious or serious?

Holden shook his head and the pink in his cheeks deepened.

"Have they seen you?"

"Baby." Holden chuckled.

Now I had to know. Holden was unusually large;

if his name would be on the bottom of the list, I feared for the safety and well-being of the women around me.

"Seriously?"

"Charleigh, he's joking."

"Thank God. I was getting ready to ask how any of them walked if *you* were—"

I didn't get the rest of what I was saying out because Holden tugged me so hard I face-planted into his chest. One of his hands rested on the back of my head and he held me in place.

"Fucking hell." His voice rumbled against my cheek and his body shook with silent laughter.

"Now I *have* to know. I *heard* the evidence of what Chasin's packin' when I lived with him and Evie. I didn't need verbal confirmation in inches," Bobby continued her tirade. "But now I'm worried about our girl here. If it's been eight years for her, I'm not worried about her walking—"

"Roberta," Genevieve muttered. "Quiet."

Holden went still, then he started vibrating, not with laughter but with something else entirely. The pressure on the back of my head increased, his other hand on my hip squeezed painfully, and for my part—I'd stopped breathing.

"Shit. I'm sorry. I was just joking around. I didn't mean...shit."

I didn't know what to say, not that I could've spoken when my face was smooshed against Holden's chest, but I felt like I needed to let Bobby off the hook. She hadn't done anything wrong. I knew she hadn't spilled my secret on purpose, she was trying to be funny.

I felt Holden press a kiss on top of my head before he released me and kissed my forehead.

"Gonna check on the girls," he muttered.

Shit.

"Holden."

"Later," he whispered. "Love you, Leigh-Leigh."

Then he was gone. Nixon followed, and once again, I was in the middle of the girl huddle.

"God, Charleigh, I'm so sorry," Bobby reiterated.

"You have nothing to be sorry for."

"I do. I don't know when to quit. I was just joking around, trying to push Nixon's buttons."

"He's so used to it, it doesn't faze him." McKenna snorted. "Besides, the guys give him so much shit about being a house kitten, your jabs are like mini-pokes."

House kitten, Nixon Swagger? Yeah, right. I didn't believe that for a second. Nixon was a man's man, meaning he was all-man, not a soft little pussy cat. More like a roaring lion.

"Charleigh?" Evie's soft tone brought my gaze to her. "I really am sorry for being such a bitch. Thank you for forgiving me."

"There was nothing to forgive," I told her. "Holden told me, he asked you to keep me out of his hospital room. He also explained how close you are; the bond the two of you share is one born out of something horrific, but it's beautiful nonetheless. I understand you wanted to protect him from me. And I think now you understand I would never hurt him."

Genevieve nodded and smiled.

"I'm really happy you're here, Charleigh. You and Faith."

"Thanks."

"Okay, not to change the subject but I have to ask, where did your parents go?" Kennedy asked.

Oh, god. I hadn't thought about them since I'd kicked them out of my room.

"I don't know." I shrugged. "I guess home."

"They're..."

"Assholes." I finished for Kennedy.

"Yeah." She scrunched her face.

"My parents are totally stuck-up. It's always been about keeping up appearances. When I was younger, I let them boss me around. I didn't like confrontation so I avoided it by doing what they told me."

"Is that why you married Paul? Did they tell you to?" McKenna inquired.

"Yeah. They didn't want a fatherless child in the family."

"Did they *say* that?" Bobby's expression was set to appalled.

"They did. And I was too scared and too weak to do what was right for me and my child. I never should've married him. We weren't in love. Hell, we were barely friends. I knew next to nothing about him."

There it was—my shame.

Yet, as I looked around the group of women, none of them was looking at me in disgust. There were varying degrees of understanding and deep loathing coming from Bobby. But I figured that emotion wasn't directed at me but my parents. She seemed to take exception to what they'd called Faith.

Kennedy flashed me a smile and added a wink of approval.

Warmth washed over me. Step one into the bonds of sisterhood complete.

Maybe step two wouldn't be so bad.

24

It's been eight years for her.

Holden couldn't get Bobby's declaration out of his mind. It was as if she'd tattooed it on his brain.

Those words had replayed the rest of the night to the point he didn't remember his friends leaving, only the house was now empty. Faith's goodnight had barely registered, but luckily he'd had the good sense to snap back to reality long enough to give her a hug before Charleigh had taken her upstairs to bed.

Eight years.

What the fuck? How was that possible?

Bobby must have been joking around, yet the way Charleigh had stopped breathing told him it was the God's honest truth.

Eight goddamned years. That meant Paul was the last man to have her.

Bile churned in his gut. Christ, he didn't want that to be true. There'd been so many times Holden had wished he'd gotten out of his truck and stopped them. He would've taken pleasure in beating the fuck out of Paul for touching his Leigh-Leigh. But like a butt-hurt coward with his ego bruised, he remained in his truck and watched the couple make their way inside.

Why didn't I stop them?

Fuck.

"Holden?"

The uncertainty in Charleigh's voice spurred Holden into action, and before he knew it, he stood in front of a wide-eyed beauty.

"Is it true?"

"Huh?"

"Has it really been eight years?"

A pretty pink tinted her cheeks and he knew the truth.

Jesus. How was that possible?

"How?" he blurted out.

"How?"

"How is it possible you haven't had a man in eight fucking years?"

"Are you mad?"

Am I mad? It sure felt like he was.

"Hell, yeah."

"Why?"

"Baby, we're gonna start with the obvious—you are outrageously sexy. That alone is enough to make a man approach. Once you open your mouth and all that wit and attitude comes out, you go from outrageously sexy, to a woman a man would betray his own brother to have."

"That's not true."

"I don't know how you can deny that, considering it happened."

If Holden could pull the words back, he would. He had to stop thinking about Paul and the past. He needed to move them into the future.

"I was pregnant," she spat. "Then I was busy with a newborn. After that, I was working hard to put food on the table and a roof over our heads. I hardly had time for men."

He hated she'd been all alone. Another regret. He should've manned up and taken care of her. Even if it was from afar. Even after she denied the financial contribution he and the others tried to make. Actually, Charleigh hadn't denied it—she'd flat-out refused it and told Nixon never to send money again.

Still, Holden should've pushed the issue. Instead, his feelings had been hurt like a baby's and he'd slithered off to lick his wounds.

God, he'd been a pussy.

Holden crowded her, one hand going to her hip, the other around the nape of her neck, and he tugged Charleigh forward, eliminating the space between them. "I never should've—"

"No more talking about the past. It's done and over."

Charleigh was right, but he was certain the nagging guilt would never go away.

"No more talking," he agreed.

The two of them stood silent. Charleigh's familiar scent surrounded him, a smell he'd always associated with home. With peace and calm and love. Desire sizzled and sparked to life. A live wire of craving that had always arced between them.

Then Charleigh attacked.

Her hands dove into his hair, fisting two large handfuls. Pain radiated over his scalp as she yanked his head down and slammed her lips onto his.

Christ. He had to be dreaming.

Charleigh's head slanted and she took what she wanted. Holden gave her a moment to control their kiss, enjoying the way her body leaned into his as she dipped her tongue into his mouth and plundered. The kiss was sloppy, it was fierce, it was full of years' worth of pent-up aggression and longing.

In other words, it was the best damn kiss of his life, but it was about to get better.

Holden's hand slid down her back, his other moved from her hip to her ass, then he hefted her up and Charleigh's legs wrapped around his waist. He didn't hesitate, he moved with the singular thought of getting the woman in his arms to a bed. To take. To please. To own. His ascent up the stairs was clumsy, the walk down the hall to his room uncoordinated. Charleigh hadn't stopped her carnal assault, and the onslaught of emotions spurred him on, need thrumming through his body. Every inch of him alive.

Finally.

He had his Leigh-Leigh back.

He kicked the door closed, locked it, and now that he had them in his room, he wanted everything at once. But first, her clothes needed to come off. He set her on her feet with absolutely no finesse—he was far beyond delicacy.

"Off," he managed to grunt as he tugged at her shirt.

Once she took over, Holden went for his own tee and yanked it over his head, tossing it aside.

Years. So many goddamned years he'd waited to have her again. Wanting and needing but never thinking he'd have her. Never believing he would have her back.

Holden had been caught up in the frenzy of ridding himself of his clothes he'd missed Charleigh doing the same, so when his gaze finally lifted and he caught sight of her, he froze and his breath left his lungs in a whoosh.

Leigh-Leigh.

No words were spoken, yet a wealth of communication whispered between them. The sight of her in front of him unbearable—so beautiful, so perfect, it burned his soul. He'd needed her for so long he couldn't wait another second.

This time, it was Holden who moved first. His advance was swift, single-minded, and when he had her on the bed, he didn't give her time to settle before he spread her legs. But at the last second, he changed direction and his lips landed on the inside of her thigh.

Sweet Jesus.

His—all for him.

When his tongue made its way to her pussy, he

gave her a long swipe from ass to clit and paused to suck the nub into his mouth, resulting in a long, low moan from Charleigh.

Oh, yeah, he was going to eat her until she screamed. His woman wasn't shy about what she wanted, never had been. Sex with Charleigh was an epic battle. It was on that thought, he swung her leg over his shoulder, giving him more room. Holden's tongue speared in, her excitement coated his tongue, and his cock painfully throbbed at the taste.

Control. He needed to find it before he exploded before he even got inside of her. Holden had barely checked the need that threatened to unman him when Charleigh fisted his hair and held his face where she wanted him.

"More," she rasped, and lifted her hips to punctuate her demand.

With pleasure.

Holden didn't let up, couldn't, even if he wanted to. The need to hear her say his name spurred him on. His tongue lashed and licked. He sucked and nibbled until her back arched and her hips bucked.

"Holden."

His eyes closed and he took a moment to savor the sound of *his* woman moaning *his* name. *His* Leigh-Leigh climaxing on *his* tongue.

I want to hear that sound for the rest of my life.

The thought washed over him as he lifted his head and Charleigh's hands fell away awkwardly, like her arms were too heavy to hold up. Boneless. He wanted her boneless and unable to get up from his bed.

The sight laid out before him was stunning. He was sure there were changes to her body since he'd seen it last, but he couldn't see a single one. All he saw was perfection. And when Charleigh's eyes finally opened and her gaze met his, a sexy, satisfied smile tipped her lips up and he knew what she was going to say before she said it. He knew because she always said it.

"That all you got?"

Holden returned her smile. The comfort of the exchange fueled his desire, but more, it fed his soul. It was like a part of him had returned. After years apart, he finally had her back, that meant he didn't delay, he didn't go slow, he didn't take his time, he didn't waste another second. Holden surged over her, hooked the back of her knee with his hand, keeping her open to him, and drove in, and buried his cock to the root. Her pussy convulsed around his length and Holden gritted his teeth.

Christ, amazing.

Overcome, Holden shoved his face in Charleigh's neck and breathed through the sudden rush of emotions. Remorse and shame mixed with happiness and ecstasy. He had her back. She was right there under him, waiting for him to do something. Holden ignored the ache in his cock, ignored the feel of her pussy enveloping him, ignored the need to pound into her until the world fell away and there was nothing left but what he could give her.

"Honey?"

Charleigh's hands slowly slid up his back and he shivered. So long he'd been without her touch. So fucking long he'd gone without her smile, her voice, her humor. She had been his everything, then he'd thrown her away.

Fuck.

"What do you need, Holden?"

Jesus, *she* was soothing *him.*

Man up, Stanford, you can't let her down—again.

"You can't leave me." There. He'd said it and it wasn't lost on him the stupidity of his statement. He'd been the one to desert her. "I can't lose you, Leigh-Leigh."

Her hands continued to roam but her touch had become tentative and he hated that. He'd done that to her. There was nothing shy or hesitant about Charleigh. His woman was sure and confident.

"Please, baby, fight *with* me, fight for this, for us. I can't live without you. I tried to do the right thing. I tried to let you go. I tried to give you what you wanted. But I can't do it. I'm selfish, Charleigh. My life is shit without you. There wasn't a day that went by I didn't look at your beautiful face and regret what I'd done. There wasn't a night I went to sleep and didn't ache to hold you. I'll do anything, baby, just please don't leave me."

Charleigh's hand cupped his cheek and her thumb stroked his jaw. It had always amazed him how her touch eased him, calmed his racing thoughts, quieted all the noise.

How could I have been so fucking stupid?

"Make love to me," she whispered.

It felt like he'd waited a lifetime to hear those words, and if her verbal request wasn't enough, Charleigh wrapped her long legs around his waist, hooked her ankles, and lifted her hips.

"No more talking, honey. Show me."

Holden slowly withdrew and groaned. He set a leisurely pace, unhurried deep thrusts that had Charleigh mewing. *The sweetest sound he'd ever heard.* He could make love to her all night long, never wanting to leave the warmth she provided. Everything made sense when she was near. She brightened his world, made it better.

Fuck, he loved this woman. Always had and always would.

"More," she urged.

"No baby, slow."

"Holden."

"Slow, Leigh-Leigh. You feel so damn beautiful I don't want it to end." Holden pulled his face out of her neck and looked down at the woman he loved. "I love you so damn much. Only you. It has always been you."

Charleigh's head tipped back, her eyes closed, and she moaned as Holden rocked into her harder.

"Open your pretty eyes and look at me." Holden waited until she complied and gave her another deep thrust. "Do you understand? Only you."

"Yes," she groaned and lifted her hips.

Holden kept his slow pace until Charleigh dug her heels into his ass and her nails raked down his back. But it was when she let an impatient whimper, he knew she was close to the edge.

"You want more, Leigh-Leigh?"

"God, yes."

He hitched her leg up higher, then finally

allowed his hand to skim her soft skin on his way to her breast. Heavy, full tits he'd been dying to play with but had refrained in fear once he started, he'd lose control. The moment his thumb grazed her hard nipple, he knew he'd been right. Charleigh gasped and arched into his touch and he snapped.

"Beautiful," he groaned as he pinched and rolled her nipple. "More?" Her eyes flared in a nonverbal answer and he smiled. "Yeah, my girl wants more."

Holden pulled back and slammed home, loving the way Charleigh moved with him, accepted him, taking what she wanted, unabashed and demanding.

"Hard...*er*," she stammered.

Slick, wet, heat coated his cock. So fucking hot it scalded, burned, set every cell in his body on fire.

Holden gave her nipple one last pinch before he slid his hand under Charleigh's shoulder so he could hold her steady as he set about fucking his woman. Gone were the gentle glides. Her body jolted under his as he slammed into her until her pussy quivered. Her climax detonated his. His ears roared, muffling the sound of their bodies coming together, drowning out her moans, dulling the sound of her chanting his name. And just like always, the world melted away. It was him and her and their connection. Insane pleasure rippled through him—nothing had ever felt so good and he thought she should know that.

"Nothing in the world feels as good as you."

Holden rolled his hips, an insatiable need to be as deep as he could get. His body shook when the first jet of come poured into her. He didn't stop trembling until he'd emptied himself fully, and only then did he feel truly whole. A carnal satisfaction washed over him. It was probably the most animalist, savage, honest thought he'd ever had. But there it was—Charleigh turned him into a barbarian, and knowing he'd bathed, marked, laved her with his release made his chest expand. It filled him with gratification that a woman as perfect as Charleigh would accept him into her beautiful body.

The only thing better would've been if our coupling resulted in a baby.

"Holden," Charleigh wheezed, and Holden quickly rolled, taking some of his weight off of her.

"Most beautiful woman on the planet."

"Hardly," she returned and tried to look away but Holden caught her chin and held her gaze.

"I'm serious, Leigh-Leigh. Everything about you calls to me. It's primal and soul-deep. You're it for me. No one in the world compares to you."

Holden saw it—uncertainty.

Fuck. No.

"Promise me you're gonna fight so we can get back what I broke."

"I can't."

Those two whispered words felt like a blade to his throat. He needed this woman to live. And if he hadn't before, he did it right then—with his spent cock still buried deep, their combined releases leaking down his balls, the smell of her surrounding him, the memory of her moaning his name still fresh in his mind—he vowed to never stop fighting. He would win her back. There was no other option.

"You can."

"I can't until you prove to me this is real. I can't let myself get so caught up in us that I lose focus on what's important. I can't let you barge in again and sweep me off my feet. This time, it's different. It's not just me." Charleigh paused to lick her lips and her eyes turned pleading. "Please be real. Please prove to me that this time you'll trust me. Please fight for us until I know that you won't turn on me again. I know we're supposed to be leaving the past in the past but, Holden, that wound is deep and it never went away. I've never stopped loving you. So, I need you to do all the work. You have to win me and Faith. And you're gonna have to fight me to let you back in."

That was all Holden needed to hear. He'd prove all of that and more. He'd show her she could trust him.

"I love you, my sweet Leigh-Leigh."

She gave him a small smile and nodded but she didn't return the words.

Those would come.

But for now, the way she was staring up at him like he was her whole world was enough. He vaguely wondered if she knew she wasn't hiding anything from him. Then he remembered she never had. Even when he'd been a douche she'd never withheld her true self. The thought both humbled and sickened him. She'd given him everything and he'd turned his back on her.

Never again. He'd make it up to her, then spend the rest of his life showing her how much he adored her. And he'd forge a relationship with Faith, he'd let the little girl guide them. He'd be anyone she wanted him to be. Friend, stepdad, daddy...whatever Faith wanted, that's what she was going to get.

Soon, he'd have his family back.

25

I sat fidgeting in Holden's Suburban, so nervous I was speechless.

The last two days had been weird.

Yesterday, I'd woken up sore in all the right places. Then I had a freak-out worrying about how Holden would behave. To say he wasn't pleased when I'd rolled out of his bed in favor of the one I was sharing with Faith was an understatement. He'd pleaded with me to stay. He even promised to wake me up early so I would be out of his room before Faith woke up, but I still said no. I was proud of myself for not giving in, even though I really, *really* wanted to sleep next to Holden. When I'd gone downstairs to make coffee, he'd had a mug ready for me. I wanted to swoon over his thoughtfulness but simply thanked him and braced. We stood in the kitchen in silence that should've been awkward but Holden just went about making breakfast like he hadn't given me two of the best orgasms of my life. I told myself they were better than normal because they weren't self-induced, but that was a lie. A big, fat lie.

They were the best because Holden knew exactly how to work my body. He knew because the two years we'd been together, he'd made it his mission to discover every secret spot that made me crazy. He'd held back, and with Faith in the house, I appreciated him not taking me where he often had, reducing me to a sobbing, blubbering mess as I begged for mercy. If there was such a thing as dying by orgasm I would've been six feet under. For the record, that wasn't a thing—after all, I was still alive—but there was such a thing as too much of a good thing. Holden could dispense pleasure like a normal man could chew gum and walk. Whether it was a conscious decision on his part or not, I was still grateful we hadn't woken up Faith.

After coffee and breakfast, we'd driven Faith to school, gone to his office where we'd parted ways—me in his office, him in the conference room—and when it was time we picked up Faith and went back to the house. We had dinner together—he cooked, I cleaned—we'd watched some TV with Faith, then I took Faith up to bed. But not before Holden had given me a knowing smile. I was using Faith's bedtime as an excuse to hide. He knew I wouldn't be coming back down.

This morning was much of the same. I woke up, left Faith sleeping so I could drink my morning coffee in peace, but like the morning before, Holden was waiting in the kitchen. However, unlike yesterday, he pulled me into his arms and kissed the ever-loving hell out of me before I could reach for the coffee pot. I wanted to protest this. Remind him I was grouchy before caffeine and it was in everyone's best interest not to derail my morning intake. But I didn't say a word. Then I wondered—if Holden had tried that when we'd been together all those years ago would my coffee addiction be as bad as it was? It seemed all I needed was a deep, plundering kiss from Holden and my morning perked right up.

I didn't divulge this information. Holden was nothing if not resourceful; if I uttered a word about how much I enjoyed that kiss, he'd exploit it. And I had to be strong, I had to keep my wits about me so I could put up at least an appearance of a fight until I knew for sure Holden was where I needed him to be.

I was beyond lying to myself. I wanted Holden back. I wanted to give my daughter a family. But I wouldn't settle. I'd wait as long as I needed and protect her as much as I could. But the truth was, Faith was falling for Holden just as fast as I had when I first met him.

There was a lot to fall for, a lot to love. Holden was a good man.

Then why did he break your heart?

I shoved that thought aside and looked over at Holden. "Why are you so quiet?" He hadn't said a word since we'd dropped Faith off at school and it was starting to irritate me.

"Because you have yourself all worked up."

"I do not," I snapped.

"Babe, you look like you're ready to jump out of the car. And just to say, I'm going fifty-five and I'm afraid that won't be a deterrent."

Okay, so maybe I was a little more on edge than I thought I was.

"I won't jump until you slow down." I smiled and added, "But anything under ten miles an hour is fair game."

"You have nothing to worry about."

Considering we were on our way to the courthouse for Patricia, Beatrice, and Chad's bail hearing,

I didn't know how he could say that. They'd be there. I'd be there. Holden would be there. We'd *all* be in the same room together.

"They hate me," I supplied a reason to worry.

"Great, then we're all on the same page since you hate them and I absolutely hate them. Jonny's not feeling particularly friendly toward them and it's gonna be a toss-up who wants to murder them more. Me, Nix, Chasin or Jameson."

Oh, hell.

"Nix, Chasin, and Jameson will be there?"

"Of course they will be. Weston's pissed he pulled the short straw to drive to Delaware to pick up a bond skip. And Alec would be there, too, but he's taking Micky to talk to Donna Lot."

The mention of Donna Lot's name was enough to sober me right up. Suddenly, having to face the Towlers didn't seem like a big deal. They hated me, so fucking what? Like Holden said, the feeling was mutual and this time I had the upper hand. They were in jail. Faith was home safe and sound—Holden had made sure of that. Donna Lot's daughter was not and never would be again. My heart broke for the woman.

"Micky told me she was nervous about talking to

her," I told Holden. "She said that when she talked to her over the phone she sounded horrible."

Holden was quiet for a moment and I thought back to McKenna's conversation with Kimberly's mother. Yesterday, I'd been in McKenna's office when she spoke to the woman. The phone call was brief, Donna had finally agreed to meet with McKenna. But apparently, McKenna hadn't liked Donna's tone. She'd described the other woman as sounding dead.

I could imagine that was exactly what Donna Lot was feeling—dead inside.

"I think the grief is finally hitting her. It's now been over a month. The shock has worn off, along with the disbelief. All that's left is a gaping hole. Donna has no family in the area. Word is, she's not seeing any of her friends, she's stopped all of Kimberly's friends from visiting her. Part of what Micky's gonna talk to her about today is allowing her daughter's friends to come over and talk to her. Micky's smart and compassionate. She'll do what she can to help."

"Can I talk to her?"

"Who?"

"Donna."

"Babe—"

"You said it yourself, she doesn't have family around. She's pushed her friends away. Sometimes, it's easier to talk about your grief with a stranger than it is with someone who knows you."

Holden's head snapped to the side and he took me in before his eyes went back to the road.

"Is that how you felt?" he asked.

"How I felt about what?"

"Your grief."

I couldn't stop the sigh. Once and for all, this needed to end.

"I didn't grieve the way you're thinking."

"Leigh-Leigh, it's okay. I don't want you hiding anything from me. I saw you at his funeral."

Paul's funeral had been horrible. Quite possibly one of the worst days of my life.

"We shouldn't talk about this. I think this needs to be one of those things that's left in the past."

My stomach started to tighten painfully and it had nothing to do with facing Paul's bitchy mother and sister.

"I don't want anything left between us. We need to talk about it so in the future, nothing pops up that can hurt us."

If he wanted to talk about it, fine.

"Well, Holden, let's see. I found out I was pregnant. Married a man I didn't love. As a matter of fact, if we're being a hundred percent honest, a man I ended up not liking all that much, yet to this day I still force myself to say he was a good man and a good friend to me so my daughter will never find out her father was a cheating asshole. And so I don't look like a bitch for speaking ill of the dead. Or saying something bad about a man who died a hero. I was very pregnant, not feeling well, Bea and Patty had been at my house the week before the funeral and had ransacked my bedroom and living room, packing up everything that belonged to Paul. I'd spent the next two days cleaning up the mess they'd made. I had made fifty-two-million phone calls, fought with the Towlers about Paul's service. And I was a pregnant widow who had been married less than a year and was tired as hell. I wanted it over. My life had turned into a sham. A total lie. I was feeling weak, hateful, and vulnerable, and to top all of that off, you were there.

"I spent half the time looking at you, wishing my life was different. I couldn't stop thinking about how handsome you looked in your dress uniform. Pretty fucked—my husband was in a coffin a few feet in front of me and I was thinking about you. Then shame hit. Then my parents were being over-the-top dramatic. I wanted to be anywhere but there. I was in shock mainly because that's what one feels when someone they know gets shot and killed."

I still hadn't paused to take a break when I finished.

"If all of that wasn't enough, I saw you and Patty's friend."

"Come again?"

"I saw you, Holden."

"Saw me doing what?"

Jerk was going to make me say it. Fine. He was right. It was better just to let it all hang out.

"I saw the two of you together. It started at the gravesite and continued on to O'Malley's."

God, I'd wanted to get out of that stupid bar. Bea and Patty insisted we have a farewell after the service at Paul's favorite bar. The only thing those two loved more than Paul's money was the attention they got from him being a SEAL. And Bea had shamelessly abused being a Gold Star Mother, garnering all the attention she could get. Paul would've been pissed as shit. And most of the men who were in attendance were biting their tongues in an effort not to blast the stupid cow.

But above all else, what I remembered about that day, the very day we put Paul into the ground, was

Holden leaving the bar with a very drunk blonde. The same woman who'd been hanging all over him all night.

"What continued?"

"Why are you being so obtuse?"

"Charleigh, the last thing I'm being is obtuse. I have no clue what the fuck you're talking about. If you're talking about Shelly, I took her home."

"I'm sure you did," I mumbled.

"To her house. Then she stayed there alone."

"Right."

"Do you remember Freddy?"

"Yeah."

Holden's friend Freddy died in a training accident the year before I'd met Holden.

"Shelly's Freddy's sister. As you can imagine, burying Paul reminded her of when we buried her brother. She wasn't acting like herself, and to top that off she got smashed at the bar. I drove her home, walked her to her door, and left. I didn't even step one foot into her place."

Oh. Well, I guess I read that situation wrong.

"I thought she was Patty's friend."

"She was. It doesn't mean she also wasn't Freddy's sister, and that's why I was putting up with a fuckton more than I would've from a woman I didn't know who liked touching me."

And Shelly had been touching him. At one point, she was trying to put her hands down his pants.

"And for the record, Shelly called me two days later to apologize. She was mortified. If memory serves, she moved back to Wisconsin to be near her family."

"You never came back to the bar."

My defense was weak. Hell, I didn't even know if I was trying to defend myself for thinking he'd taken Shelly home or if after all of these years I was still so hurt that he'd left me alone that day I still wasn't over it.

After a few beats, he said, "I drove down to Kitty Hawk. I needed to clear my head and make some decisions about my life. Clearly, that day I made the wrong choice, or maybe it was the right one at the time."

"What's that mean?"

"It means I was fucked-up. Everything had spiraled out of control. I was still trying to process the fact I'd never have kids, I'd fucked up everything with you. And I couldn't attempt to make things right because you were pregnant. Don't twist that into something ugly. The way I was, I knew I had no business being around a child. My life was toxic. I had to stay away. I spent two nights at the beach, then I came back and tried to restart my life."

I knew a little something about having to restart. The year after Holden left me was a blur. Every time I restarted, something came along and tore my life apart and I had to start all over. Until I had Faith. That day had changed my life. I had a purpose, I couldn't fail her, and it was then I stopped walking around *letting* things happen to me and started *making* what I wanted out of my life.

I'd taken control back.

Holden pulled into the parking lot at the side of the courthouse and I was grateful to end the conversation. And a part of me was happy I finally knew what really happened the day of Paul's funeral.

"You ready to do this?" he asked.

"Yep."

Holden smiled, and not for the first time I noticed the crinkles around his eyes. Lines that were not there seven years ago. I'd missed out on them forming. I'd missed out on a lot of things. Things I was not willing to miss out on in the future.

Please God, prove to me I can trust you.

"BAIL'S SET AT ONE MILLION—"

"That's absurd," Beatrice screeched and I jerked in surprise.

Patty hadn't said a word when Judge Price set her bail at the same one million dollars. However, the bitch had turned her head to glare at me before the bailiff took her away. Chad Bullock hadn't uttered a word, nor did he glance in my direction while he was in front of the judge.

But leave it to Beatrice Towler to make a complete ass out of herself.

The judge furiously pounded the gavel while Paul's mother continued to shout, "That bitch has my money. My son died protecting you and this is how I'm treated."

I rolled my eyes and heard Holden grunt his displeasure.

Oh, boy.

"And you!" Bea turned and pointed at me. "You and your bastard child won't take what's mine. Do you hear me?"

I heard the crazy woman loud and clear. Suddenly, I was no longer in my seat and Holden was pulling me down the empty row toward the aisle.

"It's you. It's always been you. You stole everything from my boy and you're stealing what's mine."

The pounding of the gavel made me wince as Holden did his best to shield me from Bea. There was a loud commotion, but before I could turn to see what was happening, Nixon was behind me. His hand went to my shoulder and I jumped in surprise.

"Easy," he murmured.

Then Jameson was there and I could only see the huge wood courtroom door. I was completely boxed in. Three men surrounded me. All I could feel was relief. The last time I had the misfortune to sit in the same room with that vile bitch, I'd been alone. There'd been no one to protect me from the vitriol she spewed. It was always the same thing. Faith was a bastard and I stole her money.

God, I hated that bitch.

The door whispered closed, silencing the banging and shouting. Once we were a few feet away, Holden stopped us. Both of his hands went to my shoulders and he held me steady.

"Are you okay?"

I shook my head.

"Damn."

Holden yanked me forward. My face hit a wall of muscle and his arms wrapped around me. "That's the last time you ever see that woman."

"The trial—"

"Bitch will take any deal put in front of her."

I loved that he wanted to shield me from her crazy, but I was strong enough to face her if I needed to. However, I was smart enough not to argue with Holden.

"Can we leave?"

"Yeah, baby. Let's get you home."

"Faith—"

"I'll take you home, get you settled, and go get Faith."

I swallowed the lump in my throat. Kennedy had watched Faith a few times while I worked, Macy had picked her up for a play date with Rory, I'd dropped her off with Evie for guitar lessons, McKenna had invited her over to play with her pony and goat, Silver and Weston had even taken her to lunch. But no one had ever picked my daughter up from school. No one. Not ever. Not for as long as she was alive and started to go to daycare. I dropped off and picked up every single day.

When I cleared my throat and Holden held my eyes. When he smiled, I knew, he knew, I was feeling something big. So when he pressed his lips against my forehead, he let them linger for a long while before he murmured, "My Leigh-Leigh."

"Mom!" Faith shouted and I rushed from the kitchen to the enormous foyer and found Faith tugging off her coat.

"Don't you drop that on the floor."

My daughter's eyes got wide and she turned to hang up her coat.

"How'd you know?" Holden chuckled.

"She had that look like she was going to drop her bag and coat and leave them there for me to pick up."

Holden nodded and I shrugged. What could I say? I knew my kid.

"Guess what?" Faith happily chirped and I glanced at Holden.

We needed to talk to Beth again. Faith was still not talking about what happened. She'd shared what she shared then clammed up about it. I was scared the longer this went on, the harder the crash would be. Now she was back to happy-go-lucky, everything-was-perfect-in-her-world as long as Holden was close.

That worried me, too. She didn't want him out of her sight while she wasn't at school. Last night, she'd even tried to get him to read her a bedtime story. Luckily, since I'd been actively trying to avoid alone time with him, I'd bribed her by telling her I would read her three chapters instead of her normal two.

"What?" I returned.

"Holden said we could get a puppy."

Faith did a cute little girl jump and twirled around as she continued imparting her news. "He said we could get a Tank. That's a...what's it called again?"

"German Shepherd," Holden helpfully supplied and smiled.

I felt it, the bubble of irritation rising, and the closer it got to the surface, the more danger there was of it bursting.

"Faith, we talked about this." My words were for my daughter but I hadn't taken my gaze from Holden's.

There was no way for him to miss the laser beams I was shooting in his direction, yet he opened his mouth and spoke. The better option would've been for him to remain silent.

"Faith told me you couldn't have a dog because

you live in an apartment. Since you won't be living there anymore—"

"I won't?"

"Leigh-Leigh—"

"No." I put my hand up to halt him and changed course since I knew he'd fight me tooth and nail about going back to the scene of the crime. "Are you going to come over and train this puppy?"

"Yes."

"Really. And you're gonna walk it, and pick up puppy poop, and feed it, and buy its food, and the bed and toys and the hundred other things that come with owning a dog?"

"Yes."

I let out a long-suffering sigh knowing he'd gladly come over and do all of those things.

"You can't make decisions without discussing them with me."

Holden's body locked and his face fell.

"Damn, Leigh-Leigh, I didn't mean to...you're right. I should've talked to you first. Faith mentioned how much she loved Tank and Axel and there's another litter from the same parents. I got ahead of myself."

Shit. Why'd he have to go and apologize and

admit he was wrong? That took the wind out of my sails and made my blood pressure lower.

Maybe a puppy wouldn't be so bad. Faith had been asking for years if she could get a pet. And I bet if Tank or Axel had been at my side when Chad knocked, the dog would've torn him apart before he'd had the chance to knock me out and take my child.

Okay, so maybe a dog was a really great idea.

"We'll go look at the puppy when they're—"

"Yippy!" Faith shouted and twirled. "Oh, yeah, I'm getting a dog." She continued to do some weird jig that included kicking her feet, flailing her arms, and contorting her body in a way that would have me in traction for a year.

Seriously worried about injury, I asked, "Do you have homework?"

"Yep. I have new spelling words. But they're easy, and two pages of math."

I had no doubt the spelling words would be easy for Faith—if I had to guess, I'd say the math would be easy for her, too. I'd been blessed with a brilliant daughter and God knows I didn't pass that gene down to her.

"Wash your hands and grab your homework and take it into the kitchen. I made you a snack."

She nodded and rushed to Holden, wrapped her

arms around his waist, and stared up at him like he hung the moon. Oh, yeah, my daughter had fallen hard for Holden.

"Thank you."

"I didn't make you the snack, doll. You should thank your mom."

"I'm talking about the puppy. I promise I'll take care of it and help you train him. I want him to sit, roll over, and play dead."

"I'm sure we can manage that."

"You're the best!" She broke the hug and ran off down the hall.

"Oh, Lord. She's wrapped you around her finger," I muttered.

"Leigh-Leigh." He smiled. "It's not my fault. I tried, I really did, but when she got this little frown and told me how much she'd always wanted a puppy, I couldn't say no."

"Right. And I'm sure she gave you sad eyes and told you all about the time she found a kitten and only had it a week before the owner contacted us and thankfully came over to pick up the beast."

"She didn't call it a beast."

"It was the devil. It clawed my couch, my curtains, it hissed and bit. I was so happy when someone finally responded to the SOS I put out."

"She played me."

"Oh, yeah, she did. You better toughen up or she'll run roughshod all over you."

"Nah."

"Seriously—"

"Baby, I was joking. I knew she was playing me and I didn't mind."

Of course, he'd know Faith's big, pleading eyes and pout. What scared the hell out of me was, he didn't mind. In a few short days, Holden had done an about-face.

Faith came skidding back into the foyer and announced, "Ready."

Neither Holden nor I moved. Our eyes locked and the old Holden was back. The one who didn't conceal how he felt about me. The man who openly loved me. And when he turned his gentle gaze on Faith, she froze and I knew she saw the difference, too.

Oh, boy, we were in trouble with a capital T and an exclamation point.

Shit.

It wasn't only my daughter that had fallen—Holden had, too.

"Come on. Let's go see what your mom made." Holden gestured to the kitchen.

Faith pulled herself from her stupor enough to nod and woodenly turn toward the kitchen.

I was thinking about what I was going to tell Faith about Holden when he walked past me and stopped.

"Babe, tonight don't even think about hiding again. Gave you last night to sort yourself. You didn't take Faith and run. You didn't tell me to leave. I want you to know I heard every word you said the other night. I'm all-in to prove to you I'm here to stay. But I also *felt* you, and, Leigh-Leigh, you cannot deny you want me to prove those things to you. Tonight, you're in my bed and this time you're staying."

With that, Holden sauntered off, not giving me a chance to reply. Not that I had anything to say. He was right; I hadn't run or kicked him out. I also really wanted to stay so he could prove he was the man I'd always thought he was.

"Christ. Your mouth," Holden growled. "Heaven."

I smiled around his cock and took him as deep as I could go. My eyes lifted to his and he groaned.

"Up," he demanded.

I didn't follow his demand. Instead, I wrapped my hand around his shaft and stroked him while I worked the head of his dick with my tongue. Past experience told me I had approximately ten seconds left to enjoy Holden in my mouth. Ten seconds to drive him crazy with need. The results of my efforts would be otherworldly.

The mere thought of him filling me up made my pussy clench.

"Up," he repeated, but this time he didn't give me a chance to obey. His hands went under my pits and he pulled me up over his lap and planted me on his dick.

"Honey," I groaned.

Holden was sitting with his back to the headboard, making us eye-to-eye, therefore, I didn't miss the flash of possession in his gaze. His pupils were dilated; inky black ate up most of the light-brown iris. And something about that sent a thrill up my spine. But beyond the possession, there was something bigger than dominance, lust, or passion. There was reverence and adoration. It was in the way he looked *into* me, not *at* me. The way his hands shook when he touched me. The way he craved the connection with the same fervor I did. I *needed* Holden. Not to complete me or make me strong, but because with him by my side, I was happier, more content, brighter. Everything was better when Holden was in my life.

One of his hands left my hip, slowly skimmed up my ribs, and brushed the side of my breast.

"Love when you suck me off, Leigh-Leigh." Holden's voice was gruff but his touch was gentle as his finger circled my nipple. "Love seeing all that hair curtain your beautiful face when my cock is in your mouth." He paused again and studied me as he rolled my nipple between his fingers. My inner muscles clenched around his cock and my skin heated. "Fuckin' love seeing those pretty lips wrapped around me." Holden lowered his head and I lost his eyes, but when he gently kissed away the sting of his pinch, my hips bucked. "But, baby, I finish in your pussy. Ride me, Leigh-Leigh."

"Holden," I cried out when he sucked my nipple back into his mouth.

I had more to say. I wanted to tell him how good it felt to be connected to him. How much I loved him. How good he made me feel with just a look and a smile. But I didn't say the words, I couldn't speak as I rocked my hips and ground down on him until my head felt too heavy and it dropped forward and my hands dove into his hair. It was softer than it looked, silkier than I'd imagined, just long enough I could grab a fistful.

Holden's mouth left my nipple long enough for him to grunt his pleasure.

"Harder, Leigh-Leigh." His hands on my ass squeezed, his fingertips dug in to the point of pain, and he drove his cock up as I slid down. "Fucking hell. Beautiful."

A tidal wave of emotion rolled over me. It came out of nowhere and I felt tears hit my eyes. Then my chest swelled until my breath hitched. Holden's head came up and he took me in. The change in him was immediate—lust to concern. Desire to apprehension.

"Charleigh?"

"I don't know what came over me," I answered his unasked question. "I've missed you so much. I've missed this. Not the sex...well, yeah, the sex...but the part where you make me feel beautiful and wanted. The part where you look at me and I feel like I'm the center of your universe."

"You are the center of my universe."

"When we're like this, I believe I am."

"Good."

Just *good*, that was all he said, but that was all he needed to say. He wanted me to believe. He wanted me to feel beautiful.

"I'm so scared, Holden. I can't lose you again."

"I could promise you, you won't, but I'd rather show you. Every day, Leigh-Leigh, I'm gonna prove to you I was worth the risk."

My eyes drifted closed and I willed myself to memorize the moment. Commit to memory the fierce determination I'd seen on his face. I never wanted to forget how I felt right then.

I took a breath and opened my eyes.

The man of my dreams was right there, his eyes were on me, his hands gently stroked my back, we were connected in the most intimate of ways. All of it was overwhelming. All of it was mine to keep if I was brave enough to stay the course. Everything I ever wanted was under me, at my fingertips. I was his. But more than that, Holden was mine. He always had been. Years of separation hadn't changed that.

"You've always been worth the risk," I told him and swiveled my hips.

Our eyes remained fixed, attached, linked. I braced my hands on Holden's shoulders and slowly worked myself up and down his shaft until my climax built to the tipping point. I let myself fall over the edge of pleasure, the enormity of my orgasm had me floating away. I needn't have worried, Holden was there with me. United as one as we both shook and trembled.

"Holden," I gasped.

"You feel that, baby? That's us. You and me. Always. I love you, always."

"Always," I echoed.

26

Two days later, Holden was still riding the high. He felt like he'd traversed a mountain taking the long way around, but now he'd reached the summit and he was looking down, and all he saw was beauty on the horizon.

There was a tap on Holden's office door but before he could call out, Nix opened the door. The look on his friend's face cut off the smartass retort about not waiting before he entered.

"What's up?" Holden asked and stood.

"Jonny and Mr. Purdy are downstairs."

"Who?"

"Ayla Purdy's father."

Ayla was one of the missing girls Cory Saddler had found.

A man who did not work on Sundays. After some poking around, Jonny still hadn't found any evidence Cory had gone in on his day off on the Sunday in question. Which left the question—what was the man really doing out driving before dawn? But more, why had he lied?

"Is Ayla okay?"

"By the look on her father's face, I'd say no."

Holden moved around his desk and followed Nixon out into the hall. They made their way down to the conference room in silence. Earlier, Holden was disappointed Charleigh hadn't come into the office with him; she had an appointment first thing. So Holden had taken Faith to school. The little girl only agreed after Holden had spent a good amount of time explaining to her that the people who had hurt her and her mom were still in jail. Throughout the conversation, Holden had to check his vocabulary and refrain from calling the Towlers Bitches From Hell. He'd managed, but barely.

He'd also been careful not to call the women aunt or grandma. As far as Holden was concerned, they were dead to Faith. And he'd do everything he could, including taking Faith and Charleigh on the run to keep the Towlers away from his girls.

But when Holden caught sight of Ayla's father,

he was happy Charleigh wasn't there. The man looked destroyed. There was no shortage of anger rolling off the older man. But it was the sadness that hit Holden in the gut.

"Mr. Purdy. What can we do for you?" Nixon asked.

"There's no easy way to say this," Mr. Purdy started. "Ayla's pregnant."

Oh, fuck.

The man swallowed and looked at his feet.

"Nix—" McKenna paused in the doorway and started to back out into the hallway. "Excuse me, I didn't realize you were in a meeting."

"You know." There was no missing Jonny's cold, hard tone.

"Um." McKenna glanced at her husband and he nodded. "Yes."

"Is there anything else we should know?"

Technically, McKenna was breaking the law by hacking into Ayla's phone. Jonny didn't ask how McKenna found the information she found and she never admitted to illegal activity.

There had been times when the proper warrants had been obtained, but this was not one of those times.

"Elliana's worried she is, too," McKenna softly said.

"How did you find out your daughter was pregnant?" Holden inquired.

"Periodically, my wife checks Ayla's phone. She's not allowed to have a passcode on it. This morning while Ayla was in the shower, KiKi looked through her phone and saw one of those disappearing messages… you know from that app… I can't remember the name. Anyway, my wife saw the last message Ayla sent to Elliana telling her she was pregnant. The message had expired before KiKi could show me. But I did read the message from Elliana that said 'he's gonna freak'."

"Did either of them say who "he" is?"

"No," Mr. Purdy answered and Holden turned to McKenna.

"No."

Fucking hell.

"Did you confront Ayla?" Nixon entered the questioning.

"No. We thought it was best to talk to the police first."

"Why is that?" McKenna asked. "I mean, why report her pregnancy to the police?"

"Because there is something wrong. She's not the

same. After that night, something changed in my little girl." There was no missing the hitch in the father's voice.

No one said a word. It was obvious he had more to say but needed a moment to compose himself.

"She was...she...something happened to her. And now she's pregnant."

"Please, Mr. Purdy, have a seat," Nix offered.

Christ. Jonny had been right.

"I want you to find the man responsible," Mr. Purdy demanded as he sat in the chair Nix had offered. The room went still at the older man's ragged voice, he struggled to keep his emotions in check but lost the battle. His shoulders sagged and he let out a gut-wrenching roar, "She's...she's..." The wounded disjointed words coming from a father undone had acid churning in Holden's stomach.

Unable to watch a father in extreme pain, Holden turned to McKenna. "What else were the girls talking about?"

"The last message Elliana sent to Ayla was reminding her they'd made a pact not to talk about what happened."

Jesus.

"Has she told anyone else?" McKenna looked at

Jonny and shook her head in a nonverbal answer. "I need to know the second she does."

Translation: If Ayla reached out to the man who violated her, if he was indeed a serial pedophile, she would be putting her life in jeopardy.

Hours later, Holden was getting ready to leave when Weston stepped into his office.

"Got a minute?"

He didn't; Charleigh had already picked up Faith from school and he was anxious to get home to them, but he needed to talk to his friend.

"Yeah."

"I need to apologize."

It took a moment for the meaning behind Weston's statement to hit him, but when it did, he decided it was time to shut this shit down once and for all.

No more talking about the past. No more hindsight, no more apologizing, no more talking about Paul.

"Appreciate what you're trying to do, but I don't want to talk about Paul."

"Good to know." Weston chuckled. "I was going to apologize for letting this whole situation go on as long as it did. I should've been a better friend. We all should've been better."

"Nothing you could've done."

"Doesn't mean we shouldn't have tried. We failed you."

"You really didn't. I wasn't ready to face what'd I done, and if you would've pressed the topic, you would've pushed me away. I'm a stubborn jackass."

"You are that," Weston agreed.

"Good. That's done." Holden's tone left no question, they were indeed done with the topic. So he made the inquiry he'd meant to the other night but hadn't had the chance. "I need the name of the realtor you and Silver used."

"Looking to finally dump that trailer?"

Holden's eyes narrowed on his friend. "Call my baby a trailer again and you'll find my foot up your ass."

"Touchy. Geez. But seriously, you thinking about moving?"

"Yeah. I need to buy a house."

"Need?"

Christ, did Weston miss anything?

"Charleigh's not going back to her apartment. I'd move them into the Airstream but that'd work for about a night. And we can't live in Evie's uncle's house indefinitely. So, I need to buy us a place."

Weston's mouth curved up into a broad smile.

"Does she know she's moving in with you?"

"Not yet. Though Leigh-Leigh's not dumb. She has to know now that I have her back I'm not letting her out of my sight."

"You mean bed."

"That, too."

"I'll text you Jodi's number. Ask her about the property next to me and Nix. The front of the house is around the block, but the property butts up to mine. Might be more house than you're looking for but you'd be close to us."

That would be perfect for Holden but Charleigh might want to live in a development where Faith could have friends in the neighborhood, not a hundred acres outside of town.

"Thanks, I'll ask her," he said even though he'd leave the final decision up to Charleigh.

"Happy for you," Weston noted.

"A lot has changed in the last few years."

"Yeah, it has. All for the better."

Weston wouldn't get any arguments from Holden about that. Who would've thought that when Nixon had suggested they all move back to his hometown in the middle of bum-fuck-Egypt, everyone's life would change?

THE WEIGHT of Holden's day crashed into him as soon as he walked into the house and saw Faith playing with her Barbies. He'd done his best to hide the anger when Faith chatted with him about her day. He'd done his best to tamp down the revulsion while they all sat around the table and ate dinner, but Holden had barely tasted his meal. He'd gone through the motions of helping Charleigh clean up the kitchen when she'd cornered him and demanded that he tell her what was wrong.

He didn't hold back when he told her. He trusted Charleigh could handle the ugliness of his day. After he'd unloaded, he couldn't say he felt any better, but he could see that while Charleigh absolutely didn't like hearing about it, she was relieved he shared. She'd placed a kiss on his cheek and left the kitchen. That was ten minutes ago and now that the last of the dishes were put away, he was ready to go find his girls. But when he turned to go search, Faith was standing there with her coat on.

What the hell?

"Where are you going?"

"Come on, I'm taking you out for an ice cream sundae." Faith waved a twenty-dollar bill in the air. "With sprinkles."

Holden glanced up and spotted Charleigh leaning against the door frame with a smile on her face.

"Ice cream?" Holden asked.

"Mom says ice cream sundaes with sprinkles make the worst days a little better," Faith chirped.

"No." Charleigh giggled. "I said, spending time with you makes the worst days a little better. But ice cream helps."

Holden took in Charleigh's bare feet and short-sleeved shirt.

"You need to get boots and a coat, baby, it's—"

"I'm gonna stay home. Faith's gonna take you out."

Ever so slowly, Holden's body tightened. The feeling started in his chest and moved upward, the swell so big it was a wonder he didn't choke. Only when the magnitude of Charleigh's gesture fully engulfed him, the trust she was giving him, the opportunity to get to know Faith, did he finally understand what he'd set out to win. He thought he knew, he thought since he'd seen his friends with their women and families he had a good idea. He thought since Charleigh had been his once, he remembered what it was like. He'd been incorrect on all accounts. He was clueless, utterly ignorant of the true emotional impact. Family wasn't a word, it wasn't a place, it wasn't blood or DNA. Family was a deep-seated feeling that rooted, blossomed, then flourished. The scale in which you measure those emotions—indescribable. But once the hugeness of the emotions hit—you just knew.

So, Holden had been wrong. He hadn't known jackshit about what exactly he'd been fighting for. He'd liked the idea of it, loved Leigh-Leigh, wanted to get to know and bond with Faith. Together with Charleigh, he wanted to watch the little girl grow up, teach her, guide her, show her wondrous things. Now, an idea had morphed into an all-encompassing precious *emotion.*

One he would die to keep—protect with his life.

"Are we going?" Faith cut through his musings.

"You buying?" he asked, and held out his hand.

"Yep." Faith proudly held up the bill.

"Then it's a date."

Faith's little hand curled around Holden's and she gave him a mighty tug. "We have to hurry."

Holden didn't know why they had to hurry and

didn't bother to ask. He simply allowed Faith to pull him through the kitchen. But as they passed Charleigh, he paused and brushed his lips against hers. "Thank you."

"You're welcome."

Her smile held him captive until Faith let out a grunt and yanked on his arm.

"We'll be back."

"Take your time."

He'd planned on it. Holden wanted to soak up as much of Faith's attention as he could.

"Told you we needed to hurry," Faith noted the crush of people inside The Freeze.

They'd waited in line, ordered, Faith paid, then she took her time counting out her change while a group of teenagers stood behind them in line. Holden waited for one of them to complain, but when Faith dropped some change, Zack Wilson, McKenna's younger brother, gathered up the coins and handed them over.

That led to Faith telling Zack and his girlfriend about their "date". As Holden listened, his heart swelled some more. He knew right then he was ass over teakettle for the little girl.

Once they'd been served their sundaes, they'd taken them out to his SUV and sat in the parking lot to eat them.

"You were right," he agreed.

"Zack brings all of his girlfriends here."

Holden didn't doubt it. McKenna's brother was a good-looking kid and seemed to always have a new girl when he saw the kid.

"Is Mom *your* girlfriend?"

Faith's inquiry both surprised and worried Holden. He hadn't thought about what he'd do if Faith rejected the idea of him being with her mother. Frankly, it never dawned on him that Faith would have a problem with him being around.

But what if she did?

Uncertainty crept in and suddenly Holden was sweating.

Shit.

He looked over at Faith and took her in. She didn't look worried or uncertain as she shoveled a huge spoonful of ice cream in her mouth. If Charleigh were here, she would likely tell her daughter to slow down, or at least remind her to wipe the chocolate off her chin.

Shit, again. He didn't know anything. He was the fun "uncle" who tossed a ball with Caleb, gave Zack condoms when he'd asked, played dolls with Rory, and spun Joss around in circles until she laughed, and he'd do the same with Holly and Dylan when they got bigger. But playing with kids and parenting were two different things. Worlds apart from each other.

"I mean, she is, right? Only boyfriends and girlfriends kiss. Andy asked me to be his girlfriend so he could kiss me. But I told him no because he smells funny."

Who the fuck was this Andy kid and why did Holden have an overwhelming need to find the boy and tell him to stay the hell away from Faith?

"Who's Andy?" he grumbled.

"A boy in my class. He's nice but I don't want to kiss him."

"Of course you don't. Boys are gross."

That was what he was supposed to say, right? That was better than telling her boys were horny little fucks with one-track minds and she was staying away from all boys until she was twenty-five. At that time, they'd reevaluate the situation, possibly extending the ban on penises until she was thirty. Yeah, that was better. Thirty. She could date when she was thirty. Most guys had their shit together by then.

"You're a boy and you kiss Mom."

Damn. That backfired.

"I'm not a boy, doll. I'm a man."

Faith tilted her cute little head in confusion and Holden quickly changed the subject, not wanting to explain the difference.

"Is it okay with you if your mom is my girlfriend?"

"Sure." Faith shrugged and Holden released the breath he'd been holding. "I heard Uncle Jameson tell Aunt Kennedy you'd make Mom happy."

It amazed him that just a week ago, he'd been deliriously jealous of his friend's relationship with Faith. Now he was eternally grateful she had good men in her life who would look out for her. And as it were, help pave the way for him being in Charleigh and Faith's lives.

"I'll make you happy, too, Faith."

An odd expression marred her pretty face, and when she averted her gaze, Holden started to worry.

"What's wrong?"

"What's a bastard?"

Holden's heart sank and he prayed to God Faith

hadn't overheard him calling Paul a bastard. "Where'd you hear that?"

"Grandma Bea called me a bastard child."

What. The. Actual. Motherfuck.

Fucking bitch.

"You're not that, Faith. Beatrice was being mean. It is not a nice word and a grandmother should never speak to her grandchild that way."

A gold medal was in Holden's future, he was sure of it. Fuck that, he deserved more than a medal, he deserved a great big, huge plaque that he could hang on his wall for holding his tongue and not saying what was really on his mind which was—Beatrice and Patricia Towler were total cunts. Who spoke like that to a child? Especially one who was your blood? Nothing could ever excuse Paul's behavior, but Holden did wonder how the man had escaped those two relatively intact. They were vipers.

"I don't want to have to see her again. She makes me feel funny."

Jesus, fuck.

"You won't ever have to see her or Patty again," he vowed. "What does that mean? She makes you feel funny?"

Holden hoped to God they hadn't hurt her more

than he already knew about or he'd post the bitches' bail himself, then he'd be the one waiting for them when they got out of jail.

"I don't know. My stomach hurts when she talks. She says bad things about Mom. I don't like it. And she always says I ruined her life. She thinks me and Mom stole something from her."

The fucking money. It always came down to the goddamned money.

"Your mom didn't steal anything from them."

"I know that. Mom says stealing is bad."

"Your mom's right, it is. I'm sorry Bea was mean to you, doll. But that's over for you and your mom. Neither of you will have to see them again."

"Because they're in jail?"

"No, honey, because I will never let them get anywhere near you guys again."

Faith looked like she had more to say, but as the seconds ticked by, she remained quiet so Holden prompted, "Do you have any other questions?"

"When can we move in with you?"

"When you and your mom are ready."

Faith nodded and went back to eating her sundae.

Holden did not eat his; anxiety churned in his gut. He was all for the three of them living together as soon as possible. But something struck him as strange that Faith would ask the question. She was eight. Sure, she was smart, Leigh-Leigh had told him she was always at the top of her class and her reading and math scores were way above grade-level, but still, something felt off that Faith would ask about moving in with him.

Or maybe he didn't know what the hell he was doing and Faith's question was totally innocent and normal.

The only thing he was sure of was, he wanted them all living together in a house with a puppy running around causing havoc. He wanted more mornings with Faith and the chaos she created when she was getting ready for school. He wanted Leigh-Leigh in the kitchen grumpy, waiting for the coffee to brew. He wanted to go to sleep and wake up next to his woman. He wanted his girl down the hall in her room. He wanted more dates with Faith and nights alone with Leigh-Leigh.

He wanted the dream.

27

Thank God for Saturdays. I wanted nothing more than to stay in my pjs and laze around all day long. That, and I needed to talk to Holden. Last night, after they got back, Faith was wired. She rambled on about seeing Zack, who incidentally she had a crush on, something that Holden had cottoned on to halfway through Faith's retelling, which led to him frowning until deep lines formed around his lips. Somehow, the fierce look only made him sexier.

But after that, Holden became watchful and contemplative. I didn't get a chance to last night, but I needed to get a read on his mood-change, stat. I wasn't worried about him running off—at least that was what I was telling myself, but my gut was telling me something was wrong. It was the way he'd studied Faith, it was almost like he was weighing each sentence and scrutinizing it.

I knew their "date" had gone well and Holden even asked Faith if he could take her to dinner next weekend—just the two of them. When she happily accepted, he told her that the following week it would be my turn and asked her if she'd be all right staying with Jameson and Kennedy. Of course, my daughter had jumped at the prospect of spending time with Tank.

So, all was good in Holden and Faith Land, but something was bugging Holden, and I intended to find out what it was. I'd learned the hard way never to let things fester or go. If we were going to make a go at being together, I needed total and complete honesty from him.

It was on that thought I walked into the kitchen and found Holden already sitting at the kitchen table with a mug of coffee in front of him.

"Morning," I greeted as I made my coffee.

"Missed you last night," he grumbled.

My lips twitched at his disgruntled tone. "Did you now?"

"You know I did."

Yeah, I knew he missed me. Faith had been wound up and it had taken me forever to get her to sleep. And by the time I knew she was down for the count, I was too tired to get out of bed.

"And a text, *really,* Leigh-Leigh?" he complained.

The carafe in my hand started to wobble, and my shoulders shook as I tried and failed to hold back my amusement.

"We need to talk." I sobered instantly at the jarring change of tone. "Would've found time last night if you'd come back down."

That was unlikely. He would've started kissing me, then the rest of the world would've fallen away. After that, I would've been a boneless, exhausted pile of goo and would've gone to sleep. Which meant he wouldn't have found the time to tell me what was bothering him. But I didn't point that out, instead, I finished making my coffee and sat across from him.

Holden didn't delay. "First, I want this kid Andy's dad's phone number. The man needs to talk to his son and tell him if he tries to kiss Faith, I'm gonna wring an eight-year-old-boy-neck."

I stared at Holden unblinking—he was serious. Totally and completely serious. And that time when my shoulders shook with humor I couldn't hold back, I busted out laughing. I did this for a long time, so long, my stomach started to cramp. Oh, boy, Holden was in for a world of hurt if an eight-year-old could get under his skin. Wait until Faith was sixteen and...

My laughter froze in my throat and I went still. So still, I didn't think I was breathing. Sixteen? That was eight years from now, eight long years and I'd naturally, without pause, thought Holden would still be with us.

"I don't know why you're laughing, Leigh-Leigh. I'm perfectly serious."

"I know you are," I whispered.

"Thankfully, Faith says the kid smells. That's good news—for now. Until he takes a shower, then Faith might not mind if the little shit tries to kiss her. And I'm telling you right now, I am not down with that shit. I was a boy, I know what boys are thinking about. Third grade is way too early for that shit to be happening, but apparently, it is. Did you know this Andy punk asked her out so he could fucking kiss her?"

That "Andy punk" was a shy, quiet boy who didn't stink. But, he did smell—from the cologne he wore because he had a sweet crush on Faith. However, at that juncture, I wasn't going to tell any of that to Holden.

"I know Andy asked Faith to be his girlfriend. We talked about it, and even though she told him no,

I still told her she wasn't allowed to have a boyfriend until she was fifteen."

"Fifteen...*fifteen*?" he sputtered. "I was thinking more like twenty-five." My jaw dropped open and I was trying to form words when he continued. "I'm sure you'll find that to be ridiculous, but by then a boy has turned into a man and has burned out all the wild."

"Um, yeah, it's ridiculous to think she's waiting until she's twenty-five to have a boyfriend. And if you keep thinking that, her teenage years are gonna be mighty painful for you."

There it was again. I was assuming he'd be around for those years, and God, I hoped he was.

"Fine, sixteen. No car dates before then."

Were we really negotiating when Faith could date? We hadn't even figured our own shit out yet. Talk about putting the cart before the horse.

"What's happening here?"

"You know what's happening, Leigh-Leigh."

"It sounds like we're talking about when Faith can date, but, Holden, there's a deeper meaning there and that's what I'm asking about."

"Again, you know what's happening."

"But—"

"Straight up, baby, you know I would not be

sitting across from you having this conversation if I didn't intend to be that man barring the door when teenage pricks come knockin'. No way in hell would I be digging my way into Faith's life if I didn't intend to be the man who's walking her down the aisle to one of those assholes. And I absolutely would never have taken you to my bed if I didn't intend to keep you there for the entirety of our lives."

He glanced down at the coffee mug still gripped in his hands then back up at me. "Full disclosure, I asked Weston for the name of his realtor. Her name is Jodi, she's got a listing near Nix and Weston. She texted me the address, I'll forward it to you so you can take a look. You don't like it, I'll ask her to send more. I'm gonna be honest, I'm not a development kinda guy. I like lots of space and no neighbors, but if you want a neighborhood for whatever reason, find a house and I'll look at it. If you're firm on living in town, I'll leave my Airstream at Chasin and Evie's. If I want to take Faith four-wheeling we can go there and ride. Bottom line, you find something you like—the more you can take on finding us a house would be appreciated. I have zero interest in talking to a realtor and no time to look at a million houses."

There was so much to that, I couldn't begin to unpack all the emotions swirling around in my mind.

But what's more, I couldn't process the fullness I felt. I thought I was going to burst.

"You're buying a house?"

"Yep. You're never going back to that apartment, all of us won't fit in my Airstream, and as Gucci as this place is, it's a damn mausoleum, it's not a home. At least not my kind of home."

I agreed with him about the house. It was spectacularly beautiful, but it was cold and grandiose. The mansion screamed money and class, not warmth and family.

I took a sip of my coffee. "So, last night you were contemplating strangling an eight-year-old when you came home?"

"No, I was contemplating all the ways I'm going to fuck the Towlers. I was also reevaluating my morals and how I felt about hitting a woman. And, Leigh-Leigh, it might make me an asshole, but I had to dig really fucking deep to remember the man I am, and that I would never strike a woman. Because if there were ever two women who deserved to be on the receiving end of my anger, it is them."

I didn't want to know but I had to ask. "Did Faith say something?"

"Did she tell you Bea called her a bastard child?"

My eyes closed and my heart sank. I hated them.

Absolutely loathed them. Bea and Patty were vile, evil, spawned-from-Satan creatures that I wished with everything inside of me would go away and never return. "They've called her that, yes."

Holden muttered a bunch of expletives that had me shrinking back. He was pissed. Super-pissed, and for the first time, I was worried about the Towlers' safety.

"You can't—"

"I'm going to destroy them," he cut me off. "I told you, this shit ends. No more, Charlotte. Their days of terror are fucking over. Before, I was going ruin them, now I'm gonna blow their shit up."

"Hold—"

"They called her a *bastard child*," he whispered and my lungs seized. "They called her that to her face. Forget the shit they talked about you. I'm no expert but I'm not stupid so I'm sure that calling a child's parent bad names has some sort of impact, most of which you can't see because it might take years for it to come out. Obviously, this shit is weighing heavy on her mind because she brought it up. I didn't ask, she straight-out told me they were mean to her and made her feel funny."

He gripped his coffee mug so tightly I was shocked he hadn't shattered it. "Now, I know you're not down with that, having your girl get a stomach ache because those bitches talked that shit to her. But I know you're a good person, a kind person, you'll turn your cheek and take care of your daughter. Me? I'm a vengeful son of a bitch. No one calls my girl a bastard child. No lip, Leigh-Leigh."

"All right," I readily agreed.

I was so down with him destroying the lives of the women who'd harmed my child. Something I wish I had the means to do myself, but since I didn't know how to ruin a person's life, I wouldn't stand in Holden's way. As a matter of fact, I'd be glad for it. I needed Faith to be safe from them.

Before Holden could reply, his phone rang and I glanced at the microwave. It was just after seven in the morning on a Saturday—way too early for a friendly chat. Apparently, Holden felt the same way because he didn't delay getting up and picking it up off the counter.

With a frown, he answered, "Rhode. Everything okay?" There was a pause and Holden's relief was palpable. "Right. Yeah, I'll talk to her and call Alec or Jameson. I'm sure one of them wouldn't mind taking Faith for the day." Another pause, this one longer. "No, it's fine. I just haven't talked to Charleigh yet. I didn't think you'd be here until tomorrow." Holden's gaze came to me and I didn't like the fear I saw. "Sure, see you then."

"What?"

"Drink your coffee, baby, I'll—"

"Oh, no." Irrational panic started to well. "Tell me what's wrong."

"I will. I need to make a call first. Just—"

"Last time you left me, there was something wrong and I missed it and then you left and I didn't know. I. Didn't. Know. For years, I didn't know, Holden. But now, I see it. Whatever this guy Rhode said, I see it—fear. It's all over your face. You said you wanted me to fight. This is me fighting to keep my family whole. You're not leaving this room until you tell me what's wrong."

All the color had bleached from Holden's face. That was all I was concentrating on, the pallor of his skin as he stalked across the room. So, I missed the other changes—the sadness in his eyes, the deep lines on his forehead, his downturned lips. I missed it all until he was right in front of me. Then everything hit me at once. The sheer terror at the thought he'd leave me again.

"Jesus, fuck."

Everything happened at once. My heart pounded and anxiety rushed through me. I was breathing heavily, yet I couldn't breathe at all. I felt hot and cold at the same time. My muscles were taut but I felt them twitching.

He was going to leave me. I knew it. This was the beginning of the end.

"Christ, Leigh-Leigh, look at me, baby." I was looking at him—*right* at him and I saw it. So much fear in his beautiful brown eyes. Then I lost sight of the fear, the worry, the trepidation when his lids closed.

Had he done that before? Simply closed me off from his pain so I couldn't see it? Had he distracted me from what was bothering him?

Slowly, he opened his eyes and his focus came back to me. The intensity rocked my world.

"You didn't miss anything, baby. Is that what you think? That there was something you should've caught?" He didn't wait for me to answer before he went on. "Jesus, Charleigh, you did nothing wrong. Everything about our life was perfect."

"It wasn't perfect or you wouldn't have left me."

"Wrong. Our life was perfect. It was me that wasn't. After Doc told me I'd most likely never have kids, I was in denial. For weeks I just—"

The world froze in place.

"Wait. What?"

Words jumbled together in my mind. My brain felt like it was on the fritz, it had to be. I had to have heard him wrong.

"I wanted a family with you so badly. I wanted the future we'd talked about. I don't know why that particular night everything crashed around me, but when it did, I couldn't stop it. I wanted you to have everything you wanted. I knew you'd be an excellent mother. I knew I couldn't deny you—"

"Stop, Holden. Most likely never have kids, or couldn't have kids?"

"Same thing, baby. I couldn't take that chance."

Same thing? It wasn't even remotely the same fucking thing. 'Most likely' and 'never' weren't even in the same ballpark. Holden left me over "most likely".

Fury consumed me. Righteous rage took over and I lost control.

"You asshole."

I barely recognized my ravaged growl. In the far corners of my mind, I heard a tiny, little rational voice telling me to calm down. But it was too late. My temper flared, my heart shattered, my vision blurred. Anger took over and I was a woman possessed. If it could've, my head would've spun around in circles and my eyes would've caught fire.

I don't remember how it happened, just that I felt the sting on my palm, heard the crack rent the air, Holden's grunt of pain. Then my arms were trapped but I wasn't done, I kicked and kneed and struggled and jerked my body this way and that, wanting to free myself so I could attack.

"Charleigh," Holden grunted.

"Most likely," I cried. "Most *fucking* likely. You left me over a *maybe*."

There was more I wanted to say but the words escaped me.

"Leigh-Leigh, please listen to me. It wasn't a maybe." He paused and adjusted his arms around me, bringing me closer. I didn't want to be closer, I wanted to be far, far away from him.

"I was exposed to radiation. My whole team was. Everyone was tested and the level was low enough, no one thought much about it. Until one of the guys reported he and his wife had been trying for a baby and they couldn't conceive. Turns out, the problem was him. That meant we all got tested again. Baby, it had been years since the accident and my sperm levels were still low. I couldn't have kids and I've made peace with it. But that night, us talking about all the babies we wanted to make, I broke. I had to admit I wasn't enough for you. I'm half a man who cannot give his woman—"

"You're so fucking stupid."

"Come again?"

I ignored the hurt in his voice. I ignored my pain and anger. I was completely detached from the situation. *This couldn't be real.* Years of heartache for nothing.

Fucking asshole.

"Low sperm count doesn't mean you can't have children. Did you get a second opinion? Did you talk to a fertility specialist or did you just take the word of an over-worked Navy doctor? I can't believe you did this to us. After you explained, part of me understood, or at least I could empathize enough to forgive you for leaving me. Never being told I couldn't have children, I couldn't fully put myself in your shoes and how the shock and pain of that would lead you to run away from me—but I could forgive you because I know it would kill me to find out I couldn't carry a baby."

I shook my head. "We had so many options, Holden. I heard you when you said you didn't want to put us through that, but you didn't get to make that choice for both of us. Yet, I still forgave you."

I pushed at his arms still encircling me. "I don't

think I can forgive you now. You took a maybe and turned it into a worst-case scenario and ran with it. You didn't trust me enough to tell me, to talk to me about what the doctor said, to have a conversation about options, to let me be there for you while you were in pain. You took all of that away from me—from us. I thought I could, I wanted to, but I can't."

"Can't what, Charleigh?" His voice had gone deathly quiet.

"Be with you. Make this work. Build a life and a family with you."

He stiffened. "You can. We can. I'm so sorry. I was wrong, so damn wrong."

"You were wrong. I love you, Holden. But—"

"Hold on to that, Leigh-Leigh, and fight. We can get through this."

"I don't—"

"Goddammit, don't give up. Don't make the same mistake I did. Fight, Charlotte. Yell at me, kick, punch, scream, but do not walk away."

It wasn't lost on me the regret that shone in his eyes. The sorrow in his words.

There was a knock on the door. Holden jolted and closed down.

Great. Splendid. More drama.

"Who's here?" I asked him.

"The guy on the phone. Rhode. Let me answer the door and I'll explain why he's here."

Dead. Cold. Distant.

Whoever this man was, he didn't come knocking first thing in the morning on a Saturday to deliver good tidings.

Holden left the kitchen but I remained rooted, wondering how my life had once again gone to shit. Just like the first time it happened, it happened in the blink of an eye. One moment, we were discussing our future, the next that future was ash.

Maybe love wasn't enough. Maybe love didn't conquer all. Maybe love wasn't kind. Maybe love was brutal and ugly. Maybe it left you in tatters.

Hours later, I would come to know the true devastation of love. It would be then, I would feel the crushing blow of regret. My life would be forever changed again.

28

With each step, Holden felt like he was walking toward his execution.

How had one bad decision rippled into catastrophe? One wrong choice, and he'd ruined everything. Dread filled him as he made his way to the front door. He'd waited too long; once again, he'd been a coward and put off telling Charleigh about the box until it was too late.

Rhode was there on the other side of the door. A panel of wood was Holden's last defense. He didn't have to open it. He could tell Rhode to go away, that they didn't want to know what Paul had left behind. Holden could bar the door and save himself from the hell that awaited him.

What was supposed to be a beautiful Saturday with his girls had turned into an epic clusterfuck.

Would there ever come a time when the past wouldn't hurt them and send their lives spiraling out of control?

When Holden opened the door and found Nixon standing beside Rhode, he knew the answer—today would not be the day he and Charleigh moved forward. Today wouldn't bring healing. The universe wasn't done fucking with him. He had more reparations to pay.

Fuck.

Holden wordlessly stepped to the side to allow the men to enter, his gaze going to the cardboard banker's box that would serve as his noose. Whatever was in that box was bad enough that Rhode felt he needed to bring Nixon along.

Christ.

"Who's that?" Faith's sleepy voice filled the foyer and Holden inhaled sharply.

He hadn't had a chance to call Alec or Jameson to ask one of them to come pick her up.

"Hey there, little lady. My name is Rhode."

"That's a funny name." Faith's cute face scrunched. Any other time, Holden would've melted seeing that look, but right then all he wanted to do was scoop her up, grab Charleigh, and flee. Take them both someplace where evil bitches and unknown horror-filled boxes didn't exist.

"Faith, that's not nice," Charleigh chastised.

"Sorry. I didn't mean it bad."

"It is a funny name," Rhode smoothly interjected. "The story goes, my mom wanted to name me Preston, but my dad was a biker and he wasn't gonna name his son Preston. So after I was born, he waited for my mom to take a shower, then went to the nurses' station and changed my name. Word has it, my momma was fit to be tied, but then my dad explained why he named me Rhode and my mom forgave him."

"Why'd he change it?" Faith asked, totally enthralled with Rhode's story.

"I don't know. Neither of them will say. But I was stuck with a funny name." Rhode winked at Faith and she smiled.

"My mom named me Faith because when I was born I gave her strength and faith after Paul died."

Paul?

Charleigh gasped, and it was a wonder she hadn't inhaled all of the oxygen in the room. When did Faith start calling her dad Paul? Holden's lungs felt like they were on fire as he struggled to breathe. And when his gaze sliced to Charleigh, he saw the same.

"What's in the box?" Faith inquired.

Fucking hell, could the room get anymore uncomfortable?

"Breathe," Holden muttered as he made his way to Charleigh.

Her startled eyes came to him and she nodded but didn't follow his orders.

"What's going on?"

"Let's you and me go for a walk, Faith," Nix said. Holden didn't take his gaze from Charleigh.

"Mom?"

Charleigh jumped and looked around. She read the room correctly when she settled on Faith and said, "It's okay. Go with Uncle Nix. Maybe you can show him the bird nest you found by the dock."

"Okay."

Moments later, the back door opened then closed and the vibe in the house changed from uncomfortable to hostile.

"What's happening?" Charleigh asked, her voice tinged with rage.

"This is Rhode," Holden began.

"I know that. Hello, Rhode, nice to meet you. Now why's he here and what's with the box?"

Fuck.

"When we were looking for Faith, Rhode was our man in Virginia Beach. Actually, before Faith was taken, he was investigating the Towlers, digging up whatever he could to help you when you went to court. But he was goin' easy so that he didn't alert Bea or Patty. After Faith was taken, easy shifted and so did our objective. Rhode searched Bea's house for clues where they'd taken Faith. He found that box and took it. Last week, he called me and told me that it belonged to Paul and we needed to see what was in it."

"What's in it?" She looked back and forth between the two men.

"That's why Rhode is here to show us."

Her brow furrowed. "I don't understand."

"I know you don't," Rhode rejoined. "And I wouldn't have insisted on bringing it to you if it wasn't important, and I'm sorry that I didn't go through it sooner. I was actually going to throw it away, but there's some stuff you both need to see."

"Fine," Charleigh snapped, then her shoulders sagged. "Sorry. I'm being a bitch to you and you helped save my daughter's life. Thank you for everything you did."

"It was my pleasure, and I don't take offense. No one wants their past to invade their present, especially when everything was starting to smooth out. I promise, I wouldn't be here unless I knew what was in this box could provide answers you both need."

Rhode handed the box to Holden but paused before he let go.

"I'm sorry, brother." *Motherfuck.* Holden felt that straight to his bones. "I'll be outside with Nixon and Faith."

Rhode let go and suddenly the box felt like it weighed a ton instead of a few pounds.

Charleigh stared at the box like it was about to explode. "We don't have to—"

"We do, Leigh-Leigh. No more running. Whatever's in here, we'll work through it." Holden walked into the sitting room off the foyer and fortified his resolve.

No matter what, Charleigh and Faith were his. He'd fight to the death to keep them. He'd beg and plead and get on his knees. Whatever it took to prove to Charleigh he wasn't ever going to leave her again.

This time, they would win.

They'd come out victorious. Even if it took until

he was eighty, he would not leave this earth until Charleigh was his wife.

Holden opened the box and tipped it over. The contents spilled out and he didn't understand why Rhode thought they were such a big deal.

"Paul's service awards?" Charleigh shuffled through the papers. "I don't get it." Then her hand landed on an envelope with her name scrolled across it in heavy block letters. When she turned it over, the envelope had been opened.

"I've never seen this," she told Holden and pulled out a piece of lined paper.

Holden's throat clogged. He knew what was in that envelope. Back in the day, he'd written one, too. His jaw clenched and his stomach roiled. Paul was reaching out from the grave.

Jesus, fuck.

There was no mistaking the tightness in Charleigh's face as she scanned the letter, tightness which triggered his. But it wasn't until he watched her start to tremble did he finally lose patience. Holden had tried to be respectful and allow her some privacy as she read the words of a dead man. But seeing his woman wracked by violent sobs was too fucking much.

"Baby." He reached for her just as she dropped the letter and her knees buckled.

"No," she cried. "No. No. No."

Holden knelt, but before he could reach for Charleigh, she launched herself at him. His ass hit the floor at the same time she crawled into his lap and shoved her face in his neck.

"No," she moaned against his throat. Her vise-like grip damn near choked him.

"Baby?"

Unbelievable fear terrorized his mind. *What the hell could be so bad?*

Holden reached for the paper and Charleigh batted it out of his hand.

"Nononono," she repeated.

"Leigh-Leigh, I need to read it," he told her and picked it up again.

Unable to do much more than hold a sobbing Charleigh in his arms, he brought the paper up enough to see Paul's simple print.

Charleigh,

If you're reading this, I didn't come home and now I owe you the truth, but first I need you to understand how much I loved you. From the first time Holden brought you to that hog roast at the beach, I was in love.

You were so beautiful, God, I couldn't take my eyes off you. I watched you all night. The way you smiled at the guys but only had eyes for Holden. The way you'd go off and talk to the wives and girlfriends but you always made your way back to his side. I'd always wanted that. A woman to love me so completely that on a crowded beach with a bunch of rowdy SEALs she only saw me. With that said, I knew it was wrong to feel the way I did and I tried to forget you, but every time I turned around you and Holden were there. You were there. And my feelings for you only grew.

I tried to do the right thing, I swear, honey. I stayed away for as long as I could. But when Holden left you, I had to take my shot. I'd regret not trying for the rest of my life. So I did, I overheard you were at the bar and I took my shot. You told me you and Holden were through and I felt like I won the lottery. Nothing was gonna stop me from showing you how much I loved you. We went back to your place—

Holden had to close his eyes against the bile rising. Fucking Christ, he didn't want to read this shit. First, because the sick fuck didn't love her, not the way she deserved to be loved. And second, he didn't need to know how Paul felt about the night they'd made Faith. He was doing his best to forget that night ever happened. But he braced and forced himself to continue because so far he hadn't read anything that warranted her reaction.

—I knew you were drunk and I knew I was taking advantage of the situation but, Charleigh I need you to understand, I loved you so much and I thought once you were over Holden I could make you happy. We were in your room, things were progressing, then you called me Holden. After that, you fell asleep. I put you in my shirt and got into bed next to you. The next morning you assumed we'd slept together and I didn't correct you. Then when you came to me and told me you were pregnant, even though the baby wasn't mine, I wanted it—

The next morning, you assumed.

Assumed.

Even though the baby wasn't mine.

Faith wasn't Paul's.

Holden's head spun until he was dizzy. His chest caught fire and burned so hot it was in literal pain. Agonizing, helpless, bitter pain that took his breath.

Motherfucker stole his life.

Stole his child.

Faith.

Inconceivable anger engulfed him.

He'd lost eight years of his child's life.

Holden shook as he pulled Charleigh off his

chest and set her aside. Then he was on his feet. His hands raked through his hair and he yanked until his scalp screamed in pain. He'd needed to do something, anything to take away the burning in his heart.

"Holden?"

His gaze sliced to Charleigh but her devastation didn't register. Nothing did. Not the way her arms were wrapped protectively around her middle. Not the tears that rolled down her cheeks. Not the sadness in her eyes.

Eyes.

Faith's eyes.

The dimple.

Jesus Christ.

"I have to go," Holden blurted and stormed out of the room.

"Please don't." Charleigh's hand wrapped around his biceps but he didn't stop.

He couldn't be there.

He couldn't stand to be in the same room as that fucking letter and Paul's from-the-grave confession.

Bastard child.

Those motherfucking bitches knew. They'd known all along that Faith wasn't Paul's. Murderous intent saturated his whole body.

"Holden, please."

He stopped with his hand on the knob and craned his neck to take in Charleigh.

So beautiful. Perfect. His.

"I need time, Leigh-Leigh."

"Stay."

"She's mine," he growled. "Mine. *What the fuck have I done?*"

Then he was gone.

29

What now?

What was I supposed to do now?

What was I supposed to tell Faith? How did I explain to my child that the man I told her was her father, was not? That he'd lied. That his family knew but didn't tell me. Why would they do that? Why wouldn't they have told me right after Paul died?

Why can't I feel my legs?

I needed to do something but my feet were rooted in place. I had to...shit, I didn't know what I needed to do. I needed Holden but he *left* me, again.

"Charleigh?" Kennedy's voice. I twirled around to find her, Jameson, Silver, and Weston behind me. "Come into the living room."

She knew.

Oh my God, they all know.

"I need to get Faith."

"Macy and McKenna are outside with her. She's fine. Let's go in the—"

"No. Nononono."

I was well aware I sounded like a crazy person. I didn't need Kennedy's wide eyes or the way Silver was approaching like I was a wild animal to confirm what I knew—I'd finally lost my mind.

"Charleigh, Macy's gonna bring Faith in to get dressed. It's not a good idea she sees you like this. Come into the living room. We'll take Faith upstairs and—"

"Nononono."

"Charlotte," Jameson's voice boomed and I jerked in surprise. No, my body jolted in horror as I took in the pity in his eyes. "Know it's a shock, Charleigh, but right now we need to see to Faith. We can't let Macy bring her in until you're in the living room. We're all gonna help you figure this out. But let's get Faith out of here first, yeah?"

No. I didn't want Faith to leave. I wanted to pack her up and leave. Holden had the right idea; running sounded like the best option. How had this happened?

"Why would he do that?" Silver came closer and

I put my hands up to ward her off. "How could he lie? He said...he said he loved me but he took everything away from me. He ruined me, he broke Holden, and Faith...ohmigod, what am I going to tell her? She'll think I'm a..."

I didn't finish partly because I couldn't utter the words but also because both women had descended. Silver's arms wrapped around me from the front and Kennedy came up from behind and in some sort of weird three-person-hug, they held on tight.

I felt my legs finally give out.

"I hate him," I whispered against Silver's shoulder. "I hate all of them. They all knew."

Kennedy's baby bump pressed against my side, the feel of it reminding me of everything Holden lost out on. All the things she and Jameson took for granted. Holden never got to feel Faith kick, he never got to see an ultrasound, he missed her coming into the world. Everything. We lost everything.

"Jesus, *fuck*," Weston grunted. "I gotta call Chasin and tell him to keep Evie away from Holden. Anyone know where Bobby is?"

"On her way and she's bringing Evie," Silver answered.

Then I was shuffled out of the foyer and guided to a chair. I sat, Jameson swept all the papers scattered on the table back into the box, and I vaguely wondered what else was in there.

I was so numb nothing felt real. How, why, why, why would Paul marry me knowing Faith was not his?

"What else is in that box?"

"Nothing that matters right now," Jameson told me.

There was more. There had to be—Jameson wouldn't be trying to get rid of the papers as fast as he was unless there was something he didn't want me to see.

"It matters, Jameson."

"Charleigh—"

"I get you're trying to protect me, but don't you think it's better if everything hits at once?"

"No, I do not. I think you need to process Paul's letter and what that means for you, Faith, and Holden. The rest of it can wait."

He was wrong. I didn't want bad news trickling in. I didn't want to draw out the pain. But before I could tell him that, I heard Faith's happy voice, then I heard Rory, then Macy telling the girls to go upstairs.

How was this my life?

I closed my eyes and thought back to the day I

told Paul I was pregnant. He was happy. He didn't so much as blink, flinch, give any indication that the baby couldn't be his. He told me he wanted to keep the baby and marry me. He was insistent. He was sympathetic and told me he knew it would take time for me to get over Holden, but in time he would make me love him. He told me he wanted to make me happy. He told me he already loved me.

Paul didn't love me, he was obsessed. What kind of man pretended to be the father of a child that was not his to get the mother to marry him? Who did that?

He knew.

Nothing made sense.

Not a damn thing.

If the Towlers knew, why didn't they use that to get the money?

"I'm gonna take Faith back to my house." Macy's soft voice pulled me from my thoughts. "She's more than welcome to spend the night."

"I should say goodbye."

"No, honey, you shouldn't." There was motherly compassion in her eyes. "Trust me, you don't want her seeing you like this. I promise we'll take good care of her."

I must've looked like hell if no one wanted Faith to see me.

"Thank you, Macy."

"No need to thank me. We love you both."

My throat started to tingle, therefore, I couldn't speak so I nodded.

"When you're ready to talk, all of us are ready to listen." And with that, Macy left the living room and my eyes went back to Jameson.

His jaw was set in an angry clench and his eyes were focused on me. I couldn't stop myself from squirming.

"I didn't know," I blurted out. "I would've told him. I never would've kept Faith from him. I swear, I had no idea."

Jameson carefully masked his fury, and with a good amount of effort, I watched him force himself to relax.

There was a commotion in the other room, the front door opened, then closed, and silence stole over the room.

I glanced out the window to see Macy helping the girls into her SUV, Alec going to the driver's side. Nixon and McKenna walked to Nix's truck. Doors slammed and vehicles drove away. All of that happened surprisingly quickly. My daughter was being whisked away so she wouldn't witness my meltdown.

I didn't know if I was grateful or if I felt like the world's worst mother. Shouldn't I have been able to keep my shit together for the sake of my child?

"None of us think that about you, Charleigh. We know you'd never do that to Holden. And more, we know you wouldn't do that to Faith. Holden knows that, too."

"Does he?" I snapped.

"Hundred percent, he knows," Weston assured me.

"Then why isn't he here? Why'd he leave me, *again*? He begged me to fight for our future, he pleaded with me to forgive him for leaving me. But he left me, again."

"I'm not making excuses for him," Jameson started. "But, Charleigh, he didn't leave you. He left so he could go somewhere and beat himself up. For him, this is the best and the worst day of his life. Finding out that Faith is his after all these years thinking she was Paul's, but knowing the true depth of Paul's betrayal, knowing that he denied a child that at the time he truly believed couldn't be his, losing you and Faith, missing eight years of his daughter's life."

"And what about me? I just found out the depth of Paul's betrayal, too. None of you understand the shame I've lived with thinking I slept with him. None of you understand the guilt I feel for wishing that night never happened. None of you understand how lonely I've been. How much I missed Holden. How fucking hurt I was."

Shouldn't the shame have been washed clean now that I knew the truth? Shouldn't I feel better knowing I never had sex with Paul? But nothing felt better or good. It felt more screwed up. How stupid could I have been? How weak? Why didn't I demand Holden take a DNA test?

Pride. I let my damn pride stand in the way. At the time, I thought Holden was rejecting me and the possibility the baby was his. His refusal to acknowledge the baby hurt so bad, I slithered away to lick my wounds and let my parents force me to marry Paul and stay quiet about Holden.

Even after Paul died, my parents pushed me to play the part of the grieving widow. A thought nagged the back of my mind, a hunch that wasn't fully formed, but pieces started to click into place. The Towlers. My parents. Court appearances.

"What else is in the box?" I demanded to know.

"Charleigh—"

Determination infused my spine and I stood. "No more hiding. I have a right to know and frankly, so does Holden."

By the time I'd walked across the room, Jameson had placed the box on the table. But he hadn't taken his hand off of it.

"You sure?"

"Positive."

With a stern jerk of his chin, he reached into the box, pulled out a stack of papers, and handed them to me.

These didn't belong to Paul. They were bank statements dated after he'd died. I shifted through the papers noting there were highlighted lines—deposits—but they were meaningless to me.

"I don't understand."

"Neither did Rhode. So he dug deeper. For eight years, there's been a reoccurring two-thousand dollar deposit." Jameson reached back into the box and handed me another stack of papers.

More statements. I scanned the first page and froze.

First National Bank.

Edward Axelson.

I didn't need to look through the bank records to

know what my parents had done. I didn't give the first fuck if the Towlers were blackmailing my parents or if it was my parents' idea to give Beatrice hush money.

I didn't give the first two shits my parents had wasted a crapton of money.

They knew.

My own fucking parents had known all along.

Fuck them. Fuck everyone.

I bolted from the room. Kennedy shouted my name, Jameson said something, but I didn't stop until I was in the room I was sharing with Faith. I locked the door, found my phone on the nightstand, and called my parents.

Luckily, my father answered.

"Charlotte," he clipped.

Asshole.

"This will be the last time I ever call you."

"What on earth—"

"I know, Father."

"I don't like your attitude."

The nerve.

The gall.

Edward didn't like my attitude? Well, I didn't like his deception. I didn't like how my whole life I'd been treated like I wasn't good enough. I didn't like how their standing at the country club was more important than me.

"Then you'll be happy to know after today, Faith and I do not exist for you. Not that we ever truly mattered, but we're gone nonetheless. You will not contact me, you will not attempt to contact Faith. And you absolutely will not reach out to Holden and cause him anymore trouble than you already have."

"Seriously, Charlotte, why does it always come down to that piece of trash?"

"You do not call him that!" I shouted. "You don't ever say his name again. You knew, all these years, you knew Holden was Faith's father and you gave money to those horrible people after all the things they did to me. They took me to court and you gave them money! You lied to me. You're the piece of trash. You and Mother are vile pieces of shit."

"Char—"

"Shut up and listen. I hope your reputation was worth losing your daughter and granddaughter. I hope you and Mother are happy knowing you destroyed my life and your granddaughter missed growing up without a father. This is your only warning—if I ever hear from either of you again, I'll make sure everyone knows what you did. If you ever try to speak to my daughter, so help me God, I'll unleash Holden on you."

"Char—"

"Fuck. Off. Father."

I disconnected the call, tossed my phone on the bed, pulled on the clothes I wore yesterday, and headed for the door.

When I opened it, my breath caught in my throat.

Evie, Bobby, Kennedy, and Silver all stood there with matching smiles. No one said a word but they didn't have to. None of them masked their approval.

"Are you ready?" Evie asked.

I didn't need her to clarify her question, therefore, I didn't.

"Yes."

"Good. He's at the farm in his Airstream. Chasin's there making sure he doesn't do something stupid."

Like hitch his rig to the back of his Suburban and drive away.

As fast as that thought flitted into my mind, it disappeared. Holden wouldn't leave Faith. Hell, I knew he wouldn't leave me.

I understood he needed time to process the news he had a daughter, but his time was up.

"I need a favor."

"Anything." Evie smiled.

Once I instructed the women, I was out the door.

I'd lost my family once.

I was not losing anymore.

30

Daughter.

The word was foreign as it rolled around in Holden's mind.

He had a daughter.

Incomparable joy morphed into pain. Sheer anguish made his heart ache.

The piss of it was, he couldn't blame Paul, not fully.

Sick fuck.

Holden stared at the shiny metal above his head. Guilt crushed him to his small mattress, and the longer he lay there contemplating his mistakes, the harder it was to comprehend how badly he'd fucked up.

Pride goes before destruction.

Long ago, Holden had destroyed his life. What he hadn't known at the time was the repercussions would be lasting and devastating. He'd hurt Leigh-Leigh, but worse, he'd unknowingly turned his back on his child.

I'm that asshole.

The door to his Airstream creaked open and he didn't bother lifting his head when he roared, "Out!"

There was no response but Holden didn't need there to be. The air around him charged and crackled with unhappiness.

"I'm not leaving."

"I thought you were Chasin," Holden explained but still didn't get up. Didn't even glance in Charleigh's direction as she walked through his small space.

"He's worried about you."

"Is that why you came over here, to tell me that Chasin's outside pacing, waiting for me to start tearing things apart?" Holden paused and blew out a breath. "Sorry, that was a dick thing to say."

"Actually, I think he's out there to make sure you don't run."

That made Holden sit upright.

"I'm not—"

"I know," she sighed.

His heart skipped a beat when he saw her red-rimmed eyes and blotchy face.

Fuck.

They stared at each other for a good long while. There was so much to say, but Holden couldn't find the words. He felt his mouth get tight and tighter still as realized in the space of a few hours, he'd been given everything only to have it taken away.

How could he ask Charleigh to forgive him yet again? For another monumental fuck-up. His first offense was bad enough—leaving her had scarred her. Leaving her *and* their unborn child—unforgivable.

"How are you?" she whispered.

"Me?"

Everything about Charleigh relaxed seeing that Holden tensed. He was about to ask her if she was shitting him asking him how he was.

He was wrecked.

Totally and completely disgusted with himself.

Eight years and some months ago, he had everything he ever wanted within his grasp. Every. Last. Thing. It had been right in front of him and he'd turned it away.

"Never mind, I know how you are."

Doubtful. She hadn't missed out on her child

being brought into this world. She hadn't denied she made a child.

"Leigh-Leigh, I think—"

"No, Holden. I gave you time to get yourself together. Now we need to talk."

He swung his legs over the side of his bed and clenched his jaw until he managed to wrangle his temper.

"Think I need a *little* more time to get myself together."

"And you'll do that with me here."

God, he wanted that so badly. Selfishly he wanted her by his side, and in return, he'd be by hers. Together, they could face the betrayal. Together, they could do anything. But it was ridiculous to believe Charleigh would stay. And he didn't blame her.

"Charleigh—"

"My parents knew," she blurted out. "I don't know how it went down, but my parents started giving Beatrice money shortly after Paul died. When I called to tell my father that Faith and I were dead to them and if they tried to contact us or you, I would ruin them, I didn't think to ask. Not that it matters whose idea it was. I don't care if Bea was blackmailing them, or my father decided the best thing to do was to throw money at the bitch to keep her quiet rather than telling his daughter that the man she loved was his granddaughter's father. No, not him, their reputation was more important than our daughter. Bottom line is, they've known all these years. You need to know that. Yes, Paul started the lie but my parents perpetuated it. I believe that Beatrice would've been all too happy to show me that letter after her son died if my parents hadn't paid her off."

He felt his body go numb. That was good; numb was better than the overwhelming urge to strangle her parents. The Axelsons had hated him from the very moment Charleigh had introduced them and they didn't hide their disdain. Holden would never be good enough for their daughter. He'd never wear polo shirts and pink shorts and belong to the damn club. He would never kiss their asses and pretend to be someone he wasn't at a cocktail party.

Paul wouldn't have played their games either, but he had something Holden didn't—honor. He'd died in combat, he was a war hero, and to them, he was nothing more than a good story they could tell at a dinner party.

Arguably, the Axelsons were worse than the Towlers.

"Did you hear me?" Charleigh mumbled. "I'm so sorry, Holden."

He felt the pressure build, the cold slide into his veins, but that chill didn't last long before it morphed into fire. Oh, he'd heard her all right. He'd heard that her parents had prolonged their misery, had deprived him of knowing his daughter, had begrudged Faith a father. But there was still no denying if Holden had done what he should've done instead of what he'd done none of this would be happening.

"I don't know how you can stand there and apologize."

Charleigh jerked and folded her arms over her chest. The protective gesture made his blood sizzle. "*You* don't have a goddamn thing to be sorry for. *You* didn't do anything wrong. *You* didn't lie. *You* weren't a fucking idiot and took the word of a fucking doctor without questioning it, without a second opinion."

Holden dropped his elbows to his knees, bowed his head, and closed his eyes. "*You* didn't miss the birth of your child. *You* didn't miss her first steps. *You* didn't miss her first day of school. *You* didn't do a fucking thing wrong, so don't you fucking apologize."

The warmth of her hands hit his shoulders and Holden felt his jaw get tight again.

"I have a lot to apologize for."

"No, you don't," he argued.

"We were both wrong, Holden. Both of us could've done a number of things differently. I could've asked for a DNA test. I could've been stronger and told my parents to fuck off. When Bea and Patty stormed my house and took Paul's stuff, including that box, I could've told them to get out. I didn't do any of those things because I was scared and hurt and so damn lost. It's embarrassing how weak I was. We are both at fault."

She squeezed his shoulders. "But you know who isn't? Faith. She's innocent in all of this. So the question is, can we get our shit sorted and give her what she deserves? Have we learned anything from the past? God knows I have. Have you?"

His head slowly lifted and he took her in.

Christ, so beautiful.

And for the second time in his life, she was right in front of him with her heart on her sleeve as they stood at the precipice of greatness—of happiness, of a beautiful future. It was right there, so close all he had to do was step off the cliff and freefall.

She'd catch him.

No. They'd catch each other.

"What if she was my only chance and I missed it?"

The question hadn't left his mouth before Charleigh was pushing him back on his bed. She wasted no time crawling in next to him. Then she pressed close, her arm went over his chest, her leg over his thigh, and she pinned him to the bed.

"Then she grows up an only child, or we adopt, or we do IVF, or we find another option."

Pain carved a path the length of his body. A sting so bad, he wasn't sure he'd ever be the same. He'd missed it, he'd hurt her. Hurt *them.*

"My pregnancy was easy." Charleigh's soft voice sliced through his thoughts. "The only thing I craved was mac and cheese. I could eat it breakfast, lunch, and dinner. I went to every doctors' appointment so excited to hear her heartbeat. I could listen to the whooshing all day. Sometimes, I'd ask to hear it a second time when the appointment was done. My water broke at seven in the morning. I was in the kitchen and I thought I peed myself." Charleigh huffed a laugh and Holden closed his eyes. "When I got to the hospital, I was so scared. I couldn't wait to finally meet my daughter but I was terrified of labor. I had great nurses. They knew I wanted an unmedicated birth so they—"

"Wait. What? You didn't want drugs?"

"Nope. I wanted to experience natural childbirth. All the nurses were great but I had this one named Rebecca. She actually stayed after her shift and helped me. If it wasn't for her coaching, I would've given in and taken the pain meds. She held my hand while I pushed, she encouraged me, and when I was crying that I couldn't do it she gave me a dose of tough love. She saw me through. I even got to help deliver Faith."

Charleigh paused again. This time when she started to giggle she didn't stop when she said, "Rebecca was insistent I could do it. She nearly crawled in the bed behind me to prop me up so I could reach between my legs. I must've looked ridiculous, Rebecca had one arm hooked around my leg holding it up, her chest was to my back almost bending me in half with this huge belly in the way. But when the doctor took my hands and guided them to Faith's body and I got to hold onto her as she came into the world, it was the most amazing experience of my life."

"I wish I was there," Holden whispered and fought back the wetness in his eyes.

"I wish you were, too."

Then Charleigh snuggled closer and told Holden a story he'd never forget. He committed every detail to memory as she gave him an accounting of his daughter's life. First tooth, when she started to crawl, walk, when she learned to draw, first day of school, all the details he should've known. It was exquisite pain, profound and agonizing.

And through it all, she clung to him and he hung on her every word, soaking it in, needing more.

"I want to know her." Holden cleared the lump in his throat. "I don't know how we tell her I'm her dad, and if you want to wait, I'll understand, but I want..." He trailed off, not knowing how to put into words exactly what he wanted. *Everything* didn't begin to scratch the surface. He wanted Faith to be the center of his universe, he wanted to be an integral part of her life, he wanted her to need him, he wanted to teach her and learn from her. He wanted to earn her forgiveness and make up for his stupidity. He needed to prove he was worthy of being her dad.

"You're her dad, Holden, of course we're going to tell her."

"I *want* to be her dad."

"You are," she said softly.

"No, Leigh-Leigh, I want to be her *dad*. I want to be the one to...fuck." He stopped and cleared his throat again but it was a losing battle.

The emotion consumed him.

"Jesus, fuck!" he roared and wrapped his arms around Charleigh.

He held on as tight as he could, his Leigh-Leigh, his lifeline, was the only thing stopping him from coming apart.

"I wanted her. I wanted her to be mine. You and her were all I thought about. I was dying inside, every fucking day, I was dying thinking that motherfucker was her dad. It ate me up. Why didn't I—"

"Stop, honey. No good comes from playing that game. We can both lie here and beat ourselves up for all the mistakes we made. Or we can decide right now to put it behind us and move forward. You wanted to fight, Holden, so now we fight for what should've been ours. And we do that by letting go of the past because we cannot change that, grab ahold of each other and get up."

Holden took a breath so big it expanded his chest, and he held it until his lungs protested. Then he exhaled. He did it again and again until he could finally breathe easy. Clean. She was right. There was nothing he could do to change the past—but he could give them a future.

"Let's get up, Leigh-Leigh," he agreed.

Before he understood she meant "get up" in a literal way, she unwrapped herself and scrambled off the bed. Once she was on her feet, she held out her hand.

"Come on. I want to introduce you to your daughter."

Jesus God.

His daughter.

Charleigh didn't have to ask him twice.

Holden surged off his bed and she let out a squeak when he pulled her into his arms. Her head tipped back, probably to ask him what he was doing. Holden decided to show her. One hand stayed at her hip, the other glided up her back and his fingers curled around the nape of her neck. His mouth slammed down and he said everything he needed to say with a bruising kiss. Charleigh's hands fisted the material of his tee, and he deepened the kiss, taking it from wet and rough to wild.

This is what forgiveness tastes like.

If he wanted to be the man Faith and Charleigh deserved, he had to forgive himself. He had to live in the now. He had to purge the hatred. And he would, he'd do any-fucking-thing for his girls.

When Charleigh moaned and pressed closer, Holden knew it was time to end the kiss. Satisfaction thrummed through him when she mewed and leaned forward, chasing his lips.

"Baby," he mumbled against her lips.

"Hm?"

"We have to get out of here," he said through a smile.

Charleigh pressed closer still, and that felt so damn good he warned, "Time to go."

"What's the rush?"

Holden flexed his hips and pushed his erection against her stomach but said nothing. He figured his hard-on said it all.

A sexy, sly smile played on her lips and his cock twitched. Her smile turned wicked.

"Still don't see what the rush is."

"How much time we got?"

"How much do you need?"

"Days."

"Days?" she parroted.

"Days," he confirmed. "Baby, I got a lot to be thankful for and I plan on expressin' that gratitude with orgasms. In other words, I'm gonna take my time reminding you how much I love you. If you wanna start that now, take your clothes off and climb that fine ass into bed. But we're not leaving until I'm convinced you understand the depth of my appreciation, and it might take me a while before I'm certain you know how grateful I am."

"I don't think we have days," she conceded.

Unfortunately, they didn't. But he'd arrange it so they did, and he'd do that quickly because he needed to show her he was indeed grateful she'd given him a second chance. And he'd do that in a way she'd never forget.

"Then cut me some slack and let's go."

"Slack?"

"Leigh-Leigh," he groaned.

"Fine. Okay. But first I want to look around."

"Later."

"Don't be ridiculous, I've never been inside your Airstream."

Holden sighed and took a step away from her, which was more like a shuffle considering the space was tight.

"There's not much to see."

Charleigh turned and she took in his home.

"Did you do all the work?" she inquired.

"Yep. When I bought her, she was a mess. I gutted it and started from an empty hull."

Nixon, Weston, and Chasin all thought he was crazy when he purchased a beat-up old trailer. Jameson got it—he, too, liked his solitude. Though Holden didn't buy the Airstream for the reasons his teammates thought he did. It wasn't an escape plan and it wasn't so he'd have a place where he could ruminate his poor life choices. Holden bought it because he needed something to occupy his time. He'd needed a project that would keep him busy and his mind off Charleigh, Paul, and their child.

It had taken years to complete the renovations. Between training, work-ups, and deployments, he was gone more than he was home. But he'd put every waking moment into creating something that was just his.

Holden looked around. He'd opted to keep the classic shiny metal walls and ceiling instead of adding coverings. He'd built the kitchen cabinets out of pine and painted them white. They were topped with black granite, and stainless steel appliances finished the modern look. Holden had even framed in the custom loveseat. Though he hired an upholsterer to fashion the cushion covers. Next to that was a slab of wood he'd found at a sawmill. He'd sanded it smooth and given it several coats of lacquer; with all the natural light the table gleamed.

"All of it?" Charleigh asked.

"Everything you see, I built."

"It's beautiful, Holden. I'm totally impressed. I had no idea you could do...well, this." She motioned around the room.

Holden knew the craftsmanship was top-notch. He knew he'd put in a great deal of effort to make something he could be proud of, and he was. But right then, seeing his Leigh-Leigh smiling, he'd never been prouder.

Fuck. They had to leave.

He tagged her hand and pulled her toward the door. But before he pushed the door open, he froze and looked back at the interior of his prized Airstream. Suddenly, it just felt like an RV. He no longer needed what it once represented—he didn't need the physical labor, he didn't need the mind-numbing repetition of polishing the metal. He didn't need the quiet. As a matter of fact, he wanted noise. He wanted to hear Faith's laughter. He wanted to hear Charleigh in the kitchen. He wanted Barbies and coloring books. He wanted mess and chaos.

"You all right?"

"Never better, baby."

Leigh-Leigh tilted her head and she smiled.

Holden returned it.

Then he pushed open the door and they went to pick up their daughter.

31

It's a strange and miraculous thing, the way a child's mind works.

When we got to Macy and Alec's, Faith was no worse for the wear. She and Rory were playing and she barely greeted me when I entered the house. After the way she'd been swept away that morning, I was concerned she would be upset. But no.

After the girls had retreated to Rory's room and were out of earshot, an uncomfortable silence fell over the four of us until Holden smiled and addressed the five-hundred-pound elephant that had been crushing my lungs by announcing, "I'm a dad."

He did this proudly and quietly so the kids wouldn't hear.

Alec's reaction was immediate and it was so

sweet I was taken aback. "Welcome to the best job in the world."

Holden's eyes cut to me and his smile said everything. He was happy—truly happy.

I, on the other hand, was terrified—ecstatic but terrified.

Now we had to find a way to tell Faith that the man I'd told her was her father wasn't and that my ex-boyfriend who happened to be the love of my life was actually her dad. Then I'd have to answer some uncomfortable questions. The uncomfortably of those questions remained to be seen. Thank the good Lord, Faith didn't know the nitty-gritty of baby-making but she knew just enough to make me dread her inquiries.

"Rhode's out back on a call," Alec weirdly said and jerked his head to the side door. "He wants to talk to you before he heads out."

"Be back," Holden muttered, and kissed the top of my head before he followed Alec.

I waited until they were outside to ask Macy, "Was that guy-code for we need to talk without the women?"

"Yep. So totally *not* obvious." She rolled her eyes. "You doing okay?"

"Yes and no. I'm...overwhelmed. And thank you for taking care of Faith for me. I appreciate it."

"Alec and I know better than most how hard it is to juggle kids and drama."

I appreciated Macy's attempt to lighten the mood. What had happened to her and Alec was more than your average everyday drama. Macy had been beaten up, and later, Rory's father had taken her without Macy's permission. Then the little girl watched her Uncle Jonny shoot and kill her father after she watched her grandfather die. Faith's kidnapping notwithstanding, what was happening to me and Holden paled in comparison.

We were both alive, healthy, and we could change our circumstances. Faith would get to know her dad.

"What's the 'no' part?" Macy asked.

"I'm scared."

"Of what? Alec told me the story. He wasn't on Holden's team, obviously you know that, so he doesn't know all the details. But from what he said, Holden never stopped loving you."

"It's weird because last week I was worried about Holden and me. You know, worried we wouldn't be able to overcome the past. But now, it's hard to explain, but I know we're gonna make it. And it has nothing to do with Paul's letter because I felt that before we found out Holden was her dad."

"All of that sounds good so I don't understand what you're scared of."

It didn't surprise me Macy was confused. Hell, I was confused. I didn't know how to articulate what I was feeling.

"I'm so bloody angry I could scream. *I want to scream.* I want Bea and Patty to rot in jail for what they did to Faith. Not just kidnapping her, but keeping her from Holden. I want to slap the shit out of my mother for being such a wretched bitch. I want to do more than tell my dad off for being a worthless father and spineless piece of shit. I'm their daughter. Forget Faith and Holden—me. I'm their only child and they lied to me. They purposefully hurt me. I'm so scared of the hate I feel."

"Ah." Macy nodded once. "I understand, and all I can tell you is in time, it fades."

"How?"

"Every day the anger fades. Every morning when you wake up next to the man you love, it dwindles a little. Every time you see Faith smile, it will retreat. When you see her happy and thriving it goes away more. There will be hundreds of small things, inconsequential things that make the anger and pain diminish. Even after what happened to us, I knew that I'd stop hating Doug. He hurt my kids, he hurt me, he hurt his brother, he killed his father. I hated him and he was dead and I felt cheated that I didn't get to tell him how much I despised him. But every day, I wake up and remember how blessed I am. I have Rory and Caleb, and Joss and Alec. I have wonderful friends, a nice home, a safe place for my kids. I'm loved, they're loved, and I think to myself I have it all. And when you are loved so completely, there is no room for hate. Give it time, Charleigh; it fades, and before you know it, it's gone."

That sounded like sound advice. It'd give it time and hope Macy was right.

"Thanks."

Macy smiled and said, "Now tell me, how happy is Holden now that he's a daddy?"

Now *that* made me smile.

Holden was a daddy.

"Over the moon comes to mind."

So did betrayed, sad, and regretful. But we weren't dwelling on the past so I let those thoughts flee and concentrated on our blessings.

And there were many.

HOLDEN STOOD in Alec's backyard. Winter had not left and there was a chill in the air, but that was not why his body trembled.

He was pissed.

Rhode had just finished filling him in on the details Charleigh had left out about her parents' part in keeping him from his daughter, from Leigh-Leigh.

"I want them to go down," Holden grounded out through gritted teeth.

"Not sure you can do that without blowback. Edward isn't stupid. Charleigh may've told the asshole off, but he knows his daughter doesn't have the means to take him on. So he'll know it was you."

Holden thought on that a moment, then he decided he didn't give the first fuck. Actually, he liked that Edward would know it was Holden—a man who Edward had deemed beneath him—was responsible for his fall.

"I don't want his business touched. When I'm done, I want them to be just as wealthy as they are right now. But I want their reputations dragged through the mud. I want them left with no friends, no country club, no dinner parties to attend, no afternoon tea. I want those two to feel betrayed by the people they thought were their friends. I want them to be the outcasts. The pariahs. I want everyone to know they're shit parents. I want them to sit in that big-ass house of theirs and know what it's like to be lonely."

Rhode jerked his chin in acknowledgment.

"I'll dig up what I can. But I'm leaving on a job tomorrow."

"You going out with Takeback?" Alec asked.

"Yeah. We got confirmation this morning from the feds they're ready to move in. Three girls, twelve, nine, and five."

Sweet Jesus.

Holden couldn't let that penetrate or he'd go ballistic.

"They offered to take me on full-time," Rhode continued. "Which means I'll be on the road more than I am now."

"Wilson still there?" Alec inquired.

"Yeah. I don't know him but he seems solid. He coordinates our jobs with the marshal's office."

"He is solid," Alec confirmed. "I worked with him at DHS."

"Good to know."

As much as Holden enjoyed shooting the shit with his friends, he wanted to take Leigh-Leigh and Faith home and spend some time alone with his girls. He was under no illusion they would tell Faith he was her dad tonight—that could wait until the time was right. But he would be having a conversation about changing Faith's last name. And while they were at it, Charleigh's as well.

"Did someone think to remove that box from the house?" Holden looked at Rhode.

"Yeah, Jameson took it."

Soon there would be no reminders of Paul Towler. None. That man had no place in their lives and he would go to great pains to make sure every memory was wiped clean.

"Appreciate everything you both did for us," he told his friends. "I'm gonna grab my girls and go home."

"Bet you are." Alec smiled.

"Good after all these years to see you happy," Rhode added.

Holden's eyes sliced to Rhode and the truth hit him, and when it did, it rocked him.

"I was happy before I knew the truth. Faith was going to be mine. I had Leigh-Leigh back and we were building a future. What you found was icing. It doesn't change the way I feel but it might help my daughter. I'm not saying I'm not forever grateful, because I am. But I've loved Charleigh all these years thinking she slept with Paul and together they made something precious. I was jealous as fuck, but I never stopped loving her. Never stopped wishing Faith was mine. You finding that intel is a dream come true, but I was already living a new dream. Knowing that the motherfucker lied doesn't make me love her more. I started all of this misery when I was stupid enough to take the word of a doctor and not trust Charleigh with what I thought was relationship-ending news. She would've made me get a second opinion, she would've been smart enough to know even doctors make mistakes. But I pussed out and ran. That's on me and I'll have to find a way to move past it."

"You will. I've learned that with the right woman by your side it doesn't matter what life throws your way—you find a way around it. You and Charleigh will come out of this stronger than you were."

Fuck yeah, they would.

Unbreakable.

He knew all too well what it was like to live without her. Never again would he be separated from his girls.

Holden turned to Rhode and offered the other man his hand.

"Be safe. And I hope you know you can always call on us if you need anything."

"I do and I will."

When their hands released, Holden slapped Alec on the shoulder.

"I still haven't read over your report. And honestly, it's doubtful I will tonight. Anything I need to know about your meet with Donna Lot? Did you get anything?"

"Nothing. She talked to us, but it was the same thing she told Jonny. And she refused to allow McKenna to look at her computer or cell. The woman is beyond traumatized. She needs serious help, but she refused that, too. Her house sold. My guess is she's either gone or packing up as we speak so she can get gone. The woman wants away from this place."

"Do you think she's been threatened?"

"I think she's a woman who lost her only child in a horrific manner and she blames herself for not seeing the signs."

Holden thought about that for a moment and could see how the mother would blame herself.

"It's not her fault."

"You know that. I know that. But Donna Lot will never see it that way."

All the more reason to catch the son of a bitch who had harmed Kimberly. Donna deserved a slice of peace. Not that it would ease what happened or stop her pain, but anything they could give her would be worth it.

"I'll see you in the morning. Thanks for taking Faith today. Hope it wasn't too much trouble."

"Get the fuck out of here with that noise. We loved that girl before we knew she was yours. She's always welcome here. And now that Rory and Faith are "BFFs To The End of Time" and that's a direct quote, you can expect my daughter at your house and yours at mine. Though you and I are gonna be having a talk about this little shit named Andy."

"Right? Leigh-Leigh told me I can't hunt him down and wring his neck, though I will be finding the kid's dad. The little fucker tries to kiss my daughter I won't care he's eight, that shit ain't happenin'."

Rhode damn near busted a gut laughing, but Holden didn't see the humor. He was dead serious. No boy was putting his lips near Holden's daughter.

32

"And this was my seventh birthday." Faith proudly pointed at the picture of herself and her friends all in silly hats on the beach.

Holden smiled and ran his finger over the edge of the plastic-covered corner. The same way he'd done with each picture Faith had stopped on to tell a story.

There was something about how he touched the images, reverently, worshipfully, adoringly. And the way he stared at the pages of the album as Faith flipped through, like he was trying to soak in the memory.

It was both heartbreaking and heartwarming. He'd missed out on everything.

Faith got to the last page and announced, "That's all of them."

"But you're eight," Holden retorted.

"Mom hasn't made that one yet."

"You haven't?"

"I make them right before her birthday," I explained.

"And on my birthday we look back over the year. It's a tradition."

I smiled at Faith's excitement. What had started as me spending my daughter's birthday looking back over the last year with a sadness only a mother understands, reminiscing, noting how much she'd changed and grown, had turned into something more. And I loved that Faith was always anxious to look at the album I made her.

"So on your ninth birthday, you'll get your eight-year-old album?"

"Yep."

Holden looked over at me and my breath caught—unbridled emotion. He wasn't hiding anything from me and in turn, he wasn't hiding anything from our daughter. He was showing us both he'd enjoyed looking over Faith's life.

"That's cool of you, Leigh-Leigh."

"Does this mean you'll stay and be my dad?"

Every muscle in my body contracted, my eyes felt like they were bugging out of my face, and I would swear I was experiencing heart failure. I couldn't feel it beating, or maybe it was beating so fast that it was one continuous flutter, making me light-headed.

"Wh...what?" I stammered, unable to get my breathing steady enough to ask more.

To Holden's credit, he didn't look as freaked out as I did. Actually, he was grinning.

"Why would you ask that, doll?"

Faith shrugged.

"Because you're my dad, right?"

No, I was experiencing heart failure *now*, and I was definitely dizzy. When neither of the two adults in the room spoke—which would've been the thing to do, except I was having an out-of-body episode and Holden looked like he was in shock—Faith looked between us, then continued.

"You'll stay this time, right?"

Holden's shoulders jerked and his torso followed. Thankfully, we were sitting down or Holden would've fallen on his ass.

There was no malice in Faith's question, just innocent intrigue.

"Yeah, Faith, I'm staying. And, yes, I'm your dad."

"And that's why you wanted to look at my books?"

"Yeah. I wanted to see everything I missed. It's not the same, nothing will ever make up for the time I missed out on being with you and being your dad. But I still want to see the pictures and hear all the stories."

Faith nodded like she was a thirty-five-year-old woman and she found Holden's answer acceptable. I, on the other hand, was confused. Unless my daughter had somehow come into magical powers that included mind reading, I wanted to know how Faith knew Holden was her dad. Unless she was just being an eight-year-old girl who wanted a dad however that came to be.

"Why'd you ask if Holden was your dad?" I'd softened my question with a smile, but when my daughter bit her lip I wasn't sure if I'd succeeded. "Honey, I'm just asking why you'd think he's your dad."

"He is, right? And he's gonna stay with us. He won't leave this time?" Faith's voice had gone shrill and her eyes darted around the room.

The eye thing was her tell—when she got upset she didn't hold eye contact.

"Yes, he's your dad. What I'm asking is, how did you know?"

When her teeth sank into her lower lip and tears sprang in her eyes, I reconsidered my line of questioning.

"C'mere." Holden lifted Faith off the couch and set her in his lap. Immediately her little body melted into his.

I wished I had my camera. I wished the situation wasn't what it was because that would've been a great picture to include in Faith's album.

Daddy and daughter. Faith leaning into Holden looking for comfort.

God, we screwed up.

"Faith, I'm not leaving, no matter what. When I left your mom, I didn't know..." Holden paused and I held my breath, waiting to see how Holden was going to explain to an eight-year-old the circumstances surrounding him leaving me. But what I didn't even think about was taking over the conversation. That wasn't because I was a chicken shit, but because I trusted Holden would do his best. And together we'd answer her questions.

"I didn't know your mom was pregnant with you. And when she found out I was..." There was another pause, this one longer, this one painful. I swallowed the lump in my throat that was so big it was a miracle it didn't choke me. Holden had tears in his eyes, then I had tears in mine when Faith reached up and placed her hand on his cheek.

"Are you sad you're my dad?"

Horror passed over Holden's face before he covered her hand with his.

Another moment I wished I could capture. The tips of Faith's tiny fingers were barely poking out from under her dad's much bigger hand.

"No. I am not sad I'm your dad. I'm sad I missed out on you growing in your mom's belly. I'm sad I didn't get to see your beautiful face when you were born. I'm sorry I didn't know you were my daughter and we missed out on so many years. But, Faith, I promise you I'm gonna make it up to you. I swear, doll, I'm gonna be the best dad. I know this is confusing, but I want you to know I didn't leave because I didn't want you."

"Do I get to live with you?"

"Yes. You and your mom."

Faith grinned, then her grin turned into a full-fledged smile and she said, "You, me, Mom, and a puppy."

Holden's face split into a matching smile and he agreed. But I wasn't thinking about life with a puppy and all that came with a small, needy dog in the house. No, I couldn't take my eyes off the similarities between the two of them. All the small things I had shoved aside over the years and eventually stopped looking for altogether. But now that I was free to compare, it was plain to see.

"Aunt Patty said that Mom was stupid," Faith announced. "She told that man that they were running out of time. That I looked like Holden and now that he was back he'd start asking questions. Then she told him all it would take was a N-A-D test and Holden would know he was my dad."

"DNA," Holden mouthed, then asked Faith, "Did Patty say anything else?"

"I was getting sleepy," Faith muttered. "And my tummy felt funny. I was scared."

"I know you were, doll. It's okay if you don't remember anything else."

"Patty was mad at the man and was yelling that he better not have...killed Mom...or they'd never get the money."

God, those bitches. Money. It was always about the money.

"They will never hurt you or your mom again."

"Patty said Mom would give them the money to get me back."

Holden stared at Faith and pulled her closer.

"Faith, your mom would've done anything to get you back. Anything, you hear that? *Any. Thing.*"

"I know. She sent you."

"She did."

Hours and hours of pent-up emotion, years and years of pent-up frustration, years of agonizing loneliness and loss finally broke free. I was tired, so damn tired I couldn't hold it in. I couldn't even hold my body upright so I slumped forward and gave Holden my weight. And just like I knew he would, his arm came around me and my arm went around Faith and together we held our daughter.

Finally.

Freaking, finally.

Holden Stanford lay awake in a big bed that was not his and stared into the dark. To his right, his daughter slept with her hand in his. To his left, his Leigh-Leigh had fallen into a restless sleep. He knew this because in the hours since they'd come upstairs, he hadn't closed his eyes, not once. He was too afraid if he did, he'd wake up to find it was all a dream.

Charleigh's body jolted and he pulled her tighter

against his chest and waited. She settled in and nuzzled his chest.

Heaven.

He held heaven in his hands.

Everything he'd ever wanted was in that bed. His Leigh-Leigh and their daughter.

His.

Then he lay there in the dark remembering all the plans they'd made, all the adventures they wanted to take, all the things they wanted to do. All of the things they were *going* to do.

Finally.

Fucking, finally.

33

"How's Faith?" Jameson asked.

Holden looked up from the report he was reading and rubbed his eyes.

"She already knew I was her dad."

"How?"

Just thinking about those bitches made Holden's skin crawl. White-hot rage took on a whole new meaning when he thought about what they'd done to Charleigh. She'd endured years of their nasty vitriol. As for Faith—they'd hurt his daughter and scared her. Holden had seen a lot, done a lot, been to battle, taken lives, but never had he wanted to commit murder. Now he could think of four people he'd gladly take out. And while the law would frown at him ridding the world of four vile pieces of shit, he would feel no remorse. Each of those four assholes played a role in keeping Faith from him, depriving his child of her father.

When Holden was done explaining last night's conversation, Jameson's face was set to stone. As always, when one of his friends expressed their loyalty, Holden sat back and remembered how lucky he was.

"Christ. And here I thought Chasin's mom was the supreme cunt. Seems to me, the bitch has company. Alec filled us in on Edward Axelson. I'll do my part and make some calls, see what I can dig up. For what it's worth, I agree with your play. Above all else, they care about their social standing."

"Appreciate it. But don't give it too much time, you have a family to worry about."

"And you're not family?"

There it was, another reminder.

"You know what I mean."

"Not sure I do. You seem to forget that when something happens to one of us it happens to all of us. That includes our wives and children. Kennedy and the girl posse are circling Charleigh, closing in tight, making sure her and Faith are okay. Whether she wants it or not, she just got six new best friends and became an aunt to a ragtag group of hellions.

Not that Faith didn't already have us, but she's got five uncles and you got your brothers at your back to help you with her. That's family, Holden. That's what we do. It's what we should've done when you left her. We should've strapped your ass to a board and tortured your stubborn ass until you told us why you left her. We should've beat you senseless when that little girl was about three, looked nothing like that douchebag but she sure as shit looked like you. We all failed you and Charleigh and Faith. That's never gonna happen again. And I'll remind you every fucking day what family means until you get it through your thick-ass skull. Do not shut us out. Do not carry the load on your own. Divvy that weight up and let us be there for you like you're always there for us."

It took extreme effort not to allow his gratitude to overwhelm him. He knew he had great friends, he knew all of them were good men, but time and time again, what he failed to remember was they were *brothers*.

He stared at Jameson, a man who used to be surly and selfish with his words, a man who elected to grunt more than he spoke, a man who'd lived behind walls and kept to himself, a man who had done an about-face when he met his wife. Not that

Jameson was chatty, but he no longer guarded his thoughts. Therefore, Holden opened up.

"I'm so fucking happy I don't know what to do."

"Live."

"Come again?"

"Just live." Jameson smiled. "Tell me, how'd you feel when you woke up this morning?"

Holden didn't tell his friend he hadn't actually woken up because he'd never gone to sleep, but he caught his drift and answered, "Unbelievably happy."

"Right. And this afternoon you'll go home and they'll be there and you'll be happy. You'll go to sleep and you'll do that happy, too. Just fucking *live*, Holden. No thinking about the past, about shit you cannot control or change. You got it now. Enjoy it. Savor it. Show your girls how much you love them and they'll wake up, go to sleep, and spend all the moments between knowing they have you so they'll be happy. It's time for you to start livin' again."

Jesus, he's right.

I hadn't truly been living for years.

"It's good to know you getting laid on the regular has turned you into a wise old man. We needed someone smart around here."

"Idiot," Jameson mumbled and shook his head.

"I've always been smarter than the rest of you fools. Better-looking, too."

"Right." Holden chuckled. "Good to know you got that big ego of yours in check."

"I know you already know this because you had it once, but you seem to have forgotten so I'll remind you. When you have a beautiful woman at your side who is strong, capable, smart, loyal, and you know you've earned her respect, that's not called ego. That, my friend, is confidence. I know Kennedy wouldn't be standing next to me with my ring on her finger and my baby in her stomach if I wasn't worth something. So that confidence is earned. Remember that, Holden. Charleigh Axelson is a warrior, and she wouldn't have waited for as long as she has for you to pull your head out of your ass if she didn't think you weren't worth that wait. You got everything you want, now all you gotta do is live."

With that, Jameson turned and left, leaving Holden reeling.

His friend was right, again. Charleigh was strong, capable, smart, loyal, and a great mom. She wouldn't accept anything but the best for herself and Faith.

Live.

He could totally do that. But while he was living,

he'd do more than show his girls how loved they were —he'd prove to them he was absolutely worth the wait.

HOLDEN WAS on his way down to the conference room when his cell vibrated. Charleigh's name flashed on the screen and his heart flip-flopped.

Damn, he had it bad.

"Hey, baby," he greeted.

"Sorry to bother you at work but I wanted to tell you Jodi called and asked if I was available today to see the property you told me about."

Holden smiled and asked, "What'd you tell her?"

"I told her I was. But, Holden, are you sure about this? She told me the list price on the house and it's—"

"Go look at it, Leigh-Leigh. If you like it, call me and I'll make an offer."

"You can't make an offer without seeing it."

"Sure I can."

"What if you don't like it?"

It seemed his woman didn't understand, so he walked past the conference room, noting everyone was already around the table, went into the reception area, and stopped in front of the big window overlooking Fountain Park.

"Okay, Charleigh, I guess I haven't made myself clear, so let me do that now. I don't care where I live as long as it's with you and Faith. I don't care what the house looks like, if it's in a development, on a farm, one-story or two. The only requirement I have is that there's a yard for Faith's dog. So, if you like the house, tell Jodi to call me. If you don't, set up more viewings and when you find what you're looking for, we'll make an offer."

"It's really expensive, and as you know—"

"Then it's a good thing your man is rich."

"You're rich?" she wheezed.

"I live in a trailer. I have minimal overhead. My Suburban's paid off. I saved money while I was in the Navy mainly because I was gone more than I was home and I had nothing to spend it on. I own Gemini Group with Nix, Jameson, Weston, Chasin, and Alec. You've seen where they live; tell me, do they look like they're hurtin'?"

"No, but—"

"Trust me, we got the money to buy the house."

"But—"

"Charleigh, baby, please find us a house. I want my family set up and settled as soon as that can happen. I know it's asking a lot for you to handle it on your own, but I'm asking all the same—find our family somewhere to live."

"Okay," she whispered. "But, Holden, I'm not alone, I have you."

His eyes lost focus and his body locked.

Jesus, Jesus.

They'd done it.

They'd won.

Just start living.

Holden let the beauty of her words wash away the bitterness of the past and he did exactly what Jameson told him to do.

"You're correct. You are not alone." Holden was well-aware his voice was gruff and he didn't give two shits it cracked when he said, "I love you, Leigh-Leigh."

"I love you, too, Holden."

Last night, he hadn't been wrong when he was lying between his girls thinking there was nothing better, but he hadn't taken into account how good it felt to hear Leigh-Leigh say those words. Having his girls close, heaven. Hearing Leigh-Leigh tell him she loved him, a mili-inch less than the best feeling in the world. And only because anytime Faith was in the equation, it was the best.

"Find us a house."

"Okay. Um..."

"What's wrong?"

"Nothing, really, but...um...the girls are here and they want to go with me."

Fuck, the velvet blows just kept coming. The girl posse had closed ranks. Six new best friends for Charleigh. Six new aunts for his daughter. Six women who would show his daughter what it meant to be strong, loyal, and loving. Hell, yeah, that blow took his breath.

"Then take them. Just don't let Evie buy us the house."

"Would she do that?"

"Absolutely, yes. She is generous with wedding gifts."

"Wedding gifts?" Charleigh breathed.

He didn't bother explaining to her she'd be wearing his ring in the next couple of days. And as soon as the weather broke, he'd be dragging her ass and all of their friends up the knoll that used to be Swagger land but now belonged to Chasin and Evie. And they'd be saying their vows in the same place everyone else had.

Nixon had once said that farm was hallowed ground. All of his childhood memories were wrapped up with that land. And when Nix's father passed, that farm became even more sacred. Nixon allowing Evie to buy the farmhouse and some of the land from him with the promise to keep it in the family was a testament to how much Nixon trusted Chasin.

Holden caught Weston's reflection in the window and told Charleigh, "Gotta run, everyone's waiting on me to start the meeting."

"Wedding gifts," she echoed.

"Baby, we'll talk when I get home. It's Sunday and no one wants to be here. Let me get this meeting done and you and your girls go buy us a house."

"Hold—"

"Love you."

Holden disconnected and pocketed his phone before he turned and caught Weston smiling at him.

"What?"

"Pleased as fuck." That was all his friend said before he walked away.

"Me, too, brother. Me fucking, too," Holden mumbled to the empty room and made his way to the conference room.

"Anything?" Holden heard Jonny ask as he walked into the room.

"No. The girls are talking about it over

messenger but they're not using his name," McKenna answered. "As you know, Donna Lot didn't give us anything new. And she wouldn't give me Kimberly's cell or laptop. Both are turned off, which means I can't access them remotely. Honestly, I think she's been through enough. She doesn't want to know what's on those devices, and as frustrating as it is from an investigation standpoint, I don't blame her."

"I agree," Alec put in. "We need to respect her right to privacy and find another way."

McKenna glanced around the room sheepishly before her eyes landed on her husband and she worried her bottom lip.

"Out with it, sweetheart."

It was safe to say, not much got by Nixon, and nothing did when it pertained to his wife. He had finely honed skills when it came to McKenna.

"Molly Buchannan, the girl Jonny found behind the barn at the party?"

"What about her?" Jonny asked.

"She has a friend, Sydney, who from what I can tell is newish to the area. Sydney was telling Molly about a party she went to. She didn't mention any names but she was bragging about this hot older guy she met." There was a twinge of recognition, but before he could suss it out, McKenna continued,

"Sydney's description was tall, built, brown hair. She told Molly for an old guy, he was ripped." Seven disgruntled male growls sounded in the room but McKenna pushed through. "Molly was engaged, asking questions and sending thumbs-up emojis until Sydney told her the guy brought a bottle of Malibu rum. After that, Molly shut down and warned Sydney to stay away from him. Sydney became angry and accused Molly of being jealous she couldn't get an older guy. Molly's last message was, and I quote, 'been there, done that, and threw the t-shirt away.'"

"Fuck," Jonny grunted.

Holden's stomach dropped. "Sydney *Powell*?"

"I don't know her last name. They use an anonymous messaging app."

"Then how did you get Molly's info?"

"I may or may not have sent Molly an email with a link to a YouTube video of a hilarious camel spitting at a zookeeper. And I may or may not have cloned her mother's email address to make sure Molly opened the link that, once clicked could hypothetically give me access to her phone."

"Jesus." That came from Jonny who was used to Micky's hypothetical scenarios but still mostly liked to be kept in the dark on how Gemini Group obtained their intel. And that 'mostly' actually meant that he absolutely didn't want to know when McKenna hacked illegally.

"I only know HotSyd4Life's name is Sydney because that's the name Molly used."

"Are there no goddamn parents that check their kids' phones?" Alec grumbled.

"Even if Molly's parents checked her phone they probably wouldn't think to check an app that's icon is a clock. Teenagers are crafty when they want to hide stuff."

"Who's Sydney Powell?" Weston asked.

"Charleigh's planning her fifty-thousand dollar birthday party," Holden answered, then asked, "The girl's turning fifteen. What the fuck is she doing at a party in the first place?"

"He's starting early," Jonny noted.

"Or he's grooming her," Jameson retorted. "Didn't think about what comes before the three-month mark and he takes the girls. This could be his normal routine."

"Jesus. Are you telling me he picks a girl and spends the next few months toying with her before..." Jonny clamped his mouth shut, unable to finish his thought.

"That's exactly what I think. And it makes sense. If he just showed up out of the blue and forced himself on the girls, even if he threatened them, more than likely they'd break. But, if he takes his time and makes the girls think he loves them, that they love him, there's nothing wrong with what they're doing, convinces them they're in some sort of sick relationship, it would be easier for him to control the girls. And when he's done he could manipulate them into thinking that the disintegration of the relationship was somehow their fault, that they weren't good enough, and he moves on to the next."

"The ultimate mindfuck," Nixon added.

"And they don't tell because they think they're in love."

"A teenage girl's emotions are fragile," McKenna said softly.

Jonny's hands went to his temples and his eyes closed. When he opened them, his expression was tortured. "Been a cop a long time. I thought I'd seen pretty much all there was to see. I know we live in a small town and we don't have the same crime as they do in big cities. But people still rob, kill, and harm around here. Never did it occur to me that..." Jonny gritted his teeth. "Fuck, what else have I missed?"

"You can't find things that people don't want you to find," Chasin told Jonny.

"Then what the fuck am I doing?" Jonny stood

and shook his head once. "Appreciate you all coming in on a Sunday."

"Jonny," Alec called out, and Jonny stopped in the doorway but didn't turn back.

"Whatever you're gonna say, don't. I'm a fucking cop and this sick shit has been happening in my town, under my watch for a long goddamn time. If I can't even protect my own fucking father from my piece of shit brother, then what fucking good am I?" With that parting shot, Jonny was gone.

And there it was—the truth.

Jonny was still struggling with the death of his father and brother.

"We've gotta get his ass sorted," Alec said.

"Agreed. This shit's gone on too long and he's retreating more and more," Holden said.

All eyes swung to Holden. There were varying degrees of the same 'what the fuck' expression. Jameson's was accompanied by a smirk. Weston's was a frown. Nixon had narrowed his eyes. Alec was shaking his head. But it was Chasin who was smiling.

"Pot, have you met kettle? His name is Holden," Chasin jabbed.

"Never said I was a smart man," he admitted. "But I'm sure as fuck not stupid. So just to clear the air, I know my head was up my ass. I know I was wrong. I know I should've opened up. I know I should've told you all the truth, but more, I should've told Charleigh. Now, can we please move on and talk about Jonny?"

"Sure, after you explain to us why you still haven't put a ring on that woman's finger," Weston asked.

"It's been about a minute since our world was rocked. I figured I'd come in, participate in a meeting like I actually worked here, then I'd hit the jewelry store on High Street. I know it's hard for a man like you to understand, since you clapped eyes on your woman, knocked her up the second she let you into bed, then had your band on her finger before the haze had cleared. Which was a smart move on your part, because Silver is way out of your league, friend, so you had to be speedy before she figured it out. But some of us like to bask in the moment."

"Bask in the moment?" Nixon sputtered. "Holy fucking shit, Holden just said bask. Do you know what that word even means?"

Holden leaned back in his chair and took in the scene around him.

Some of the good-natured insults hurled his way were hard to understand seeing as they were said through laughter. Others were things he'd said to his friends as they struggled through the beginnings of their relationships. But the bottom line was, Holden enjoyed every minute—dare he say, he was basking in a brotherhood he was blessed to be a part of.

But Holden wouldn't be Holden if he didn't do it with his middle finger extended.

34

"You've lost your mind," I told Holden.

And the room exploded into laughter. Everyone was back at the house—that was Evie's uncle's house, not the house that Holden was currently putting a bid on.

"You like it?" he asked.

"Well, yeah, it's beautiful. But it's also more house than we need and expensive and you haven't seen it."

"Told you I didn't care."

Obviously, he was telling the truth because right then, he had his phone to his ear and he was talking to Jodi. To bid on a house he'd never seen—not even a picture on the internet, nothing. He was actually going to purchase a house sight unseen because I liked it. Or maybe he was buying it because Faith had prattled on and on about how much she loved it. And then Rory put in her two-cents about how awesome the finished room above the garage was, which I learned was called a FROG. Faith had declared that room would be her playroom and had even picked out which room she wanted for her bedroom.

Next, the women had all added commentary about all the great things about the house. McKenna and Silver were all for it, since the house's property butted up against theirs. Kennedy and Macy both admitted the house was beautiful but wasn't close to their houses so they voted to keep looking and find something close to them.

But it was Evie who'd cinched the deal when she told Holden I'd absentmindedly said the house felt like home. And it did. The house was big, but it just had this homey vibe. The interior was stunning but it didn't feel like you were in a showroom. And the living room with the big fireplace made you want to lounge on the couch and watch a movie. And the firepit out back screamed Holden and the guys. I could totally see them hanging around the fire, shooting the shit, enjoying a beer.

Of course, there was also the fact Faith could

have her dog. She could have ten dogs, a horse, a goat, and a few donkeys and there'd still be leftover land. Thankfully, I'd refrained from mentioning this, or we'd have a menagerie in our backyard.

"Right, I appreciate it. Tell me what they say." Holden ended his call and tossed his phone on the counter. "Are we ordering in or braving taking the kids to a restaurant?"

My mouth dropped open at Holden's question. He had lost his mind. He'd potentially just purchased a house, hung up the phone, and essentially asked what was for dinner.

"You..." I snapped my mouth shut and tried again. "You just..."

Nope. I was still at a loss for words.

"I what, Leigh-Leigh?"

"Just bought a house." I told him something he very well knew but I felt it bore repeating.

"Actually, *we* just put a bid in. It remains to be seen if *our* offer is accepted."

"Oh, no, *you* just bought a house like a crazy person. You need to go see—"

"You gonna marry me?"

The room fell silent and someone sucked in a momentous lungful of air, or maybe it was me who'd removed all the oxygen from the room. And did someone light a fire, because suddenly I was sweating, as in profusely.

"What?"

"Are you gonna marry me?" he repeated but offered no further explanation.

Was he serious? Throwing out a theoretical question as it pertained to the future? Did he mean right this second? And again, was he seriously asking me that in a room full of our friends?

Then I got pissed, because I wanted to marry him. I had wanted that ten years ago the moment I laid eyes on him. I had obsessively wanted to marry him the years we were together, and in the years we'd been apart I'd mourned the death of my dream. Now he was just tossing it out there willy-nilly like it wasn't the most important question he'd ever ask me, without giving me the opportunity to express how much it meant to me he wanted to spend his life with me.

That was why my eyes narrowed, my hands went to my hips, and my attitude flared.

"I don't know, Holden Clarence Stanford. Are you gonna ask me properly or is it a leading question before you enlighten me on how we bought a house, when really you bought it because I certainly don't have the money to—"

I didn't get to finish my rant. Holden's hands went to my face and he tipped my head back so he was looking in my eyes.

"Take a breath, Leigh-Leigh."

My eyes got squintier and Holden smiled.

Jerk.

Then I lost his hands and his eyes. I tucked my chin and looked down. Once again, my breath caught, but this time I was positive I was the one who extracted the air from the room.

"Leigh-Leigh, baby, I knew the moment I saw you we were going to spend our lives together. It was your beauty that caught my attention but it was your spirit that captured me. And since that day, there hasn't been a single one that has passed that I haven't thought about you. Marry me, Charleigh, and let me—"

"Yes," I interrupted the rest of the proposal I thought I wanted when really all I wanted was the man. "Yes. Yes. Yes."

Instead of standing, he reached into his pocket, then grabbed my left hand and slid an enormous diamond on my finger. But I knew he wasn't done when he looked up at me and said, "This one is us.

Uncut, a diamond is rough, but when it's polished it's beautiful and strong. When you're not by my side, I'm jagged and raw. But when we're together," Holden tapped the ring, "nothing but beauty."

He slid a second ring on my finger, brought my hand to his mouth, and kissed the rings he'd slipped on. "Faith. It's said that an amethyst is the bridge between the concrete and the divine. The antidote for clumsiness and foolery. It's fitting that it's our girl's birthstone. She certainly has brought my life into brilliant clarity."

I didn't look down at the new ring, I was sure it was pretty, but Holden's glassy, brown eyes held me hostage.

"Beautiful," I muttered.

"Stunning," he returned and winked.

Holden rose to his feet and brushed his mouth against mine while he told me how much he loved me. Before I could return the sentiment, I felt arms wrap around my thighs and looked down.

"So we're moving into the house?"

I nodded.

"And we're for sure getting a puppy?"

God help me, one of the best moments of my life was being interrupted for confirmation a puppy was forthcoming.

I nodded again.

"And it's gonna be a Tank dog?"

"Yes." I changed tactics, hoping my verbal answer would appease my child.

"Awesome." Her accompanying dance, if it could be called that, had the room laughing again. "I'm getting a pup-py," she chanted and jerked her body this way and that way.

"Lord, save me."

"Anyone else in shock that Holden's middle name is Clarence?" Weston hooted.

I opened my mouth to defend my man but Holden stopped me. "No, baby, let them have this."

"But, there's nothing wrong with Clarence. Besides, it's a family name."

"Trust me. Let Weston dig his hole." I tilted my head, not understanding. "I know what his is."

"Is it bad?"

Holden leaned close and whispered, "Orville."

I tried, I really did, but I couldn't stop the laughter from bubbling up.

"Dad?" Faith's voice rang out sure and strong like she'd been calling Holden that since she could talk. When in actuality, she'd never in her life called a man dad.

The laughter died down and I felt all eyes come

to me, including Holden's, before his gaze slid to his daughter. It was at that moment, Holden changed. I saw it happen right before my very eyes. Everything about him softened, and if Faith hadn't already had Holden wrapped around her pinkie, calling him dad would've done it.

"Yeah, doll?"

"If Mom will buy me a bike, will you teach me how to ride so me and Rory can have a race?"

What my child didn't know was, I wouldn't have to buy her anything. I had a feeling by tomorrow morning there would be five bikes sitting outside.

"Absolutely," Holden answered in a rough voice.

"Yay!" Faith did her signature jig and turned to Rory. "My dad's gonna teach me to ride a bike. Then we can race."

The girls' chatter faded into the background. Dinner plans, house buying, engagement, company, all forgotten. Everyone except Holden ceased to exist for me. I never wanted to forget this moment, the look on his face, the happiness that radiated from him. So I took my time and memorized the moment. I committed every nuance to memory and I locked it away nice and tight in a secret place that was just for me.

It was then some of the hatred faded.

It was then I realized that with all of the people conspiring against us, we'd won. Sure, we lost some time, but we hadn't lost it all.

There was a lot of life to live. There was more to our story. And we were finally going to live it.

35

"Dad?"

Holden forced his body to stay relaxed as he looked over at Faith. He wasn't entirely successful in this endeavor, seeing as his neck muscles had stiffened and his heart pounded violently, but he didn't think his daughter noticed.

This wasn't the first time he'd heard Faith call him "Dad" and it wasn't even the third. Over the last few hours, it seemed once she'd broken the seal she was using every available opportunity to call out to him even if he was right next to her. Case in point, they were side by side on the bed Faith and Charleigh shared and Holden had been reading her a bedtime story.

"Right here, doll."

"I just like calling you that."

Jesus, Jesus.

"That's good, 'cause I like hearing it."

"Why was Paul my dad if you really were?"

Fuck.

How in the hell did he explain to an eight-year-old the mess he'd created?

With honesty. But how did he break it down in a way she could understand?

"When I was in the Navy, I got hurt and had to go see a doctor." *Okay, that was a good start. Now what?* Holden studied his daughter and wondered how it was possible he'd had his head so twisted he'd missed really *seeing* her. It had been right in front of him the whole time, all he had to do was look. Faith wasn't a carbon copy of him—most of her features came from her mom—but he was there, too. The shape of her eyes, her skin tone, her hair color, she even had his nose. Holden shook those thoughts from his mind and came back to her question. "The doctor had to give me a bunch of tests. And he told me I couldn't have children."

"But...you're my dad, right?"

Goddammit. He was screwing this up. He needed Charleigh, she'd know what to say.

"Yes, Faith. You are my daughter. The doctor

was wrong. But at the time I didn't know that. I didn't leave because I didn't want you or your mom. I left because I wanted you so badly to be mine, but at the time, I believed the doctor. I didn't ask the right questions and because of that I missed a lot of your life."

"I asked Mom for a brother or sister and she told me no."

Holden's gut clenched at what was coming next.

"Now that you're my dad and we're gonna live together, can I have a brother or sister?"

Punch to the throat.

"I'd like that very much, but that's something I have to talk to your mom about."

"She'll say yes." Faith solemnly nodded.

He had no doubt. Charleigh had wanted kids—plural, as in as many as they could have and still live a life that was full of adventures and outings. The problem wouldn't be talking her into more, it would be whether or not Holden was capable of producing them. Not that Holden would explain that to Faith. Nor would he tell her that for the time being she would be an only child. He wanted time to get to know her and build a solid relationship before they added to their family.

Then a thought hit him—he'd taken Charleigh

bare. Not once had he used a condom. It hadn't occurred to him he could get her pregnant and he hadn't asked if she was on birth control.

She could be pregnant right now.

It was a whisper that fluttered over him. A fantasy, a wish that even in his darkest days without her had never gone away. Knowing Faith was his, and there was a possibility they could have more, revived his dream.

Maybe.

That was the best he could hope for until things settled down and he sought a second opinion.

"Time for bed. It's been a busy weekend and you have school tomorrow."

"I can't wait to tell Andy I have a dad."

Good Christ, that felt good.

"You do that. And make sure you tell him that your dad owns—"

"Holden," Charleigh snapped and his gaze went to the door.

"What?"

"We talked about this."

Had they? He didn't think they did. They'd talked about when Faith could date, which he was holding firm on sixteen—eighteen if he could push it and get away with it. And they'd talked about him not being allowed to threaten a little boy. But they had not talked about Faith telling Andy and all the other little twits in her class that he owned guns and a lot of them. They hadn't even touched on the fact that he knew a multitude of ways to inflict bodily harm. Nor had they discussed that he had zero issue kicking teenager ass if one of them tried to put his filthy hands on his girl. But if Charleigh frowned upon that, he would make sure Alec's boy, Caleb, was up for the task. He smiled at his fiancée and added giving Caleb hand-to-hand combat lessons on his mental to-do list. Alec would be all for it—as a matter of fact, Alec might have started his training already.

"We didn't, but I'm sensing you don't like the idea of Faith telling—"

"No, I don't like the idea. Unless of course, you want our daughter's classmates to think you're Rambo."

Holden took a moment to consider her question.

"I see you like that idea."

"I do," he admitted.

"Who's Rambo?"

"Who's Rambo?" Holden mock gasped. "Only the best action hero of all-time."

"Never heard of him."

"Charleigh, you've deprived our child of Rambo?"

Faith giggled and Charleigh smiled.

"Yeah. Call me crazy but I think she's got a few more years before she's ready for blood, guts, and gore."

"Well, there's something to look forward to." Holden tousled Faith's hair and said. "In five years you and me got a date. Rambo marathon and popcorn."

"Try seven," Charleigh returned.

"Six," he countered.

"Fine, six. But only if you promise not to call Andy's father."

"Deal," he gritted out because he really did want to call Andy's father but he couldn't wait to introduce his daughter to action movies.

"Time for bed, sweets."

"I know, Dad already told me."

Holden chuckled and Charleigh huffed.

Then Faith did the third best thing that ever happened to him, when she scrambled up on her knees on the bed next to him, grabbed his face, and rubbed her nose against his. "Eskimo kiss." She bent his head forward and pressed her lips to his forehead. "Sweet dream kiss." Then she righted his head and kissed both cheeks. "French kisses until the morning comes."

Holden sat in stunned silence as a golden stream flowed through him.

"Your turn," Faith declared, looking at him expectantly.

"Um..."

"Watch," Charleigh said, and made her way to Faith's side of the bed.

Faith moved to her mom and repeated the routine, then Charleigh did it back and his two girls scrunched their noses and giggled.

Jesus fuck. That had to be the most beautiful thing he'd ever witnessed. That was, until Faith scooted back to him, repeated the process, and he returned the gesture and saw up close his daughter's eyes light with happiness.

That was the most beautiful thing he'd ever seen in his whole damn life.

"Goodnight, Dad."

"Goodnight, doll."

"Night, Mom."

"Night, sweets."

Holden scooted to the edge of the bed and threw his legs over the side. He had to wait a moment for the dizzy spell to pass.

Did that just happen?

Hell, yes, it did.

His daughter had just initiated him into her bedtime ritual. A ritual she'd only ever shared with her mom.

Sweet Christ, that felt good.

Holden didn't look back as he exited the room. On shaky legs, he walked to his room, fire pumping through his body with each beat of his heart. He stopped in the middle of the room, his head dropped forward, his hand went to the back of his neck, and he thought back over his life. This time without compunction or regret, but searching. He loved Charleigh, he knew it down to his bones, he loved that woman something fierce. But never had he felt a love so pure and sweet. Never had he loved so completely, without hesitation or pause.

"You okay?" Charleigh asked.

The door clicked shut, he heard her approach, but he didn't move.

"Holden?"

"No."

"No?"

"No, baby, I'm not all right."

"Hold—"

"I just fell in love with my daughter." He felt

rather than heard Charleigh's swift intake of oxygen. "I reckon it happened for you the second your hands wrapped around her tiny body. A moment when you and she were still one. Mine happened with Eskimo kisses."

Holden righted his head.

"I love you, Leigh-Leigh. Down to my soul, I love you. It's a consuming, undying, unwavering love. But that girl in there, I love her more than that. I love her in a way that I never thought was possible. Different than how I love you."

"Good," she whispered.

"Thank you."

"You don't—"

"Thank you for being such a great mother."

"Honey, you never have to thank me for that."

"I need you to teach me how to be a good dad."

"You don't need me to teach you anything. She's happy in a way I've never seen her. All she needs is you."

All she needs is you.

He hoped like hell Charleigh was right.

Unable to wait another second, he tagged Charleigh around the waist and hauled her closer, then closer still until she was plastered against him.

Then he thanked her properly.

The kiss wasn't sweet, there was no slow gradual build-up. He went straight to deep and wild, even though Faith was still awake and he couldn't take it where he *really* wanted, which was hot and wild with Charleigh on her back, his tongue not in her mouth but in her pussy.

That would have to wait.

Holden broke the kiss but kept her close and told her, "I have to talk to you about something. But first, let me go lock up the house."

Charleigh burrowed closer, giving no indication she'd heard him so he repeated, "Gotta lock up the house."

Her head tipped back and she pressed a kiss under his jaw while asking, "Will this talk take long?"

Fuck, he hoped not.

"It'll go faster if you let me go lock up and get back to you."

Holden felt her smile against his throat before she gave him another lip touch and stepped away.

He caught her before she could get too far, brushed her hair over her shoulder, and let his fingers glide through the soft strands.

So damn beautiful, his Leigh-Leigh.

"In the interest of saving time, it wouldn't go

unappreciated if you got into bed without your panties on."

Holden watched her lips quirk before she nodded. "Noted."

"Bra, too."

"Your wish is my command."

"We'll see if you're still saying that later when I get you on your knees." He watched with no small amount of satisfaction when she shivered. "Not in the mood for gentle tonight," he warned.

"Good, because neither am I."

"Bed, baby," he growled and turned to leave.

"You know it's sexy when you grunt your demands."

Fuck, now his dick was rock-hard and facing a long wait before he found any relief. His hand went into his jeans to make the necessary adjustments before he attempted to walk down a flight of stairs and he heard Charleigh's soft giggle.

"You keep laughing, baby."

And she did, she kept at it as he exited the bedroom. Even though he could no longer hear her as he walked around checking that the doors were locked and the lights were off, he was sure she was still up in his room laughing herself sick, thinking it was funny she could get his dick hard and ready with a few words.

He used the time it took to get back upstairs wisely and plotted his revenge. There would be a whole lot of begging on her part before the night was over.

By the time he got back to the room, Charleigh was in bed, her back to the headboard, blanket up to her waist, and she obviously rummaged through his bag and nabbed one of his tees, something she used to do when they lived together, but something she hadn't done since they'd been back together. Mainly because he'd done his best to keep her naked, making good use of their limited alone time.

But right then he appreciated the tee—her naked would distract him from the talk they needed to have.

Once he'd stripped off his clothes, he climbed in next to her, and even knowing it was a fool thing to do, Holden's arm went around Charleigh and he tugged her to his side. Further, he continued the lunacy and cupped her bare ass.

It took three deep breaths to get his body under control, then he started.

"Sydney Powell."

Charleigh jerked and her head tipped up.

"The girl I'm planning the party for?"

"Yeah. What are her parents like?"

"Rich."

"No. What are they *like*? Good people, attentive parents, watchful?"

"Um...negative. They're planning a blowout fifteenth birthday party so they can brag about having the party of the decade. They're doing this because from what I've witnessed they mostly ignore her. Her dad is a workaholic and her mom likes to spend his money as fast as she can. Of course, I don't know them well, but I do know a spoiled brat when I see one."

Shit. That was what he was afraid of.

"What's she look like?"

"Why?"

"I'll explain in a second."

"Okay, she's tall, only a couple inches shorter than I am. She's very pretty though she has a heavy hand with makeup and her clothes are far too skimpy, especially for a teenager."

"What color hair?"

"She's a blonde and she has blue eyes."

"Fuck."

"You're scaring me."

Holden squeezed her but refrained from telling her she should be scared because if he was right, the fifteen-year-old was being groomed by a sick fuck who intended to harm her.

"I don't know for sure, I reckon there are a lot of high school girls with the name Sydney in Kent County but..."

Over the next ten minutes, he ran down the case for her, leaving out some of the details she didn't know, but giving her enough to understand Jonny needed this guy off the street.

"Oh my God. I don't know what to say."

"Nothing to say, baby. We need to find him, but none of the girls are talking. And the messages they're sending are cryptic, leaving out his name. All we know is he's older, he has a car, and he gave Sydney Malibu rum at a party hosted by a teenager. No description, no make or model or his car, nothing." Holden gave her another squeeze then added, "And we know he's seriously fucked in the head and he's hurting these girls. I need you to do something for me."

"Anything."

"Do you have Sydney's email or cell number?"

"Yes, to both."

"If McKenna gives you something to text Sydney, will you do it?"

"Sure. What do you want me to send her?"

"You find a video or picture, it can be of anything, and McKenna will embed a virus so when Sydney opens it, McKenna will have access to her cell or computer. Though she'd prefer her cell."

"She wants to hack her phone," Charleigh surmised.

"Yeah. The kids are using a hidden messaging app and Micky's been trying but hasn't had any luck finding a way to break into the app. We need access to Sydney's phone to see if she's communicating with this guy."

"I know the perfect video to send her. The party's next week and we're finalizing the song list for the DJ."

"That's perfect. Thank you."

Charleigh tipped her head back and gave him a small, sad smile.

"She's kinda a brat, totally spoiled, has zero respect for the adults in her life, acts like she's thirty, not fifteen. But she doesn't deserve to be preyed on by some gross old man."

"No, baby, she doesn't. No kid deserves that. Jonny's doing his best and feels like shit this has been going on for as long as it has and he didn't see the pattern."

"It's not Jonny's fault."

"No, it's not. But that doesn't mean *he* doesn't feel like it is. After everything that happened with his brother, Doug, and his dad dying, Jonny's been in a bad way. He feels guilt over what his niece Rory saw and what Caleb endured. But mostly, he's feeling like he's useless. And that's the worst thing a man like Jonny can feel."

"Macy told me what happened. I knew a little bit of the story because Kennedy told me but I didn't know Rory was kidnapped and witnessed her dad kill her grandfather, or that she was in the room when her dad died, until after Faith was taken. Macy told me everything and gave me the name of the counselor Rory's been seeing."

Alec had come apart the day he found Caleb hiding in the woods after the boy had narrowly escaped Doug. Only to find that Doug had gotten his hands on Rory. From there, the events of the day went downhill. Jonny was left bleeding on his parents' living room floor, his dad was dead, he killed his brother. Jonny's emotional scars were so deep, Holden was worried he'd never recover. Rory had been traumatized, too. But the difference was, the little girl was surrounded by love. And Alec and Macy had found someone for her to talk to. Jonny had refused counseling.

"I'm afraid if we don't find this guy before he hurts another girl, Jonny will do something stupid."

"Like what?"

That was something he wasn't talking about with Charleigh. He and the guys had had a long talk after Jonny had taken off and they'd come up with three likely scenarios. The first was that Jonny would quit the force. There was a place at Gemini Group for Jonny if he left the sheriff's department. Option two was Jonny would find the guy on his own and mete out justice. That justice would not be going through the proper legal channels, which would land Jonny's ass in jail. And the third was something Holden didn't want to think about. That outcome was unacceptable and all the men would go to great lengths to ensure it didn't happen.

Knowing he needed to answer, Holden went with the least of the three and told her.

"Like quit the department. Jonny's a good cop. He cares about the citizens of Kent County. It'd be a shame if he quit."

"I agree. I don't know him well, but I like him. And Rory adores her uncle Jonny. She talks about him all the time."

Rory adored everyone. The girl came by it honestly—Macy was the same way.

Silence fell and Holden figured he'd give her a minute to digest everything he'd told her, process it, and file it away before he moved their night along. He didn't want to rush her but there was only so much a man could take, between her soft tits pressing against his side and her bare ass under his palm, which meant her bare pussy was a mere slide of his hand away.

Charleigh's hand did a slow glide down Holden's stomach while simultaneously pressing her lips to his chest.

"Are we done talking?"

"Oh, yeah."

"Good," she mumbled and engaged her tongue, swirling it around his nipple.

Holden shifted and curled his hand around Charleigh's thigh, but before he could maneuver her where he wanted, she slanted her leg across his, opening herself to Holden. Without delay, he accepted her invitation and slid his hand around and down and found her pussy already wet. He pushed two fingers in and he felt her moan vibrate across his chest.

"Mouth, baby," Holden demanded.

She gave him one last swipe around his nipple and tipped her head back. Holden tucked his chin and captured her mouth at the same time her hand wrapped around his cock. He'd meant to start slow and work her up but when Charleigh's fist started stroking him hard and fast, he deepened the kiss and pumped his fingers until she was rocking her hips, chasing an orgasm he wasn't going to let her have.

He slowed his hand but slanted his head and took more of her mouth. The kiss went straight to out-of-control—deep, wet, and wild. Charleigh's hips bucked, still on the verge of coming but Holden keeping her on the edge.

He tore his mouth from hers and stroked faster.

"Knees," he grunted.

Charleigh scrambled to the side, got to her knees, ripped his tee off, tossed it aside, then her hands hit the mattress and she presented him with her fine, round ass.

He took a moment to appreciate the beauty before he moved in behind her.

"You wanna come, Charleigh?" he asked as he curled his body over hers and moved one hand around to her front and flicked his thumb over her clit.

With his chest pressed to her back, he didn't miss her body jolt, he didn't miss the growl of need, and he really didn't miss her ass pressing against his aching cock.

"Yes," she hissed.

"You sure you're ready? We can play awhile longer," he teased and toyed with her clit until her legs were trembling and her groans were near-constant.

"You have one second to get inside of me, Holden, before I finish myself."

"Oh, yeah? How will you finish yourself, baby? Will you rub here?" He lightly circled her clit. "Or do you need to be filled up?" He roughly pushed his finger in her wetness and finger-fucked her until her back arched and her head fell forward.

"I need both."

Holden pulled his fingers free, grabbed his cock, and once he was lined up, he slammed home.

Charleigh was so primed and ready, she came around his shaft on his second stroke. She continued to come as he roughly drove in. After the weekend's events, having her back—really having her in a permanent way, her agreeing to be his wife—he couldn't hold back so he didn't. He didn't take her slow and sweetly, he just took. He took everything that had always been his. He gave her everything that they'd missed.

"Honey," she moaned.

"Not done, Leigh-Leigh."

"Okay."

"Hold on, baby, it's gonna be a long night."

"Okay, honey."

One hand gripped her hip, the other glided over her ass until his palm was in the middle of her back, then he pushed her down while he told her, "Chest to the bed and tip your ass up."

"Holden," she groaned and did what he asked.

Christ, but he loved it when she groaned his name.

Nowhere near done, Holden slammed into her, roughly making love to his woman. He hadn't lied, it was a long fucking night—literally.

36

"Daisy, no!" Faith shouted and I turned to find a furry puppy attacking a stuffed animal.

"Faith, get that."

"Trying!" she yelled and chased the dog out the front door.

Jameson paused with a box in hand and shook his head. "And that's why I don't want another one."

"Another child or puppy?" Kennedy asked.

"Dog. Killer was a maniac when he was a puppy."

"Tank," she snapped, and my eyes went to my friend. "Sorry. I'm starving and grumpy."

"The guys already brought the couch in. Go sit down."

It was moving day. Obviously, Holden's bid was

accepted. Yet, he'd waited another week for the inspector to show to view the property. I still thought it was crazy he'd bought a house sight unseen, but I'd stopped mentioning it to him. As luck had it, he loved the house, so all's well that ends well.

"The pizzas should be in here any minute," McKenna said as she placed a stack of plates in the cabinet.

"Maybe you should go home and rest," I told Kennedy, feeling guilty she'd been on her feet all day. "We're done anyway."

"And miss your welcome home party? No way. Speaking of parties, Jameson told me you got a ton of business from the Powell gig."

"I did." I smiled.

Thankfully, Sydney's party had gone off without a hitch. Everything had been perfect despite the last-minute changes to the menu. And the fact that Lizza and Stone were less than pleased their daughter had received an alcohol citation the week before her party. But like any spoil-the-child parent, they blamed Jonny for his "heavy-handed" treatment of their princess. I'm not exactly sure what had gone down, just that a deal had been made that if Stone and Lizza kept Sydney on home restriction, he wouldn't ask the

State's Attorney to file charges which could've landed Sydney in juvenile detention until her hearing. I had a feeling that was Jonny's way of keeping Sydney safe since there hadn't been a break in the case in the last month, even after I'd sent the text with McKenna's virus. McKenna confirmed Sydney had been talking to a guy using an anonymous messaging app, but since it was anonymous, there was no email or cell number to sign up for the service, so all she had was a screen name. She'd spent a week researching the name but so far she hadn't found that name associated with any other forum or social media.

Now after a month, I, too, was worried about Jonny. He looked horrible. Not his appearance. He was still as good-looking as ever, but it was in his eyes—devastation. Everyone saw it and all of the guys had been working extra hours trying to help Jonny. Holden had explained there was a deadline—there was a three-month pattern between assaults, and that day was drawing near. Another reason I believed Jonny was behind Sydney getting in trouble. Not that he could've done anything if she hadn't been breaking the law first and been drunk and in possession of alcohol, but he was relentless in his demands that the teenager not be allowed out of her house.

"Pizza's here, babe," Holden said, coming into the dining room. "Do you know where my wallet is?"

I glanced around my new house and took in the boxes scattered around the room. I forgot all about Holden's wallet when my eyes rolled up to the fantastic pine boards that made up the vaulted ceiling, then over to the stone fireplace that was a magnificent work of art and focal point of the big living room, then farther down to the knotted wood floors that had been refinished and glossed to a shine. The living room was so huge we needed more furniture to fill it up. Even my dining room table that leafed out to sit eight looked ridiculously small in the space it was now in.

McKenna's soft laugh drew my attention to her still standing in the kitchen. It was a chef's dream with granite countertops, double ovens, and a six-burner gas stovetop.

All of it open, so I could be in the kitchen and have an unobstructed view out the huge windows in the living room. The house was perfect. I loved it. But I really loved that Holden was happy. He'd been on top of the world as he moved our stuff into the house, never once complaining about the boxes of junk I'd accumulated over the years. True to his word, I'd never stepped foot back into my apartment.

He and the guys had packed everything up and brought it to the house without me lifting a finger. All that was left to do was return the moving truck, bring his Airstream over—which I'd flatly refused to allow him to sell when he'd brought it up, and unpack.

Then we'd just be living.

"I already paid for it," Evie said and Holden growled. "Oh, shut up, you wouldn't let me buy you a housewarming present. You don't get to bitch about me buying pizza."

"New bedroom furniture isn't a housewarming present," Holden returned and I settled in for the same argument I'd heard three times already.

I'd politely declined her generous offer. Holden hadn't declined politely, he'd told her she was nuts and she absolutely couldn't buy us a ten-thousand-dollar gift. Yes, ten grand, I'd nearly fallen over when I saw the price tag. His comment had led into a thirty-minute dispute about Holden saving Evie's life. Seeing as Chasin was present for this disagreement and he hated being reminded his friend had been shot and almost killed protecting his woman, he thankfully ended the tiff by pulling a still-shouting Evie out the door.

"It is to me," she retorted.

"Well, it isn't to me. Love you like a sister, Genevieve, but you are not now nor are you ever buying us furniture."

"Fine," she huffed, and tears sprang in her eyes.

Holden's face fell and he took a step to her but she put up her hands to stop him.

"Evie, sweetheart, I didn't—"

"I know you didn't," she hissed and angrily swiped at her face. "Stupid pregnancy hormones."

Evie's eyes widened in shock and she slammed her hand over her mouth like she could shove the words back in, but it was too late. The whole room was stunned into silence.

"Come again?" Chasin barked, and Evie jumped and her eyes sliced to her best friend, Bobby. The look could only be identified as "eek".

Thank God, Bobby broke the tension and roared in hysterics.

"You suck at..." Bobby stammered, "keeping secrets. It hasn't even been an hour and you've already blown it."

"An hour?" Chasin growled. "Why does she know you're having my baby before I know you're having my baby?"

Holden stepped closer, put his arms around me, and tucked me to his side. When he had me where he wanted, he bent down and whispered, "It's a shame Nixon and Alec went to Nix's to get a toolbox."

"Why's that?"

"Because they're gonna miss Chasin throwing a tantrum."

"That's not nice," I mumbled and glanced back at a red-faced Chasin.

"It might not be nice but it's gonna be hilarious."

"You say that, but how mad would you be if you found out I told Kennedy I was pregnant before I told you?"

Just as I expected, Holden went solid and his hand went to my chin and forced me to look up at him.

"Did you tell Kennedy you're...are you?"

I shrugged and smiled. "No. I didn't tell her. But I am three weeks late, so I asked her to pick me up a test."

All the color bleached from my man's face and his beautiful brown eyes went lazy.

"Have you taken it?" he whispered.

"Nope. I thought we'd wait until everyone was gone."

"Party's over!" Holden shouted. "Everyone out."

"Don't be ridiculous." I smacked him on the

chest and glanced around the room at our startled friends.

Our friends.

Mine and his.

And Faith's.

Friends that were more than friends—they were family.

Blessed.

"Dad, why's the party over when we haven't had pizza yet?" Faith asked, holding a squirming ball of fur that was licking her face and mouth.

"Daisy, stop. Faith, don't let her lick your mouth, that's gross. And the party's not over, your Dad's being silly."

"No, I'm not. I want—"

"To enjoy a house full of friends and thank them all for helping us move in because we appreciate all their hard work."

"Yeah," Holden muttered. "What she said."

"I'm unclear how you got him as far as you did," Silver said. "I've been trying to get Weston to behave for-freaking-ever and I still can't get him to—"

"That's because you like it when I misbehave."

"See? Little ears, Weston."

"Sorry." He smiled, not looking sorry at all.

"Hello? Anyone care that my woman told her

best friend we're having a baby before she told me?" Chasin griped.

"No," McKenna tossed out and went to Evie to pull her into a hug. "Congratulations."

"What'd we miss?" Nixon asked, coming into the house. "Pizza's here, cool."

"Chasin and Evie are having a kid," Jameson informed the newcomers. "And Chasin's salty because Bobby knew first."

"Right, like that's a surprise, those two are surgically attached," Alec added.

"Let's eat!" Macy shouted. "Paper plates are on the counter."

The gang shuffled into the kitchen and helped themselves to the food, but Holden and I remained where we were.

"Dad, tomorrow can we put together my new bike?"

"Yep. And we'll start your first lesson."

"Awe-some!"

Daisy barked her agreement then licked Faith's face and I groaned.

"Gonna have to get over that, Leigh-Leigh."

"It's gross."

Holden's smile died and he stared at me with a

look I knew well. It was full of love and gratitude. It was hopeful and happy.

"Welcome home, Holden."

"Welcome home, Leigh-Leigh."

Much later that night…

Holden carefully rolled away from Charleigh and on silent feet made his way into the master bathroom.

The house was sweet, the women in the house, sweeter.

He picked up the pregnancy test he'd insisted Charleigh keep and looked down at the white plastic stick in his hand.

Pregnant.

He let the warmth wash over him, savoring it, then he smiled and set it back on the counter.

Holden made his way back to the bed, slid in, and pulled Leigh-Leigh close.

"Still positive?" she whispered sleepily.

"Yep."

"That's the third time you've checked."

"Yep."

"You think you're done checkin' for the night?"

"Nope."

His pregnant woman giggled in his arms and Holden thought he had it all.

"Dream come true," he told her.

"Yeah."

Charleigh was awake the fourth time Holden went to check the test. She didn't make a peep when he crawled back in next to her but she did smile.

Dream come true.

37

Jonny

The 911 call came in when Jonny was leaving the hospital. Jameson and Kennedy's little boy, Noah, couldn't wait until his due date to make his appearance. Four weeks early, but perfect.

Thank fuck.

Everyone had been at the hospital for hours waiting to see what the doctor was going to do, then waiting on news about Noah, therefore no one was paying attention to what was going on with Ayla Purdy.

Not even him.

Once again, he'd fucked up and dropped the ball.

While his ass was sitting in a hospital waiting room, Ayla had done the one thing they'd all prayed she wouldn't do. She'd reached out to her baby's father. The results of that phone call were disastrous.

By the time Jonny had made it to the scene, Cory Saddler was in cuffs. But it was Ayla's bruised face and bloody lip Jonny couldn't get out of his mind.

For forty-five days, Jonny had followed Cory when he wasn't on shift. He'd been studious in making sure he kept tabs on the man's whereabouts, and when the opportunity arose, Jonny had pushed an alcohol citation as far as he could to get Sydney Powell clear of danger. Sure, her parents were pissed and threatened to make a complaint but Jonny didn't give the first fuck if they took his badge as long as Sydney didn't fall victim to Saddler.

But Ayla had been keeping her head down, doing what her parents had asked, and not telling anyone she was pregnant.

Until she didn't listen and she contacted that sick fuck, who fed her a bunch of bullshit about loving her and wanting their baby. So when he asked to meet her, she'd snuck out and gone to him.

Then he attempted to beat her until...

No.

Fuck. No.

Jonny shook his head to knock the thought clean away.

He picked up his half-full glass of vodka and took a healthy swig. It would take more than a few glasses to wipe his mind clear of the compounding guilt.

He heard a car door slam but he didn't bother to move from his back deck. His eyes remained unfocused into the darkness.

The wicker love seat groaned under the weight of a second occupant.

Still, he didn't look.

He didn't need to.

And when her head hit his shoulder and the faint smell of peaches filled his nostrils he greedily took in another breath.

It wasn't working.

Not this time.

Maybe not ever again would the scent of her calm his restless soul.

He took another pull of his drink before he silently passed it to her. She took the glass, he felt her head tip back, then the glass was back in his hand.

Silence.

But no peace.

In a perfect world, he would've been good enough for a woman like Bobby Layne.

But the world wasn't perfect. It was evil, cruel, and inhumane.

Jonny went back to his vodka.

Bobby remained silent, loaning him her strength.

Next up is Jonny and Bobby in

Jonny's Redemption

Grab your copy here

ALSO BY RILEY EDWARDS

Riley Edwards

www.RileyEdwardsRomance.com

Romantic Suspense

Gemini Group

Nixon's Promise

Jameson's Salvation

Weston's Treasure

Alec's Dream

Chasin's Surrender

Holden's Resurrection

Jonny's Redemption

Red Team

Nightstalker

Protecting Olivia - Susan Stoker Universe

Redeeming Violet - Susan Stoker Universe

Recovering Ivy - Susan Stoker Universe

Rescuing Erin - Susan Stoker Universe

The Gold Team

Brooks - Susan Stoker Universe

Thaddeus - Susan Stoker Universe

Kyle - Susan Stoker Universe

Maximus - Susan Stoker Universe

Declan - Susan Stoker Universe

The 707 Freedom Series

Free

Freeing Jasper

Finally Free

Freedom

The Next Generation (707 spinoff)

Saving Meadow

Chasing Honor

Finding Mercy

Claiming Tuesday

Adoring Delaney

Keeping Quinn

Taking Liberty

Triple Canopy

Damaged

Flawed

The Collective

Unbroken

Trust

Standalone

Romancing Rayne - Susan Stoker Universe

BE A REBEL

Riley Edwards is a USA Today bestselling author, wife, and military mom. Riley was born and raised in Los Angeles but now resides on the east coast with her fantastic husband and children.

Riley writes heart-stopping romance with sexy alpha heroes and even stronger heroines. Riley's favorite genres to write are romantic suspense and military romance.

Don't forget to sign up for Riley's newsletter and never miss another release, sale, or exclusive bonus material. https://www.subscribepage.com/RRsignup

Facebook Fan Group

www.rileyedwardsromance.com

facebook.com/Novelist.Riley.Edwards
twitter.com/rileyedwardsrom
instagram.com/rileyedwardsromance
bookbub.com/authors/riley-edwards
amazon.com/author/rileyedwards

Printed in Great Britain
by Amazon

63135069R00292